DOVER · THRIFT · EDITIONS

Classic Mystery Stories

EDITED BY
DOUGLAS G. GREENE

DOVER PUBLICATIONS, INC.
Mineola, New York

DOVER THRIFT EDITIONS

GENERAL EDITOR: PAUL NEGRI

EDITOR OF THIS VOLUME: DOUGLAS G. GREENE

Bibliographical Note

This Dover edition, first published in 1999, is a new anthology of works reprinted from standard sources. A new introductory Note and prefaces to the stories have been specially prepared for this edition.

Library of Congress Cataloging-in-Publication Data

Classic mystery stories / edited by Douglas G. Greene.
    p.   cm. — (Dover thrift editions)
  ISBN 0-486-40881-7 (pbk.)
  1. Detective and mystery stories, American. 2. Detective and mystery stories, English. I. Greene, Douglas G. II. Series.
PS648.D4C56 1999
813'.087208 — dc21
                                            99–44254
                                             CIP

Manufactured in the United States of America
Dover Publications, Inc., 31 East 2nd Street, Mineola, N.Y. 11501

A Celebration of the Detective Story

This anthology is a collection of detective stories, tales in which the mystery is mysterious, the crime is criminous, and above all the detective actually detects. We may well enjoy suspense thrillers and psychological probings of diseased brains and even (in our guiltier moments) shoot-'em-ups with plenty of AK-47s and car chases. But when it comes to the mystery story, there is nothing to rival the genuine tale of—to use Edgar Allan Poe's word—ratiocination, wherein the detective solves the crime by investigation and observation, by using his or her wits. In this genre fisticuffs may occasionally be acceptable—but only *after* the detective has already worked things out through brainpower.

The tales in *Classic Mystery Stories* are taken from almost eighty years (from 1841 to 1920) of fictional sleuthing. The book begins with the very first detective story, Poe's "The Murders in the Rue Morgue" (1841), continues through the gaslit eras of Victorian and Edwardian England and America, and concludes with stories that feature E. C. Bentley's Philip Trent and H. C. Bailey's Reggie Fortune, two of the fictional detectives who point the way to the flapper era of Agatha Christie's Hercule Poirot and Dorothy Sayers' Lord Peter Wimsey. We meet police detectives, amateur detectives, a seer-sleuth, an investigator from pre-Civil War Virginia, Scotland Yard's premier female detective, and even a leopard-trainer who unravels a crime. They are as colorful a cast of characters as the genre they represent.

DOUGLAS G. GREENE

Contents

Edgar Allan Poe

(1809–1849)

EDGAR ALLAN POE invented the detective story. Industrious scholars have, of course, found precursors, ranging from Daniel's primitive investigations in the Bible, to anecdotes in Greek and medieval literature, and (more persuasively) inductions and deductions in Renaissance and Enlightenment literature. Strong arguments can be—and have been—presented that a scene in Shakespeare's *Henry V*, some instant deductions in Voltaire's *Zadig,* and the psychological pinning of guilt in William Godwin's *Caleb Williams* and in William Gilmore Simms's *Martin Faber* are examples of detection before Poe. In none of these works, however, is the rational investigation of a crime the major subject of the narrative. But in Poe, detection *is* the subject, and the detective is the main character. Or, to be more precise, as Poe indicates in the opening pages of "The Murders in the Rue Morgue," the subject is Poe's theories of analysis. And he explains those theories by creating a genius detective (whose powers of observation and cryptic remarks are recorded with undisguised admiration by the narrator) and inventing a seemingly insoluble mystery for him to investigate.

"The Murders in the Rue Morgue" was published in *Graham's Magazine,* March 1841, and it was followed by two other stories about Monsieur C. Auguste Dupin, "The Mystery of Marie Rogêt" and "The Purloined Letter," as well as a detective story which does not feature Dupin, "Thou Art the Man," and a puzzle story, "The Gold-Bug."

The Murders in the Rue Morgue

What Song the Syrens sang or what name Achilles assumed when
he hid himself among women, although puzzling questions are
not beyond *all* conjecture.

SIR THOMAS BROWNE, Urn-Burial

THE MENTAL FEATURES discoursed of as the analytical, are, in themselves, but little susceptible of analysis. We appreciate them only in
their effects. We know of them, among other things, that they are
always to their possessor, when inordinately possessed, a source of the
liveliest enjoyment. As the strong man exults in his physical ability,
delighting in such exercises as call his muscles into action, so glories
the analyst in that moral activity which *disentangles*. He derives pleasure
from even the most trivial occupations bringing his talents into play.
He is fond of enigmas, of conundrums, of hieroglyphics; exhibiting in
his solutions of each a degree of *acumen* which appears to the ordinary
apprehension preternatural. His results, brought about by the very soul
and essence of method, have, in truth, the whole air of intuition. The
faculty of re-solution is possibly much invigorated by mathematical
study, and especially by that highest branch of it which, unjustly, and
merely on account of its retrograde operations, has been called, as if *par
excellence*, analysis. Yet to calculate is not in itself to analyse. A chess-
player, for example, does the one without effort at the other. It follows
that the game of chess, in its effects upon mental character, is greatly
misunderstood. I am not now writing a treatise, but simply prefacing a
somewhat peculiar narrative by observations very much at random;
I will, therefore, take occasion to assert that the higher powers of the

reflective intellect are more decidedly and more usefully tasked by the unostentatious game of draughts than by all the elaborate frivolity of chess. In this latter, where the pieces have different and *bizarre* motions, with various and variable values, what is only complex is mistaken (a not unusual error) for what is profound. The *attention* is here called powerfully into play. If it flag for an instant, an oversight is committed, resulting in injury or defeat. The possible moves being not only manifold but involute, the chances of such oversights are multiplied; and in nine cases out of ten it is the more concentrative rather than the more acute player who conquers. In draughts, on the contrary, where the moves are *unique* and have but little variation, the probabilities of inadvertence are diminished, and the mere attention being left comparatively unemployed, what advantages are obtained by either party are obtained by superior *acumen*. To be less abstract—Let us suppose a game of draughts where the pieces are reduced to four kings, and where, of course, no oversight is to be expected. It is obvious that here the victory can be decided (the players being at all equal) only by some *recherché* movement, the result of some exertion of the intellect. Deprived of ordinary resources, the analyst throws himself into the spirit of his opponent, identifies himself therewith, and not unfrequently sees thus, at a glance, the sole methods (sometimes indeed absurdly simple ones) by which he may seduce into error or hurry into miscalculation.

Whist has long been noted for its influence upon what is termed the calculating power; and men of the highest order of intellect have been known to take an apparently unaccountable delight in it, while eschewing chess as frivolous. Beyond doubt there is nothing of a similar nature so greatly tasking the faculty of analysis. The best chess-player in Christendom *may* be little more than the best player of chess; but proficiency in whist implies capacity for success in all these more important undertakings where mind struggles with mind. When I say proficiency, I mean the perfection in the game which includes a comprehension of *all* the sources whence legitimate advantage may be derived. These are not only manifold but multiform, and lie frequently among recesses of thought altogether inaccessible to the ordinary understanding. To observe attentively is to remember distinctly; and, so far, the concentrative chess-player will do very well at whist; while the rules of Hoyle (themselves based upon the mere mechanism of the game) are sufficiently and generally comprehensible. Thus to have a retentive memory, and to proceed by "the book," are points commonly regarded as the sum total of good playing. But it is in matters beyond the limits of mere rule that the skill of the analyst is evinced. He makes, in silence, a host of observations and inferences. So, perhaps, do his companions; and the difference in the extent of the information obtained, lies not so much in the validity of the inference as in the quality of the observation. The necessary knowledge is that of *what* to observe. Our player confines himself not at all; nor, because the game is the object, does he reject deductions from things external to the game. He examines the countenance of his partner, comparing it carefully with that of each of his opponents. He considers the mode of assorting the cards in each hand; often counting trump by trump, and honour by honour, through the glances bestowed by their holders upon each. He notes every variation of face as the play progresses, gathering a fund of thought from the differences in the expression of certainty, of surprise, of triumph, or chagrin. From the manner of gathering up a trick he judges whether the person taking it can make another in the suit. He recognizes what is played through feint, by the air with which it is thrown upon the table. A casual or inadvertent word; the accidental dropping or turning of a card, with the accompanying anxiety or carelessness in regard to its concealment; the counting of the tricks, with the order of their arrangement; embarrassment, hesitation, eagerness or trepidation—all afford, to his apparently intuitive perception, indications of the true state of affairs. The first two or three rounds have been played, he is in full possession of the contents of each hand, and thenceforward puts down his cards with as absolute a precision of purpose as if the rest of the party had turned outward the faces of their own.

The analytical power should not be confounded with simple ingenuity; for while the analyst is necessarily ingenious, the ingenious man is often remarkably incapable of analysis. The consecutive or combining power, by which ingenuity is usually manifested, and to which the phrenologists (I believe erroneously) have assigned a separate organ, supposing it a primitive faculty, has been so frequently seen in those whose intellect bordered otherwise upon idiocy, as to have attracted general observations among writers on morals. Between ingenuity and the analytic ability there exists a difference far greater, indeed, than that between the fancy and the imagination, but of a character very strictly analogous. It will be found, in fact, that the ingenious are always fanciful, and the *truly* imaginative never otherwise than analytic.

The narrative which follows will appear to the reader somewhat in the light of a commentary upon the propositions just advanced.

Residing in Paris during the spring and part of the summer of 18——, I there became acquainted with a Monsieur C. Auguste Dupin. This young gentleman was of an excellent—indeed of an illustrious family, but, by a variety of untoward events, had been reduced to such poverty that the energy of his character succumbed beneath it, and he ceased to bestir himself in the world, or to care for the retrieval of his fortunes. By courtesy of his creditors, there still remained in his possession a small remnant of his patrimony; and, upon the income arising from this, he managed, by means of a rigorous economy, to procure the necessaries of life, without troubling himself about its superfluities. Books, indeed, were his sole luxuries, and in Paris these are easily obtained.

Our first meeting was at an obscure library in the Rue Montmartre, where the accident of our both being in search of the same very rare and very remarkable volume, brought us into closer communion. We saw each other again and again. I was deeply interested in the little family history which he detailed to me with all that candour which a Frenchman indulges whenever mere self is the theme. I was astonished, too, at the vast extent of his reading; and, above all, I felt my soul enkindled within me by the wild fervour, and the vivid freshness of his imagination. Seeking in Paris the objects I then sought, I felt that the society of such a man would be to me a treasure beyond price; and this feeling I frankly confided to him. It was at length arranged that we should live together during my stay in the city; and as my worldly circumstances were somewhat less embarrassed than his own, I was permitted to be at the expense of renting, and furnishing in a style which suited the rather fantastic gloom of our common temper, a time-eaten and grotesque mansion, long deserted through superstitions into which we did not inquire, and tottering to its fall in a retired and desolate portion of the Faubourg St. Germain.

Had the routine of our life at this place been known to the world, we should have been regarded as madmen—although, perhaps, as madmen of a harmless nature. Our seclusion was perfect. We admitted no visitors. Indeed the locality of our retirement had been carefully kept a secret from my own former associates; and it had been many years since Dupin had ceased to know or be known in Paris. We existed within ourselves alone.

It was a freak of fancy in my friend (for what else shall I call it?) to be enamoured of the Night for her own sake; and into this *bizarrerie*, as into all his others, I quietly fell; giving myself up to his wild whims with a perfect *abandon*. The sable divinity would not herself dwell with us always; but we could counterfeit her presence. At the first dawn of the morning we closed all the massy shutters of our old building; lighted a couple of tapers which, strongly perfumed, threw out only the ghastliest and feeblest of rays. By the aid of these we then busied our souls in dreams—reading, writing, or conversing, until warned by the clock of the advent of the true Darkness. Then we sallied forth into the streets, arm in arm, continuing the topics of the day, or roaming far and wide until a late hour, seeking, amid the wild lights and shadows of the populous city, that infinity of mental excitement which quiet observation can afford.

At such times I could not help remarking and admiring (although from his rich ideality I had been prepared to expect it) a peculiar analytic ability in Dupin. He seemed, too, to take an eager delight in its exercise—if not exactly in its display—and did not hesitate to confess the pleasure thus derived. He boasted to me, with a low chuckling laugh, that most men, in respect to himself, wore windows in their bosoms, and was wont to follow up such assertions by direct and very startling proofs of his intimate knowledge of my own. His manner at these moments was frigid and abstract; his eyes were vacant in expression; while his voice, usually a rich tenor, rose into a treble which would have sounded petulantly but for the deliberateness and entire distinctness of the enunciation. Observing him in these moods, I often dwelt meditatively upon the old philosophy of the Bi-Part Soul, and amused myself with the fancy of a double Dupin—the creative and the resolvent.

Let it not be supposed, from what I have just said, that I am detailing any mystery, or penning any romance. What I have described in the Frenchman, was merely the result of an excited, or perhaps of a diseased intelligence. But of the character of his remarks at the periods in question an example will best convey the idea.

We were strolling one night down a long dirty street, in the vicinity of the Palais Royal. Being both, apparently, occupied with thought, neither of us had spoken a syllable for fifteen minutes at least. All at once Dupin broke forth with these words:

"He is a very little fellow, that's true, and would do better for the *Théâtre des Variétés.*"

"There can be no doubt of that," I replied unwittingly, and not at first observing (so much had I been absorbed in reflection) the extraordinary manner in which the speaker had chimed in with my meditations. In an instant afterwards I recollected myself, and my astonishment was profound.

"Dupin," said I, gravely, "this is beyond my comprehension. I do not hesitate to say that I am amazed, and can scarcely credit my senses. How was it possible you should know I was thinking of——?" Here I paused, to ascertain beyond a doubt whether he really knew of whom I thought.

—"of Chantilly," said he, "why do you pause? You were remarking to yourself that his diminutive figure unfitted him for tragedy."

This was precisely what had formed the subject of my reflections. Chantilly was a *quondam* cobbler of the Rue St. Denis, who, becoming stage-mad, had attempted the *rôle* of Xerxes, in Crébillon's tragedy so called, and been notoriously Pasquinaded for his pains.

"Tell me, for Heaven's sake," I exclaimed, "the method—if method there is—by which you have been enabled to fathom my soul in this matter." In fact I was even more startled than I would have been willing to express.

"It was the fruiterer," replied my friend, "who brought you to the conclusion that the mender of soles was not of sufficient height for Xerxes *et id genus omne.*"

"The fruiterer!—you astonish me—I know no fruiterer whomsoever."

"The man who ran up against you as we entered the street—it may have been fifteen minutes ago."

I now remembered that, in fact, a fruiterer, carrying upon his head a large basket of apples, had nearly thrown me down, by accident, as we passed from the Rue C——, into the thoroughfare where we stood; but what this had to do with Chantilly I could not possibly understand.

There was not a particle of *charlatanerie* about Dupin. "I will explain," he said, "and that you may comprehend all clearly, we will first retrace the course of your meditations, from the moment in which I spoke to you until that of the *rencontre* with the fruiterer in question. The larger links of the chain run thus—Chantilly, Orion, Dr. Nicols, Epicurus, Stereotomy, the street stones, the fruiterer."

There are few persons who have not, at some period of their lives, amused themselves in retracing the steps by which particular conclusions of their own minds have been attained. The occupation is often full of interest; and he who attempts it for the first time is astonished by the apparently illimitable distance and incoherence between the starting-point and the goal. What, then, must have been my amazement when I heard the Frenchman speak what he had just spoken, and when I could not help acknowledging that he had spoken the truth. He continued:

"We had been talking of horses, if I remember aright, just before leaving the Rue C——. This was the last subject we discussed. As we crossed into this street, a fruiterer, with a large basket upon his head, brushing quickly past us, thrust you upon a pile of paving-stones collected at a spot where the causeway is undergoing repair. You stepped upon one of the loose fragments, slipped, slightly strained your ankle, appeared vexed or sulky, muttered a few words, turned to look at the pile, and then proceeded in silence. I was not particularly attentive to what you did; but observation has become with me, of late, a species of necessity.

"You kept your eyes upon the ground—glancing, with a petulant expression, at the holes and ruts in the pavement (so that I saw you were still thinking of the stones), until we reached the little alley called Lamartine, which has been paved, by way of experiment, with the overlapping and riveted blocks. Here your countenance brightened up, and, perceiving your lips move, I could not doubt that you murmured the word 'stereotomy,' a term very affectedly applied to this species of pavement. I knew that you could not say to yourself 'stereotomy' without being brought to think of atomies, and thus of the theories of Epicurus; and since, when we discussed this subject not very long ago, the vague guesses of that noble Greek had met with confirmation in the late nebular cosmogony, I felt that you could not avoid casting your eyes upwards to the great *nebula* in Orion, and I certainly expected that you would do so. You did look up; and I was now assured that I had correctly followed your steps. But in that bitter *tirade* upon Chantilly, which appeared in yesterday's '*Musée*,' the satirist, making some disgraceful allusions to the cobbler's change of name upon assuming the buskin, quoted a Latin line about which we have often conversed. I mean the line

Perdidit antiquum litera prima sonum.

I had told you that this was in reference to Orion, formerly written Urion; and, from certain pungencies connected with this explanation, I was aware that you could not have forgotten it. It was clear, therefore, that you would not fail to combine the two ideas of Orion and Chantilly. That you did combine them I saw by the character of the smile which passed over your lips. You thought of the poor cobbler's immolation. So far, you had been stooping in your gait; but now I saw you draw yourself up to your full height. I was then sure that you reflected upon the diminutive figure of Chantilly. At this point I interrupted your meditations to remark that as, in fact, he was a very little fellow—that Chantilly—he would do better at the *Théâtre des Variétés.*"

Not long after this, we were looking over an evening edition of the *Gazette des Tribunaux*, when the following paragraphs arrested our attention.

"EXTRAORDINARY MURDERS.—This morning, about three o'clock, the inhabitants of the Quartier St. Roch were aroused from sleep by a succession of terrific shrieks, issuing, apparently, from the fourth story of a house in the Rue Morgue, known to be in the sole occupancy of one Madame L'Espanaye, and her daughter, Mademoiselle Camille L'Espanaye. After some delay, occasioned by a fruitless attempt to procure admission in the usual manner, the gateway was broken in with a crowbar, and eight or ten of the neighbours entered, accompanied by two *gendarmes*. By this time the cries had ceased; but, as the party rushed up the first flight of stairs, two or more rough voices, in angry contention, were distinguished, and seemed to proceed from the upper part of the house. As the second landing was reached, these sounds, also, had ceased, and everything remained perfectly quiet. The party spread themselves, and hurried from room to room. Upon arriving at a large back chamber in the fourth story (the door of which, being found locked, with the key inside, was forced open), a spectacle presented itself which struck every one present not less with horror than with astonishment.

"The apartment was in the wildest disorder—the furniture broken and thrown about in all directions. There was only one bedstead; and from this the bed had been removed, and thrown into the middle of the floor. On a chair lay a razor, besmeared with blood. On the hearth were two or three long and thick tresses of grey human hair, also dabbled in blood, and seeming to have been pulled out by the roots. Upon the floor were found four Napoleons, an ear-ring of topaz, three large silver spoons, three smaller of *métal d'Alger*, and two bags, containing nearly four thousand francs in gold. The drawers of a *bureau*, which stood in one corner, were open, and had been, apparently, rifled, although many articles still remained in them. A small iron safe was discovered under the *bed* (not under the bedstead). It was open, with the key still in the door. It had no contents beyond a few old letters, and other papers of little consequence.

"Of Madame L'Espanaye no traces were here seen; but an unusual quantity of soot being observed in the fireplace, a search was made in the chimney, and (horrible to relate!) the corpse of the daughter, head downwards, was dragged therefrom; it having been thus forced up the narrow aperture for a considerable distance. The body was quite warm. Upon examining it, many excoriations were perceived, no doubt occasioned by the violence with which it had been thrust up and down. Upon the face were many severe scratches, and, upon the throat, dark bruises, and deep indentations of fingernails, as if the deceased had been throttled to death.

"After a thorough investigation of every portion of the house, without farther discovery, the party made its way into a small paved yard in the rear of the building, where lay the corpse of the old lady, with her throat so entirely cut that, upon an attempt to raise her, the head fell off. The body, as well as the head, was fearfully mutilated—the former so much so as scarcely to retain any semblance of humanity.

"To this horrible mystery there is not as yet, we believe, the slightest clue."

The next day's paper had these additional particulars.

"*The Tragedy in the Rue Morgue*. Many individuals have been examined in relation to this most extraordinary and frightful affair" (the word "*affaire*" has not yet, in France, that levity of import which it conveys with us), "but nothing whatever has transpired to throw light upon it. We give below all the material testimony elicited.

"*Pauline Dubourg,* laundress, deposes that she has known both the deceased for three years, having washed for them during that period. The old lady and her daughter seemed on good terms—very affectionate towards each other. They were excellent pay. Could not speak in regard to their mode or means of living. Believed that Madame L. told fortunes for a living. Was reputed to have money put by. Never met any persons in the house when she called for the clothes or took them home. Was sure that they had no servant in employ. There appeared to be no furniture in any part of the building except in the fourth story.

"*Pierre Moreau,* tobacconist, deposes that he has been in the habit of selling small quantities of tobacco and snuff to Madame L'Espanaye for nearly four years. Was born in the neighbourhood, and has always resided there. The deceased and her daughter had occupied the house in which the corpses were found, for more than six years. It was formerly occupied by a jeweller, who under-let the upper rooms to various persons. The house was the property of Madame L. She became dissatisfied with the abuse of the premises by her tenant, and moved into them herself, refusing to let any portion. The old lady was childish. Witness had seen the daughter some five or six times during the six years. The two lived an exceedingly retired life—were reputed to have money. Had heard it said among the neighbours that Madame L. told fortunes—did not believe it. Had never seen any person enter the door except the old lady and her daughter, a porter once or twice, and a physician some eight or ten times.

"Many other persons, neighbours, gave evidence to the same effect. No one was spoken of as frequenting the house. It was not known whether there were any living connections of Madame L. and her daughter. The shutters of the front windows were seldom opened. Those in the rear were always closed, with the exception of the large back room, fourth story. The house was a good house—not very old.

"*Isidore Musèt, gendarme,* deposes that he was called to the house about three o'clock in the morning, and found some twenty or thirty persons at the gateway, endeavouring to gain admittance. Forced it open, at length, with a bayonet—not with a crowbar. Had but little difficulty in getting it open, on account of its being a double or folding gate, and bolted neither at bottom nor top. The shrieks were continued until the gate was forced—and then suddenly ceased. They seemed to be screams of some person (or persons) in great agony—were loud and drawn out, not short and quick. Witness led the way upstairs. Upon reaching the first landing, heard two voices in loud and angry contention—the one a gruff voice, the other much shriller—a very strange voice. Could distinguish some words of the former, which was that of a Frenchman. Was positive that it was not a woman's voice.

Could distinguish the words '*sacré*' and '*diable.*' The shrill voice was that of a foreigner. Could not be sure whether it was the voice of a man or of a woman. Could not make out what was said, but believed the language to be Spanish. The state of the room and of the bodies was described by this witness as we described them yesterday.

"*Henri Duval*, a neighbour, and by trade a silversmith, deposes that he was one of the party who first entered the house. Corroborates the testimony of Musèt in general. As soon as they forced an entrance, they reclosed the door, to keep out the crowd, which collected very fast, notwithstanding the lateness of the hour. The shrill voice, the witness thinks, was that of an Italian. Was certain it was not French. Could not be sure that it was a man's voice. It might have been a woman's. Was not acquainted with the Italian language. Could not distinguish the words, but was convinced by the intonation that the speaker was an Italian. Knew Madame L. and her daughter. Had conversed with both frequently. Was sure that the shrill voice was not that of either of the deceased.

"—— *Odenheimer, restaurateur*. This witness volunteered his testimony. Not speaking French, was examined through an interpreter. Is a native of Amsterdam. Was passing the house at the time of the shrieks. They lasted for several minutes—probably ten. They were long and loud—very awful and distressing. Was one of those who entered the building. Corroborated the previous evidence in every respect but one. Was sure that the shrill voice was that of a man—of a Frenchman. Could not distinguish the words uttered. They were loud and quick—unequal—spoken apparently in fear as well as anger. The voice was harsh—not so much shrill as harsh. Could not call it a shrill voice. The gruff voice said repeatedly '*sacré*,' '*diable*,' and once '*mon Dieu.*'

"*Jules Mignaud*, banker, of the firm of Mignaud et Fils, Rue Deloraine. Is the elder Mignaud. Madame L'Espanaye had some property. Had opened an account with his banking house in the spring of the year —— (eight years previously). Made frequent deposits in small sums. Had checked for nothing until the third day before her death, when she took out in person the sum of 4000 francs. This sum was paid in gold, and a clerk sent home with the money.

"*Adolphe Le Bon*, clerk to Mignaud et Fils, deposes that on the day in question, about noon, he accompanied Madame L'Espanaye to her residence with the 4000 francs, put up in two bags. Upon the door being opened, Mademoiselle L. appeared and took from his hands one of the bags, while the old lady relieved him of the other. He then bowed and departed. Did not see any person in the street at the time. It is a bye-street—very lonely.

"*William Bird*, tailor, deposes that he was one of the party who entered the house. Is an Englishman. Has lived in Paris two years. Was one of the first to ascend the stairs. Heard the voices in contention. The gruff voice was that of a Frenchman. Could make out several words, but cannot now remember all. Heard distinctly '*sacré*' and '*mon Dieu.*' There was a sound at the moment as if of several persons struggling— a scraping and scuffling sound. The shrill voice was very loud—louder than the gruff one. Is sure that it was not the voice of an Englishman. Appeared to be that of a German. Might have been a woman's voice. Does not understand German.

"Four of the above-named witnesses, being recalled, deposed that the door of the chamber in which was found the body of Mademoiselle L. was locked on the inside when the party reached it. Everything was perfectly silent—no groans or noises of any kind. Upon forcing the door no person was seen. The windows, both of the back and front room, were down and firmly fastened from within. A door between the two rooms was closed, but not locked. The door leading from the front room into the passage was locked, with the key on the inside. A small room in the front of the house, on the fourth story, at the head of the passage, was open, the door being ajar. This room was crowded with old beds, boxes, and so forth. These were carefully removed and searched. There was not an inch of any portion of the house which was not care-fully searched. Sweeps were sent up and down the chimneys. The house was a four-story one, with garrets (*mansardes*). A trap-door on the roof was nailed down very securely—did not appear to have been opened for years. The time elapsing between the hearing of the voices in contention and the breaking open of the room door, was variously stated by the witnesses. Some made it as short as three minutes—some as long as five. The door was opened with difficulty.

"*Alfonzo Carcio*, undertaker, deposes that he resides in the Rue Morgue. Is a native of Spain. Was one of the party who entered the house. Did not proceed up-stairs. Is nervous, and was apprehensive of the consequences of agitation. Heard the voices in contention. The gruff voice was that of a Frenchman. Could not distinguish what was said. The shrill voice was that of an Englishman—is sure of that. Does not understand the English language, but judges by the intonation.

"*Alberto Montani*, confectioner, deposes that he was among the first to ascend the stairs. Heard the voices in question. The gruff voice was that of a Frenchman. Distinguished several words. The speaker appeared to be expostulating. Could not make out the words of the shrill voice. Spoke quick and unevenly. Thinks it the voice of a Russian. Corroborates the general testimony. Is an Italian. Never conversed with a native of Russia.

"Several witnesses, recalled, here testified that the chimneys of all the rooms on the fourth story were too narrow to admit the passage of a human being. By 'sweeps' were meant cylindrical sweeping-brushes, such as are employed by those who clean chimneys. These brushes were passed up and down every flue in the house. There is no back passage by which any one could have descended while the party proceeded upstairs. The body of Mademoiselle L'Espanaye was so firmly wedged in the chimney that it could not be got down until four or five of the party united their strength.

"*Paul Dumas*, physician, deposes that he was called to view the bodies about daybreak. They were both then lying on the sacking of the bedstead in the chamber where Mademoiselle L. was found. The corpse of the young lady was much bruised and excoriated. The fact that it had been thrust up the chimney would sufficiently account for these appearances. The throat was greatly chafed. There were several deep scratches just below the chin, together with a series of livid spots which were evidently the impression of fingers. The face was fearfully discoloured, and the eyeballs protruded. The tongue had been partially bitten through. A large bruise was discovered upon the pit of the stomach, produced, apparently, by the pressure of a knee. In the opinion of M. Dumas, Mademoiselle L'Espanaye had been throttled to death by some person or persons unknown. The corpse of the mother was horribly mutilated. All the bones of the right leg and arm were more or less shattered. The left *tibia* much splintered, as well as all the ribs of the left side. Whole body dreadfully bruised and discoloured. It was not possible to say how the injuries had been inflicted. A heavy club of wood, or a broad bar of iron—a chair—any large, heavy, and obtuse weapon would have produced such results, if wielded by the hands of a very powerful man. No woman could have inflicted the blows with any weapon. The head of the deceased, when seen by witness, was entirely separated from the body, and was also greatly shattered. The throat had evidently been cut with some very sharp instrument— probably with a razor.

"*Alexandre Etienne*, surgeon, was called with M. Dumas to view the bodies. Corroborated the testimony, and the opinions of M. Dumas.

"Nothing farther of importance was elicited, although several other persons were examined. A murder so mysterious, and so perplexing in all its particulars, was never before committed in Paris—if indeed a murder has been committed at all. The police are entirely at fault—an unusual occurrence in affairs of this nature. There is not, however, the shadow of a clue apparent."

The evening edition of the paper stated that the greatest excitement still continued in the Quartier St. Roch—that the premises in question had been carefully re-searched, and fresh examinations of witnesses instituted, but all to no purpose. A postscript, however, mentioned that Adolphe Le Bon had been arrested and imprisoned—although nothing appeared to criminate him, beyond the facts already detailed.

Dupin seemed singularly interested in the progress of this affair—at least so I judged from his manner, for he made no comments. It was only after the announcement that Le Bon had been imprisoned, that he asked me my opinion respecting the murders.

I could merely agree with all Paris in considering them an insoluble mystery. I saw no means by which it would be possible to trace the murderer.

"We must not judge of the means," said Dupin, "by this shell of an examination. The Parisian police, so much extolled for *acumen*, are cunning, but no more. There is no method in their proceedings, beyond the method of the moment. They make a vast parade of measures; but, not unfrequently, these are so ill adapted to the objects proposed, as to put us in mind of Monsieur Jourdain's calling for his *robe-de-chambre—pour mieux entendre la musique*. The results attained by them are not unfrequently surprising, but, for the most part, are brought about by simple diligence and activity. When these qualities are unavailing, their schemes fail. Vidocq, for example, was a good guesser, and a persevering man. But, without educated thought, he erred continually by the very intensity of his investigations. He impaired his vision by holding the object too close. He might see, perhaps, one or two points with unusual clearness, but in so doing he, necessarily, lost sight of the matter as a whole. Thus there is such a thing as being too profound. Truth is not always in a well. In fact, as regards the more important knowledge, I do believe that she is invariably superficial. The depth lies in the valleys where we seek her, and not upon the mountain-tops where she is found. The modes and sources of this kind of error are well typified in the contemplation of the heavenly bodies. To look at a star by glances—to view it in a side-long way, by turning towards it the exterior portions of the *retina* (more susceptible of feeble impressions of light than the interior), is to behold the star distinctly— is to have the best appreciation of its lustre—a lustre which grows dim just in proportion as we turn our vision *fully* upon it. A greater number of rays actually fall upon the eye in the latter case, but, in the former, there is the more refined capacity for comprehension. By undue profundity we perplex and enfeeble thought; and it is possible to make even Venus herself vanish from the firmament by a scrutiny too sustained, too concentrated, or too direct.

"As for these murders, let us enter into some examinations for ourselves, before we make up an opinion respecting them. An inquiry will afford us amusement" (I thought this an odd term, so applied, but said nothing), "and, besides, Le Bon once rendered me a service for which I am not ungrateful. We will go and see the premises with our own eyes. I know G——, the Prefect of Police, and shall have no difficulty in obtaining the necessary permission."

The permission was obtained, and we proceeded at once to the Rue Morgue. This is one of those miserable thoroughfares which intervene between the Rue Richelieu and the Rue St. Roch. It was late in the afternoon when we reached it; as this quarter is at a great distance from that in which we resided. The house was readily found; for there were still many persons gazing up at the closed shutters, with an objectless curiosity, from the opposite side of the way. It was an ordinary Parisian house, with a gateway, on one side of which was a glazed watch-box, with a sliding panel in the window, indicating a *loge de concierge*. Before going in we walked up the street, turned down an alley, and then, again, turning, passed in the rear of the building—Dupin, meanwhile, examining the whole neighbourhood, as well as the house, with a minuteness of attention for which I could see no possible object.

Retracing our steps, we came again to the front of the dwelling, rang, and, having shown our credentials, were admitted by the agents in charge. We went upstairs—into the chamber where the body of Mademoiselle L'Espanaye had been found, and where both the deceased still lay. The disorders of the room had, as usual, been suffered to exist. I saw nothing beyond what had been stated in the *Gazette des Tribunaux*. Dupin scrutinized everything—not excepting the bodies of the victims. We then went into the other rooms, and into the yard; a *gendarme* accompanying us throughout. The examination occupied us until dark, when we took our departure. On our way home my companion stopped in for a moment at the office of one of the daily papers.

I have said that the whims of my friend were manifold, and that *Je les ménageais:*—for this phrase there is no English equivalent. It was his humour, now, to decline all conversation on the subject of the murder, until about noon the next day. He then asked me, suddenly, if I had observed anything *peculiar* at the scene of the atrocity.

There was something in his manner of emphasizing the word "peculiar," which caused me to shudder, without knowing why.

"No, nothing *peculiar*," I said; "nothing more, at least, than we both saw stated in the paper."

"The *Gazette*," he replied, "has not entered, I fear, into the unusual horror of the thing. But dismiss the idle opinions of this print. It appears to me that this mystery is considered insoluble, for the very reason which should cause it to be regarded as easy of solution—I mean for the *outré* character of its features. The police are confounded by the seeming absence of motive—not for the murder itself—but for the atrocity of

the murder. They are puzzled, too, by the seeming impossibility of rec-
onciling the voices heard in contention, with the facts than no one was
discovered upstairs but the assassinated Mademoiselle L'Espanaye, and
that there were no means of egress without the notice of the party
ascending. The wild disorder of the room; the corpse thrust, with the
head downwards, up the chimney; the frightful mutilation of the body
of the old lady; these considerations, with those just mentioned and
others which I need not mention, have sufficed to paralyse the powers,
by putting completely at fault the boasted *acumen*, of the government
agents. They had fallen into the gross but common error of confound-
ing the unusual with the abstruse. But it is by these deviations from the
plane of the ordinary, that reason feels its way, if at all, in its search for
the true. In investigations such as we are now pursuing, it should not
be so much asked 'what has occurred,' as 'what has occurred that has
never occurred before.' In fact, the facility with which I shall arrive, or
have arrived, at the solution of the mystery, is in the direct ratio of its
apparent insolubility in the eyes of the police."

I stared at the speaker in mute astonishment.

"I am now awaiting," continued he, looking towards the door of our
apartment—"I am now awaiting a person who, although perhaps not
the perpetrator of these butcheries, must have been in some measure
implicated in their perpetration. Of the worst portion of the crimes
committed, it is probable that he is innocent. I hope that I am right in
this supposition; for upon it I build my expectation of reading the
entire riddle. I look for the man here—in this room—every moment.
It is true that he may not arrive; but the probability is that he will.
Should he come, it will be necessary to detain him. Here are pistols;
and we both know how to use them when occasion demands their use."

I took the pistols, scarcely knowing what I did, or believing what I
heard, while Dupin went on, very much as if in a soliloquy. I have
already spoken of his abstract manner at such times. His discourse was
addressed to myself; but his voice, although by no means loud, had that
intonation which is commonly employed in speaking to some one at a
great distance. His eyes, vacant in expression, regarded only the wall.

"That the voices heard in contention," he said, "by the party upon
the stairs, were not the voices of the women themselves, was fully
proved by the evidence. This relieves us of all doubt upon the question
whether the old lady could have first destroyed the daughter, and afterward have committed suicide. I speak of this point chiefly for the sake
of method; for the strength of Madame L'Espanaye would have been
utterly unequal to the task of thrusting her daughter's corpse up the
chimney as it was found; and the nature of the wounds upon her own
person entirely precluded the idea of self-destruction. Murder, then,

has been committed by some third party; and the voices of this third party were those heard in contention. Let me now advert—not to the whole testimony respecting these voices—but to what was *peculiar* in that testimony. Did you observe anything peculiar about it?"

I remarked that, while all the witnesses agreed in supposing the gruff voice to be that of a Frenchman, there was much disagreement in regard to the shrill, or, as one individual termed it, the harsh voice.

"That was the evidence itself," said Dupin, "but it was not the peculiarity of the evidence. You have observed nothing distinctive. Yet there *was* something to be observed. The witnesses, as you remark, agreed about the gruff voice; they were here unanimous. But in regard to the shrill voice, the peculiarity is—not that they disagreed—but that, while an Italian, an Englishman, a Spaniard, a Hollander, and a Frenchman attempted to describe it, each one spoke of it as that of a *foreigner*. Each is sure that it was not the voice of one of his own countrymen. Each likens it—not to the voice of an individual of any nation with whose language he is conversant—but the converse. The Frenchman supposes it the voice of a Spaniard, and 'might have distinguished some words *had he been acquainted with the Spanish.*' The Dutchman maintains it to have been that of a Frenchman; but we find it stated that '*not understanding French this witness was examined through an interpreter.*' The Englishman thinks it the voice of a German, and '*does not understand German.*' The Spaniard 'is sure' that it was that of an Englishman, but 'judges by the intonation' altogether, '*as he has no knowledge of the English.*' The Italian believes it the voice of a Russian, but '*has never conversed with a native of Russia.*' A second Frenchman differs, however, with the first, and is positive that the voice is that of an Italian, but, '*not being cognizant of that tongue,* is, like the Spaniard, convinced by the intonation.' Now, how strangely unusual must that voice have really been, about which such testimony as this *could* have been elicited!—in whose *tones,* even, denizens of the five great divisions of Europe could recognize nothing familiar! You will say that it might have been the voice of an Asiatic—of an African. Neither Asiatics nor Africans abound in Paris; but, without denying the inference, I will now merely call your attention to three points. The voice is termed by one witness 'harsh rather than shrill.' It is represented by two others to have been 'quick and *unequal.*' No words—no sounds resembling words—were by any witness mentioned as distinguishable.

"I know not," continued Dupin, "what impression I may have made, so far, upon your own understanding; but I do not hesitate to say that legitimate deductions even from this portion of the testimony—the portion respecting the gruff and shrill voices—are in themselves sufficient to engender a suspicion which should give direction to all farther progress in the investigation of the mystery. I said 'legitimate deductions'; but my meaning is not thus fully expressed. I designed to imply that the deductions are the *sole* proper ones, and that the suspicion rises *inevitably* from them as the single result. What the suspicion is, however, I will not say just yet. I merely wish you to bear in mind that, with myself, it was sufficiently forcible to give a definite form—a certain tendency—to my inquires in the chamber.

"Let us now transport ourselves, in fancy, to this chamber. What shall we first seek here? The means of egress employed by the murderers. It is not too much to say that neither of us believe in preternatural events. Madame and Mademoiselle L'Espanaye were not destroyed by spirits. The doers of the deed were material, and escaped materially. Then how? Fortunately, there is but one mode of reasoning upon the point, and that mode *must* lead us to a definite decision.—Let us examine, each by each, the possible means of egress. It is clear that the assassins were in the room where Mademoiselle L'Espanaye was found, or at least in the room adjoining, when the party ascended the stairs. It is then only from these two apartments that we have to seek issues. The police have laid bare the floors, the ceilings, and the masonry of the walls, in every direction. No *secret* issues could have escaped their vigilance. But not trusting *their* eyes, I examined with my own. There were, then, *no* secret issues. Both doors leading from the rooms into the passage were securely locked, with the keys inside. Let us turn to the chimneys. These, although of ordinary width for some eight or ten feet above the hearths, will not admit, throughout their extent, the body of a large cat. The impossibility of egress, by means already stated, being thus absolute, we are reduced to the windows. Through those of the front rooms no one could have escaped without notice from the crowd in the street. The murderers *must* have passed, then, through those of the back room. Now, brought to this conclusion in so unequivocal a manner as we are, it is not our part, as reasoners, to reject it on account of apparent impossibilities. It is only for us to prove that these apparent 'impossibilities' are, in reality, not such.

"There are two windows in the chamber. One of them is unobstructed by furniture, and is wholly visible. The lower portion of the other is hidden from view by the head of the unwieldy bedstead which is thrust close up against it. The former was found securely fastened from within. It resisted the utmost force of those who endeavoured to raise it. A large gimlet-hole had been pierced in its frame to the left, and a very stout nail was found fitted therein, nearly to the head. Upon examining the other window, a similar nail was seen similarly fitted in it; and a vigorous attempt to raise this sash, failed also. The police were now entirely satisfied that egress had not been in these directions. And, *therefore*, it was thought a matter of supererogation to withdraw the nails and open the windows.

"My own examination was somewhat more particular, and was so for the reason I have just given—because here it was, I knew, that all apparent impossibilities *must* be proved to be not such in reality.

"I proceeded to think thus—*a posteriori*. The murderers *did* escape from one of these windows. This being so, they could not have re-fastened the sashes from the inside, as they were found fastened;—the consideration which put a stop, through its obviousness, to the scrutiny of the police in this quarter. Yet the sashes *were* fastened. They *must*, then, have the power of fastening themselves. There was no escape from this conclusion. I stepped to the unobstructed casement, withdrew the nail with some difficulty, and attempted to raise the sash. It resisted all my efforts, as I had anticipated. A concealed spring must, I now knew, exist; and this corroboration of my idea convinced me that my premises, at least, were correct, however mysterious still appeared the circumstances attending the nails. A careful search soon brought to light the hidden spring. I pressed it, and, satisfied with the discovery, forbore to upraise the sash.

"I now replaced the nail and regarded it attentively. A person passing out through this window might have reclosed it, and the spring would have caught—but the nail could not have been replaced. The conclusion was plain, and again narrowed in the field of my investigations. The assassins *must* have escaped through the other window. Supposing, then, the springs upon each sash to be the same, as was probable, there *must* be found a difference between the nails, or at least between the modes of their fixture. Getting upon the sacking of the bedstead, I looked over the head-board minutely at the second casement. Passing my hand down behind the board, I readily discovered and pressed the spring, which was, as I had supposed, identical in character with its neighbour. I now looked at the nail. It was as stout as the other, and apparently fitted in the same manner—driven in nearly up to the head.

"You will say that I was puzzled; but, if you think so, you must have misunderstood the nature of the inductions. To use a sporting phrase, I had not been once 'at fault.' The scent had never for an instant been lost. There was no flaw in any link of the chain. I had traced the secret to its ultimate result,—and that result was *the nail.* It had, I say, in every respect, the appearance of its fellow in the other window; but this fact was an absolute nullity (conclusive as it might seem to be) when compared with the consideration that here, at this point, terminated the clue. 'There *must* be something wrong,' I said, 'about the nail.' I touched it; and the head, with about a quarter of an inch of the shank, came off in my fingers. The rest of the shank was in the gimlet-hole, where it had been broken off. The fracture was an old one (for its edges were incrusted with rust), and had apparently been accomplished by the blow of a hammer, which had partially imbedded, in the top of the bottom sash, the head portion of the nail. I now carefully replaced this head portion in the indentation whence I had taken it, and the resemblance to a perfect nail was complete—the fissure was invisible. Pressing the spring, I gently raised the sash for a few inches; the head went up with it, remaining firm in its bed. I closed the window, and the semblance of the whole nail was again perfect.

"The riddle, so far, was now unriddled. The assassin had escaped through the window which looked upon the bed. Dropping of its own accord upon his exit (or perhaps purposely closed), it had become fastened by the spring; and it was the retention of this spring which had been mistaken by the police for that of the nail,—farther inquiry being thus considered unnecessary.

"The next question is that of the mode of descent. Upon this point I had been satisfied in my walk with you around the building. About five feet and a half from the casement in question there runs a lightning-rod. From this rod it would have been impossible for any one to reach the window itself, to say nothing of entering it. I observed, however, that the shutters of the fourth story were of the peculiar kind called by Parisian carpenters *ferrades*—a kind rarely employed at the present day, but frequently seen upon very old mansions at Lyons and Bordeaux. They are in the form of an ordinary door (a single, not a folding door), except that the upper half is latticed or worked in open trellis—thus affording an excellent hold for the hands. In the present instance these shutters are fully three feet and a half broad. When we saw them from the rear of the house, they were both about half open—that is to say, they stood off at right angles from the wall. It is probable that the police, as well as myself, examined the back of the tenement; but, if so, in looking at these *ferrades* in the line of their breadth (as they must have done), they did not perceive this great breadth itself, or, at all events, failed to take it into consideration. In fact, having once satisfied themselves that no egress could have been made in this quarter, they would naturally bestow here a very cursory examination. It was clear to me, however, that the shutter belonging to the window at the head of the bed, would, if swung fully back to the wall, reach to within two feet of the lightning-rod. It was also evident that, by exertion of a very unusual degree of activity and courage, an entrance into the window, from the rod, might have been thus effected.—By reaching to the distance of two feet and a half (we now suppose the shutter open to its whole extent) a robber might have taken a firm grasp upon the trellis-work. Letting go, then, his hold upon the rod, placing his feet securely against the wall, and springing boldly from it, he might have swung the shutter so as to close it, and, if we imagine the window open at the time, might even have swung himself into the room.

"I wish you to bear especially in mind that I have spoken of a *very* unusual degree of activity as requisite to success in so hazardous and so difficult a feat. It is my design to show you, first, that the thing might possibly have been accomplished:—but, secondly and *chiefly*, I wish to impress upon your understanding the *very extraordinary*—the almost preternatural character of that agility which could have accomplished it.

"You will say, no doubt, using the language of the law, that 'to make out my case' I should rather undervalue, than insist upon a full estimation of the activity required in this matter. This may be the practice in law, but it is not the usage of reason. My ultimate object is only the truth. My immediate purpose is to lead you to place in juxtaposition that *very unusual* activity of which I have just spoken, with that *very peculiar* shrill (or harsh) and *unequal* voice, about whose nationality no two persons could be found to agree, and in whose utterances no syllabification could be detected."

At these words a vague and half-formed conception of the meaning of Dupin flitted over my mind. I seemed to be upon the verge of comprehension, without power to comprehend—as men, at times, find themselves upon the brink of remembrance, without being able, in the end, to remember. My friend went on with his discourse.

"You will see," he said, "that I have shifted the question from the mode of egress to that of ingress. It was my design to suggest that both were effected in the same manner, at the same point. Let us now revert to the interior of the room. Let us survey the appearances here. The drawers of the bureau, it is said, had been rifled, although many articles of apparel still remained within them. The conclusion here is absurd. It is a mere guess—a very silly one—and no more. How are we to know that the articles found in the drawers were not all these drawers had originally contained? Madame L'Espanaye and her daughter lived an exceedingly retired life—saw no company—seldom went out—had little use for numerous changes of habiliment. Those found were at least of as good quality as any likely to be possessed by these ladies. If a thief had taken any, why did he not take the best—why did he not take all? In a word, why did he abandon four thousand francs in gold to encumber himself with a bundle of linen? The gold *was* abandoned. Nearly the whole sum mentioned by Monsieur Mignaud, the banker, was discovered, in bags, upon the floor. I wish you, therefore, to discard from your thoughts the blundering idea of *motive*, engendered in the brains of the police by that portion of the evidence which speaks of money delivered at the door of the house. Coincidences ten times as remarkable as this (the delivery of the money, and murder committed within three days upon the party receiving it), happen to all of us every hour of our lives, without attracting even momentary notice. Coincidences, in general, are great stumbling-blocks in the way of that class of thinkers who have been educated to know nothing of the theory of probabilities—that theory to which the most glorious objects of human research are indebted for the most glorious of illustration. In the present instance, had the gold been gone, the fact of its delivery three days before would have formed something more than a coincidence. It would have been corroborative of this idea of motive. But, under the real circumstances of the case, if we are to suppose gold the motive of this outrage, we must also imagine the perpetrator so vacillating an idiot as to have abandoned his gold and his motive together.

"Keeping now steadily in mind the points to which I have drawn your attention—that peculiar voice, that unusual agility, and that startling absence of motive in a murder so singularly atrocious as this—let us glance at the butchery itself. Here is a woman strangled to death by manual strength, and thrust up a chimney, head downwards. Ordinary assassins employ no such modes of murder as this. Least of all, do they thus dispose of the murdered. In the manner of thrusting the corpse up the chimney, you will admit that there was something *excessively outré*—something altogether irreconcilable with our common notions of human action, even when we suppose the actors the most depraved of men. Think, too, how great must have been that strength which could have thrust the body *up* such an aperture so forcibly that the united vigour of several persons was found barely sufficient to drag it *down!*

"Turn, now, to other indications of the employment of a vigour most marvellous. On the hearth were thick tresses—very thick tresses—of grey human hair. These had been torn out by the roots. You are aware of the great force in tearing thus from the head even twenty or thirty hairs together. You saw the locks in question as well as myself. Their roots (a hideous sight!) were clotted with fragments of the flesh of the scalp—sure token of the prodigious power which had been exerted in uprooting perhaps half a million of hairs at a time. The throat of the old lady was not merely cut, but the head absolutely severed from the body: the instrument was a mere razor. I wish you also to look at the *brutal* ferocity of these deeds. Of the bruises upon the body of Madame L'Espanaye I do not speak. Monsieur Dumas, and his worthy coadjutor Monsieur Etienne, have pronounced that they were inflicted by some obtuse instrument; and so far these gentlemen are very correct. The obtuse instrument was clearly the stone pavement in the yard, upon which the victim had fallen from the window which looked in upon the bed. This idea, however simple it may now seem, escaped the police for the same reason that the breadth of the shutters escaped them—because, by the affair of the nails, their perceptions had been hermetically sealed against the possibility of the windows having ever been opened at all.

"If now, in addition to all these things, you have properly reflected upon the odd disorder of the chamber, we have gone so far as to combine the ideas of an agility astounding, a strength superhuman, a ferocity brutal, a butchery without motive, a *grotesquerie* in horror absolutely alien from humanity, and a voice foreign in tone to the ears of men of many nations, and devoid of all distinct or intelligible syllabification. What result, then, has ensued? What impression have I made upon your fancy?"

I felt a creeping of the flesh as Dupin asked me the question. "A madman," I said, "has done this deed—some raving maniac, escaped from a neighbouring *Maison de Santé.*"

"In some respects," he replied, "your idea is not irrelevant. But the voices of madmen, even in their wildest paroxysms, are never found to tally with that peculiar voice heard upon the stairs. Madmen are of some nation, and their language, however incoherent in its words, has always the coherence of syllabification. Besides, the hair of a madman is not such as I now hold in my hand. I disentangled this little tuft from the rigidly clutched fingers of Madame L'Espanaye. Tell me what you can make of it."

"Dupin!" I said, completely unnerved; "this hair is most unusual—this is no *human* hair."

"I have not asserted that it is," said he; "but, before we decide this point, I wish you to glance at the little sketch I have here traced upon the paper. It is a *fac-simile* drawing of what has been described in one portion of the testimony as 'dark bruises, and deep indentations of finger-nails,' upon the throat of Mademoiselle L'Espanaye, and in another (by Messrs. Dumas and Etienne), as a 'series of livid spots, evidently, the impression of fingers.'

"You will perceive," continued my friend, spreading out the paper upon the table before us, "that this drawing gives the idea of a firm and fixed hold. There is no *slipping* apparent. Each finger has retained—possibly until the death of the victim—the fearful grasp by which it originally imbedded itself. Attempt, now to place all your fingers, at the same time, in the respective impressions as you see them."

I made the attempt in vain.

"We are possibly not giving this matter a fair trial," he said. "The paper is spread out upon a plane surface; but the human throat is cylindrical. Here is a billet of wood, the circumference of which is about that of the throat. Wrap the drawing around it, and try the experiment again."

I did so, but the difficulty was even more obvious than before.

"This," I said, "is the mark of no human hand."

"Read now," replied Dupin, "this passage from Cuvier."

It was a minute anatomical and generally descriptive account of the large fulvous Ourang-Outang of the East Indian Islands. The gigantic stature, the prodigious strength and activity, the wild ferocity, and the imitative propensities of these mammalia are sufficiently well known to all. I understood the full horrors of the murder at once.

"The description of the digits," said I, as I made an end of reading, "is in exact accordance with this drawing. I see that no animal but an Ourang-Outang, of the species here mentioned, could possibly have impressed the indentations as you have traced them. This tuft of tawny hair, too, is identical with that of the beast of Cuvier. But I cannot possibly comprehend the particulars of this frightful mystery. Besides, there were *two* voices heard in contention, and one of them was unquestionably the voice of a Frenchman."

"True; and you will remember an expression attributed almost unanimously, by the evidence, to this voice,—the expression, '*mon Dieu!*' This, under the circumstances, has been justly characterized by one of the witnesses (Montani, the confectioner), as an expression of remonstrance or expostulation. Upon these two words, therefore, I have mainly built my hopes of a full solution of the riddle. A Frenchman was cognizant of the murder. It is possible—indeed it is far more than probable—that he was innocent of all participation in the bloody transactions which took place. The Ourang-Outang may have escaped from him. He may have traced it to the chamber; but, under the agitating circumstances which ensued, he could never have recaptured it. It is still at large. I will not pursue these guesses—for I have no right to call them more—since the shades of reflection upon which they are based are scarcely of sufficient depth to be appreciable by my own intellect, and since I could not pretend to make them intelligible to the understanding of another. We will call them guesses then, and speak of them as such. If the Frenchman in question is indeed, as I suppose, innocent of this atrocity, this advertisement, which I left last night, upon our return home, at the office of *Le Monde* (a paper devoted to the shipping interest, and much sought by sailors), will bring him to our residence."

He handed me a paper, and I read thus:

> CAUGHT—*In the Bois de Boulogne, early in the morning of the —— inst.* (the morning of the murder), *a very large, tawny Ourang-Outang of the Bornese species. The owner (who is ascertained to be a sailor, belonging to a Maltese vessel), may have the animal again, upon identifying it satisfactorily and paying a few charges arising from its capture and keeping. Call at No. ——, Rue ——, Faubourg St. Germain —— au troisième.*

"How was it possible," I asked, "that you should know the man to be a sailor, and belonging to a Maltese vessel?"

"I do *not* know it," said Dupin. "I am not *sure* of it. Here, however, is a small piece of ribbon, which from its form, and from its greasy appearance, has evidently been used in tying the hair in one of those long *queues* of which sailors are so fond. Moreover, this knot is one which few besides sailors can tie, and is peculiar to the Maltese. I picked the ribbon up at the foot of the lightning-rod. It could not have belonged to either of the deceased. Now if, after all, I am wrong in my induction from this ribbon, that the Frenchman was a sailor belonging to a Maltese vessel, still I can have no harm in saying what I did in the advertisement. If I am in error, he will merely suppose that I have been misled by some circumstance into which he will not take the trouble to inquire. But if I am right, a great point is gained. Cognizant although innocent of the murder, the Frenchman will naturally hesitate about replying to the advertisement—about demanding the Ourang-Outang. He will reason thus:—'I am innocent; I am poor; my Ourang-Outang is of great value—to one in my circumstances a fortune of itself—why should I lose it through idle apprehensions of danger? Here it is, within my grasp. It was found in the Bois de Boulogne—at a vast distance from the scene of that butchery. How can it ever be suspected that a brute beast should have done the deed? The police are at fault—they have failed to procure the slightest clue. Should they even trace the animal, it would be impossible to prove me cognizant of the murder, or to implicate me in guilt on account of that cognizance. Above all, *I am known*. The advertiser designates me as the possessor of the beast. I am not sure to what limit his knowledge may extend. Should I avoid claiming a property of so great value, which it is known that I possess, I will render the animal, at least, liable to suspicion. It is not my policy to attract attention either to myself or to the beast. I will answer the advertisement, get the Ourang-Outang, and keep it close until this matter has blown over.'"

At this moment we heard a step upon the stairs.

"Be ready," said Dupin, "with your pistols, but neither use them nor show them until at a signal from myself."

The front door of the house had been left open, and the visitor had entered, without ringing, and advanced several steps upon the staircase. Now, however, he seemed to hesitate. Presently, we heard him descending. Dupin was moving quickly to the door, when we again heard him coming up. He did not turn back a second time, but stepped up with decision and rapped at the door of our chamber.

"Come in," said Dupin, in a cheerful and hearty tone.

A man entered. He was a sailor, evidently,—a tall, stout, and muscular-looking person, with a certain dare-devil expression of countenance, not altogether unprepossessing. His face, greatly sunburnt, was more than half hidden by whisker and *mustachio*. He had with him a huge oaken cudgel, but appeared to be otherwise unarmed. He bowed awkwardly, and bade us "good evening," in French accents, which, although somewhat Neufchatelish, were still sufficiently indicative of a Parisian origin.

"Sit down, my friend," said Dupin. "I suppose you have called about the Ourang-Outang. Upon my word, I almost envy you the possession of him; a remarkably fine, and no doubt a very valuable animal. How old do you suppose him to be?"

The sailor drew a long breath, with the air of a man relieved of some intolerable burthen, and then replied, in an assured tone:

"I have no way of telling—but he can't be more than four or five years old. Have you got him here?"

"Oh, no; we had no conveniences for keeping him here. He is at a livery stable in the Rue Dubourg, just by. You can get him in the morning. Of course you are prepared to identify the property?"

"To be sure I am, sir."

"I shall be sorry to part with him," said Dupin.

"I don't mean that you should be at all this trouble for nothing, sir," said the man. "Couldn't expect it. Am very willing to pay a reward for the finding of the animal—that is to say, anything in reason."

"Well," replied my friend, "that is all very fair, to be sure. Let me think!—what should I have? Oh! I will tell you. My reward shall be this. You shall give me all the information in your power about these murders in the Rue Morgue."

Dupin said the last words in a very low tone, and very quietly. Just as quietly, too, he walked toward the door, locked it, and put the key in his pocket. He then drew a pistol from his bosom and placed it, without the least flurry, upon the table.

The sailor's face flushed up as if he were struggling with suffocation. He started to his feet and grasped his cudgel; but the next moment he fell back into his seat, trembling violently, and with the countenance of death itself. He spoke not a word. I pitied him from the bottom of my heart.

"My friend," said Dupin, in a kind tone, "you are alarming yourself unnecessarily—you are indeed. We mean you no harm whatever. I pledge you the honour of a gentleman, and of a Frenchman, that we intend you no injury. I perfectly well know that you are innocent of the atrocities in the Rue Morgue. It will not do, however, to deny that you are in some measure implicated in them. From what I have already said, you must know that I have had means of information about this matter—means of which you could never have dreamed. Now the thing stands thus. You have done nothing which you could have avoided—nothing, certainly, which renders you culpable. You were not even guilty of robbery, when you might have robbed with impunity. You have nothing to conceal. You have no reason for concealment. On the other hand, you are bound by every principle of honour to confess all you know. An innocent man is now imprisoned, charged with that crime of which you can point out the perpetrator."

The sailor had recovered his presence of mind, in a great measure, while Dupin uttered these words; but his original boldness of bearing was all gone.

"So help me God," said he, after a brief pause, "I *will* tell you all I know about this affair;—but I do not expect you to believe one half I say—I would be a fool indeed if I did. Still, I *am* innocent, and I will make a clean breast if I die for it."

What he stated was, in substance, this. He had lately made a voyage to the Indian Archipelago. A party, of which he formed one, landed at Borneo, and passed into the interior on an excursion of pleasure. Himself and a companion had captured the Ourang-Outang. This companion dying, the animal fell into his own exclusive possession. After great trouble, occasioned by the intractable ferocity of his captive during the home voyage, he at length succeeded in lodging it safely at his own residence in Paris, where, not to attract toward himself the unpleasant curiosity of his neighbours, he kept it carefully secluded, until such time as it should recover from a wound in the foot, received from a splinter on board ship. His ultimate design was to sell it.

Returning home from some sailors' frolic on the night, or rather in the morning of the murder, he found the beast occupying his own bed-room, into which it had broken from a closet adjoining, where it had been, as was thought, securely confined. Razor in hand, and fully lathered, it was sitting before a looking-glass, attempting the operation of shaving, in which it had no doubt previously watched its master through the keyhole of the closet. Terrified at the sight of so dangerous a weapon in the possession of an animal so ferocious, and so well able to use it, the man, for some moments, was at a loss what to do. He had been accustomed, however, to quiet the creature, even in its fiercest moods, by the use of a whip, and to this he now resorted. Upon sight of it, the Ourang-Outang sprang at once through the door of the chamber, down the stairs, and thence, through a window, unfortunately open, into the street.

The Frenchman followed in despair; the ape, razor still in hand, occasionally stopping to look back and gesticulate at its pursuer, until the latter had nearly come up with it. It then again made off. In this manner the chase continued for a long time. The streets were profoundly quiet, as it was nearly three o'clock in the morning. In passing down an alley in the rear of the Rue Morgue, the fugitive's attention was arrested by a light gleaming from the open window of Madame L'Espanaye's chamber, in the fourth story of her house. Rushing to the building, it perceived the lightning-rod, clambered up with inconceivable agility, grasped the shutter, which was thrown fully back against the wall, and, by its means, swung itself directly upon the head-board of the bed. The whole feat did not occupy a minute. The shutter was kicked open again by the Ourang-Outang as it entered the room.

The sailor, in the meantime, was both rejoiced and perplexed. He had strong hopes of now recapturing the brute, as it could scarcely escape from the trap into which it ventured, except by the rod, where it might be intercepted as it came down. On the other hand, there was much cause for anxiety as to what it might do in the house. This latter reflection urged the man still to follow the fugitive. A lightning-rod is ascended without difficulty, especially by a sailor; but, when he had arrived as high as the window, which lay far to his left, his career was stopped; the most that he could accomplish was to reach over so as to obtain a glimpse of the interior of the room. At this glimpse he nearly fell from his hold through excess of horror. Now it was that those hideous shrieks arose upon the night, which had startled from slumber the inmates of the Rue Morgue. Madame L'Espanaye and her daughter, habituated in their night clothes, had apparently been arranging some papers in the iron chest already mentioned, which had been wheeled into the middle of the room. It was open, and its contents lay beside it on the bed. The victims must have been sitting with their backs toward the window; and, from the time elapsing between the ingress of the beast and the screams, it seems probable that it was not immediately perceived. The flapping-to of the shutter would naturally have been attributed to the wind.

As the sailor looked in, the gigantic animal had seized Madame L'Espanaye by the hair (which was loose, as she had been combing it), and was flourishing the razor about her face, in imitation of the motions of a barber. The daughter lay prostrate and motionless: she had swooned. The screams and struggles of the old lady (during which the hair was torn from her head) had the effect of changing the proba- bly pacific purposes of the Ourang-Outang into those of wrath. With one determined sweep of its muscular arm it nearly severed her head from her body. The sight of blood inflamed its anger into frenzy. Gnashing its teeth, and flashing fire from its eyes, it flew upon the body of the girl, and imbedded its fearful talons in her throat, retaining its grasp until she expired. Its wandering and wild glances fell at this moment upon the head of the bed, over which the face of its master, rigid with horror, was just discernible. The fury of the beast, who no doubt bore still in mind the dreaded whip, was instantly converted into fear. Conscious of having deserved punishment, it seemed desirous of concealing its bloody deeds, and skipped about the chamber in an agony of nervous agitation; throwing down and breaking the furniture as it moved, and dragging the bed from the bedstead. In conclusion, it seized first the corpse of the daughter, and thrust it up the chimney, as it was found; then that of the old lady, which it immediately hurled through the window headlong.

As the ape approached the casement with its mutilated burthen, the sailor shrank aghast to the rod, and, rather gliding than clambering down it, hurried at once home—dreading the consequences of the butchery, and gladly abandoning, in his terror, all solicitude about the fate of the Ourang-Outang. The words heard by the party upon the staircase were the Frenchman's exclamations of horror and affright, commingled with the fiendish jabberings of the brute.

I have scarcely anything to add. The Ourang-Outang must have escaped from the chamber by the rod, just before the breaking of the door. It must have closed the window as it passed through it. It was subsequently caught by the owner himself, who obtained for it a very large sum at the *Jardin des Plantes*. Le Bon was instantly released, upon our narration of the circumstances (with some comments from Dupin) at the *bureau* of the Prefect of Police. This functionary, however well disposed to my friend, could not altogether conceal his chagrin at the turn which affairs had taken, and was fain to indulge in a sarcasm or two, about the propriety of every person minding his own business.

"Let him talk," said Dupin, who had not thought it necessary to reply. "Let him discourse; it will ease his conscience. I am satisfied with having defeated him in his own castle. Nevertheless, that he failed in the solution of this mystery is by no means that matter for wonder which he supposes it; for in truth, our friend the Prefect is somewhat too cunning to be profound. In his wisdom is no *stamen*. It is all head and no body, like the pictures of the Goddess Laverna,—or, at best, all head and shoulders, like a codfish. But he is a good creature after all. I like him especially for one master stroke of cant, by which he has attained his reputation for ingenuity. I mean the way he has '*de nier ce qui est, et d'expliquer ce qui n'est pas.*'"*

---

*"of denying that which is, and explaining that which is not." Rousseau, *Nouvelle Héloise*.

Charles Dickens

(1812–1870)

POE'S STORIES WERE POPULAR, but for detective fiction to become a major form of popular literature, public attitudes toward crime had to turn from sympathy for the criminal (as had been the response to the picaresque romances and Newgate Calendar tales of previous centuries) toward admiration for the law-enforcer. It was, however, difficult to find anything to admire in London's corrupt Bow Street Runners or the often superannuated night watchmen in many cities. This would change with the creation of Scotland Yard in 1829, to be followed thirteen years later by the office that would develop into the plain-clothes Criminal Investigation Department. As the success and relative honesty of the Detective Police became known, the old image of the crooked thief-taker was gradually replaced by the upright Bobby.

With his interest in crime, Charles Dickens had introduced not-always respectable characters as investigators in *Barnaby Rudge* (1841) and *Martin Chuzzlewit* (1843), but it was in journalism that he gained a genuine knowledge of police activities. As editor of *Household Words*, he spent nights with the police, invited almost the entire C.I.D. to the magazine's offices for a party, and recorded the investigations of the police in "Three Detective Anecdotes," in 1850. These experiences led to the positive depiction of Inspector Bucket in *Bleak House* (1853), and it was Dickens who began the process of creating the policeman as detective hero.

Three "Detective" Anecdotes

I.—The Pair of Gloves

"IT'S A SINGLER STORY, Sir," said Inspector Wield, of the Detective Police, who, in company with Sergeants Dornton and Mith, paid us another twilight visit, one July evening; "and I've been thinking you might like to know it.

"It's concerning the murder of the young woman, Eliza Grimwood, some years ago, over in the Waterloo Road. She was commonly called The Countess, because of her handsome appearance and her proud way of carrying of herself; and when I saw the poor Countess (I had known her well to speak to), lying dead, with her throat cut, on the floor of her bed-room, you'll believe me that a variety of reflections calculated to make a man rather low in his spirits, came into my head.

"That's neither here nor there. I went to the house the morning after the murder, and examined the body, and made a general observation of the bed-room where it was. Turning down the pillow of the bed with my hand, I found, underneath it, a pair of gloves. A pair of gentlemen's dress gloves, very dirty; and inside the lining, the letters TR, and a cross.

"Well, Sir, I took them gloves away, and I showed 'em to the magistrate, over at Union Hall, before whom the case was. He says 'Wield,' he says, 'there's no doubt this is a discovery that may lead to something very important; and what you have got to do, Wield, is, to find out the owner of these gloves.'

"I was of the same opinion, of course, and I went at it immediately. I looked at the gloves pretty narrowly, and it was my opinion that they had been cleaned. There was a smell of sulphur and rosin about 'em, you know, which cleaned gloves usually have, more or less. I took 'em over to a friend of mine at Kennington, who was in that line, and I put

it to him. 'What do you say now? Have these gloves been cleaned?'
'These gloves have been cleaned,' says he. 'Have you any idea who
cleaned them?' says I. 'Not at all,' says he; 'I've a very distinct idea who
didn't clean 'em, and that's myself. But I'll tell you what, Wield, there
ain't above eight or nine reg'lar glove cleaners in London,'—there were
not, at that time, it seems—'and I think I can give you their addresses,
and you may find out, by that means, who did clean 'em.' Accordingly,
he gave me the directions, and I went here, and I went there, and I
looked up this man, and I looked up that man; but, though they all
agreed that the gloves had been cleaned, I couldn't find the man,
woman, or child, that had cleaned that aforesaid pair of gloves.

"What with this person not being at home, and that person being
expected home in the afternoon, and so forth, the inquiry took me three
days. On the evening of the third day, coming over Waterloo Bridge
from the Surrey side of the river, quite beat, and very much vexed and
disappointed, I thought I'd have a shilling's worth of entertainment at
the Lyceum Theatre to freshen myself up. So I went into the Pit, at
half-price and I sat myself down next to a very quiet, modest sort of a
young man. Seeing I was a stranger (which I thought it just as well to
appear to be) he told me the names of the actors on the stage, and we
got into conversation. When the play was over, we came out together,
and I said, 'We've been very companionable and agreeable, and perhaps you wouldn't object to a drain?' 'Well, you're very good,' says he;
'I *shouldn't* object to a drain.' Accordingly, we went to a public-house,
near the Theatre, sat ourselves down in a quiet room up stairs on the
first floor, and called for a pint of half-and-half, apiece, and a pipe.

"Well, Sir, we put our pipes aboard, and we drank our half-and-half,
and sat a talking, very sociably, when the young man says, 'You must
excuse me stopping very long,' he says, 'because I'm forced to go
home in good time. I must be at work all night.' 'At work all night?'
says I. 'You ain't a Baker?' 'No,' he says, laughing, 'I ain't a baker.'
"I thought not,' says I, 'you haven't the looks of a baker.' 'No,' says he,
'I'm a glove-cleaner.'

"I never was more astonished in my life, than when I heard them
words come out of his lips. 'You're a glove-cleaner, are you?' says I. 'Yes,'
he says, 'I am.' 'Then, perhaps,' says I, taking the gloves out of my
pocket, 'you can tell me who cleaned this pair of gloves? It's a rum
story,' I says. 'I was dining over at Lambeth, the other day, at a free-and-
easy—quite promiscuous—with a public company—when some
gentleman, he left these gloves behind him! Another gentleman
and me, you see, we laid a wager of a sovereign, that I wouldn't find out
who they belong to. I've spent as much as seven shillings already, in trying to discover; but, if you could help me, I'd stand another seven and

welcome. You see there's TR and a cross, inside.' '*I* see,' he says. 'Bless you, *I* know these gloves very well! I've seen dozens of pairs belonging to the same party.' 'No?' says I. 'Yes,' says he. 'Then you know who cleaned 'em?' says I. 'Rather so,' says he. 'My father cleaned 'em.'

"'Where does your father live?' says I. 'Just round the corner,' says the young man, 'near Exeter Street, here. He'll tell you who they belong to, directly.' 'Would you come round with me now?' says I. 'Certainly,' says he, 'but you needn't tell my father that you found me at the play, you know, because he mightn't like it.' 'All right!' We went round to the place, and there we found an old man in a white apron, with two or three daughters, all rubbing and cleaning away at lots of gloves, in a front parlor. 'Oh, Father!' says the young man, 'here's a person been and made a bet about the ownership of a pair of gloves, and I've told him you can settle it.' 'Good-evening, Sir,' says I to the old gentleman. 'Here's the gloves your son speaks of. Letters TR, you see, and a cross.' 'Oh yes,' he says, 'I know these gloves very well; I've cleaned dozens of pairs of 'em. They belong to Mr. Trinkle, the great upholsterer in Cheapside.' 'Did you get 'em from Mr. Trinkle, direct,' says I, 'if you'll excuse my asking the question?' 'No,' says he; 'Mr. Trinkle always sends 'em to Mr. Phibbs's, the haberdasher's, opposite his shop, and the haberdasher sends 'em to me.' 'Perhaps *you* wouldn't object to a drain?' says I. 'Not in the least!' says he. So I took the old gentleman out, and had a little more talk with him and his son, over a glass, and we parted excellent friends.

"This was late on a Saturday night. First thing on the Monday morning, I went to the haberdasher's shop, opposite Mr. Trinkle's the great upholsterer's in Cheapside. 'Mr. Phibbs in the way?' 'My name is Phibbs.' 'Oh! I believe you sent this pair of gloves to be cleaned?' 'Yes, I did, for young Mr. Trinkle over the way. There he is, in the shop!' 'Oh! that's him in the shop, is it? Him in the green coat?' 'The same individual.' 'Well, Mr. Phibbs, this is an unpleasant affair; but the fact is, I am Inspector Wield of the Detective Police, and I found these gloves under the pillow of the young woman that was murdered the other day, over in the Waterloo Road!' 'Good Heaven!' says he. 'He's a most respectable young man, and if his father was to hear of it, it would be the ruin of him!' 'I'm very sorry for it,' says I, 'but I must take him into custody.' 'Good Heaven!' says Mr. Phibbs, again; 'can nothing be done?' 'Nothing,' says I. 'Will you allow me to call him over here,' says he, 'that his father may not see it done?' 'I don't object to that,' says I; 'but unfortunately, Mr. Phibbs, I can't allow of any communication between you. If any was attempted, I should have to interfere directly. Perhaps you'll beckon him over here?' Mr. Phibbs went to the door and beckoned, and the young fellow came across the street directly; a smart, brisk young fellow.

"'Good-morning, Sir,' says I. 'Good-morning, Sir,' says he. 'Would you allow me to inquire, Sir,' says I, 'if you ever had any acquaintance with a party of the name of Grimwood?' 'Grimwood! Grimwood!' says he, 'No!' 'You know the Waterloo Road?' 'Oh! of course I know the Waterloo Road!' 'Happen to have heard of a young woman being murdered there?' 'Yes, I read it in the paper, and very sorry I was to read it.' 'Here's a pair of gloves belonging to you, that I found under her pillow the morning afterward!'

"He was in a dreadful state, Sir; a dreadful state! 'Mr. Wield,' he says, 'upon my solemn oath I never was there. I never so much as saw her, to my knowledge, in my life!' 'I am very sorry,' says I. 'To tell you the truth, I don't think you *are* the murderer; but I must take you to Union Hall in a cab. However, I think it's a case of that sort, that, at present, at all events, the magistrate will hear it in private.'

"A private examination took place, and then it came out that this young man was acquainted with a cousin of the unfortunate Eliza Grimwood, and that, calling to see this cousin a day or two before the murder, he left these gloves upon the table. Who should come in, shortly afterward, but Eliza Grimwood! 'Whose gloves are these?' she says, taking 'em up. 'Those are Mr. Trinkle's gloves,' says her cousin. 'Oh!' says she, 'they are very dirty, and of no use to him, I am sure. I shall take 'em away for my girl to clean the stoves with.' And she put 'em in her pocket. The girl had used 'em to clean the stoves, and, I have no doubt, had left 'em lying on the bed-room mantel-piece, or on the drawers, or somewhere; and her mistress, looking round to see that the room was tidy, had caught 'em up and put 'em under the pillow where I found 'em.

"That's the story, Sir."

II. — The Artful Touch

"One of the most *beautiful* things that ever was done, perhaps," said Inspector Wield, emphasizing the adjective, as preparing us to expect dexterity or ingenuity rather than strong interest, "was a move of Sergeant Witchem's. It was a lovely idea!

"Witchem and me were down at Epsom one Derby Day, waiting at the station for the Swell Mob. As I mentioned, when we were talking about these things before, we are ready at the station when there's races, or an Agricultural Show, or a Chancellor sworn in for an university, or Jenny Lind, or anything of that sort; and as the Swell Mob come down, we send 'em back again by the next train. But some of the

Swell Mob, on the occasion of this Derby that I refer to, so far kiddied us as to hire a horse and shay; start away from London by Whitechapel, and miles round; come into Epsom from the opposite direction; and go to work, right and left, on the course, while we were waiting for 'em at the Rail. That, however, ain't the point of what I'm going to tell you.

"While Witchem and me were waiting at the station, there comes up one Mr. Tatt; a gentleman formerly in the public line, quite an amateur Detective in his way, and very much respected. 'Halloa, Charley Wield,' he says. 'What are you doing here? On the look out for some of your old friends?' 'Yes, the old move, Mr. Tatt.' 'Come along,' he says, 'you and Witchem, and have a glass of sherry.' 'We can't stir from the place,' says I, 'till the next train comes in; but after that, we will with pleasure.' Mr. Tatt waits, and the train comes in, and then Witchem and me go off with him to the Hotel. Mr. Tatt he's got up quite regardless of expense, for the occasion; and in his shirt-front there's a beautiful diamond prop, cost him fifteen or twenty pound—a very handsome pin indeed. We drink our sherry at the bar, and have had our three or four glasses, when Witchem cries suddenly, 'Look out Mr. Wield! stand fast!' and a dash is made into the place by the Swell Mob—four of 'em—that have come down as I tell you, and in a moment Mr. Tatt's prop is gone! Witchem, he cuts 'em off at the door, I lay about me as hard as I can, Mr. Tatt shows fight like a good 'un, and there we are, all down together, heads and heels, knocking about on the floor of the bar—perhaps you never see such a scene of confusion! However, we stick to our men (Mr. Tatt being as good as any officer), and we take 'em all, and carry 'em off to the station. The station's full of people, who have been took on the course; and it's a precious piece of work to get 'em secured. However, we do it at last, and we search 'em; but nothing's found upon 'em, and they're locked up; and a pretty state of heat we are in by that time, I assure you!

"I was very blank over it, myself, to think that the prop had been passed away; and I said to Witchem, when we had set 'em to rights, and were cooling ourselves along with Mr. Tatt, 'we don't take much by *this* move, anyway, for nothing's found upon 'em, and it's only the braggadocia* after all.' 'What do you mean, Mr. Wield,' says Witchem. 'Here's the diamond pin!' and in the palm of his hand there it was, safe and sound! 'Why, in the name of wonder,' says me and Mr. Tatt, in astonishment, 'how did you come by that?' 'I'll tell you how I come by it,' says he. 'I saw which of 'em took it; and when we were all down on the floor together, knocking about, I just gave him a little touch on the

*Three months' imprisonment as reputed thieves.

back of his hand, as I knew his pal would; and he thought it *was* his pal; and gave it me!' It was beautiful, beau-ti-ful!

"Even that was hardly the best of the case, for that chap was tried at the Quarter Sessions at Guilford. You know what Quarter Sessions are, Sir. Well, if you'll believe me, while them slow justices were looking over the Acts of Parliament, to see what they could do to him, I'm blowed if he didn't cut out of the dock before their faces! He cut out of the dock, Sir, then and there; swam across a river; and got up into a tree to dry himself. In the tree he was took—an old woman having seen him climb up—and Witchem's artful touch transported him!"

III.—The Sofa

"What young men will do, sometimes, to ruin themselves and break their friends' hearts," said Sergeant Dornton, "it's surprising! I had a case at Saint Blank's Hospital which was of this sort. A bad case, indeed, with a bad end!"

"The Secretary, and the House-Surgeon, and the Treasurer, of Saint Blank's Hospital, came to Scotland Yard to give information of numerous robberies having been committed on the students. The students could leave nothing in the pockets of their great-coats, while the great-coats were hanging at the hospital, but it was almost certain to be stolen. Property of various descriptions was constantly being lost; and the gentlemen were naturally uneasy about it, and anxious, for the credit of the institution, that the thief or thieves should be discovered. The case was entrusted to me, and I went to the hospital.

"'Now, gentlemen,' said I, after we had talked it over; 'I understand this property is usually lost from one room.'

"Yes, they said. It was.

"'I should wish, if you please,' said I, 'to see the room.'

"It was a good-sized bare room downstairs, with a few tables and forms in it, and a row of pegs, all round, for hats and coats.

"'Next, gentlemen,' said I, 'do you suspect anybody?'

"Yes, they said. They did suspect somebody. They were sorry to say, they suspected one of the porters.

"'I should like,' said I, 'to have that man pointed out to me, and have a little time to look after him.'

"He was pointed out, and I looked after him, and then I went back to the hospital, and said, 'Now, gentlemen, it's not the porter. He's, unfortunately for himself, a little too fond of drink, but he's nothing worse. My suspicion is, that these robberies are committed by one of the students; and if you'll put me a sofa into that room where the pegs are—as there's no closet—I think I shall be able to detect the thief. I wish the sofa, if you please, to be covered with chintz, or something of that sort, so that I may lie on my chest, underneath it, without being seen.'

"The sofa was provided, and next day at eleven o'clock, before any of the students came, I went there, with those gentlemen, to get underneath it. It turned out to be one of those old-fashioned sofas with a great cross-beam at the bottom, that would have broken my back in no time if I could ever have got below it. We had quite a job to break all this away in time; however, I fell to work, and they fell to work, and we broke it out, and made a clear place for me. I got under the sofa, lay down on my chest, took out my knife, and made a convenient hole in the chintz to look through. It was then settled between me and the gentlemen that when the students were all up in the wards, one of the gentlemen should come in, and hang up a great-coat on one of the pegs. And that the great-coat should have, in one of the pockets, a pocket-book containing marked money.

"After I had been there some time, the students began to drop into the room, by ones, and twos, and threes, and to talk about all sorts of things, little thinking there was anybody under the sofa—and then go upstairs. At last there came in one who remained until he was alone in the room by himself. A tallish, good-looking young man of one or two and twenty, with a light whisker. He went to a particular hat-peg, took off a good hat that was hanging there, tried it on, hung his own hat in its place, and hung that hat on another peg, nearly opposite to me. I then felt quite certain that he was the thief, and would come back by-and-bye.

"When they were all upstairs, the gentleman came in with the great-coat. I showed him where to hang it, so that I might have a good view of it; and he went away; and I lay under the sofa on my chest, for a couple of hours or so, waiting.

"At last, the same young man came down. He walked across the room, whistling—stopped and listened—took another walk and whistled—stopped again, and listened—then began to go regularly round the pegs, feeling in the pockets of all the coats. When he came to *the* great-coat, and felt the pocket-book, he was so eager and so hurried that he broke the strap in tearing it open. As he began to put the money in his pocket, I crawled out from under the sofa, and his eyes met mine.

"My face, as you may perceive, is brown now, but it was pale at that time, my health not being good; and looked as long as a horse's. Besides which, there was a great draught of air from the door, underneath the sofa, and I had tied a handkerchief round my head; so what I looked like, altogether, I don't know. He turned blue—literally blue—when he saw me crawling out, and I couldn't feel surprised at it.

"'I am an officer of the Detective Police,' said I, 'and have been lying here, since you first came in this morning. I regret, for the sake of yourself and your friends, that you should have done what you have; but this case is complete. You have the pocket-book in your hand and the money upon you; and I must take you into custody.

"It was impossible to make out any case in his behalf, and on his trial he pleaded guilty. How or when he got the means I don't know; but while he was awaiting his sentence, he poisoned himself in Newgate."

We inquired of this officer, on the conclusion of the foregoing anecdote, whether the time appeared long, or short, when he lay in that constrained position under the sofa?

"Why, you see, sir," he replied, "if he hadn't come in, the first time, and I had not been quite sure he was the thief, and would return, the time would have seemed long. But, as it was, I being dead-certain of my man, the time seemed pretty short."

Wilkie Collins

(1824–1889)

WILLIAM WILKIE COLLINS was probably the finest constructor of plots of all Victorian novelists. It is difficult to find the dovetailing of as many elements, and as many voices, as Collins was able to achieve in *The Woman in White* (1860). However, although this novel contains a great deal of detective-investigation, the identity of Count Fosco as a villain is too obvious to make much of the story mysterious. It was eight years later, that Collins wrote what has been hailed as the first full-length detective novel: *The Moonstone*. And though there were (as with Poe's contributions) some precursors—most notably Mary Elizabeth Braddon's *The Trail of the Serpent* (1861), and Charles Felix's *The Notting Hill Mystery* (1865)—Collins's great novel does deserve pride of place. The mystery of who stole the Moonstone is central throughout the book; there are many clues to the ultimate solution; and the detection—shared by many characters, including a finely drawn police detective, Sergeant Cuff—drives much of the plot.

Before he wrote *The Moonstone*, Collins had made gentle fun of the idea, promulgated by his friend Charles Dickens, of the near infallibility of the new police force. "The Biter Bit" was first collected in Collins's book *The Queen of Hearts* (1859).

The Biter Bit

(Extracted from the Correspondence of the London Police.)

FROM CHIEF INSPECTOR THEAKSTONE, OF THE DETECTIVE POLICE,
TO SERGEANT BULMER, OF THE SAME FORCE.

London, 4th July, 18—.
SERGEANT BULMER,—This is to inform you that you are wanted to assist
in looking up a case of importance, which will require all the attention
of an experienced member of the force. The matter of the robbery on
which you are now engaged you will please to shift over to the young
man who brings you this letter. You will tell him all the circumstances
of the case, just as they stand; you will put him up to the progress
you have made (if any) toward detecting the person or persons by
whom the money has been stolen; and you will leave him to make the
best he can of the matter now in your hands. He is to have the whole
responsibility of the case, and the whole credit of his success if he
brings it to a proper issue.

So much for the orders that I am desired to communicate to you.

A word in your ear, next, about this new man who is to take your
place. His name is Matthew Sharpin, and he is to have the chance
given him of dashing into our office at one jump—supposing he turns
out strong enough to take it. You will naturally ask me how he comes
by this privilege. I can only tell you that he has some uncommonly
strong interest to back him in certain high quarters, which you and I
had better not mention except under our breaths. He has been a lawyer's
clerk, and he is wonderfully conceited in his opinion of himself, as well

as mean and underhand to look at. According to his own account, he leaves his old trade and joins ours of his own free will and preference. You will no more believe that than I do. My notion is, that he has managed to ferret out some private information in connection with the affairs of one of his master's clients, which makes him rather an awkward customer to keep in the office for the future, and which, at the same time, gives him hold enough over his employer to make it dangerous to drive him into a corner by turning him away. I think the giving him this unheard-of chance among us is, in plain words, pretty much like giving him hush-money to keep him quiet. However that may be, Mr. Matthew Sharpin is to have the case now in your hands, and if he succeeds with it he pokes his ugly nose into our office as sure as fate. I put you up to this, sergeant, so that you may not stand in your own light by giving the new man any cause to complain of you at head-quarters, and remain yours,

FRANCIS THEAKSTONE.

FROM MR. MATTHEW SHARPIN TO CHIEF INSPECTOR THEAKSTONE.

London, 5th July, 18—.

DEAR SIR,—Having now been favored with the necessary instructions from Sergeant Bulmer, I beg to remind you of certain directions which I have received relating to the report of my future proceedings which I am to prepare for examination at head-quarters.

The object of my writing, and of your examining what I have written before you send it to the higher authorities, is, I am informed, to give me, as an untried hand, the benefit of your advice in case I want it (which I venture to think I shall not) at any stage of my proceedings. As the extraordinary circumstances of the case on which I am now engaged make it impossible for me to absent myself from the place where the robbery was committed until I have made some progress toward discovering the thief, I am necessarily precluded from consulting you personally. Hence the necessity of my writing down the various details, which might, perhaps, be better communicated by word of mouth. This, if I am not mistaken, is the position in which we are now placed. I state my own impressions on the subject in writing, in order that we may clearly understand each other at the outset; and have the honor to remain your obedient servant,

MATTHEW SHARPIN.

FROM CHIEF INSPECTOR THEAKSTONE TO MR. MATTHEW SHARPIN.

London, 5th July, 18—.

SIR,—You have begun by wasting time, ink, and paper. We both of us perfectly well knew the position we stood in toward each other when I sent you with my letter to Sergeant Bulmer. There was not the least need to repeat it in writing. Be so good as to employ your pen in future on the business actually in hand.

You have now three separate matters on which to write me. First, you have to draw up a statement of your instructions received from Sergeant Bulmer, in order to show us that nothing has escaped your memory, and that you are thoroughly acquainted with all the circumstances of the case which has been intrusted to you. Secondly, you are to inform me what it is you propose to do. Thirdly, you are to report every inch of your progress (if you make any) from day to day, and, if need be, from hour to hour as well. This is *your* duty. As to what *my* duty may be, when I want you to remind me of it, I will write and tell you so. In the mean time, I remain, yours,

FRANCIS THEAKSTONE.

FROM MR. MATTHEW SHARPIN TO CHIEF INSPECTOR THEAKSTONE.

London, 6th July, 18—.

SIR,—You are rather an elderly person, and, as such, naturally inclined to be a little jealous of men like me, who are in the prime of their lives and their faculties. Under these circumstances, it is my duty to be considerate toward you, and not to bear too hardly on your small failings. I decline, therefore, altogether to take offense at the tone of your letter; I give you the full benefit of the natural generosity of my nature; I sponge the very existence of your surly communication out of my memory—in short, Chief Inspector Theakstone, I forgive you, and proceed to business.

My first duty is to draw up a full statement of the instructions I have received from Sergeant Bulmer. Here they are at your service, according to my version of them.

At number Thirteen Rutherford Street, Soho, there is a stationer's shop. It is kept by one Mr. Yatman. He is a married man, but has no family. Besides Mr. and Mrs. Yatman, the other inmates in the house are a lodger, a young single man named Jay, who occupies the front room on the second floor—a shopman, who sleeps in one of the attics, and a servant-of-all-work, whose bed is in the back kitchen. Once a week a charwoman comes to help this servant. These are all the persons who, on ordinary occasions, have means of access to their interior of the house, placed, as a matter of course, at their disposal.

Mr. Yatman has been in business for many years, carrying on his affairs prosperously enough to realize a handsome independence for a person in his position. Unfortunately for himself, he endeavored to increase the amount of his property by speculating. He ventured boldly in his investments; luck went against him; and rather less than two years ago he found himself a poor man again. All that was saved out of the wreck of his property was the sum of two hundred pounds.

Although Mr. Yatman did his best to meet his altered circumstances, by giving up many of the luxuries and comforts to which he and his wife had been accustomed, he found it impossible to retrench so far as to allow of putting by any money from the income produced by his shop. The business has been declining of late years, the cheap advertising stationers having done it injury with the public. Consequently, up to the last week, the only surplus property possessed by Mr. Yatman consisted of the two hundred pounds which had been recovered from the wreck of his fortune. This sum was placed as a deposit in a joint-stock bank of the highest possible character.

Eight days ago Mr. Yatman and his lodger, Mr. Jay, held a conversation on the subject of the commercial difficulties which are hampering trade in all directions at the present time. Mr. Jay (who lives by supplying the newspapers with short paragraphs relating to accidents, offenses, and brief records of remarkable occurrences in general—who is, in short, what they call a penny-a-liner) told his landlord that he had been in the city that day and heard unfavorable rumors on the subject of the joint-stock banks. The rumors to which he alluded had already reached the ears of Mr. Yatman from other quarters, and the confirmation of them by his lodger had such an effect on his mind—predisposed as it was to alarm by the experience of his former losses—that he resolved to go at once to the bank and withdraw his deposit. It was then getting on toward the end of the afternoon, and he arrived just in time to receive his money before the bank closed.

He received the deposit in bank-notes of the following amounts: one fifty-pound note, three twenty-pound notes, six ten-pound notes, and six five-pound notes. His object in drawing the money in this form was to have it ready to lay out immediately in trifling loans, on good security, among the small tradespeople of his district, some of whom are sorely pressed for the very means of existence at the present time. Investments of this kind seemed to Mr. Yatman to be the most safe and the most profitable on which he could now venture.

He brought the money back in an envelope placed in his breast pocket, and asked his shopman, on getting home, to look for a small, flat, tin cash-box, which had not been used for years, and which, as Mr. Yatman remembered it, was exactly of the right size to hold the bank-notes. For some time the cash-box was searched for in vain.

Mr. Yatman called to his wife to know if she had any idea where it was. The question was overheard by the servant-of-all-work, who was taking up the tea-tray at the time, and by Mr. Jay, who was coming down stairs on his way out to the theatre. Ultimately the cash-box was found by the shopman. Mr. Yatman placed the bank-notes in it, secured them by a padlock, and put the box in his coat pocket. It stuck out of the coat pocket a very little, but enough to be seen. Mr. Yatman remained at home, up stairs, all that evening. No visitors called. At eleven o'clock he went to bed, and put the cash-box under his pillow.

When he and his wife woke the next morning the box was gone. Payment of the notes was immediately stopped at the Bank of England, but no news of the money has been heard of since that time.

So far the circumstances of the case are perfectly clear. They point unmistakably to the conclusion that the robbery must have been committed by some person living in the house. Suspicion falls, therefore, upon the servant-of-all-work, upon the shopman, and upon Mr. Jay. The two first knew that the cash-box was being inquired for by their master, but did not know what it was he wanted to put into it. They would assume, of course, that it was money. They both had opportunities (the servant when she took away the tea, and the shopman when he came, after shutting up, to give the keys of the till to his master) of seeing the cash-box in Mr. Yatman's pocket, and of inferring naturally, from its position there, that he intended to take it into his bedroom with him at night.

Mr. Jay, on the other hand, had been told, during the afternoon's conversation on the subject of joint-stock banks, that his landlord had a deposit of two hundred pounds in one of them. He also knew that Mr. Yatman left him with the intention of drawing that money out; and he heard the inquiry for the cash-box afterward, when he was coming down stairs. He must, therefore, have inferred that the money was in the house, and that the cash-box was the receptacle intended to contain it. That he could have had any idea, however, of the place in which Mr. Yatman intended to keep it for the night is impossible, seeing that he went out before the box was found, and did not return till his landlord was in bed. Consequently, if he committed the robbery, he must have gone into the bedroom purely on speculation.

Speaking of the bedroom reminds me of the necessity of noticing the situation of it in the house, and the means that exist of gaining easy access to it at any hour of the night.

The room in question is the back room on the first floor. In consequence of Mrs. Yatman's constitutional nervousness on the subject of fire, which makes her apprehend being burned alive in her room, in case of accident, by the hampering of the lock if the key is turned in it, her husband has never been accustomed to lock the bedroom door. Both he and his wife are, by their own admission, heavy sleepers; consequently, the risk to be run by any evil-disposed persons wishing to plunder the bedroom was of the most trifling kind. They could enter the room by merely turning the handle of the door; and, if they moved with ordinary caution, there was no fear of their waking the sleepers inside. This fact is of importance. It strengthens our conviction that the money must have been taken by one of the inmates of the house, because it tends to show that the robbery, in this case, might have been committed by persons not possessed of the superior vigilance and cunning of the experienced thief.

Such are the circumstances, as they were related to Sergeant Bulmer when he was first called in to discover the guilty parties, and, if possible, to recover the lost bank-notes. The strictest inquiry which he could institute failed of producing the smallest fragment of evidence against any of the persons on whom suspicion naturally fell. Their language and behavior on being informed of the robbery was perfectly consistent with the language and behavior of innocent people. Sergeant Bulmer felt from the first that this was a case for private inquiry and secret observation. He began by recommending Mr. and Mrs. Yatman to affect a feeling of perfect confidence in the innocence of the persons living under their roof, and he then opened the campaign by employing himself in following the goings and comings, and in discovering the friends, the habits, and the secrets of the maid-of-all-work.

Three days and nights of exertion on his own part, and on that of others who were competent to assist his investigations, were enough to satisfy him that there was no sound cause for suspicion against the girl.

He next practiced the same precaution in relation to the shopman. There was more difficulty and uncertainty in privately clearing up this person's character without his knowledge, but the obstacles were at last smoothed away with tolerable success; and, though there is not the same amount of certainty in this case which there was in the case of the girl, there is still fair reason for supposing that the shopman has had nothing to do with the robbery of the cash-box.

As a necessary consequence of these proceedings, the range of suspicion now becomes limited to the lodger, Mr. Jay.

When I presented your letter of introduction to Sergeant Bulmer, he had already made some inquiries on the subject of this young man. The result, so far, has not been at all favorable. Mr. Jay's habits are irregular; he frequents public houses, and seems to be familiarly acquainted with a great many dissolute characters; he is in debt to most of the trades-people whom he employs; he has not paid his rent to Mr. Yatman for the last month; yesterday evening he came home excited by liquor, and last week he was seen talking to a prize-fighter; in short, though Mr. Jay does call himself a journalist, in virtue of his penny-a-line contributions to the newspapers, he is a young man of low tastes, vulgar manners, and bad habits. Nothing has yet been discovered in relation to him which redounds to his credit in the smallest degree.

I have now reported, down to the very last details, all the particulars communicated to me by Sergeant Bulmer. I believe you will not find an omission any where; and I think you will admit, though you are prejudiced against me, that a clearer statement of facts was never laid before you than the statement I have now made. My next duty is to tell you what I propose to do now that the case is confided to my hands.

In the first place, it is clearly my business to take up the case at the point where Sergeant Bulmer has left it. On his authority, I am justified in assuming that I have no need to trouble myself about the maid-of-all-work and the shopman. Their characters are now to be considered as cleared up. What remains to be privately investigated is the question of the guilt or innocence of Mr. Jay. Before we give up the notes for lost, we must make sure, if we can, that he knows nothing about them.

This is the plan that I have adopted, with the full approval of Mr. and Mrs. Yatman, for discovering whether Mr. Jay is or is not the person who has stolen the cash-box:

I propose to-day to present myself at the house in the character of a young man who is looking for lodgings. The back room on the second floor will be shown to me as the room to let, and I shall establish my-self there to-night as a person from the country who has come to London to look for a situation in a respectable shop or office.

By this means I shall be living next to the room occupied by Mr. Jay. The partition between us is mere lath and plaster. I shall make a small hole in it, near the cornice, through which I can see what Mr. Jay does in his room, and hear every word that is said when any friend happens to call on him. Whenever he is at home, I shall be at my post of obser-vation; whenever he goes out, I shall be after him. By employing these means of watching him, I believe I may look forward to the discovery of his secret—if he knows any thing about the lost bank-notes—as to a dead certainty.

What you may think of my plan of observation I can not undertake to say. It appears to me to unite the invaluable merits of boldness and simplicity. Fortified by this conviction, I close the present communica-tion with feelings of the most sanguine description in regard to the future, and remain your obedient servant,

MATTHEW SHARPIN.

FROM THE SAME TO THE SAME.

7th July.

SIR,—As you have not honored me with any answer to my last communication, I assume that, in spite of your prejudices against me, it has produced the favorable impression on your mind which I ventured to anticipate. Gratified and encouraged beyond measure by the token of approval which your eloquent silence conveys to me, I proceed to report the progress that has been made in the course of the last twenty-four hours.

I am now comfortably established next door to Mr. Jay, and I am delighted to say that I have two holes in the partition instead of one. My natural sense of humor has led me into the pardonable extravagance of giving them both appropriate names. One I call my peep-hole, and the other my pipe-hole. The name of the first explains itself; the name of the second refers to a small tin pipe or tube inserted in the hole, and twisted so that the mouth of it comes close to my ear while I am standing at my post of observation. Thus, while I am looking at Mr. Jay through my peep-hole, I can hear every word that may be spoken in his room through my pipe-hole.

Perfect candor—a virtue which I have possessed from my childhood—compels me to acknowledge, before I go any farther, that the ingenious notion of adding a pipe-hole to my proposed peep-hole originated with Mrs. Yatman. This lady—a most intelligent and accomplished person, simple, and yet distinguished in her manners, has entered into all my little plans with an enthusiasm and intelligence which I can not too highly praise. Mr. Yatman is so cast down by his loss that he is quite incapable of affording me any assistance. Mrs. Yatman, who is evidently most tenderly attached to him, feels her husband's sad condition of mind even more acutely than she feels the loss of the money, and is mainly stimulated to exertion by her desire to assist in raising him from the miserable state of prostration into which he has now fallen.

"The money, Mr. Sharpin," she said to me yesterday evening, with tears in her eyes, "the money may be regained by rigid economy and strict attention to business. It is my husband's wretched state of mind that makes me so anxious for the discovery of the thief. I may be wrong, but I felt hopeful of success as soon as you entered the house; and I believe that, if the wretch who robbed us is to be found, you are the man to discover him." I accepted this gratifying compliment in the spirit in which it was offered, firmly believing that I shall be found, sooner or later, to have thoroughly deserved it.

Let me now return to business—that is to say, to my peep-hole and my pipe-hole.

I have enjoyed some hours of calm observation of Mr. Jay. Though rarely at home, as I understand from Mrs. Yatman, on ordinary occasions, he has been in-doors the whole of this day. That is suspicious, to begin with. I have to report, farther, that he rose at a late hour this morning (always a bad sign in a young man), and that he lost a great deal of time, after he was up, in yawning and complaining to himself of headache. Like other debauched characters, he ate little or nothing for breakfast. His next proceeding was to smoke a pipe—a dirty clay pipe, which a gentleman would have been ashamed to put between his lips. When he had done smoking he took out pen, ink, and paper, and sat down to write with a groan—whether of remorse for having taken the bank-notes, or of disgust at the task before him, I am unable to say. After writing a few lines (too far away from my peep-hole to give me a chance of reading over his shoulder), he leaned back in his chair, and amused himself by humming the tunes of popular songs. I recognized "My Mary Anne," "Bobbin' around," and "Old Dog Tray," among other melodies. Whether these do or do not represent secret signals by which he communicates with his accomplices remains to be seen. After he had amused himself for some time by humming, he got up and began to walk about the room, occasionally stopping to add a sentence to the paper on his desk. Before long he went to a locked cupboard and opened it. I strained my eyes eagerly, in expectation of making a discovery. I saw him take something carefully out of the cupboard—he turned round—and it was only a pint bottle of brandy! Having drunk some of the liquor, this extremely indolent reprobate lay down on his bed again, and in five minutes was fast asleep.

After hearing him snoring for at least two hours, I was recalled to my peep-hole by a knock at his door. He jumped up and opened it with suspicious activity.

A very small boy, with a very dirty face, walked in, said, "Please, sir, they're waiting for you," sat down with his legs a long way from the ground, and instantly fell asleep! Mr. Jay swore an oath, tied a wet towel round his head, and, going back to his paper, began to cover it with writing as fast as his fingers could move the pen. Occasionally getting up to dip the towel in water and tie it on again, he continued at this employment for nearly three hours; then folded up the leaves of writing, woke the boy, and gave them to him, with this remarkable expression: "Now, then, young sleepyhead, quick march! If you see the governor, tell him to have the money ready for me when I call for it." The boy grinned and disappeared. I was sorely tempted to follow "sleepy-head," but, on reflection, considered it safest still to keep my eye on the proceedings of Mr. Jay.

In half an hour's time he put on his hat and walked out. Of course,

I put on my hat and walked out also. As I went down stairs I passed Mrs. Yatman going up. The lady has been kind enough to undertake, by previous arrangement between us, to search Mr. Jay's room while he is out of the way, and while I am necessarily engaged in the pleasing duty of following him wherever he goes. On the occasion to which I now refer, he walked straight to the nearest tavern, and ordered a couple of mutton-chops for his dinner. I placed myself in the next box to him, and ordered a couple of mutton-chops for my dinner. Before I had been in the room a minute, a young man of highly suspicious manners and appearance, sitting at a table opposite, took his glass of porter in his hand and joined Mr. Jay. I pretended to be reading the newspaper, and listened, as in duty bound, with all my might.

"Jack has been here inquiring after you," says the young man.

"Did he leave any message?" asks Mr. Jay.

"Yes," says the other. "He told me, if I met with you, to say that he wished very particularly to see you to-night, and that he would give you a look in at Rutherford Street at seven o'clock."

"All right," says Mr. Jay. "I'll get back in time to see him."

Upon this, the suspicious-looking young man finished his porter, and saying that he was rather in a hurry, took leave of his friend (perhaps I should not be wrong if I said his accomplice?), and left the room.

At twenty-five minutes and a half past six—in these serious cases it is important to be particular about time—Mr. Jay finished his chops and paid his bill. At twenty-six minutes and three quarters I finished my chops and paid mine. In ten minutes more I was inside the house in Rutherford Street, and was received by Mrs. Yatman in the passage. That charming woman's face exhibited an expression of melancholy and disappointment which it quite grieved me to see.

"I am afraid, ma'am," says I, "that you have not hit on any little criminating discovery in the lodger's room?"

She shook her head and sighed. It was a soft, languid, fluttering sigh—and, upon my life, it quite upset me. For the moment I forgot business, and burned with envy of Mr. Yatman.

"Don't despair, ma'am," I said, with an insinuating mildness which seemed to touch her. "I have heard a mysterious conversation—I know of a guilty appointment—and I expect great things from my peep-hole and my pipe-hole to-night. Pray don't be alarmed, but I think we are on the brink of a discovery."

Here my enthusiastic devotion to business got the better part of my tender feelings. I looked—winked—nodded—left her.

When I got back to my observatory, I found Mr. Jay digesting his mutton-chops in an arm-chair, with his pipe in his mouth. On his table were two tumblers, a jug of water, and the pint bottle of brandy. It was then close upon seven o'clock. As the hour struck the person described as "Jack" walked in.

He looked agitated—I am happy to say he looked violently agitated. The cheerful glow of anticipated success diffused itself (to use a strong expression) all over me, from head to foot. With breathless interest I looked through my peep-hole, and saw the visitor—the "Jack" of this delightful case—sit down, facing me, at the opposite side of the table to Mr. Jay. Making allowance for the difference in expression which their countenances just now happened to exhibit, these two abandoned villains were so much alike in other respects as to lead at once to the conclusion that they were brothers. Jack was the cleaner man and the better dressed of the two. I admit that, at the outset. It is, perhaps, one of my failings to push justice and impartiality to their utmost limits. I am no Pharisee; and where Vice has its redeeming point, I say, let vice have its due—yes, yes, by all manner of means, let Vice have its due.

"What's the matter now, Jack?" says Mr. Jay.

"Can't you see it in my face?" says Jack. "My dear fellow, delays are dangerous. Let us have done with suspense, and risk it, the day after to-morrow."

"So soon as that?" cries Mr. Jay, looking very much astonished. "Well, I'm ready, if you are. But, I say, Jack, is somebody else ready too? Are you quite sure of that?"

He smiled as he spoke—a frightful smile—and laid a very strong emphasis on those two words, "Somebody else." There is evidently a third ruffian, a nameless desperado, concerned in the business.

"Meet us to-morrow," says Jack, "and judge for yourself. Be in the Regent's Park at eleven in the morning, and look out for us at the turning that leads to the Avenue Road."

"I'll be there," says Mr. Jay. "Have a drop of brandy and water? What are you getting up for? You're not going already?"

"Yes, I am," says Jack. "The fact is, I'm so excited and agitated that I can't sit still any where for five minutes together. Ridiculous as it may appear to you, I'm in a perpetual state of nervous flutter. I can't, for the life of me, help fearing that we shall be found out. I fancy that every man who looks twice at me in the street is a spy—"

At these words I thought my legs would have given way under me. Nothing but strength of mind kept me at my peep-hole—nothing else, I give you my word of honor.

"Stuff and nonsense!" cries Mr. Jay, with all the effrontery of a veteran in crime. "We have kept the secret up to this time, and we will manage cleverly to the end. Have a drop of brandy and water, and you will feel as certain about it as I do."

Jack steadily refused the brandy and water, and steadily persisted in taking his leave.

"I must try if I can't walk it off," he said. "Remember to-morrow morning—eleven o'clock, Avenue Road, side of the Regent's Park."

With those words he went out. His hardened relative laughed desperately and resumed the dirty clay pipe.

I sat down on the side of my bed, actually quivering with excitement.

It is clear to me that no attempt has yet been made to change the stolen bank-notes, and I may add that Sergeant Bulmer was of that opinion also when he left the case in my hands. What is the natural conclusion to draw from the conversation which I have just set down? Evidently that the confederates meet to-morrow to take their respective shares in the stolen money, and to decide on the safest means of getting the notes changed the day after. Mr. Jay is, beyond a doubt, the leading criminal in this business, and he will probably run the chief risk—that of changing the fifty-pound note. I shall, therefore, still make it my business to follow him—attending at the Regent's Park to-morrow, and doing my best to hear what is said there. If another appointment is made for the day after, I shall, of course, go to it. In the mean time, I shall want the immediate assistance of two competent persons (supposing the rascals separate after their meeting) to follow the two minor criminals. It is only fair to add that, if the rogues all retire together, I shall probably keep my subordinates in reserve. Being naturally ambitious, I desire, if possible, to have the whole credit of discovering this robbery to myself.

8th July.

I have to acknowledge, with thanks, the speedy arrival of my two subordinates—men of very average abilities, I am afraid; but, fortunately, I shall always be on the spot to direct them.

My first business this morning was necessarily to prevent possible mistakes by accounting to Mr. and Mrs. Yatman for the presence of two strangers on the scene. Mr. Yatman (between ourselves, a poor, feeble man) only shook his head and groaned. Mrs. Yatman (that superior woman) favored me with a charming look of intelligence.

"Oh, Mr. Sharpin!" she said, "I am so sorry to see those two men! Your sending for their assistance looks as if you were beginning to be doubtful of success."

I privately winked at her (she is very good in allowing me to do so without taking offense), and told her, in my facetious way, that she labored under a slight mistake.

"It is because I am sure of success, ma'am, that I send for them. I am determined to recover the money, not for my own sake only, but for Mr. Yatman's sake—and for yours."

I laid a considerable amount of stress on those last three words. She said, "Oh, Mr Sharpin!" again, and blushed of a heavenly red, and looked down at her work. I could go to the world's end with that woman if Mr. Yatman would only die.

I sent off the two subordinates to wait until I wanted them at the Avenue Road gate of the Regent's Park. Half an hour afterward I was following the same direction myself at the heels of Mr. Jay.

The two confederates were punctual to the appointed time. I blush to record it, but it is nevertheless necessary to state that the third rogue—the nameless desperado of my report, or, if you prefer it, the mysterious "somebody else" of the conversation between the two brothers—is—a woman! and, what is worse, a young woman! and, what is more lamentable still, a nice-looking woman! I have long resisted a growing conviction that, wherever there is mischief in this world, an individual of the fair sex is inevitably certain to be mixed up in it. After the experience of this morning, I can struggle against that sad conclusion no longer. I give up the sex—excepting Mrs. Yatman, I give up the sex.

The man named "Jack" offered the woman his arm. Mr. Jay placed himself on the other side of her. The three then walked away slowly among the trees. I followed them at a respectful distance. My two subordinates, at a respectful distance also, followed me.

It was, I deeply regret to say, impossible to get near enough to them to overhear their conversation without running too great a risk of being discovered. I could only infer from their gestures and actions that they were all three talking with extraordinary earnestness on some subject which deeply interested them. After having been engaged in this way a full quarter of an hour, they suddenly turned round to retrace their steps. My presence of mind did not forsake me in this emergency. I signed to the two subordinates to walk on carelessly and pass them, while I myself slipped dexterously behind a tree. As they came by me, I heard "Jack" address these words to Mr. Jay:

"Let us say half past ten to-morrow morning. And mind you come in a cab. We had better not risk taking one in this neighborhood."

Mr. Jay made some brief reply which I could not overhear. They walked back to the place at which they had met, shaking hands there with an audacious cordiality which it quite sickened me to see. They then separated. I followed Mr. Jay. My subordinates paid the same delicate attention to the other two.

Instead of taking me back to Rutherford Street, Mr. Jay led me to the Strand. He stopped at a dingy, disreputable-looking house, which, according to the inscription over the door, was a newspaper office, but which, in my judgment, had all the external appearance of a place devoted to the reception of stolen goods.

After remaining inside for a few minutes, he came out whistling, with his finger and thumb in his waistcoat pocket. Some men would now have arrested him on the spot. I remembered the necessity of catching the two confederates, and the importance of not interfering with the appointment that had been made for the next morning. Such coolness as this, under trying circumstances, is rarely to be found, I should imagine, in a young beginner, whose reputation as a detective policeman is still to make.

From the house of suspicious appearance Mr. Jay betook himself to a cigar-divan, and read the magazines over a cheroot. From the divan he strolled to the tavern and had his chops. I strolled to the tavern and had my chops. When he had done he went back to his lodgings. When I had done I went back to mine. He was overcome with drowsiness early in the evening, and went to bed. As soon as I heard him snoring, I was overcome with drowsiness and went to bed also.

Early in the morning my two subordinates came to make their report. They had seen the man named "Jack" leave the woman at the gate of an apparently respectable villa residence not far from the Regent's Park. Left to himself, he took a turning to the right, which led to a sort of suburban street, principally inhabited by shopkeepers. He stopped at the private door of one of the houses, and let himself in with his own key—looking about him as he opened the door, and staring suspiciously at my men as they lounged along the opposite side of the way. These were all the particulars which the subordinates had to communicate. I kept them in my room to attend on me, if needful, and mounted to my peep-hole to have a look at Mr. Jay.

He was occupied in dressing himself, and was taking extraordinary pains to destroy all traces of the natural slovenliness of his appearance. This was precisely what I expected. A vagabond like Mr. Jay knows the importance of giving himself a respectable look when he is going to run the risk of changing a stolen bank-note. At five minutes past ten o'clock he had given the last brush to his shabby hat and the last scouring with bread-crumb to his dirty gloves. At ten minutes past ten he was in the street, on his way to the nearest cab-stand, and I and my subordinates were close on his heels.

He took a cab, and we took a cab. I had not overheard them appoint a place of meeting when following them in the Park on the previous day, but I soon found that we were proceeding in the old direction of the Avenue Road gate. The cab in which Mr. Jay was riding turned into the Park slowly. We stopped outside, to avoid exciting suspicion. I got out to follow the cab on foot. Just as I did so, I saw it stop, and detected the two confederates approaching it from among the trees. They got in, and the cab was turned about directly. I ran back to my own cab, and told the driver to let them pass him, and then to follow as before.

The man obeyed my directions, but so clumsily as to excite their suspicions. We had been driving after them about three minutes (returning along the road by which we had advanced) when I looked out of the window to see how far they might be ahead of us. As I did this, I saw two hats popped out of the windows of their cab, and two faces looking back at me. I sank into my place in a cold sweat; the expression is coarse, but no other form of words can describe my condition at that trying moment.

"We are found out!" I said, faintly, to my two subordinates. They stared at me in astonishment. My feelings changed instantly from the depth of despair to the height of indignation.

"It is the cabman's fault. Get out, one of you," I said, with dignity— "get out, and punch his head."

Instead of following my directions (I should wish this act of disobedience to be reported at head-quarters) they both looked out of the window. Before I could pull them back they both sat down again. Before I could express my just indignation, they both grinned, and said to me, "Please to look out, sir!"

I did look out. Their cab had stopped.

Where?

At a church door!

What effect this discovery might have had upon the ordinary run of men I don't know. Being of a strong religious turn myself, it filled me with horror. I have often read of the unprincipled cunning of criminal persons, but I never before heard of three thieves attempting to double on their pursuers by entering a church! The sacrilegious audacity of that proceeding is, I should think, unparalleled in the annals of crime.

I checked my grinning subordinates by a frown. It was easy to see what was passing in their superficial minds. If I had not been able to look below the surface, I might, on observing two nicely-dressed men and one nicely-dressed woman enter a church before eleven in the morning on a week day, have come to the same hasty conclusion at which my inferiors had evidently arrived. As it was, appearances had no power to impose on *me*. I got out, and, followed by one of my men, entered the church. The other man I sent round to watch the vestry door. You may catch a weasel asleep, but not your humble servant, Matthew Sharpin!

We stole up the gallery stairs, diverged to the organ-loft, and peered through the curtains in front. There they were, all three, sitting in a pew below—yes, incredible as it may appear, sitting in a pew below!

Before I could determine what to do, a clergyman made his appearance in full canonicals from the vestry door, followed by a clerk. My brain whirled and my eyesight grew dim. Dark remembrances of robberies committed in vestries floated through my mind. I trembled for the excellent man in full canonicals—I even trembled for the clerk.

The clergyman placed himself inside the altar rails. The three desperadoes approached him. He opened his book, and began to read. What? you will ask.

I answer, without the slightest hesitation, the first lines of the Marriage Service.

My subordinate had the audacity to look at me, and then to stuff his pocket-handkerchief into his mouth. I scorned to pay any attention to him. After I had discovered that the man "Jack" was the bridegroom, and that the man Jay acted the part of father, and gave away the bride, I left the church, followed by my men, and joined the other subordinate outside the vestry door. Some people in my position would now have felt rather crestfallen, and would have begun to think that they had made a very foolish mistake. Not the faintest misgiving of any kind troubled me. I did not feel in the slightest degree depreciated in my own estimation. And even now, after a lapse of three hours, my mind remains, I am happy to say, in the same calm and hopeful condition.

As soon as I and my subordinates were assembled together outside the church, I intimated my intention of still following the other cab in spite of what had occurred. My reason for deciding on this course will appear presently. The two subordinates appeared to be astonished at my resolution. One of them had the impertinence to say to me,

"If you please, sir, who is it that we are after? A man who has stolen money, or a man who has stolen a wife?"

The other low person encouraged him by laughing. Both have deserved an official reprimand, and both, I sincerely trust, will be sure to get it.

When the marriage ceremony was over, the three got into their cab, and once more our vehicle (neatly hidden round the corner of the church, so that they could not suspect it to be near them) started to follow theirs.

We traced them to the terminus of the Southwestern Railway. The newly-married couple took tickets for Richmond, paying their fare with a half sovereign, and so depriving me of the pleasure of arresting them, which I should certainly have done if they had offered a bank-note. They parted from Mr. Jay, saying, "Remember the address—

14 Babylon Terrace. You dine with us to-morrow week." Mr. Jay accepted the invitation, and added, jocosely, that he was going home at once to get off his clean clothes, and to be comfortable and dirty again for the rest of the day. I have to report that I saw him home safely, and that he is comfortable and dirty again (to use his own disgraceful language) at the present moment.

Here the affair rests, having by this time reached what I may call its first stage.

I know very well what persons of hasty judgment will be inclined to say of my proceedings thus far. They will assert that I have been deceiving myself all through in the most absurd way; they will declare that the suspicious conversations which I have reported referred solely to the difficulties and dangers of successfully carrying out a runaway match; and they will appeal to the scene in the church as offering undeniable proof of the correctness of their assertions. So let it be. I dispute nothing up to this point. But I ask a question, out of the depths of my own sagacity as a man of the world, which the bitterest of my enemies will not, I think, find it particularly easy to answer.

Granted the fact of the marriage, what proof does it afford me of the innocence of the three persons concerned in that clandestine transaction? It gives me none. On the contrary, it strengthens my suspicions against Mr. Jay and his confederates, because it suggests a distinct motive for their stealing the money. A gentleman who is going to spend his honeymoon at Richmond wants money; and a gentleman who is in debt to all his tradespeople wants money. Is this an unjustifiable imputation of bad motives? In the name of outraged Morality, I deny it. These men have combined together, and have stolen a woman. Why should they not combine together and steal a cash-box? I take my stand on the logic of rigid Virtue, and I defy all the sophistry of Vice to move me an inch out of my position.

Speaking of virtue, I may add that I have put this view of the case to Mr. and Mrs. Yatman. That accomplished and charming woman found it difficult at first to follow the close chain of my reasoning. I am free to confess that she shook her head, and shed tears, and joined her husband in premature lamentation over the loss of the two hundred pounds. But a little careful explanation on my part, and a little attentive listening on hers, ultimately changed her opinion. She now agrees with me that there is nothing in this unexpected circumstance of the clandestine marriage which absolutely tends to divert suspicion from Mr. Jay, or Mr. "Jack," or the runaway lady. "Audacious hussy" was the term my fair friend used in speaking of her; but let that pass. It is more to the purpose to record that Mrs. Yatman has not lost confidence in me, and that Mr. Yatman promises to follow her example, and do his best to look hopefully for future results.

I have now, in the new turn that circumstances have taken, to await advice from your office. I pause for fresh orders with all the composure of a man who has got two strings to his bow. When I traced the three confederates from the church door to the railway terminus, I had two motives for doing so. First, I followed them as a matter of official business, believing them still to have been guilty of the robbery. Secondly, I followed them as a matter of private speculation, with a view of discovering the place of refuge to which the runaway couple intended to retreat, and of making my information a marketable commodity to offer to the young lady's family and friends. Thus, whatever happens, I may congratulate myself beforehand on not having wasted my time. If the office approves of my conduct, I have my plan ready for farther proceedings. If the office blames me, I shall take myself off, with my marketable information, to the genteel villa residence in the neighborhood of the Regent's Park. Any way, the affair puts money into my pocket, and does credit to my penetration as an uncommonly sharp man.

I have only one word more to add, and it is this: If any individual ventures to assert that Mr. Jay and his confederates are innocent of all share in the stealing of the cash-box, I, in return, defy that individual—though he may even be Chief Inspector Theakstone himself—to tell me who has committed the robbery at Rutherford Street, Soho.

Strong in that conviction, I have the honor to be your very obedient servant,

MATTHEW SHARPIN.

FROM CHIEF INSPECTOR THEAKSTONE TO SERGEANT BULMER.

Birmingham, July 9th.
SERGEANT BULMER,—That empty-headed puppy, Mr. Matthew Sharpin, has made a mess of the case at Rutherford Street, exactly as I expected he would. Business keeps me in this town, so I write to you to set the matter straight. I inclose with this the pages of feeble scribble-scrabble which the creature Sharpin calls a report. Look them over; and when you have made your way through all the gabble, I think you will agree with me that the conceited booby has looked for the thief in every direction but the right one. You can lay your hand on the guilty person in five minutes, now. Settle the case at once; forward your report to me at this place, and tell Mr. Sharpin that he is suspended till farther notice.

Yours,   FRANCIS THEAKSTONE.

FROM SERGEANT BULMER TO CHIEF INSPECTOR THEAKSTONE.

London, July 10th.

INSPECTOR THEAKSTONE,—Your letter and inclosure came safe to hand. Wise men, they say, may always learn something even from a fool. By the time I had got through Sharpin's maundering report of his own folly, I saw my way clear enough to the end of the Rutherford Street case, just as you thought I should. In half an hour's time I was at the house. The first person I saw there was Mr. Sharpin himself.

"Have you come to help me?" says he.

"Not exactly," says I. "I've come to tell you that you are suspended till farther notice."

"Very good," says he, not taken down by so much as a single peg in his own estimation. "I thought you would be jealous of me. It's very natural; and I don't blame you. Walk in, pray, and make yourself at home. I'm off to do a little detective business on my own account, in the neighborhood of the Regent's Park. Ta-ta, sergeant, ta-ta!"

With those words he took himself out of the way, which was exactly what I wanted him to do.

As soon as the maid-servant had shut the door, I told her to inform her master that I wanted to say a word to him in private. She allowed me into the parlor behind the shop, and there was Mr. Yatman all alone, reading the newspaper.

"About this matter of the robbery, sir," says I.

He cut me short, peevishly enough, being naturally a poor, weak, womanish sort of man. "Yes, yes, I know," say he. "You have come to tell me that your wonderfully clever man, who has bored holes in my second-floor partition, has made a mistake, and is off the scent of the scoundrel who has stolen my money."

"Yes, sir," says I. "That *is* one of the things I came to tell you. But I have got something else to say besides that."

"Can you tell me who the thief is?" says he, more pettish than ever.

"Yes, sir," says I, "I think I can."

He put down the newspaper, and began to look rather anxious and frightened.

"Not my shopman?" says he. "I hope, for the man's own sake, it's not my shopman."

"Guess again, sir," says I.

"That idle slut, the maid?" says he.

"She is idle, sir," says I, "and she is also a slut; my first inquiries about her proved as much as that. But she's not the thief."

"Then, in the name of heaven, who is?" says he.

"Will you please to prepare yourself for a very disagreeable surprise, sir?" says I. "And, in case you lose your temper, will you excuse my remarking that I am the stronger man of the two, and that, if you allow yourself to lay hands on me, I may unintentionally hurt you, in pure self-defense."

He turned as pale as ashes, and pushed his chair two or three feet away from me.

"You have asked me to tell you, sir, who has taken your money," I went on. "If you insist on my giving you an answer—"

"I do insist," he said, faintly. "Who has taken it?"

"Your wife has taken it," I said, very quietly, and very positively at the same time.

He jumped out of the chair as if I had put a knife into him, and struck his fist on the table so heavily that the wood cracked again.

"Steady, sir," says I. "Flying into a passion won't help you to the truth."

"It's a lie!" says he, with another smack of his fist on the table—"a base, vile, infamous lie! How dare you—"

He stopped, and fell back into the chair again, looked about him in a bewildered way, and ended by bursting out crying.

"When your better sense comes back to you, sir," says I, "I am sure you will be gentleman enough to make an apology for the language you have just used. In the mean time, please to listen, if you can, to a word of explanation. Mr. Sharpin has sent in a report to our inspector of the most irregular and ridiculous kind, setting down not only all his own foolish doings and sayings, but the doings and sayings of Mrs. Yatman as well. In most cases, such a document would have been fit only for the waste-paper basket; but in this particular case it so happens that Mr. Sharpin's budget of nonsense leads to a certain conclusion, which the simpleton of a writer has been quite innocent of suspecting from the beginning to the end. Of that conclusion I am so sure that I will forfeit my place if it does not turn out that Mrs. Yatman has been practicing upon the folly and conceit of this young man, and that she has tried to shield herself from discovery by purposely encouraging him to suspect the wrong persons. I tell you that confidently; and I will even go farther. I will undertake to give a decided opinion as to why Mrs. Yatman took the money, and what she has done with it, or with a part of it. Nobody can look at that lady, sir, without being struck by the great taste and beauty of her dress—"

As I said those last words, the poor man seemed to find his powers of speech again. He cut me short directly as haughtily as if he had been a duke instead of a stationer.

"Try some other means of justifying your vile calumny against my wife," says he. "Her milliner's bill for the past year is on my file of receipted accounts at this moment."

"Excuse me, sir," says I, "but that proves nothing. Milliners, I must tell you, have a certain rascally custom which comes within the daily experience of our office. A married lady who wishes it can keep two accounts at her dressmaker's: one is the account which her husband sees and pays; the other is the private account, which contains all the extravagant items, and which the wife pays secretly, by installments, whenever she can. According to our usual experience, these installments are mostly squeezed out of the housekeeping money. In your case, I suspect, no installments have been paid; proceedings have been threatened; Mrs. Yatman, knowing your altered circumstances, has felt herself driven into a corner, and she has paid her private account out of your cash-box."

"I won't believe it," says he. "Every word you speak is an abominable insult to me and my wife."

"Are you man enough, sir," says I, taking him up short, in order to save time and words, "to get that receipted bill you spoke of just now off the file, and come with me at once to the milliner's shop where Mrs. Yatman deals?"

He turned red in the face at that, got the bill directly, and put on his hat. I took out of my pocket-book the list containing the numbers of the lost notes, and we left the house together immediately.

Arrived at the milliner's (one of the expensive West-end houses, as I expected), I asked for a private interview, on important business, with the mistress of the concern. It was not the first time that she and I had met over the same delicate investigation. The moment she set eyes on me she sent for her husband. I mentioned who Mr. Yatman was, and what we wanted.

"This is strictly private?" inquires the husband. I nodded my head.

"And confidential?" says the wife. I nodded again.

"Do you see any objection, dear, to obliging the sergeant with a sight of the books?" says the husband.

"None in the world, love, if you approve of it," says the wife.

All this while poor Mr. Yatman sat looking the picture of astonishment and distress, quite out of place at our polite conference. The books were brought, and one minute's look at the pages in which Mrs. Yatman's name figured was enough, and more than enough, to prove the truth of every word that I had spoken.

There, in one book, was the husband's account which Mr. Yatman had settled; and there, in the other, was the private account, crossed off also, the date of settlement being the very day after the loss of the cash-box. This said private account amounted to the sum of a hundred and seventy-five pounds, odd shillings, and it extended over a period of three years. Not a single installment had been paid on it. Under the last line was an entry to this effect: "Written to for the third time, June 23rd." I pointed to it, and asked the milliner if that meant "last June." Yes, it did mean last June; and she now deeply regretted to say that it had been accompanied by a threat of legal proceedings.

"I thought you gave good customers more than three years' credit?" says I.

The milliner looks at Mr. Yatman, and whispers to me, "Not when a lady's husband gets into difficulties."

She pointed to the account as she spoke. The entries after the time when Mr. Yatman's circumstances became involved were just as extravagant, for a person in his wife's situation, as the entries for the year before that period. If the lady had economized in other things, she had certainly not economized in the matter of dress.

There was nothing left now but to examine the cash-book, for form's sake. The money had been paid in notes, the amounts and numbers of which exactly tallied with the figures set down in my list.

After that, I thought it best to get Mr. Yatman out of the house immediately. He was in such a pitiable condition that I called a cab and accompanied him home in it. At first he cried and raved like a child; but I soon quieted him; and I must add, to his credit, that he made me a most handsome apology for his language as the cab drew up at his house door. In return, I tried to give him some advice about how to set matters right for the future with his wife. He paid very little attention to me, and went up stairs muttering to himself about a separation. Whether Mrs. Yatman will come cleverly out of the scrape or not seems doubtful. I should say myself that she would go into screeching hysterics, and so frighten the poor man into forgiving her. But this is no business of ours. So far as we are concerned, the case is now at an end, and the present report may come to a conclusion along with it.

I remain, accordingly, yours to command,

THOMAS BULMER.

P.S.—I have to add that, on leaving Rutherford Street, I met Mr. Matthew Sharpin coming to pack up his things.

"Only think!" says he, rubbing his hands in great spirits, "I've been to the genteel villa residence, and the moment I mentioned my business they kicked me out directly. There were two witnesses of the assault, and it's worth a hundred pounds to me if its worth a farthing."

"I wish you joy of your luck," says I.

"Thank you," says he. "When may I pay you the same compliment on finding the thief?"

"Whenever you like," says I, "for the thief is found."

"Just what I expected," says he. "I've done all the work, and now you cut in and claim all the credit—Mr. Jay, of course."

"No," says I.

"Who is it then?" says he.

"Ask Mrs. Yatman," says I. "She's waiting to tell you."

"All right! I'd much rather hear it from that charming woman than from you," says he, and goes into the house in a mighty hurry.

What do you think of that, Inspector Theakstone? Would you like to stand in Mr. Sharpin's shoes? I shouldn't, I can promise you.

FROM CHIEF INSPECTOR THEAKSTONE TO MR. MATTHEW SHARPIN.

July 12th.

SIR,—Sergeant Bulmer has already told you to consider yourself suspended until farther notice. I have now authority to add that your services as a member of the Detective Police are positively declined. You will please to take this letter as notifying officially your dismissal from the force.

I may inform you, privately, that your rejection is not intended to cast any reflections on your character. It merely implies that you are not quite sharp enough for our purposes. If we *are* to have a new recruit among us, we should infinitely prefer Mrs. Yatman.

Your obedient servant,   FRANCIS THEAKSTONE.

NOTE ON THE PRECEDING CORRESPONDENCE,
ADDED BY MR. THEAKSTONE.

The inspector is not in a position to append any explanations of importance to the last of the letters. It has been discovered that Mr. Matthew Sharpin left the house in Rutherford Street five minutes after his interview outside of it with Sergeant Bulmer, his manner expressing the liveliest emotions of terror and astonishment, and his left cheek displaying a bright patch of red, which looked as if it might have been the result of what is popularly termed a smart box on the ear. He was also heard by the shopman at Rutherford Street to use a very shocking expression in reference to Mrs. Yatman, and was seen to clench his fist vindictively as he ran round the corner of the street. Nothing more has been heard of him; and it is conjectured that he has left London with the intention of offering his valuable services to the provincial police.

On the interesting domestic subject of Mr. and Mrs. Yatman still less is known. It has, however, been positively ascertained that the medical attendant of the family was sent for in a great hurry on the day when

Mr. Yatman returned from the milliner's shop. The neighboring chemist received, soon afterward, a prescription of a soothing nature to make up for Mrs. Yatman. The day after, Mr. Yatman purchased some smelling-salts at the shop, and afterward appeared at the circulating library to ask for a novel descriptive of high life that would amuse an invalid lady. It has been inferred from these circumstances that he has not thought it desirable to carry out his threat of separating from his wife, at least in the present (presumed) condition of that lady's sensitive nervous system.

Rodrigues Ottolengui

(1861–1937)

IT IS NOT KNOWN why Rodrigues Ottolengui, a successful dentist, decided to try his hand at detective fiction. Perhaps he had the same motivation as a physician named Arthur Conan Doyle—too few patients and consequently too much time. Whatever the background, Ottolengui was important as a mystery writer shortly before the turn of the century, beginning with *An Artist in Crime* (1892), which introduced a professional detective, Jack Barnes, and the amateur Leroy Mitchel. This novel was followed in 1893 by *A Conflict of Evidence* and the next year by *A Modern Wizard*. In *A Catalogue of Crime* (revised edition, 1989) Jacques Barzun and Wendell Hertig Taylor complain that Ottolengui's novels sometimes have "excessive incident" and may end up "badly scrambled." The same criticisms cannot be made of Ottolengui's short stories, which seem to have first appeared in magazines in 1894, but were collected in book form as *Final Proof; or, The Value of Evidence*, in 1898.

Ottolengui was also the author of *Methods of Filling Teeth*, a standard manual for dentists which was frequently reprinted between 1891 and 1899, and the editor of *Items of Interest: A Monthly Magazine of Dental Art, Science and Literature*, from which he drew a series of articles to form a book called *Table Talk on Dentistry*.

A Singular Abduction

MR. BARNES was alone in his sanctum when an elderly gentleman of cultured manners was ushered in. The visitor sank into a seat and began his appeal at once.

"Oh! Mr. Barnes," said he, "I am in great distress. I hardly dared to hope that assistance were possible until I met my friend Mr. Leroy Mitchel. You remember him?" Mr. Barnes assented with a smile. "Well," continued the old gentleman, "Mr. Mitchel said that you could surely assist me."

"Certainly I will do all that is in my power," said the detective.

"You are very kind. I hope you can aid me. But let me tell you the story. I am Richard Gedney, the broker. Perhaps you have heard the name?" Mr. Barnes nodded. "I thought so. 'Old Dick,' they call me on the street, and sometimes 'Old Nick,' but that is only their joke. I do not believe they really dislike me, though I have grown rich. I have never cheated any one, nor wronged a friend in my life. But that is immaterial, except that it makes it hard to understand how any one could have done me the great injury of stealing my daughter."

"Stealing your daughter?" interrupted the detective. "Abduction?"

"Abduction I suppose is your technical term. I call it plain stealing. To take a girl of fourteen away from her father's home is stealing, plain and simple."

"When did this occur?"

"Two days ago. Tuesday morning we missed her, though she may have been taken in the night. She was slightly ill on Monday evening, and her maid sent for the doctor, who ordered her to be put to bed and kept there. Next morning, that is Tuesday, he called early, as he was going out on his rounds. He was admitted by the butler and went straight up to her room. He came down a few minutes later, rang the door-bell to call a servant and reported that the child was not in her room. He left word that she must be put back to bed and that he would return in an hour. The butler gave the message to her maid, who became alarmed, as she supposed her mistress to be in bed. A search was begun, but the child had vanished."

"How is it, Mr. Gedney, that the doctor did not speak to you personally instead of to the servant?"

"I cannot too much condemn myself. You see I am an old whist player, and the temptation to play made me linger so late with some friends on Monday night that I preferred to remain in Newark where I was, and so did not reach home till ten o'clock Tuesday morning. By that time the misfortune had occurred."

"Have you made no discoveries as to what has become of her?"

"None. We have sent to all of our friends in the vain hope that she might have risen early and gone out, but no one has seen her. She has disappeared as thoroughly as though she had been swallowed by an earthquake. Here, however, is a letter which reached me this morning. I cannot tell whether there is anything in it, or whether it is merely a cruel joke perpetrated by some crank who has heard of my loss." He handed the letter to the detective, who read as follows:

"Your daughter is safe if you are sensible. If you want her back all you have to do is to state your figures. Make them high enough, and she'll be with you. Put a personal in *Herald* for D. M., and I will answer."

"Mr. Gedney," said Mr. Barnes, "I am afraid this is a serious case. What has been done has been so thoroughly well accomplished, that I believe we have no fool to deal with. His is a master hand. We must begin our work at once. I will take this up personally. Come, we must go out."

They proceeded first to the *Herald* up town office, and Mr. Barnes inserted the following advertisement:

"D. M. Communicate at once stating lowest terms. Gedney."

"Now we will go to your home, Mr. Gedney," said Mr. Barnes; and thither they went.

Seating himself in a comfortable leather chair in the library, Mr. Barnes asked that the butler should be called. The man entered the room, and it was apparent at once that here was a good servant of the English type.

"Moulton," began Mr. Barnes, "I am a detective. I am going to find out where your young mistress has been taken."

"I hope so, sir," said the butler.

"Very well," said the detective. "Now answer a few questions explicitly, and you may give me great assistance. On Tuesday morning you admitted the doctor. At what time was it?"

"It was about eight o'clock, sir. We had just taken our seats at breakfast in the servants' hall, when the bell rang. That is how I know the hour. We are regular about meals in this house. We eat at eight, and the master at nine."

"What happened when you admitted the doctor?"

"He asked for Miss Nora, and I told him she was not down yet. He said he supposed he could go up, and I said I supposed so, and he went."

"What did you do next?"

"I went back to my breakfast."

"Did you tell the maid that the doctor had called?"

"Not just then, sir, for she had not come into the breakfast room."

"When did you tell her?"

"After I saw the doctor the second time. I heard the door-bell again and went up, when, to my surprise, there was the doctor. He said he rang because he did not know how else to call me. Then he said that Miss Nora had left her room, which was against the orders he gave the night before, and that I was to tell the maid to have her back to bed, and he would call again. I went back to the breakfast room. This time the maid was there, and frightened she was when I gave her the message."

"How long was it after you admitted the doctor the first time, that you answered his second ring?"

"I should think five minutes, sir; though it might have been ten."

"And during this five or ten minutes the maid was not in the breakfast room?"

"No, sir."

"Send her to me!" The butler left the room, and, whilst waiting for the maid, Mr. Barnes addressed Mr. Gedney.

"Mr. Gedney," said he, "you have not told me the name of the doctor."

"His name is Donaldson. Everybody knows Dr. Donaldson."

"Has he served you long?"

"Ever since I came to live in this neighbourhood. About two years, I should say. He has seemed to be very fond of Elinora. Why, he has been here a half-dozen times asking for news of her since her disappearance. He has a curious theory which I can hardly credit. He thinks she may have wandered off in the night asleep. But then he has not seen this letter from 'D. M.' yet."

"I would like to speak to him about his somnambulistic idea. Do you think he will drop in to-day?"

"He may be in at any moment, as he has not called yet this morning. Here is my daughter's maid." This directed the attention of Mr. Barnes to a young woman who at that moment entered. She was evidently dreadfully alarmed at being summoned to meet a detective, and her eyes showed that she had been weeping.

"Come, my girl," said Mr. Barnes, reassuringly. "You need not be frightened. I am not an ogre. I only wish to ask you a few questions. You are willing to help me find your mistress, are you not?"

"Oh, indeed, indeed yes, sir!"

"Then begin by telling me how she was on Monday night when you sent for the doctor."

The girl composed herself with an effort, evidently satisfied that a detective was just like any ordinary man, and replied,—

"Miss Nora acted rather odd all Monday, and was melancholy like. She could sit there and stare out of the window and not answer when she was spoken to. I thought perhaps something had bothered her, and so I left her alone, meaning to speak to her father at dinner time. But he sent a telegram saying he had to go out of town. So when Miss Nora wouldn't come down to dinner, and wouldn't answer me, but just kept staring out of the window, I got scared a little, and thought it best to send for Dr. Donaldson."

"What did he say when he came?"

"He talked to her, but she wouldn't answer him either. He patted her on the head, and said she was sulky. Then he told me perhaps she was angry because her father hadn't come home, but that she must not be allowed to brood over trifles. He said I must put her to bed, and he gave her some medicine that he said would put her to sleep."

"Did you have any trouble to get her to bed?"

"No, sir, though that was strange. She just stood still and let me do everything. She did not help me or prevent me."

"When did you see her after that?"

"I never saw her after that," and she began to cry softly.

"Come, come, don't cry. Your mistress is all right. I will bring her back. Now tell me why you did not see her again. Is it not your business to attend her in the morning?"

"Yes, sir, but she only gets up about eight o'clock, and the doctor told me he would call the first thing in the morning, and that I must not disturb her till he came. He said he wanted to wake her himself and see how she acted."

"You were not in the breakfast room at eight o'clock," said the detective, watching her closely; "where were you?"

The girl turned crimson, and stammered a few words inaudibly.

"Come, tell me where you were? You were somewhere, you know. Where were you?"

"I was in the downstairs hallway," she said, slowly.

"Doing what?"

"I was talking to the policeman," she replied, more reluctantly.

"Your beau?" asked Mr. Barnes, significantly.

"No, sir. He is my husband." She tossed her head defiantly, now that her secret was divulged.

"Your husband?" said Mr. Barnes, slightly surprised. "Why, then, did you hesitate to tell me of him?"

"Because, because," she stammered again much troubled, "because maybe, if I hadn't been talking to him, Miss Nora wouldn't have been carried off. He might have seen the thief."

"Just so," said Mr. Barnes. "Well, that will do." The girl retired only too gladly.

Mr. Barnes asked to be shown the room where the missing girl had slept, and made minute examinations of everything. Up in the room a thought occurred to him, and he once more asked for the maid.

"Can you tell me," he asked, "whether your mistress took any of her clothing with her?"

"Well, sir," she replied, "I miss the whole suit that she wore on Monday. It looks as though she must have dressed herself."

Mr. Barnes made a few notes in his memorandum-book, and then with Mr. Gedney returned to the library. Here they found Dr. Donaldson, who had arrived whilst they were upstairs. Mr. Gedney introduced the doctor, a genial, pleasant man, who shook Mr. Barnes cordially by the hand, saying:

"I am delighted, Mr. Barnes, that my old friend Gedney has been sensible enough to engage you to unravel this affair, rather than call in the police. The police are bunglers anyway, and only make scandal and publicity. You have looked into the matter, eh? What do you think?"

"That is precisely the question, doctor, which I wish to ask you. What do you think? Mr. Gedney says you suspect somnambulism?"

"I only said it might be that. I would not like to be too positive. You know that I was called to see the dear girl Monday night. Well! I found her in a strange mood. In fact, thinking it over, I have almost convinced myself that what we took for stubbornness, sulks I think I called it, was somnambulism. That in fact she was asleep when I saw her. That would account for her not replying to questions, and offering no resistance when her maid removed her clothing to put her to bed. Still it is merely a guess. It is possible that she got up in the night and wandered out of the house. I only venture it as a possibility. A chance clue for you to work on."

"What do you think of this letter?" asked Mr. Barnes, handing the doctor the anonymous communication from "D. M."

The doctor read it over twice, and then said:

"Looks more like somnambulism than ever. Don't you see? She

dressed herself in the night, and wandered off. Some scoundrel has found her and taken her to his home. Knowing that her father has money, he holds her for ransom."

"How do you know, doctor," said Mr. Barnes quietly, "that 'D. M.' is a he? The communication is in type-writing, so that nothing can be learned from the chirography."

"Of course I don't know it," said the doctor testily. "Still I'll wager that no woman ever concocted this scheme."

"Again, doctor, how should her abductor know that her father is rich?"

"Why, I suppose her name may be on her clothing, and once he discovered her parentage, he would know that. How ever they found it out, it is plain that he does know, or how could they, or he, or she, if you wish me to be so particular, have written this letter?"

This was unanswerable, so Mr. Barnes remained silent.

"What move will you make first?" asked the doctor.

Mr. Barnes told him of the advertisement which he had inserted, and took his departure, requesting that if Mr. Gedney received any answer, he should be notified at once.

About half-past ten the next morning, Mr. Gedney presented himself to the detective and handed him the following letter: —

"I am glad you are sensible. Saw your advertisement and I answer at once. I want twenty thousand dollars. That is my price. Now note what I have to say, and let me emphasize the fact that I mean every word. This is my first offer. Any dickering will make me increase my price, and I will never decrease it. To save time, let me tell you something else. I have no partner in this, so there is no one to squeal on me. No one on earth but myself knows where the girl is. Now for future arrangements. You will want to communicate with me. I don't mean you to have any chance to catch me with decoy letters or anything of that sort. I know already that you have that keen devil Barnes helping you. But he'll meet his match this time. Here is my plan. You, or your detective, I don't care which, must go to the public telephone station in the Hoffman House at two o'clock sharp. I will go to another, never mind where, and will ring you up. When you answer, I will simply say, 'D. M.' You will recognize the signal and can do the talking. I will not answer except by letter, because I won't even run the risk of that detective's hearing my voice, and some time in the future recognising it. You see I may need Barnes myself some day, and wouldn't like to be deprived of his valuable services. I enclose a piece of the girl's cloth dress and a lock of her hair to show that I am dealing square. D. M."

"Mr. Gedney," said Mr. Barnes, "make your mind easy. Your daughter is safe, at all events. I suppose this bit of cloth and the hair satisfy you that the scoundrel really has her?"

"Yes, I am convinced of that. But how does that make the girl safe?"

"The fellow wants the money. It is to his interest to be able to restore your daughter. My business shall be to get her without payment of ransom, and to catch the abductor. I'll meet you at the Hoffman House at two o'clock."

As soon as Mr. Gedney had gone, Mr. Barnes wrote the following note:

"Dr. Donaldson—Dear Sir, I believe that I am on the right track, and all through the clue supplied by yourself. Please aid me a little further. I would like to know the exact size of the missing girl. As a physician, you will supply this even better than the father. Also inform me of any mark or peculiarity by which I might recognize her, alive or dead. Please answer at once. Yours truly, J. Barnes."

This he sent by a messenger, and received the following in reply:

"Mr. Barnes—Dear Sir, I hope you will succeed. Elinora is small and slim, being rather undersized for her age. I should say about four feet ten inches, or thereabout. I know of no distinctive mark whereby her body could be recognized, and hope that nothing of the sort seemingly suggested may be necessary. Yours truly, Robert Donaldson, M.D."

Mr. Barnes read this, and appeared more pleased than its contents seemed to authorize. At the appointed time he went to the Hoffman House. He found Mr. Gedney impatiently walking up and down the lobby.

"Mr. Gedney," said he, "at the beginning of this case you offered me my own price for recovering your daughter. Now, supposing that you pay this ransom, it would appear that you would have had little need of my services. If, however, I get your daughter, and save you the necessity of paying any ransom at all, I suppose you will admit that I have earned my reward?"

"Most assuredly."

After this, Mr. Gedney was rather startled when he heard what the detective said to "D. M." through the telephone. They shut themselves up in the little box, and very soon received the call and then the signal "D. M." as agreed. Mr. Barnes spoke to the abductor, who presumably was listening:

"We agree to your terms," said he. "That is, we will pay twenty thousand dollars for the return of the girl unharmed. You are so shrewd that we suppose you will invent some scheme for receiving the money which will protect you from arrest, but at the same time we must be assured that the girl will be returned to us unharmed. In fact she must be given to us as soon as the money is paid. Notify us immediately, as the father is in a hurry."

Mr. Barnes put up the instrument and "rang off." Then he turned to Mr. Gedney and said:

"That may surprise you. But what may astonish you more is that you must go about obtaining twenty thousand dollars in cash at once. We will need it. Ask no questions, but depend upon me and trust me."

On the next day Mr. Gedney received the following letter:

"You have more sense than I gave you credit for. So has that Barnes fellow, for it was his voice I heard through the phone. You accept my terms. Very well. I'll deal square and not raise you, though I ought to have made it twenty-five thousand at least. Come to the phone again to-day, same hour, and I'll ring you up from a different station. Then you can tell me if you will be ready to-night, or to-morrow night. Either will suit me. Then here is the plan. You want to be sure the girl is all right. Then better let the ambassador be your friend, Doctor Donaldson. He knows the girl, and can tell she is all right. Let him start from his house at midnight, and drive from his office up Madison Avenue rapidly till hailed by the signal "D. M." He must go fast enough to prevent being followed on foot. If there is no detective with him, or following him, he will be hailed. Otherwise he will be allowed to pass. I will be in hiding with the girl. Warn the doctor that I will be armed, and will have a bead on him all the time. Any treachery will mean death. I will take the cash, give up the girl, and the transaction will be ended."

When this was shown to the detective, he proposed that he and Mr. Gedney should call upon the doctor. This they did, and, after some argument, persuaded him to undertake the recovery of the girl that same night.

"Mr. Gedney has decided to obtain his child at any sacrifice," said Mr. Barnes, "and this scoundrel is so shrewd that there seems to be no way to entrap him. No effort will be made to follow you, so you need have no fear of any trouble from the thief. Only be sure that you obtain the right girl. It would be just possible that a wrong one might be given to you, and a new ransom demanded."

"Oh, I shall know Elinora," said the doctor. "I will do this, but I think we ought to arrest the villain if possible."

"I do not despair of doing so," said Mr. Barnes. "Get a glimpse of his face if you can, and be sure to note where you receive the girl. When we get her she may give me a clue upon which an arrest may be made. We will wait for you at Mr. Gedney's house."

After midnight that night, Mr. Gedney paced the floor anxiously, while Mr. Barnes sat at a desk looking over some memoranda. Presently he went into the hall and had a long talk with the butler. One o'clock passed and still no news. At half past, however, horses' hoofs sounded upon the asphalt pavement, and a few minutes later the door-bell jingled. The door was quickly opened, and the doctor entered, bearing little Elinora asleep in his arms.

"My daughter!" exclaimed the excited father. "Thank God she is restored to me."

"Yes," said the doctor, "here she is safe and sound. I think though, that she has been drugged, for she has slept ever since I received her."

"Did you have any trouble?" asked Mr. Barnes, entering at this moment. He had lingered outside in the hall long enough to exchange a word with the butler.

"None," said the doctor. "At one-hundred-and-second street I heard the signal and stopped. A man came out of the shadow of a building, looked into the carriage, said, 'All right' and asked if I had the cash. I replied affirmatively. He went back to the side-walk and returned with the child in his arms, but with a pistol pointed at me. Then he said, 'Pass out the money.' I did so, and he seemed satisfied, for he gave me the child, took the package, and ran off. I saw his face, but I fear my description will not avail you, for I am sure he was disguised."

"Very possibly your description will be useless," said Mr. Barnes; "but I have discovered the identity of the abductor."

"Impossible," cried the doctor, amazed.

"Let me prove that I am right," said Mr. Barnes. He went to the door and admitted the butler, accompanied by the policeman who had been off his beat talking with the maid. Before his companions understood what was about to happen, Mr. Barnes said:—

"Officer, arrest that man!" Whereupon the policeman seized the doctor and held him as though in a vice.

"What does this outrage mean?" screamed the doctor, after ineffectually endeavouring to release himself.

"Put on the manacles, officer," said Mr. Barnes, "then we can talk. He is armed and might become dangerous." With the assistance of the detective this was accomplished, and then Mr. Barnes addressed himself to Mr. Gedney.

"Mr. Gedney, I had some slight suspicion of the truth after questioning the butler and the maid, but the first clue came with the answer to the personal. You brought that to me in the morning, and I noted that it was postmarked at the main office down town at six A.M. Of course it was possible that it might have been written after the appearance of the newspaper, but if so, the thief was up very early. The doctor, however, knew of the personal on the day previous, as I told him in your presence. That letter was written in typewriting, and I observed a curious error in the spelling of three words. I found the words 'emphasize,' 'recognize,' and 'recognizing.' In each, instead of the 'z,' we have a repetition of the 'i,' that letter being doubled. I happen to know something about writing machines. I felt certain that this letter had been written upon a caligraph. In that machine the bar which carries the letter 'i' is next to that which carries the letter 'z.' It is not an uncommon thing when a typewriter is out of order for two bars to fail to pass one another. Thus in writing 'emphasize' the rapid writer would strike the 'z' key before the 'i' had fully descended. The result would be that the 'z' rising would strike the 'i' bar and carry it up again, thus doubling the 'i' instead of writing 'iz.' The repetition of the mistake was evidence that it was a faulty machine. I also noted that this anonymous letter was upon paper from which the top had been torn away. I wrote to the doctor here, asking about the 'size' of the girl and for any marks whereby the body could be 'recognized.' I used the words 'size' and 'recognized,' hoping to tempt him to use them also in reply. In his answer I find the word 'recognized' and also a similar word, 'undersized.' In both we have a repetition of the double 'i' error. Moreover the paper of this letter from the doctor matched that upon which the anonymous communication had been written, provided I tore off the top, which bore his letterhead. This satisfied me that the doctor was our man. When the last letter came, proposing that he should be the ambassador, the trick was doubly sure. It was ingenious, for the abductor of course assured himself that he was not followed and simply brought the girl home. But I set another trap. I secretly placed a cyclometer upon the doctor's carriage. He says that to-night he drove to one-hundred-and-second street, and back here, a total of ten miles. The cyclometer, which the butler obtained for me when the doctor arrived awhile ago, shows that he drove less than a mile. He simply waited at his house until the proper time to come, and then drove here bringing the girl with him."

The doctor remained silent, but glared venomously at the man who had outwitted him.

"But how did he get Elinora?" asked Mr. Gedney.

"That queer yarn which he told us about somnambulism first suggested to me that he was possibly less ignorant than he pretended to be. I fear, Mr. Gedney, that your daughter is ill. I judge from the description of her condition, given by her maid, and admitted by this man, that she was suffering from an attack of catalepsy, when he was summoned. When he called the next day, finding the girl still in a trance, he quickly dressed her and took her out to his carriage. Then he coolly returned, announced that she was not in her room, and drove away with her."

"It seems incredible," exclaimed Mr. Gedney. "I have known the doctor so long that it is hard to believe that he is a criminal."

"Criminals," said Mr. Barnes, "are often created by opportunity. That was probably the case here. The case is most peculiar. It is a crime which none but a physician could have conceived, and that one fact makes possible what to a casual observer might seem most improbable.

An abduction is rarely successful, because of the difficulties which attend the crime, not the least of which are the struggles of the victim, and the story which will be told after the return of the child. Here all this was obviated. The doctor recognized catalepsy at the first visit. Perhaps during the night, the possibility of readily compelling you to pay him a large sum of money, grew into a tremendous temptation. With the project half formed, he called the next morning. Circumstances favoured the design. He found the girl unattended, and unresistant because of her condition. He likewise knew that when he should have returned her, she would tell nothing of where she had been, because of her trance. He started downstairs with her. There was no risk. If he had met any one, any excuse for bringing her from her room would have been accepted, because uttered by the family physician. He placed her in the carriage unobserved; and the most difficult part of the affair was accomplished. Many men of high degree are at heart rascals, but through fear, either of law or loss of position, they lead fairly virtuous lives. Temptation, accompanied by opportunity, coming to one of these, compasses his downfall, as has occurred in this instance. Criminals are recruited from all classes."

The ransom-money was recovered by searching the apartments of the doctor, and his guilt was thus indubitably proved. Mr. Mitchel, commenting upon the affair, simply said:

"I have sent you to him, Mr. Gedney, because Mr. Barnes is above his kind. He is no ordinary detective."

Jack London

(1876–1916)

JOHN GRIFFITH LONDON was, in his day, the most popular adventure story writer and the highest paid author in the United States. Born in San Francisco, he had a varied career: he traveled to Japan and later participated in the Alaska Gold Rush before achieving literary success with *The Call of the Wild* in 1903.

Many of London's stories, even those set in the most exotic locations, emphasize crime and, occasionally, detection. For example, "The Master of Mystery" (*Children of the Frost*, 1902) features an Eskimo shaman as a sleuth. At his death in 1916, London left unfinished *The Assassination Bureau*, a novel about the head of a group of professional assassins who is hired to kill himself; the book was completed by Robert L. Fish in 1963.

"The Leopard Man's Story" was first published in the August 1903 issue of *Leslie's Magazine* and collected in *Moon-Face and Other Stories* (1906). It features a murder method that must be unique.

The Leopard Man's Story

HE HAD A DREAMY, far-away look in his eyes, and his sad, insistent voice, gentle-spoken as a maid's, seemed the placid embodiment of some deep-seated melancholy. He was the Leopard Man, but he did not look it. His business in life, whereby he lived, was to appear in a cage of performing leopards before vast audiences, and to thrill those audiences by certain exhibitions of nerve for which his employers rewarded him on a scale commensurate with the thrills he produced.

As I say, he did not look it. He was narrow-hipped, narrow-shouldered, and anæmic, while he seemed not so much oppressed by gloom as by a sweet and gentle sadness, the weight of which was as sweetly and gently borne. For an hour I had been trying to get a story out of him, but he appeared to lack imagination. To him there was no romance in his gorgeous career, no deeds of daring, no thrills — nothing but a gray sameness and infinite boredom.

Lions? Oh, yes! he had fought with them. It was nothing. All you had to do was to stay sober. Anybody could whip a lion to a standstill with an ordinary stick. He had fought one for half an hour once. Just hit him on the nose every time he rushed, and when he got artful and rushed with his head down, why, the thing to do was to stick out your leg. When he grabbed at the leg you drew it back and hit him on the nose again. That was all.

With the far-away look in his eyes and his soft flow of words he showed me his scars. There were many of them, and one recent one where a tigress had reached for his shoulder and gone down to the bone. I could see the neatly mended rents in the coat he had on. His right arm, from the elbow down, looked as though it had gone through a threshing machine, what of the ravage wrought by claws and fangs. But it was nothing, he said, only the old wounds bothered him somewhat when rainy weather came on.

Suddenly his face brightened with a recollection, for he was really as anxious to give me a story as I was to get it.

"I suppose you've heard of the lion-tamer who was hated by another man?" he asked.

He paused and looked pensively at a sick lion in the cage opposite.

"Got the toothache," he explained. "Well, the lion-tamer's big play to the audience was putting his head in a lion's mouth. The man who hated him attended every performance in the hope sometime of seeing that lion crunch down. He followed the show about all over the country. The years went by and he grew old, and the lion-tamer grew old, and the lion grew old. And at last one day, sitting in a front seat, he saw what he had waited for. The lion crunched down, and there wasn't any need to call a doctor."

The Leopard Man glanced casually over his finger nails in a manner which would have been critical had it not been so sad.

"Now, that's what I call patience," he continued, "and it's my style. But it was not the style of a fellow I knew. He was a little, thin, sawed-off, sword-swallowing and juggling Frenchman. De Ville, he called himself, and he had a nice wife. She did trapeze work and used to dive from under the roof into a net, turning over once on the way as nice as you please.

"De Ville had a quick temper, as quick as his hand, and his hand was as quick as the paw of a tiger. One day, because the ring-master called him a frog-eater, or something like that and maybe a little worse, he shoved him against the soft pine background he used in his knife-throwing act, so quick the ring-master didn't have time to think, and there, before the audience, De Ville kept the air on fire with his knives, sinking them into the wood all around the ring-master so close that they passed through his clothes and most of them bit into his skin.

"The clowns had to pull the knives out to get him loose, for he was pinned fast. So the word went around to watch out for De Ville, and no one dared be more than barely civil to his wife. And she was a sly bit of baggage, too, only all hands were afraid of De Ville.

"But there was one man, Wallace, who was afraid of nothing. He was the lion-tamer, and he had the self-same trick of putting his head into the lion's mouth. He'd put it into the mouths of any of them, though he preferred Augustus, a big, good-natured beast who could always be depended upon.

"As I was saying, Wallace—'King' Wallace we called him—was afraid of nothing alive or dead. He was a king and no mistake. I've seen him drunk, and on a wager go into the cage of a lion that'd turned nasty, and without a stick beat him to a finish. Just did it with his fist on the nose.

"Madame De Ville—"

At an uproar behind us the Leopard Man turned quietly around. It was a divided cage, and a monkey, poking through the bars and around the partition, had had its paw seized by a big gray wolf who was trying to pull it off by main strength. The arm seemed stretching out longer and longer like a thick elastic, and the unfortunate monkey's mates were raising a terrible din. No keeper was at hand, so the Leopard Man stepped over a couple of paces, dealt the wolf a sharp blow on the nose with the light cane he carried, and returned with a sadly apologetic smile to take up his unfinished sentence as though there had been no interruption.

"—looked at King Wallace and King Wallace looked at her, while De Ville looked black. We warned Wallace, but it was no use. He laughed at us, and he laughed at De Ville one day when he shoved De Ville's head into a bucket of paste because he wanted to fight.

"De Ville was in a pretty mess—I helped to scrape him off; but he was cool as a cucumber and made no threats at all. But I saw a glitter in his eyes which I had seen often in the eyes of wild beasts, and I went out of my way to give Wallace a final warning. He laughed, but he did not look so much in Madame De Ville's direction after that.

"Several months passed by. Nothing had happened and I was beginning to think it all a scare over nothing. We were West by that time, showing in 'Frisco. It was during the afternoon performance, and the big tent was filled with women and children, when I went looking for Red Denny, the head canvas-man, who had walked off with my pocket-knife.

"Passing by one of the dressing tents I glanced in through a hole in the canvas to see if I could locate him. He wasn't there, but directly in front of me was King Wallace, in tights, waiting for his turn to go on with his cage of performing lions. He was watching with much amusement a quarrel between a couple of trapeze artists. All the rest of the people in the dressing tent were watching the same thing, with the exception of De Ville, whom I noticed staring at Wallace with undisguised hatred. Wallace and the rest were all too busy following the quarrel to notice this or what followed.

"But I saw it through the hole in the canvas. De Ville drew his handkerchief from his pocket, made as though to mop the sweat from his face with it (it was a hot day), and at the same time walked past Wallace's back. He never stopped, but with a flirt of the handkerchief kept right on to the doorway, where he turned his head, while passing out, and shot a swift look back. The look troubled me at the time, for not only did I see hatred in it, but I saw triumph as well.

"De Ville will bear watching," I said to myself, and I really breathed easier when I saw him go out the entrance to the circus grounds and board an electric car for down town. A few minutes later I was in the big tent, where I had overhauled Red Denny. King Wallace was doing his turn and holding the audience spellbound. He was in a particularly vicious mood, and he kept the lions stirred up till they were all snarling, that is, all of them except old Augustus, and he was just too fat and lazy and old to get stirred up over anything.

"Finally Wallace cracked the old lion's knees with his whip and got him into position. Old Augustus, blinking good-naturedly, opened his mouth and in popped Wallace's head. Then the jaws came together, *crunch*, just like that."

The Leopard Man smiled in a sweetly wistful fashion, and the far-away look came into his eyes.

"And that was the end of King Wallace," he went on in his sad, low voice. "After the excitement cooled down I watched my chance and bent over and smelled Wallace's head. Then I sneezed."

"It . . . it was . . .?" I queried with halting eagerness.

"Snuff—that De Ville dropped on his hair in the dressing tent. Old Augustus never meant to do it. He only sneezed."

Jacques Futrelle

(1875–1912)

BECAUSE HE WENT DOWN with the *Titanic*, Jacques Futrelle has been the subject of some publicity in recent years. He was bringing back with him some recently written detective short stories about Professor S. F. X. Van Dusen (The Thinking Machine), and a few people hold out hope that they might have survived their nearly eighty years' immersion. That would be a plot so strange as to be worthy of The Thinking Machine.

A Georgia newspaperman who spent most of his working life in Boston, Jacques Futrelle created some of the most imaginative detective stories of the Edwardian era. His most famous "Thinking Machine" tale is the spectacular "The Problem of Cell 13" in which Van Dusen "thinks" his way out of a prison cell. (It is not a detective story, and thus is out of bounds for this book.) Just as extraordinary is the tale that follows, which was first published in *The Sunday Magazine* and collected in *The Thinking Machine on the Case* (1908).

The Phantom Motor

TWO DAZZLING white eyes bulged through the night as an automobile swept suddenly around a curve in the wide road and laid a smooth, glaring pathway ahead. Even at the distance the rhythmical crackling-chug informed Special Constable Baker that it was a gasoline car, and the headlong swoop of the unblinking lights toward him made him instantly aware of the fact that the speed ordinance of Yarborough County was being a little more than broken—it was being obliterated.

Now the County of Yarborough was a wide expanse of summer estates and superbly kept roads, level as a floor, and offered distracting temptations to the dangerous pastime of speeding. But against this was the fact that the county was particular about its speed laws, so particular in fact that it had stationed half a hundred men upon its highways to abate the nuisance. Incidentally it had found that keeping record of the infractions of the law was an excellent source of income.

"Forty miles an hour if an inch," remarked Baker to himself.

He arose from a camp stool where he was wont to make himself comfortable from six o'clock until midnight on watch, picked up his lantern, turned up the light and stepped down to the edge of the road. He always remained on watch at the same place—at one end of a long stretch which autoists had unanimously dubbed The Trap. The Trap was singularly tempting—a perfectly macadamized road bed lying between two tall stone walls with only enough of a sinuous twist in it to make each end invisible from the other. Another man, Special Constable Bowman, was stationed at the other end of The Trap and there was telephonic communication between the points, enabling the men to check each other and incidentally, if one failed to stop a car or get its number, the other would. That at least was the theory.

So now, with the utmost confidence, Baker waited beside the road. The approaching lights were only a couple of hundred yards away. At the proper instant he would raise his lantern, the car would stop, its occupants would protest and then the county would add a mite to its general fund for making the roads even better and tempting autoists still more. Or sometimes the cars didn't stop. In that event it was part of the Special Constable's duties to get the number as it flew past, and reference to the monthly automobile register would give the name of the owner. An extra fine was always imposed in such cases.

Without the slightest diminution of speed the car came hurtling on toward him and swung wide so as to take the straight path of The Trap at full speed. At the psychological instant Baker stepped out into the road and waved his lantern.

"Stop!" he commanded.

The crackling-chug came on, heedless of the cry. The auto was almost upon him before he leaped out of the road—a feat at which he was particularly expert—then it flashed by and plunged into The Trap. Baker was, at the instant, so busily engaged in getting out of the way that he couldn't read the number, but he was not disconcerted because he knew there was no escape from The Trap. On the one side a solid stone wall eight feet high marked the eastern boundary of the John Phelps Stocker country estate, and on the other side a stone fence nine feet high marked the western boundary of the Thomas Q. Rogers country estate. There was no turnout, no place, no possible way for an auto to get out of The Trap except at one of the two ends guarded by the special constables. So Baker, perfectly confident of results, seized the 'phone.

"Car coming through sixty miles an hour," he bawled. "It won't stop. I missed the number. Look out!"

"All right," answered Special Constable Bowman.

For ten, fifteen, twenty minutes Baker waited expecting a call from Bowman at the other end. It didn't come and finally he picked up the 'phone again. No answer. He rang several times, battered the box and did some tricks with the receiver. Still no answer. Finally he began to feel worried. He remembered that at that same post one Special Constable had been badly hurt by a reckless chauffeur who refused to stop or turn his car when the officer stepped out into the road. In his mind's eye he saw Bowman now lying helpless, perhaps badly injured. If the car held the pace at which it passed him it would be certain death to whoever might be unlucky enough to get in its path.

With these thoughts running through his head and with genuine solicitude for Bowman, Baker at last walked on along the road of The Trap toward the other end. The feeble rays of the lantern showed the unbroken line of the cold, stone walls on each side. There was no shrubbery of any sort, only a narrow strip of grass close to the wall. The more Baker considered the matter the more anxious he became and he increased his pace a little. As he turned a gentle curve he saw a lantern in the distance coming slowly toward him. It was evidently being carried by some one who was looking carefully along each side of the road.

"Hello!" called Baker, when the lantern came within distance. "That you, Bowman?"

"Yes," came the hallooed response.

The lanterns moved on and met. Baker's solicitude for the other constable was quickly changed to curiosity.

"What're you looking for?" he asked.

"That auto," replied Bowman. "It didn't come through my end and I thought perhaps there had been an accident so I walked along looking for it. Haven't seen anything."

"Didn't come through your end?" repeated Baker in amazement. "Why it must have. It didn't come back my way and I haven't passed it so it must have gone through."

"Well, it didn't," declared Bowman conclusively. "I was on the lookout for it, too, standing beside the road. There hasn't been a car through my end in an hour."

Special Constable Baker raised his lantern until the rays fell full upon the face of Special Constable Bowman and for an instant they stared at each other. Suspicion glowed from the keen, avaricious eyes of Baker.

"How much did they give you to let 'em by?" he asked.

"Give me?" exclaimed Bowman, in righteous indignation. "Give me nothing. I haven't seen a car."

A slight sneer curled the lips of Special Constable Baker.

"Of course that's all right to report at headquarters," he said, "but I happen to know that the auto came in here, that it didn't go back my way, that it couldn't get out except at the ends, therefore it went your way." He was silent for a moment. "And whatever you got, Jim, seems to me I ought to get half."

Then the worm—i.e., Bowman—turned. A polite curl appeared about his lips and was permitted to show through the grizzled moustache.

"I guess," he said deliberately, "you think because you do that everybody else does. I haven't seen any autos."

"Don't I always give you half, Jim?" Baker demanded, almost pleadingly.

"Well I haven't seen any car and that's all there is to it. If it didn't go back your way there wasn't any car." There was a pause; Bowman was framing up something particularly unpleasant. "You're seeing things, that's what's the matter."

So was sown discord between two officers of the County of Yarborough. After awhile they separated with mutual sneers and open derision and went back to their respective posts. Each was thoughtful in his own way. At five minutes of midnight when they went off duty Baker called Bowman on the 'phone again.

"I've been thinking this thing over, Jim, and I guess it would be just as well if we didn't report it or say anything about it when we go in," said Baker slowly. "It seems foolish, and if we did say anything about it it would give the boys the laugh on us."

"Just as you say," responded Bowman.

Relations between Special Constable Baker and Special Constable Bowman were strained on the morrow. But they walked along side by side to their respective posts. Baker stopped at his end of The Trap; Bowman didn't even look around.

"You'd better keep your eyes open to-night, Jim," Baker called as a last word.

"I had 'em open last night," was the disgusted retort.

Seven, eight, nine o'clock passed. Two or three cars had gone through The Trap at moderate speed and one had been warned by Baker. At a few minutes past nine he was staring down the road which led into The Trap when he saw something that brought him quickly to his feet. It was a pair of dazzling white eyes, far away. He recognized them—the mysterious car of the night before.

"I'll get it this time," he muttered grimly, between closed teeth.

Then when the onrushing car was a full two hundred yards away Baker planted himself in the middle of the road and began to swing the lantern. The auto seemed, if anything, to be travelling even faster than on the previous night. At a hundred yards Baker began to shout. Still the car didn't lessen speed, merely rushed on. Again at the psychological instant Baker jumped. The auto whisked by as the chauffeur gave it a dexterous twist to prevent running down the Special Constable.

Safely out of its way Baker turned and stared after it, trying to read the number. He could see there was a number because a white board swung from the tail axle but he could not make out the figures. Dust and a swaying car conspired to defeat him. But he did see that there were four persons in the car dimly silhouetted against the light reflected from the road. It was useless, of course, to conjecture as to sex for even as he looked the fast receding car swerved around the turn and was lost to sight.

Again he rushed to the telephone; Bowman responded promptly.

"That car's gone in again," Baker called. "Ninety miles an hour. Look out!"

"I'm looking," responded Bowman.

"Let me know what happens," Baker shouted.

With the receiver to his ear he stood for ten or fifteen minutes, then Bowman hallooed from the other end.

"Well?" Baker responded. "Got 'em?"

"No car passed through and there's none in sight," said Bowman.

"But it went in," insisted Baker.

"Well, it didn't come out here," declared Bowman. "Walk along the road till I meet you and look out for it."

Then was repeated the search of the night before. When the two men met in the middle of The Trap their faces were blank—blank as the high stone walls which stared at them from each side.

"Nothing!" said Bowman.

"Nothing!" echoed Baker.

Special Constable Bowman perched his head on one side and scratched his grizzly chin.

"You're not trying to put up a job on me?" he inquired coldly. "You did see a car?"

"I certainly did," declared Baker, and a belligerent tone underlay his manner. "I certainly saw it, Jim, and if it didn't come out your end, why—why——"

He paused and glanced quickly behind him. The action inspired a sudden similar caution on Bowman's part.

"Maybe—maybe—" said Bowman after a minute, "maybe it's a—a spook auto?"

"Well, it must be," mused Baker. "You know as well as I do that no car can get out of this trap except at the ends. That car came in here, it isn't here now and it didn't go out your end. Now where is it?"

Bowman stared at him a minute, picked up his lantern, shook his head solemnly, and wandered along the road back to his post. On his way he glanced around quickly, apprehensively three times—Baker did the same thing four times.

On the third night the phantom car appeared and disappeared precisely as it had done previously. Again Baker and Bowman met half way between posts and talked it over.

"I'll tell you what, Baker," said Bowman in conclusion, "maybe you're just imagining that you see a car. Maybe if I was at your end I couldn't see it."

Special Constable Baker was distinctly hurt at the insinuation.

"All right, Jim," he said at last, "if you think that way about it we'll swap posts to-morrow night. We won't have to say anything about it when we report."

"Now that's the talk," exclaimed Bowman with an air approaching enthusiasm. "I'll bet I don't see it."

On the following night Special Constable Bowman made himself comfortable on Special Constable Baker's camp-stool. And *he* saw the phantom auto. It came upon him with a rush and a crackling-chug of engine and then sped on leaving him nerveless. He called Baker over the wire and Baker watched half an hour for the phantom. It didn't appear.

Ultimately all things reach the newspapers. So with the story of the phantom auto, Hutchinson Hatch, reporter, smiled incredulously when his City Editor laid aside an inevitable cigar and tersely stated the known facts. The known facts in this instance were meagre almost to the disappearing point. They consisted merely of a corroborated statement that an automobile, solid and tangible enough to all appearances, rushed into The Trap each night and totally disappeared.

But there was enough of the bizarre about it to pique the curiosity, to make one wonder, so Hatch journeyed down to Yarborough County, an hour's ride from the city, met and talked to Baker and Bowman and then, in broad daylight strolled along The Trap twice. It was a leisurely, thorough investigation with the end in view of finding out how an automobile once inside might get out again without going out either end.

On the first trip through Hatch paid particular attention to the Thomas Q. Rogers side of the road. The wall, nine feet high, was an unbroken line of stone with not the slightest indication of a secret wagon-way through it anywhere. Secret wagon-way! Hatch smiled at the phrase. But when he reached the other end—Bowman's end—of The Trap he was perfectly convinced of one thing—that no automobile had left the hard, macadamized road to go over, under or through the Thomas Q. Rogers wall. Returning, still leisurely, he paid strict attention to the John Phelps Stocker side, and when he reached the other end—Baker's end—he was convinced of another thing—that no automobile had left the road to go over, under or through the John Phelps Stocker wall. The only opening of any sort was a narrow foot-path, not more than 16 inches wide.

Hatch saw no shrubbery along the road, nothing but a strip of scrupulously cared for grass, therefore the phantom auto could not be hidden any time, night or day. Hatch failed, too, to find any holes in the road so the automobile didn't go down through the earth. At this point he involuntarily glanced up at the blue sky above. Perhaps, he thought whimsically, the automobile was a strange sort of bird, or— or—and he stopped suddenly.

"By George!" he exclaimed. "I wonder if—"

And the remainder of the afternoon he spent systematically making enquiries. He went from house to house, the Stocker house, the Rogers house both of which were at the time unoccupied, then to cottage, cabin and hut in turn. But he didn't seem overladen with information when he joined Special Constable Baker at his end of The Trap that evening about seven o'clock.

Together they rehearsed the strange points of the mystery and the shadows grew about them until finally the darkness was so dense that Baker's lantern was the only bright spot in sight. As the chill of evening closed in a certain awed tone crept into their voices. Occasionally an auto bowled along and each time as it hove in sight Hatch glanced at Baker questioningly. And each time Baker shook his head. And each time, too, he called Bowman, in this manner accounting for every car that went into The Trap.

"It'll come all right," said Baker after a long silence, "and I'll know it the minute it rounds the curve coming toward us. I'd know its two lights in a thousand."

They sat still and smoked. After awhile two dazzling white lights burst into view far down the road and Baker, in excitement, dropped his pipe.

"That's her!" he declared. "Look at her coming!"

And Hatch did look at her coming. The speed of the mysterious car was such as to make one look. Like the eyes of a giant the two lights came on toward them, and Baker perfunctorily went through the motions of attempting to stop it. The car fairly whizzed past them and the rush of air which tugged at their coats was convincing enough proof of its solidity. Hatch strained his eyes to read the number as the auto flashed past. But it was hopeless. The tail of the car was lost in an eddying whirl of dust.

"She certainly does travel," commented Baker, softly.

"She does," Hatch assented.

Then, for the benefit of the newspaper man, Baker called Bowman on the wire.

"Car's coming again," he shouted. "Look out and let me know."

Bowman, at his end, waited twenty minutes, then made the usual report—the car had not passed. Hutchinson Hatch was a calm, cold, dispassionate young man, but now a queer, creepy sensation stole along his spinal column. He lighted a cigarette and pulled himself together with a jerk.

"There's one way to find out where it goes," he declared at last, emphatically, "and that's to place a man in the middle just beyond the bend of The Trap and let him wait and see. If the car goes up, down, or evaporates he'll see and can tell us."

Baker looked at him curiously.

"I'd hate to be the man in the middle," he declared. There was something of uneasiness in his manner.

"I rather think I would, too," responded Hatch.

On the following evening, consequent upon the appearance of the story of the phantom auto in Hatch's paper, there were twelve other reporters on hand. Most of them were openly, flagrantly sceptical; they even insinuated that no one had seen an auto. Hatch smiled wisely.

"Wait!" he advised with deep conviction.

So when the darkness fell that evening the newspaper men of a great city had entered into a conspiracy to capture the phantom auto. Thirteen of them, making a total of fifteen men with Baker and Bowman, were on hand and they agreed to a suggestion for all to take positions along the road of The Trap from Baker's post to Bowman's, watch for the auto, see what happened to it and compare notes afterwards. So they scattered themselves along a few hundred feet apart and waited. That night the phantom auto didn't appear at all and twelve reporters jeered at Hutchinson Hatch and told him to light his pipe with the story. And next night when Hatch and Baker and Bowman alone were watching the phantom auto reappeared.

The Gap in the Trail

Like a child with a troublesome problem, Hatch took the entire matter and laid it before Professor Augustus S. F. X. Van Dusen, the master brain. The Thinking Machine, with squint eyes turned steadily upward and long, slender fingers pressed tip to tip listened to the end.

"Now I know of course that automobiles don't fly," Hatch burst out savagely in conclusion, "and if this one doesn't fly, there is no earthly way for it to get out of The Trap as they call it. I went over the thing carefully—I even went so far as to examine the ground and the tops of the walls to see if a runway had been let down for the auto to go over."

The Thinking Machine squinted at him inquiringly.

"Are you sure you saw an automobile?" he demanded irritably.

"Certainly I saw it," blurted the reporter. "I not only saw it—I smelled it. Just to convince myself that it was real I tossed my cane in front of the thing and it smashed it to tooth-picks."

"Perhaps, then, if everything is as you say the auto actually *does* fly," remarked the scientist.

The reporter stared into the calm, inscrutable face of The Thinking Machine, fearing first that he had not heard aright. Then he concluded that he had.

"You mean," he inquired eagerly, "that the phantom may be an auto-aeroplane affair, and that it actually does fly?"

"It's not at all impossible," commented the scientist.

"I had an idea something like that myself," Hatch explained, "and questioned every soul within a mile or so, but I didn't get anything."

"The perfect stretch of road there might be the very place for some daring experimenter to get up sufficient speed to soar a short distance in a light machine," continued the scientist.

"Light machine?" Hatch repeated. "Did I tell you that this car had four people in it?"

"Four people!" exclaimed the scientist. "Dear me! Dear me! That makes it very different. Of course four people would be too great a lift for an——"

For ten minutes he sat silent, and tiny, cobwebby lines appeared in his dome-like brow. Then he arose and passed into the adjoining room. After a moment Hatch heard the telephone bell jingle. Five minutes later The Thinking Machine appeared, and scowled upon him unpleasantly.

"I suppose what you really want to learn is if the car is a—a material one, and to whom it belongs?" he queried.

"That's it," agreed the reporter, "and of course why it does what it does, and how it gets out of The Trap."

'Do you happen to know a fast, long-distance bicycle rider?" demanded the scientist abruptly.

"A dozen of them," replied the reporter promptly. "I think I see the idea, but——"

"You haven't the faintest inkling of the idea," declared The Thinking Machine positively. "If you can arrange with a fast rider who can go a distance—it might be thirty, forty, fifty miles—we may end this little affair without difficulty."

Under these circumstances Professor Augustus S. F. X. Van Dusen, Ph.D., LL.D., F.R.S., M.D., etc., etc., scientist and logician, met the famous Jimmie Thalhauer, the world's champion long distance bicyclist. He held every record from five miles up to and including six hours, and twice won the six-day race, and was altogether a master in his field. He came in chewing a tooth-pick. There were introductions.

"You ride the bicycle?" inquired the crusty little scientist.

"Well, *some*," confessed the champion modestly with a wink at Hatch.

"Can you keep up with an automobile for a distance of, say, thirty or forty miles?"

"I can keep up with anything that ain't got wings," was the response.

"Well, to tell you the truth," volunteered The Thinking Machine, "there is a growing belief that this particular automobile has wings. However if you can keep up with it——"

"Ah, quit your kiddin'," said the champion, easily. "I can ride rings around anything on wheels. I'll start behind it and beat it where it's going."

The Thinking Machine examined the champion, Jimmie Thalhauer as a curiosity. In the seclusion of his laboratory he had never had an opportunity of meeting just such another worldly young person.

"How fast *can* you ride, Mr. Thalhauer?" he asked at last.

"I'm ashamed to tell you," confided the champion in a hushed voice. "I can ride so fast that I scare myself." He paused a moment. "But it seems to me," he said, "if there's thirty or forty miles to do I ought to do it on a motor-cycle."

"Now that's just the point," explained The Thinking Machine. "A motor-cycle makes noise and if it could have been used we would have hired a fast automobile. This proposition briefly is: I want you to ride without lights behind an automobile which may also run without lights and find out where it goes. No occupant of the car must suspect that it is followed."

"Without lights?" repeated the champion. "Gee! Rubber shoe, eh?"

The Thinking Machine looked his bewilderment.

"Yes, that's it," Hatch answered for him.

"I guess it's good for a four column head? Hunh?" inquired the champion. "Special pictures posed by the champion? Hunh?"

"Yes," Hatch replied.

"'Tracked on a Bicycle' sounds good to me. Hunh?"

Hatch nodded.

So arrangements were concluded, and then and there The Thinking Machine gave definite and conclusive instructions to the champion. While these apparently bore broadly on the problem in hand they conveyed absolutely no inkling of his plan to the reporter. At the end the champion arose to go.

"You're a most extraordinary young man, Mr. Thalhauer," commented The Thinking Machine, not without admiration for the sturdy, powerful figure.

And as Hatch accompanied the champion out the door and down the steps Jimmie smiled with easy grace.

"Nutty old guy, ain't he? Huhn?"

* * *

Night! Utter blackness, relieved only by a white, ribbon like road which winds away mistily under a starless sky. Shadowy hedges line either side and occasionally a tree thrusts itself upward out of the sombreness. The murmur of human voices in the shadows, then the crackling-chug of an engine and an automobile moves slowly, without lights, into the road.

There is the sudden clatter of an engine at high speed and the car rushes away.

From the hedge comes the faint rustle of leaves as of wind stirring, then a figure moves impalpably. A moment and it becomes a separate entity; a quick movement and the creak of a leather bicycle saddle. Silently the single figure, bent low over the handle bars, moves after the car with ever increasing momentum.

Then a long, desperate race. For mile after mile, mile after mile the auto goes on. The silent cyclist has crept up almost to the rear axle and hangs there doggedly as a racer to his pace. On and on they rush together through the darkness, the chauffeur moving with a perfect knowledge of his road, the single rider behind clinging on grimly with set teeth. The powerful, piston-like legs move up and down to the beat of the engine.

At last, with dust-dry throat and stinging, aching eyes the cyclist feels the peace slacken and instantly he drops back out of sight. It is only by sound that he follows now. The car stops; the cyclist is lost in the shadows.

For two or three hours the auto stands deserted and silent. At last the voices are heard again, the car stirs, moves away, and the cyclist drops in behind. Another race which leads off in another direction. Finally, from a knoll, the lights of a city are seen. Ten minutes elapse, the auto stops, the head lights flare up and more leisurely it proceeds on its way.

* * *

On the following evening The Thinking Machine and Hutchinson Hatch called upon Fielding Stanwood, President of the Fordyce National Bank. Mr. Stanwood looked at them with interrogative eyes.

"We called to inform you, Mr. Stanwood," explained The Thinking Machine, "that a box of securities, probably United States bonds, is missing from your bank."

"What?" exclaimed Mr. Stanwood, and his face paled. "Robbery?"

"I only know the bonds were taken out of the vault to-night by Joseph Marsh, your assistant cashier," said the scientist, "and that he, together with three other men, left the bank with the box and are now at—a place I can name."

Mr. Stanwood was staring at him in amazement.

"You know where they are?" he demanded.

"I said I did," replied the scientist, shortly.

"Then we must inform the police at once, and—"

"I don't know that there has been an actual crime," interrupted the scientist. "I do know that every night for a week these bonds have been taken out through the connivance of your watchman, and in each instance have been returned, intact, before morning. They will be returned to-night. Therefore I would advise, if you act, not to do so until the four men return with the bonds."

It was a singular party which met in the private office of President Stanwood at the bank just after midnight. Marsh and three companions formally under arrest, were present as were President Stanwood, The Thinking Machine and Hatch, besides detectives. Marsh had the bonds under his arms when he was taken. He talked freely when questioned.

"I will admit," he said without hesitating, "that I have acted beyond my rights in removing the bonds from the vault here, but there is no ground for prosecution. I am a responsible officer of this bank and have violated no trust. Nothing is missing, nothing is stolen. Every bond that went out of the bank is here."

"But why—why did you take the bonds?" demanded Mr. Stanwood.

Marsh shrugged his shoulders.

"It's what has been called a get-rich-quick scheme," said The Thinking Machine. "Mr. Hatch and I made some investigations today. Mr. Marsh and these other three are interested in a business venture which is ethically dishonest but which is within the law. They have sought backing for the scheme amounting to about a million dollars. Those four or five men of means with whom they have discussed the matter have called each night for a week at Marsh's country place. It was necessary to make them believe that there was already a million or so in the scheme, so these bonds were borrowed and represented to be owned by themselves. They were taken to and fro between the bank and his home in a kind of an automobile. This is really what happened, based on knowledge which Mr. Hatch has gathered and what I myself developed by the use of a little logic."

And his statement of the affair proved to be correct. Marsh and the others admitted the statement to be true. It was while The Thinking Machine was homeward bound that he explained the phantom auto affair to Hatch.

"The phantom auto as you call it," he said, "is the vehicle in which the bonds were moved about. The phantom idea came merely by chance. On the night the vehicle was first noticed it was rushing along—we'll say to reach Marsh's house in time for an appointment. A road map will show you that the most direct line from the bank to Marsh's was through The Trap. If an automobile should go half way through there, then out across the Stocker estate to the other road, the distance would be lessened by a good five miles. This saving at first was of course valuable, so the car in which they rushed into the trap was merely taken across the Stocker estate to the road in front."

"But how?" demanded Hatch. "There's no road there."

"I learned by 'phone from Mr. Stocker that there is a narrow walk from a very narrow foot-gate in Stocker's wall on The Trap leading through the grounds to the other road. The phantom auto wasn't really an auto at all—it was merely two motor-cycles arranged with seats and a steering apparatus. The French Army has been experimenting with them. The motor-cycles are, of course, separate machines and as such it was easy to trundle them through a narrow gate and across to the other road. The seats are light; they can be carried under the arm."

"Oh!" exclaimed Hatch suddenly, then after a minute: "But what did Jimmie Thalhauer do for you?"

"He waited in the road at the other end of the foot-path from The Trap," the scientist explained. "When the auto was brought through and put together he followed it to Marsh's home and from there to the bank. The rest of it you and I worked out today. It's merely logic, Mr. Hatch, logic."

There was a pause.

"That Mr. Thalhauer is really a marvellous young man, Mr. Hatch, don't you think?"

Samuel Hopkins Adams

(1871–1948)

SAMUEL HOPKINS ADAMS was a crusading journalist with *McClure's Magazine* whose exposés played a role in the passage of the Pure Food and Drug Act, as well as a prolific novelist and short story writer. He always claimed that he took the names of his characters from tombstones.

Adams's works in the mystery field were few but imaginative. His short story "The Flying Death" (1903), later expanded into a novel of the same name (1908), is about murders on sand marked only by the prints of a giant prehistoric bird. A bald account of the solution, involving a juggler who can walk on his hands, does not do justice to this enjoyable period piece. *The Mystery* (1907), written with Stewart Edward White, combines science fiction and mystery as a detective tries to discover why crews disappear from a ship. The situation is similar to the real-life case of the *Mary Celeste*, but the solution, involving radioactivity, is original.

In 1911, Adams wrote a short story collection, entitled *Average Jones*, about a young man about town with the misfortune to be named Adrian von Reypen Egerton Jones, the A.V.R.E.J. leading to his nickname. Bored with doing nothing, Jones hits on a unique occupation. He becomes the "Ad-Visor," investigating advertising scams.

The Million-Dollar Dog

TO THIS DAY, Average Jones maintains that he felt a distinct thrill at first sight of the advertisement. Yet Fate might well have chosen a more appropriate ambush in any one of a hundred of the strange clippings which were grist to the Ad-Visor's mill. Out of a bulky pile of the day's paragraphs, however, it was this one that leaped, significant, to his eye.

WANTED—Ten thousand loathly black beetles, by a leaseholder who contracted to leave a house in the same condition as he found it. ACKROYD, 100 W. Sixteenth St., New York.

"Black beetles, eh?" observed Average Jones. "This Ackroyd person seems to be a merry little jester. Well, I'm feeling rather jocular, myself, this morning. How does one collect black beetles, I wonder? When in doubt, inquire of the resourceful Simpson."

He pressed a button and his confidential clerk entered.

"Good morning, Simpson," said Average Jones. "Are you acquainted with that shy but pervasive animal, the domestic black beetle?"

"Yes, sir; I board," said Simpson simply.

"I suppose there aren't ten thousand black beetles in your boarding-house, though?" inquired Average Jones.

Simpson took it under advisement. "Hardly," he decided.

"I've got to have 'em to fill an order. At least, I've got to have an instalment of 'em, and to-morrow."

Being wholly without imagination, the confidential clerk was impervious to surprise or shock. This was fortunate, for otherwise, his employment as practical aide to Average Jones would probably have driven him into a madhouse. He now ran his long, thin, clerkly hands through his long, thin, clerkly hair.

"Ramson, down on Fulton Street, will have them, if any one has," he said presently. "He does business under the title of the Insect Nemesis, you know. I'll go there at once."

Returning to his routine work, Average Jones found himself unable to dislodge the advertisement from his mind. So presently he gave way to temptation, called up Bertram at the Cosmic Club, and asked him to come to the Astor Court Temple offices at his convenience. Scenting more adventure, Bertram found it convenient to come promptly. Average Jones handed him the clipping. Bertram read it with ascending eyebrows.

"Hoots!" he said. "The man's mad."

"I didn't ask you here to diagnose the advertiser's trouble. That's plain enough—though you've made a bad guess. What I want of you is to tap your flow of information about old New York. What's at One Hundred West Sixteenth Street?"

"One Hundred West Sixteenth; let me see. Why, of course; it's the old Feltner mansion. You must know it. It has a walled garden at the side; the only one left in the city, south of Central Park."

"Any one named Ackroyd there?"

"That must be Hawley Ackroyd. I remember, now, hearing that he had rented it. Judge Ackroyd, you know, better known as 'Oily' Ackroyd. He's a smooth old rascal."

"Indeed? What particular sort?"

"Oh, most sorts, in private. Professionally, he's a legislative crook; head lobbyist of the Consolidated."

"Ever hear of his collecting insects?"

"Never heard of his collecting anything but graft. In fact, he'd have been in jail years ago, but for his family connections. He married a Van Haltern. You remember the famous Van Haltern will case, surely; the million-dollar dog. The papers fairly reeked of it a year ago. Sylvia Graham had to take the dog and leave the country to escape the notoriety. She's back now, I believe."

"I've heard of Miss Graham," remarked Average Jones, "through friends of mine whom she visits."

"Well, if you've only heard of her and not seen her," returned Bertram, with something as nearly resembling enthusiasm as his habitual languor permitted, "you've got something to look forward to. Sylvia Graham is a distinct asset to the Scheme of Creation."

"An asset with assets of her own, I believe," said Average Jones. "The million dollars left by her grandmother, old Mrs. Van Haltern, goes to her eventually, doesn't it?"

"Provided she carries out the terms of the will, keeps the dog in proper luxury and buries him in the grave on the family estate at Schuylkill designated by the testator. If these terms are not rigidly carried out, the fortune is to be divided, most of it going to Mrs. Hawley Ackroyd, which would mean the judge himself. I should say that the dog was as good as sausage meat if 'Oily' ever gets hold of him."

"H'm. What about Mrs. Ackroyd?"

"Poor, sickly, frightened lady! She's very fond of Sylvia Graham, who is her niece. But she's completely dominated by her husband."

"Information is your long suit, Bert. Now, if you only had intelligence to correspond—" Average Jones broke off and grinned mildly, first at his friend, then at the advertisement.

Bertram caught up the paper and studied it. "Well, what *does* it mean?" he demanded.

"It means that Ackroyd, being about to give up his rented house, intends to saddle it with a bad name. Probably he's had a row with the agent or owner, and is getting even by making the place difficult to rent again. Nobody wants to take a house with the reputation of an entomological resort."

"It would be just like 'Oily' Ackroyd," remarked Bertram. "He's a vindictive scoundrel. Only a few days ago, he nearly killed a poor devil of a drug clerk, over some trifling dispute. He managed to keep it out of the newspapers but he had to pay a stiff fine."

"That might be worth looking up, too," ruminated Average Jones thoughtfully.

He turned to his telephone in answer to a ring. "All right, come in, Simpson," he said.

The confidential clerk appeared. "Ramson says that regular black beetles are out of season, sir," he reported. "But he can send to the country and dig up plenty of red-and-black ones."

"That will do," returned the Ad-Visor. "Tell him to have two or three hundred here to-morrow morning."

Bertram bent a severe gaze on his friend. "Meaning that you're going to follow up this freak affair?" he inquired.

"Just that. I can't explain why, but—well, Bert, it's a hunch. At the worst, Ackroyd's face when he sees the beetles should be worth the money."

"When you frivol, Average, I wash my hands of you. But I warn you, look out for Ackroyd. He's as big as he is ugly; a tough customer."

"All right. I'll just put on some old clothes, to dress the part of a beetle-purveyor correctly, and also in case I get 'em torn in my meeting with Judge 'Oily.' I'll see you later and report, if I survive his wrath."

Thus it was that, on the morning after this dialogue, a clean-built young fellow walked along West Sixteenth Street, appreciatively sniffing the sunny crispness of the May air. He was rather shabby-looking, yet his demeanor was by no means shabby. It was confident and easy. On the evidence of the bandbox which he carried, his mission should have been menial; but he bore himself wholly unlike one subdued to petty employments. His steady, gray eyes showed a glint of anticipation as he turned in at the gate of the high, broad, brown house standing back, aloof and indignant, from the roaring encroachments of trade. He set his burden down and pulled the bell.

The door opened promptly to the deep, far-away clangor. A flashing impression of girlish freshness, vigor, and grace was disclosed to the caller against a background of interior gloom. He stared a little more patiently than was polite. Whatever his expectation of amusement, this, evidently, was not the manifestation looked for. The girl glanced not at him, but at the box, and spoke a trifle impatiently.

"If it's my hat, it's very late. You should have gone to the basement."

"It isn't, miss," said the young man, in a form of address, the semi-servility of which seemed distinctly out of tone with the quietly clear and assured voice. "It's the insects."

"The *what?*"

"The bugs, miss."

He extracted from his pocket a slip of paper, looked from it to the numbered door, as one verifying an address, and handed it to her.

"From yesterday's copy of the *Banner,* miss. You're not going back on that, surely," he said somewhat reproachfully.

She read, and as she read her eyes widened to lakes of limpid brown. Then they crinkled at the corners, and her laugh rose from the mid-tone contralto, to a high, bird-like trill of joyousness. The infection of it tugged at the young man's throat, but he successfully preserved his mask of flat and respectful dullness.

"It must have been Uncle," she gasped finally. "He said he'd be quits with the real estate agent before he left. How perfectly absurd! And are those the creatures in that box?"

"The first couple of hundred of 'em, miss."

"Two hundred!" Again the access of laughter swelled the rounded bosom as the breeze fills a sail. "Where did you get them?"

"Woodpile, ash-heap, garbage-pail," said the young man stolidly. "Any particular kind preferred, Miss Ackroyd?"

The girl looked at him with suspicion, but his face was blankly innocent.

"I'm not Miss Ackroyd," she began with emphasis, when a querulous voice from an inner room called out: "Whom are you talking to, Sylvia?"

"A young man with a boxful of beetles," returned the girl, adding in brisk French: *"Il est tres amusant ce farceur. Je ne le comprends pas du tout. C'est une blague, peut-être. Si on l'invitait dans la maison pour un moment?"*

Through one of the air-holes, considerately punched in the cardboard cover of the box, a sturdy crawler had succeeded in pushing himself. He was, in the main, of a shiny and well-groomed black, but two large patches of crimson gave him the festive appearance of being garbed in a brilliant sash. As he stood rubbing his fore-legs together in self-congratulation over his exploit, his bearer addressed him in French quite as ready as the girl's:

"Permettez-moi, Monsieur le Coléoptère, de vous presenter mes excuses pour cette demoiselle qui s'exprime en langue étrangère chez elle."

"Don't apologize to the beetle on my account," retorted the girl with spirit. "You're here on your own terms, you know, both of you."

Average Jones mutely held up the box in one hand and the advertisement in the other. The adventurer-bug flourished a farewell to the girl with his antennæ, and retired within to advise his fellows of the charms of freedom.

"Very well," said the girl, in demure tones, though lambent mirth still flickered, golden, in the depths of the brown eyes. "If you persist, I can only suggest that you come back when Judge Ackroyd is here. You won't find him particularly amenable to humor, particularly when perpetrated by a practical joker in masquerade."

"Discovered," murmured Average Jones. "I shouldn't have vaunted my poor French. But must I really take my little friends all the way back? You suggested to the mystic voice within that I might be invited inside."

"You seem a decidedly unconventional person," began the other with dawning disfavor.

"Conventionality, like charity, begins at home," he replied quickly. "And one would hardly call this advertisement a pattern of formal etiquette."

"True enough," she admitted, dimpling, and Average Jones was congratulating himself on his diplomacy, when the querulous voice broke in again, this time too low for his ears.

"I don't ask you the real reason for your extraordinary call," pursued the girl with a glint of mischief in her eyes, after she had responded in an aside, "but auntie thinks you've come to steal my dog. She thinks that of every one lately."

"Auntie? Your dog? Then you're Sylvia Graham. I might have known it."

"I don't know how you might have known it. But I am Sylvia Graham—if you insist on introducing me to yourself."

"Miss Graham," said the visitor promptly and gravely, "let me present A. V. R. E. Jones, a friend—"

"Not the famous Average Jones!" cried the girl. "That is why your face seemed so familiar. I've seen your picture at Edna Hale's. You got her 'blue fires' back for her. But really, that hardly explains your being here, in this way, you know."

"Frankly, Miss Graham, it was just as a lark that I answered the advertisement. But now that I'm here and find you here, it looks—er— as if it might—er—be more serious."

A tinge of pink came into the girl's cheeks, but she answered lightly enough:

"Indeed, it may, for you, if uncle finds you here with those beetles."

"Never mind me or the beetles. I'd like to know about your dog that your aunt is worrying over. Is he here with you?"

The soft curve of Miss Graham's lips straightened a little. "I really think," she said with decision, "that you had better explain further before questioning."

"Nothing simpler. Once upon a time there lived a crack-brained young Don Quixote who wandered through an age of buried romance piously searching for trouble. And, twice upon a time, there dwelt in an enchanted stone castle in West Sixteenth Street an enchanting young damsel in distress—"

"I'm not a damsel in distress," interrupted Miss Graham, passing over the adjective.

The young man leaned to her. The half smile had passed from his lips, and his eyes were very grave.

"Not—er—if your dog were to—er—disappear?" he drawled quietly.

The swift unexpectedness of the counter broke down the girl's guard.

"You mean Uncle Hawley," she said.

"And your suspicions jump with mine."

"They don't!" she denied hotly. "You're very unjust and impertinent."

"I don't mean to be impertinent," he said evenly. "And I have no monopoly of injustice."

"What do you know about Uncle Hawley?"

"Your aunt—"

"I won't hear a word against my aunt."

"Not from me, be assured. Your aunt, so you have just told me, believes that your dog is in danger of being stolen. Why? Because she knows that the person most interested has been scheming against the animal, and yet she is afraid to warn you openly. Doesn't that indicate who it is?"

"Mr. Jones, I've no right even to let you talk like this to me. Have you anything definite against Judge Ackroyd?"

"In this case, only suspicion."

Her head went up. "Then I think there is nothing more to be said."

The young man flushed, but his voice was steady as he returned:

"I disagree with you. And I beg you to cut short your visit here, and return to your home at once."

In spite of herself the girl was shaken by his persistence.

"I can't do that," she said uneasily. And added, with a flash of anger, "I think you had better leave this house."

"If I leave this house now I may never have a chance to see you again."

The girl regarded him with level, non-committal eyes.

"And I have every intention of seeing you again—and again—and again. Give me a chance; a moment."

Average Jones' mind was of the emergency type. It summoned to its aid, without effort of cerebration on the part of its owner, whatever was most needed at the moment. Now it came to his rescue with the memory of Judge Ackroyd's encounter with the drug clerk, as mentioned by Bertram. There was a strangely hopeful suggestion of some link between a drug store quarrel and the arrival of a million-dollar dog, "better dead" in the hopes of his host.

"Miss Graham, I've gone rather far, I'll admit," said Jones; "but, if you'll give me the benefit of the doubt, I think I can show you some basis to work on. If I can produce something tangible, may I come back here this afternoon? I'll promise not to come unless I have good reason."

"Very well," conceded Miss Graham reluctantly, "it's a most unusual thing. But I'll agree to that."

"*Au revoir*, then," he said, and was gone.

Somewhat to her surprise and uneasiness, Sylvia Graham experienced a distinct satisfaction when, late that afternoon, she beheld her unconventional acquaintance mounting the steps with a buoyant and assured step. Upon being admitted, he went promptly to the point.

"I've got it."

"Your justification for coming back?" she asked.

"Exactly. Have you heard anything of some trouble in which Judge Ackroyd was involved last week?"

"Uncle has a very violent temper," admitted the girl evasively. "But I don't see what—"

"Pardon me. You will see. That row was with a drug clerk."

"Well?"

"In an obscure drug store several blocks from here."

"Yes?"

"The drug clerk insisted—as the law requires—on Judge Ackroyd registering for a certain purchase."

"Perhaps he was impertinent about it."

"Possibly. The point is that the prospective purchase was cyanide of potassium, a deadly and instantaneous poison."

"Are you sure?" asked the girl, in a low voice.

"I've just come from the store. How long have you been here at your uncle's?"

"A week."

"Then just about the time of your coming with the dog, your uncle undertook to obtain a swift and sure poison. Have I gone far enough?"

"I—I don't know."

"Well, am I still ordered out of the house?"

"N-n-no."

"Thank you for your enthusiastic hospitality," said Average Jones so dryly that a smile relaxed the girl's troubled face. "With that encouragement we'll go on. What is your uncle's attitude toward the dog?"

"Almost what you might call ingratiating. But Peter Paul—that's my dog's name, you know—doesn't take to uncle. He's a crotchety old doggie."

"He's a wise old doggie," amended the other, with emphasis. "Has your uncle taken him out, at all?"

"Once he tried to. I met them at the corner. All four of Peter Paul's poor old fat legs were braced, and he was hauling back as hard as he could against the leash."

"And the occurrence didn't strike you as peculiar?"

"Well, not then."

"When does your uncle give up this house?"

"At the end of the week. Uncle and aunt leave for Europe."

"Then let me suggest again that you and Peter Paul go at once."

Miss Graham pondered. "That would mean explanations and a quarrel, and more strain for auntie, who is nervous enough, anyway. No, I can't do that."

"Do you realize that every day Peter Paul remains here is an added opportunity for Judge Ackroyd to make a million dollars, or a big share of it, by some very simple stratagem?"

"I haven't admitted yet that I believe my uncle to be a—a murderer," Miss Graham quietly reminded him.

"A strong word," said Average Jones smiling. "The law would hardly support your view. Now, Miss Graham, would it grieve you very much if Peter Paul were to die?"

"I won't have him put to death," said she quickly. "That would be cheating my grandmother's intentions."

"I supposed you wouldn't. Yet it would be the simplest way. Once dead, and buried in accordance with the terms of the will, the dog would be out of his troubles, and you would be out of yours."

"It would really be a relief. Peter Paul suffers so from asthma, poor old beastie. The vet. says he can live only a month or two longer, anyway. But I've got to do as Grandmother wished, and keep Peter Paul alive as long as possible."

"Admitted." Average Jones fell into a baffled silence, studying the pattern of the rug with restless eyes. When he looked up into Miss Graham's face again it was with a changed expression.

"Miss Graham," he said slowly, "won't you try to forget, for the moment, the circumstances of our meeting, and think of me only as a friend of your friends who is very honestly eager to be a friend to you, when you most need one?"

Now, Average Jones's birth-fairy had endowed him with one priceless gift: the power of inspiring an instinctive confidence in himself. Sylvia Graham felt, suddenly, that a hand, sure and firm, had been outstretched to guide her on a dark path. In one of those rare flashes of companionship which come only when clean and honorable spirits recognize one another, all consciousness of sex was lost between them. The girl's gaze met the man's level, and was held in a long, silent regard.

"Yes," she said simply; and the heart of Average Jones rose and swore a high loyalty.

"Listen, then. I think I see a clear way. Judge Ackroyd will kill the dog if he can, and so effectually conceal the body that no funeral can be held over it, thereby rendering your grandmother's bequest to you void. He has only a few days to do it in, but I don't think that all your watchfulness can restrain him. Now, on the other hand, if the dog should die a natural death and be buried, he can still contest the will. But if he should kill Peter Paul and hide the body where we could discover it, the game would be up for him, as he then wouldn't even dare to come into court with a contest. Do you follow me?"

"Yes. But you wouldn't ask me to be a party to any such thing."

"You're a party, involuntarily, by remaining here. But do your best to save Peter Paul, if you will. And please call me up immediately at the Cosmic Club, if anything in my line turns up."

"What is your line?" asked Miss Graham, the smile returning to her lips. "Creepy, crawly bugs? Or imperiled dogs? Or rescuing prospectively distressed damsels?"

"Technically it's advertising," replied Average Jones, who had been formulating a shrewd little plan of his own. "Let me recommend to you the advertising columns of the daily press. They're often amusing. Moreover, your uncle might break out in print again. Who knows?"

"Who, indeed? I'll read religiously."

"And, by the way, my beetles. I forgot and left them here. Oh, there's the box. I may have a very specific use for them later. *Au revoir*—and may it be soon!"

The two days succeeding seemed to Average Jones, haunted as he was by an importunate craving to look again into Miss Graham's limpid and changeful eyes, a dull and sodden period of probation. The messenger boy who finally brought her expected note, looked to him like a Greek godling. The note enclosed this clipping:

LOST—Pug dog answering to the name of Peter Paul. Very old and asthmatic. Last seen on West 16th Street. Liberal reward for information to ANXIOUS. Care of *Banner* office.

Dear Mr. Jones (she had written):
Are you a prophet? (Average Jones chuckled, at this point.) *The enclosed seems to be distinctly in our line. Could you come some time this afternoon? I'm puzzled and a little anxious.*
                    Sincerely yours,

                              Sylvia Graham.

Average Jones could, and did. He found Miss Graham's piquant face under the stress of excitement, distinctly more alluring than before.

"Isn't it strange?" she said, holding out a hand in welcome. "Why should any one advertise for my Peter Paul? He isn't lost."

"I am glad to hear that," said the caller gravely.

"I've kept my promise, you see," pursued the girl. "Can you do as well, and live up to your profession of aid?"

"Try me."

"Very well, do you know what that advertisement means?"

"Perfectly."

"Then you're a very extraordinary person."

"Not in the least. I wrote it."

"Wrote it! You? Well—really! Why in the world did *you* write it?"

"Because of an unconquerable longing to see"—Average Jones paused, and his quick glance caught the storm signal in her eyes—"your uncle," he concluded calmly.

For one fleeting instant a dimple flickered at the corner of her mouth. It departed. But departing, it swept the storm before it.

"What do you want to see uncle about, if it isn't an impertinent question?"

"It is, rather," returned the young man judicially. "Particularly, as I'm not sure, myself. I may want to quarrel with him."

"You won't have the slightest difficulty in that," the girl assured him.

She rang the bell, despatched a servant, and presently Judge Ackroyd stalked into the room. As Average Jones was being presented, he took comprehensive note and estimate of the broad-cheeked, thin-lipped face; the square shoulders and corded neck, and the lithe and formidable carriage of the man. Judge 'Oily' Ackroyd's greeting of the guest within his gates did not bear out the *sobriquet* of his public life. It was curt to the verge of harshness.

"What is the market quotation on beetles, Judge?" asked the young man, tapping the rug with his stick.

"What are you talking about?" demanded the other, drawing down his heavy brows.

"The black beetle; the humble but brisk haunter of household crevices," explained Average Jones. "You advertised for ten thousand specimens. I've got a few thousand I'd like to dispose of, if the inducements are sufficient."

"I'm in no mood for joking, young man," retorted the other, rising.

"You seldom are, I understand," replied Average Jones blandly. "Well, if you won't talk about bugs, let's talk about dogs."

"The topic does not interest me, sir," retorted the other, and the glance of his eye was baleful, but uneasy.

The tapping of the young man's cane ceased. He looked up into his host's glowering face with a seraphic and innocent smile.

"Not even if it—er—touched upon a device for guarding the street corners in case—er—Peter Paul went walking—er—once too often?"

Judge Ackroyd took one step forward. Average Jones was on his feet instantly, and, even in her alarm, Sylvia Graham noticed how swiftly and naturally his whole form "set." But the big man turned away, and abruptly left the room.

"Were you wise to anger him?" asked the girl, as the heavy tread died away on the stairs.

"Sometimes open declaration of war is the soundest strategy."

"War?" she repeated. "You make me feel like a traitor to my own family."

"That's the unfortunate part of it," he said; "but it can't be helped."

"You spoke of having some one guard the corners of the block," continued the girl, after a thoughtful silence. "Do you think I'd better arrange for that?"

"No need. There'll be a hundred people on watch."

"Have you called out the militia?" she asked, twinkling.

"Better than that. I've employed the tools of my trade."

He handed her a galley proof marked with many corrections. She ran through it with growing amazement.

HAVE YOU SEEN THE DOG?

$100—One Hundred Dollars—$100

FOR THE BEST ANSWER IN 500 WORDS

OPEN TO ALL HIGH SCHOOL BOYS

Between now and next Saturday an old Pug
Dog will come out of a big House on West 16th
Street, between 5th and 6th Avenues. It may
be by Day. It may be any hour of the Night.
Now, you Boys, get to work.

REMEMBER: $100 IN CASH

HERE ARE THE POINTS TO MIND—

    1—Description of Dog.
    2—Description of Person with him.
    3—Description of House he Comes from.
    4—Account of Where they Go.
    5—Account of What they Do.

Manuscripts must be written plainly and
mailed within twenty-four hours of the discovery of the dog to

A. JONES : AD-VISOR,
ASTOR COURT TEMPLE, NEW YORK

"That will appear in every New York paper tomorrow morning,"
explained its deviser.

"I see," said the girl. "Any one who attempts to take Peter Paul away
will be tracked by a band of boy detectives. A stroke of genius, Mr.
Average Jones."

She curtsied low to him. But Average Jones was in no mood for play-
fulness now.

"That restricts the judge's endeavors to the house and garden," said
he, "since, of course he'll see the advertisement."

"I'll see that he does," said Miss Graham maliciously.

"Good! I'll also ask you to watch the garden for any suspicious
excavating."

"Very well. But is that all?" Miss Graham's voice was wistful.

"Isn't it enough?"

"You've been so good to me," she said hesitantly. "I don't like to
think of you as setting those boys to an impossible task."

"Oh, bless you!" returned the Ad-Visor heartily; "that's all arranged for. One of my men will duly parade with a canine especially obtained for the occasion. I'm not going to swindle the youngsters."

"It didn't seem like you," returned Miss Graham warmly. "But you must let me pay for it, that and the advertising bill."

"As an unauthorized expense—" he began.

She laid a small, persuasive hand on his arm.

"You must let me pay it. Won't you?"

Average Jones was conscious of a strange sensation, starting from the point where the firm, little hand lay. It spread in his veins and thickened his speech.

"Of course," he drawled, uncertainly, "if you—er—put it—er—that way!"

The hand lifted. "Mr. Average Jones," said the owner, "do you know you haven't once disappointed me in speech or action during our short but rather eventful acquaintance?"

"I hope you'll be able to say the same ten years from now," he returned significantly.

She flushed a little at the implication. "What am I to do next?" she asked.

"Do as you would ordinarily do; only don't take Peter Paul into the street, or you'll have a score of high-school boys trailing you. And—this is the most important—if the dog fails to answer your call at any time, and you can't readily find him by searching, telephone me, at once, at my office. Good-by."

"I think you are a very staunch friend to those who need you," she said, gravely and sweetly, giving him her hand.

She clung in his mind like a remembered fragrance, after he had gone back to Astor Court Temple to wait. And though he plunged into an intricate scheme of political advertising which was to launch a new local party, her eyes and her voice haunted him. Nor had he banished them, when, two days later, the telephone brought him her clear accents, a little tremulous now.

"Peter Paul is gone."

"Since when?"

"Since ten this morning. The house is in an uproar."

"I'll be up in half an hour at the latest."

"Do come quickly. I'm—I'm a little frightened."

"Then you must have something to do," said Average Jones decisively. "Have you been keeping an eye on the garden?"

"Yes."

"Go through it again, looking carefully for signs of disarranged earth. I don't think you'll find it, but it's well to be sure. Let me in at the basement door at half-past one. Judge Ackroyd mustn't see me."

It was a strangely misshapen presentation of the normally spick-and-span Average Jones that gently rang the basement bell of the old house at the specified hour. All his pockets bulged with lumpy angles. Immediately, upon being admitted by Miss Graham herself, he proceeded to disemburden himself of box after box, such as elastic bands come in, all exhibiting a homogeneous peculiarity, a hole at one end thinly covered with a gelatinous substance.

"Be very careful not to let that get broken," he instructed the mystified girl. "In the course of an hour or so it will melt away itself. Did you see anything suspicious in the garden?"

"No!" replied the girl. She picked up one of the boxes. "How odd!" she cried. "Why, there's something in it that's alive!"

"Very much so. Your friends, the beetles, in fact."

"What! Again? Aren't you carrying the joke rather far?"

"It's not a joke any more. It's deadly serious. I'm quite sure," he concluded in the manner of one who picks his words carefully, "that it may turn out to be just the most serious matter in the world to me."

"As bad as that?" she queried, but the color that flamed in her cheeks belied the lightness of her tone.

"Quite. However, that must wait. Where is your uncle?"

"Up-stairs in his study."

"Do you think you could take me all through the house sometime this afternoon without his seeing me?"

"No, I'm sure I couldn't. He's been wandering like an uneasy spirit since Peter Paul disappeared. And he won't go out, because he is packing."

"So much the worse, either for him or me. Where are your rooms?"

"On the second floor."

"Very well. Now, I want one of these little boxes left in every room in the house, if possible, except on your floor, which is probably out of the reckoning. Do you think you could manage it soon?"

"I think so. I'll try."

"Do most of the rooms open into one another?"

"Yes, all through the house."

"Please see that they're all unlocked, and as far as possible, open. I'll be here at four o'clock, and will call for Judge Ackroyd. You must be sure that he receives me. Tell him it is a matter of great importance. It is."

"You're putting a fearful strain on my feminine curiosity," said Miss Graham, the provocative smile quirking at the corners of her mouth.

"Doubtless," returned the other dryly. "If you strictly follow directions, I'll undertake to satisfy it in time. Four o'clock sharp, I'll be here. Don't be frightened whatever happens. You keep ready, but out of the way, until I call you. Good-by."

With even more than his usual nicety was Average Jones attired, when, at four o'clock, he sent his card to Judge Ackroyd. Small favor, however, did his appearance find, in the scowling eyes of the judge.

"What do *you* want?" he growled.

"I'll take a cigar, thank you very much," said Average Jones innocently.

"You'll take your leave, or state your business."

"It has to do with your niece."

"Then what do you take my time for, damn your impudence?"

"Don't swear." Average Jones was deliberately provoking the older man to an outbreak. "Let's—er—sit down and—er—be chatty."

The drawl, actually an evidence of excitement, had all the effect of studied insolence. Judge Ackroyd's big frame shook.

"I'm going to k-k-kick you out into the street, you young p-p-p-pup," he stuttered in his rage.

His knotted fingers writhed out for a hold on the other's collar. With a sinuous movement, the visitor swerved aside and struck the other man, flat-handed, across the face. There was an answering howl of demoniac fury. Then a strange thing happened. The assailant turned and fled, not to the ready egress of the front door, but down the dark stairway to the basement. The judge thundered after, in maddened, unthinking pursuit. Average Jones ran fleetly and easily. And his running was not for the purpose of flight alone, for as he sped through the basement rooms, he kept casting swift glances from side to side, and up and down the walls. The heavyweight pursuer could not get nearer than half-a-dozen paces.

From the kitchen Average Jones burst into the hallway, doubled back up the stairs and made a tour of the big drawing-rooms and living-rooms of the first floor. Here, too, his glance swept room after room, from floor to ceiling. The chase then led upward to the second floor, and by direct ascent to the third. Breathing heavily, Judge Ackroyd lumbered after the more active man. In his dogged rage, he never thought to stop and block the hall-way; but trailed his quarry like a bloodhound through every room of the third floor, and upward to the fourth. Half-way up this stairway, Average Jones checked his speed and surveyed the hall above. As he started again he stumbled and sprawled. A more competent observer than the infuriated pursuer might have noticed that he fell cunningly. But Judge Ackroyd gave a shout of savage triumph and increased his speed. He stretched his hand to grip the fugitive. It had almost touched him when he leaped to his feet and resumed his flight.

"I'll get you now!" panted the judge.

The fourth floor of the old house was almost bare. In a hall-embrasure hung a full-length mirror. All along the borders of this, Average Jones' quick-ranging vision had discerned small red-banded objects which moved and shifted. As the glass reflected his extended figure, it showed, almost at the same instant, the outstretched, bony-hand of 'Oily' Ackroyd. With a snarl, half rage, half satisfaction, the pursuer hurled himself forward—and fell, with a plunge that rattled the house's old bones. For, as he reached, Jones, trained on many a foot-ball field, had whirled and dived at his knees. Before the fallen man could gather his shaken wits, he was pinned with the most disabling grip known in the science of combat, a strangle-hold with the assailant's wrist clamped in below and behind the ear. Average Jones lifted his voice and the name that came to his lips was the name that had lurked subconsciously, in his heart, for days.

"Sylvia!" he cried. "The fourth floor! Come!"

There was a stir and a cry from two floors below. Sylvia Graham had broken from the grasp of her terrified aunt, and now came up the sharp ascent like a deer, her eyes blazing with resolve and courage.

"The mirror," said Average Jones. "Push it aside. Pull it down. Get behind it somehow. Lie quiet, Ackroyd or I'll have to choke your worthless head off!"

With an effort of nervous strength, the girl lifted aside the big glass. Behind it a hundred scarlet-banded insects swarmed and scampered.

"It's a panel. Open it."

She tugged at the woodwork with quick, clever fingers. A section loosened and fell outward with a bang. The red-and-black beetles fled in all directions. And now, Judge Ackroyd found his voice.

"Help!" he roared. "Murder!"

The sinewy pressure of Average Jones' wrist smothered further attempts at vocality to a gurgle. He looked up into Sylvia Graham's tense face, and jerked his head toward the opening.

"Unless my little detectives have deceived me," he said, "you'll find the body in there."

She groped, and drew forth a large box. In it was packed the body of Peter Paul. There was a cord about the fat neck.

"Strangled," whispered the girl. "Poor old doggie!" Then she whirled upon the prostrate man. "You murderer!" she said very low.

"It's not murder to put a dying brute out of the way," said the shaken man sullenly.

"But it's fraud, in this case," retorted Average Jones. "A fraud of which you're self-convicted. Get up." He himself rose and stepped back, but his eye was intent, and his muscles were in readiness.

There was no more fight in Judge 'Oily' Ackroyd. He slunk to the stairs and limped heavily down to his frightened and sobbing wife. Miss Graham leaned against the wall, white and spent. Average Jones, his heart in his eyes, took a step forward.

"No!" she said peremptorily. "Don't touch me. I shall be all right."

"Do you mind my saying," said he, very low, "that you are the bravest and finest human being I've met in a-a-somewhat varied career."

The girl shuddered. "I could have stood it all," she said, "but for those awful, crawling, red creatures."

"Those?" said Average Jones. "Why, they were my bloodhounds, my little detectives. There's nothing very awful about those, Sylvia. They've done their work as nature gave 'em to do it. I knew that as soon as they got out, they would find the trail."

"And what are they?"

"Carrion beetles," said Average Jones. "Where the vultures of the insect kingdom are gathered together, there the quarry lies."

Sylvia Graham drew a long breath. "I'm all right now," she pronounced. "There's nothing left, I suppose, but to leave this house. And to thank you. How am I ever to thank you?" She lifted her eyes to his.

"Never mind the thanks," said Average Jones unevenly. "It was nothing."

"It was—everything! It was wonderful!" cried the girl, and held out her slender hands to him.

As they clasped warmly upon his, Average Jones' reason lost its balance. He forgot that he was in that house on an equivocal footing; he forgot that he had exposed and disgraced Sylvia Graham's near relative; he forgot that this was but his third meeting with Sylvia Graham herself; he forgot everything except that the sum total of all that was sweetest and finest and most desirable in womanhood stood warm and vivid before him; and, bending over the little, clinging hands, he pressed his lips to them. Only for a moment. The hands slipped from his. There was a quick, frightened gasp, and the girl's face, all aflush with a new, sweet fearfulness and wondering confusion, vanished behind a ponderous swinging door.

The young man's knees shook a little as he walked forward and put his lips close to the lintel.

"Sylvia."

There was a faint rustle from within.

"I'm sorry. I mean, I'm glad. Gladder than of anything I've ever done in my life."

Silence from within.

"If I've frightened you, forgive me. I couldn't help it. It was stronger than I. This isn't the place where I can tell you. Sylvia, I'm going now."

No answer.

"The work is done," he continued. "You won't need me any more. (Did he hear, from within, a faint indrawn breath?) Not for any help that I can give. But I—I shall need you always, and long for you. Listen, there mustn't be any misunderstanding about this, dear. If you send for me, it must be because you want me; knowing that, when I come, I shall come for you. Good-by, dear."

"Good-by." It was the merest whisper from behind the door. But it echoed in the tones of a thousand golden hopes and dismal fears in the whirling brain of Average Jones as he walked, unseeingly, back to his offices.

Two days later he sat at his desk, in a murk of woe. Nor word nor sign had come to him from Miss Sylvia Graham. He frowned heavily as Simpson entered the inner sanctum with the usual packet of clippings.

"Leave them," he ordered.

"Yes, sir." The confidential clerk lingered; looking uncomfortable. "Anything from yesterday's lot, sir?"

"Haven't looked them over yet."

"Or day before's?"

"Haven't taken those up either."

"Pardon me, Mr. Jones, but—are you ill, sir?"

"No," snapped Average Jones.

"Ramson is inquiring whether he shall ship more beetles. I see in the paper that Judge Ackroyd has sailed for Europe on six hours' notice, so I suppose you won't want any more?"

Average Jones mentioned a destination for Ramson's beetles deeper than they had ever digged for prey.

"Yes, sir," assented Simpson. "But if I might suggest, there's a very interesting advertisement in yesterday's paper repeated this morn—"

"I don't want to see it."

"No, sir. But—but still—it—it seems to have a strange reference to the burial of the million-dollar dog, and an invitation that I thought—"

"Where is it? Give it to me!" For once in his life, high pressure of excitement had blotted out Average Jones' drawl. His employee thrust into his hand this announcement from the *Banner* of that morning:

DIED—At 100 West 16th Street, Sept. 14, Peter Paul, a dog, for many years the faithful and fond companion of the late Amelia Van Haltern. Burial in accordance with the wish and will of Mrs. Van Haltern, at the family estate, Schuylkill, Sept. 17, at 3 o'clock. His friend, Don Quixote, is especially bidden to come, if he will.

Average Jones leaped to his feet. "My parable," he cried. "Don Quixote and the damsel in distress. Where's my hat? Where's the time-table?

Get a cab! Simpson, you idiot, why didn't you make me read this before, confound you! I mean God bless you. Your salary's doubled from
to-day. I'm off."

"Yes, sir," said the bewildered Simpson, "but about Ramson's beetles?"

"Tell him to turn 'em out to pasture and keep 'em as long as they
live, at my expense," called back Average Jones as the door slammed
behind him.

Miss Sylvia Graham looked down upon a slender finger ornamented
with the oddest and the most appropriate of engagement rings, a scarab
beetle red-banded with three deep-hued rubies.

"But, Average," she said, and the golden laughter flickered again in
the brown depths of her eyes, "not even you could expect a girl to
accept a man through a keyhole."

"I suppose not," said Average Jones with a sigh of profoundest content. "Some are for privacy in these matters; others for publicity. But I
suppose I'm the first man in history who ever got his heart's answer in
an advertisement."

Baroness Orczy

(1865–1947)

THE HUNGARIAN-BORN Emma Magdalena Rosalia Marie Josepha Barbara, Baroness Orczy, is remembered for two great fictional creations—Sir Percy Blakeney, known as the Scarlet Pimpernel, who rescues aristocrats from the guillotine during the French Revolution; and the Old Man in the Corner, the first armchair detective who solves crimes while rarely leaving his table in a coffee shop. Often overlooked among Orczy's creations is Lady Molly who heads the "Female Department of Scotland Yard." *Lady Molly of Scotland Yard* (1910) begins: "Well, you know, some say she is the daughter of a duke, others that she was born in the gutter, and that the handle ['Lady'] has been soldered onto her name in order to give her style and influence." Lady Molly's cases are narrated by her friend and a fellow member of the Female Department, Mary Grannard. "My firm belief," Mary explains, "is that we shouldn't have half so many undetected crimes if some of the so-called mysteries were put to the test of feminine investigation." Mary, like most sleuthing sidekicks of this period "carried obedience to the level of a fine art."

The Bag of Sand

1

OF COURSE, I knew at once by the expression of her face that morning that my dear lady had some important business on hand.

She had a bundle in her arms, consisting of a shabby-looking coat and skirt, and a very dowdy hat trimmed with bunches of cheap, calico roses.

"Put on these things at once, Mary," she said curtly, "for you are going to apply for the situation of 'good plain cook,' so mind you look the part."

"But where in the world——?" I gasped in astonishment.

"In the house of Mr. Nicholas Jones, in Eaton Terrace," she interrupted dryly, "the one occupied until recently by his sister, the late Mrs. Dunstan. Mrs. Jones is advertising for a cook, and you must get that place."

As you know, I have carried obedience to the level of a fine art. Nor was I altogether astonished that my dear lady had at last been asked to put one of her dainty fingers in that Dunstan pie, which was puzzling our fellows more completely than any other case I have ever known.

I don't know if you remember the many circumstances, the various contradictions which were cropping up at every turn, and which baffled our ablest detectives at the very moment when they thought themselves most near the solution of that strange mystery.

Mrs. Dunstan herself was a very uninteresting individual; self-righteous, self-conscious and fat, a perfect type of the moneyed middle-class woman whose balance at the local bank is invariably heavier than that of her neighbours. Her niece, Violet Frostwicke, lived with her: a smart,

116

pretty girl, inordinately fond of dainty clothes and other luxuries which money can give. Being totally impecunious herself, she bore with the older woman's constantly varying caprices with almost angelic patience, a fact probably attributable to Mrs. Dunstan's testamentary intentions, which, as she often averred, were in favour of her niece.

In addition to these two ladies, the household consisted of three servants and Miss Cruikshank. The latter was a quiet, unassuming girl who was by way of being secretary and lady-help to Mrs. Dunstan, but who, in reality, was nothing but a willing drudge. Up betimes in the morning, she combined the work of a housekeeper with that of an upper servant. She interviewed the tradespeople, kept the servants in order, and ironed and smartened up Miss Violet's blouses. A Cinderella, in fact.

Mrs. Dunstan kept a cook and two maids, all of whom had been with her for years. In addition to these, a charwoman came very early in the morning to light fires, clean boots, and do the front steps.

On November 22nd, 1907—for the early history of this curious drama dates back to that year—the charwoman who had been employed at Mrs. Dunstan's house in Eaton Terrace for some considerable time, sent word in the morning that in future she would be unable to come. Her husband had been obliged to move to lodgings nearer to his work, and she herself could not undertake to come the greater distance at the early hour at which Mrs. Dunstan required her.

The woman had written a very nice letter explaining these facts, and sent it by hand, stating at the same time that the bearer of the note was a very respectable woman, a friend of her own, who would be very pleased to "oblige" Mrs. Dunstan by taking on the morning's work.

I must tell you that the message and its bearer arrived at Eaton Terrace somewhere about 6.00 a.m., when no one was down except the Cinderella of the house, Miss Cruikshank.

She saw the woman, liked her appearance, and there and then engaged her to do the work, subject to Mrs. Dunstan's approval.

The woman, who had given her name as Mrs. Thomas, seemed very quiet and respectable. She said that she lived close by, in St. Peter's Mews, and therefore could come as early as Mrs. Dunstan wished. In fact, from that day, she came every morning at 5.30 a.m., and by seven o'clock had finished her work, and was able to go home.

If, in addition to these details, I tell you that, at that time, pretty Miss Violet Frostwicke was engaged to a young Scotsman, Mr. David Athol, of whom her aunt totally disapproved, I shall have put before you all the personages who, directly or indirectly, were connected with that drama, the final act of which has not yet been witnessed either by the police or the public.

2

On the following New Year's Eve, Mrs. Dunstan, as was her invariable custom on that day, went to her married brother's house to dine and see the New Year in.

During her absence the usual thing occurred at Eaton Terrace. Miss Violet Frostwicke took the opportunity of inviting Mr. David Athol to spend the evening with her.

Mrs. Dunstan's servants, mind you, all knew of the engagement between the young people, and with the characteristic sentimentality of their class, connived at these secret meetings and helped to hood-wink the irascible old aunt.

Mr. Athol was a good-looking young man, whose chief demerit lay in his total lack of money or prospects. Also he was by way of being an actor, another deadly sin in the eyes of the puritanically-minded old lady.

Already on more than one occasion, there had been vigorous wordy warfare 'twixt Mr. Athol and Mrs. Dunstan, and the latter had declared that if Violet chose to take up with this mountebank, she should never see a penny of her aunt's money now or in the future.

The young man did not come very often to Eaton Terrace, but on this festive New Year's Eve, when Mrs. Dunstan was not expected to be home until long after midnight, it seemed too splendid an opportunity for an ardent lover to miss.

As ill-luck would have it, Mrs. Dunstan had not felt very well after her copious dinner, and her brother, Mr. Nicholas Jones, escorted her home soon after ten o'clock.

Jane, the parlour-maid who opened the front door, was, in her own graphic language, "knocked all of a heap" when she saw her mistress, knowing full well that Mr. Athol was still in the dining-room with Miss Violet, and that Miss Cruikshank was at that very moment busy getting him a whiskey and soda.

Meanwhile the coat and hat in the hall had revealed the young man's presence in the house.

For a moment Mrs. Dunstan paused, whilst Jane stood by trembling with fright. Then the old lady turned to Mr. Nicholas Jones, who was still standing on the doorstep, and said quietly:

"Will you telephone over to Mr. Blenkinsop, Nick, the first thing in the morning, and tell him I'll be at his office by ten o'clock?"

Mr. Blenkinsop was Mrs. Dunstan's solicitor, and as Jane explained to the cook later on, what could such an appointment mean but a determination to cut Miss Violet out of the missis's will with the prover-bial shilling?

After this Mrs. Dunstan took leave of her brother and went straight into the dining-room.

According to the subsequent testimony of all three servants, the mistress "went on dreadful." Words were not easily distinguishable from behind the closed door, but it seems that, immediately she entered, Mrs. Dunstan's voice was raised as if in terrible anger, and a few moments later Miss Violet fled crying from the dining-room, and ran quickly upstairs.

Whilst the door was thus momentarily opened and shut, the voice of the old lady was heard saying, in majestic wrath:

"That's what you have done. Get out of this house. As for her, she'll never see a penny of my money, and she may starve for aught I care!"

The quarrel seems to have continued for a short while after that, the servants being too deeply awed by those last vindictive words which they had heard to take much note of what went on subsequently.

Mrs. Dunstan and Mr. Athol were closeted together for some time; but apparently the old lady's wrath did not subside, for when she marched up to bed an hour later she was heard to say:

"Out of this house she shall go, and the first thing in the morning, too. I'll have no goings-on with a mountebank like you."

Miss Cruikshank was terribly upset.

"It is a frightful blow for Miss Violet," she said to cook, "but perhaps Mrs. Dunstan will feel more forgiving in the morning. I'll take her up a glass of champagne now. She is very fond of that, and it will help her to get to sleep."

Miss Cruikshank went up with the champagne, and told cook to see Mr. Athol out of the house; but the young man, who seemed very anxious and agitated, would not go away immediately. He stayed in the dining-room, smoking, for a while, and when the two younger servants went up to bed, he asked cook to let him remain until he had seen Miss Violet once more, for he was sure she would come down again—he had asked Miss Cruikshank to beg of her to do so.

Mrs. Kennett, the cook, was a kind-hearted old woman. She had taken the young people under her special protection, and felt very vexed that the course of true love should not be allowed to run quite smoothly. So she told Mr. Athol to make himself happy and comfortable in the dining-room, and she would sit up by the fire in the library until he was ready to go.

The good soul thereupon made up the fire in the library, drew a chair in front of it, and—went fast to sleep.

Suddenly something awoke her. She sat up and looked round in that dazed manner peculiar to people just aroused from deep sleep.

She looked at the clock; it was past three. Surely, she thought, it must have been Mr. Athol calling to her which had caused her to wake. She went into the hall, where the gas had not yet been turned off, and there she saw Miss Violet, fully dressed and wearing a hat and coat, in the very act of going out the front door.

In the cook's own words, before she could ask a question or even utter a sound, the young girl had opened the front door, which was still on the latch, and then banged it to again, she herself having disappeared in the darkness of the street beyond.

Mrs. Kennett ran to the door and out into the street as fast as her old legs would let her; but the night was an exceptionally foggy one. Violet, no doubt, had walked rapidly away, and there came no answer to Mrs. Kennett's repeated calls.

Thoroughly upset, and not knowing what to do, the good woman went back into the house. Mr. Athol had evidently left, for there was no sign of him in the dining-room or elsewhere. She then went upstairs and knocked at Mrs. Dunstan's door. To her astonishment the gas was still burning in her mistress's room, as she could see a thin ray of light filtering through the keyhole. At her first knock there came a quick, impatient answer:

"What is it?"

"Miss Violet, 'm," said the cook, who was too agitated to speak very coherently, "she is gone——"

"The best thing she could do," came promptly from the other side of the door. "You go to bed, Mrs. Kennett, and don't worry."

Whereupon the gas was suddenly turned off inside the room, and, in spite of Mrs. Kennett's further feeble protests, no other word issued from the room save another impatient:

"Go to bed."

The cook then did as she was bid; but before going to bed she made the round of the house, turned off all the gas, and finally bolted the front door.

3

Some three hours later the servants were called, as usual by Miss Cruikshank, who then went down to open the area door to Mrs. Thomas, the charwoman.

At half-past six when Mary the housemaid came down, candle in hand, she saw the charwoman a flight or two lower down, also apparently in the act of going downstairs. This astonished Mary not a little, as the woman's work lay entirely in the basement, and she was supposed never to come to the upper floors.

The woman, though walking rapidly down the stairs, seemed, moreover, to be carrying something heavy.

"Anything wrong, Mrs. Thomas?" asked Mary, in a whisper.

The woman looked up, pausing a moment immediately under the gas bracket, the by-pass of which shed a feeble light upon her and upon her burden. The latter Mary recognized as the bag containing the sand which, on frosty mornings, had to be strewn on the front steps of the house.

On the whole, though she certainly was puzzled, Mary did not think very much about the incident then. As was her custom, she went into the housemaid's closet, got the hot water for Miss Cruikshank's bath, and carried it to the latter's room, where she also pulled up the blinds and got things ready generally. For Miss Cruikshank usually ran down in her dressing-gown, and came up to tidy herself later on.

As a rule, by the time the three servants got downstairs, it was nearly seven, and Mrs. Thomas had generally gone by that time; but on this occasion Mary was earlier. Miss Cruikshank was busy in the kitchen getting Mrs. Dunstan's tea ready. Mary spoke about seeing Mrs. Thomas on the stairs with the bag of sand, and Miss Cruikshank, too, was very astonished at the occurrence.

Mrs. Kennett was not yet down, and the charwoman apparently had gone; her work had been done as usual, and the sand was strewn over the stone steps in front, as the frosty fog had rendered them very slippery.

At a quarter-past seven Miss Cruikshank went up with Mrs. Dunstan's tea, and less than two minutes later a fearful scream rang through the entire house, followed by the noise of breaking crockery.

In an instant the two maids ran upstairs, straight to Mrs. Dunstan's room, the door of which stood wide open.

The first thing Mary and Jane were conscious of was a terrific smell of gas, then of Miss Cruikshank, with eyes dilated with horror, staring at the bed in front of her, whereon lay Mrs. Dunstan, with one end of a piece of indiarubber piping still resting in her mouth, her jaw having dropped in death. The other end of that piece of piping was attached to the burner of a gas-bracket on the wall close by.

Every window in the room was fastened and the curtains drawn. The whole room reeked of gas.

Mrs. Dunstan had been asphyxiated by its fumes.

4

A year went by after the discovery of the mysterious tragedy, and I can assure you that our fellows at the Yard had one of the toughest jobs in connexion with the case that ever fell to their lot. Just think of all the contradictions which met them at every turn.

Firstly, the disappearance of Miss Violet.

No sooner had the women in the Dunstan household roused themselves sufficiently from their horror at the terrible discovery which they had just made, than they were confronted with another almost equally awful fact—awful, of course, because of its connexion with the primary tragedy.

Miss Violet Frostwicke had gone. Her room was empty, her bed had not been slept in. She herself had been seen by the cook, Mrs. Kennett, stealing out of the house at dead of night.

To connect the pretty, dainty young girl even remotely with a crime so hideous, so callous, as the deliberate murder of an old woman, who had been as a mother to her, seemed absolutely out of the question, and by tacit consent the four women, who now remained in the desolate and gloom-laden house at Eaton Terrace, forbore to mention Miss Violet Frostwicke's name either to police or doctor.

Both these, of course, had been summoned immediately; Miss Cruikshank sending Mary to the police-station and then to Dr. Folwell, in Eaton Square, whilst Jane went off in a cab to fetch Mr. Nicholas Jones, who, fortunately, had not yet left for his place of business.

The doctor's and the police-inspector's first thought, on examining the *mise en scène* of the terrible tragedy, was that Mrs. Dunstan had committed suicide. It was practically impossible to imagine that a woman in full possession of health and strength would allow a piece of indiarubber piping to be fixed between her teeth, and would, without a struggle, continue to inhale the poisonous fumes which would mean certain death. Yet there were no marks of injury upon the body, nothing to show how sufficient unconsciousness had been produced in the victim to permit of the miscreant completing his awesome deed.

But the theory of suicide set up by Dr. Folwell was promptly refuted by the most cursory examination of the room.

Though the drawers were found closed, they had obviously been turned over, as if the murderer had been in search of money or papers, or the key of the safe.

The latter, on investigation, was found to be open, whilst the key lay on the floor close by. A brief examination of the safe revealed the fact that the tin boxes must have been ransacked, for they contained neither money nor important papers now, whilst the gold and platinum settings of necklaces, bracelets, and a tiara showed that the stones—which, as Mr. Nicholas Jones subsequently averred, were of considerable value—had been carefully if somewhat clumsily taken out by obviously inexperienced hands.

On the whole, therefore, appearances suggested deliberate, systematic, and very leisurely robbery, which wholly contradicted the theory of suicide.

Then suddenly the name of Miss Frostwicke was mentioned. Who first brought it on the *tapis* no one subsequently could say; but in a moment the whole story of the young girl's engagement to Mr. Athol, in defiance of her aunt's wishes, the quarrel of the night before, and the final disappearance of both young people from the house during the small hours of the morning, was dragged from the four unwilling witnesses by the able police-inspector.

Nay, more. One very little unpleasant circumstance was detailed by one of the maids and corroborated by Miss Cruikshank.

It seems that when the latter took up the champagne to Mrs. Dunstan, the old lady desired Miss Violet to come to her room. Mary, the housemaid, was on the stairs when she saw the young girl, still dressed in her evening gown of white chiffon, her eyes still swollen with tears, knocking at her aunt's door.

The police-inspector was busy taking notes, already building up in his mind a simple, if very sensational, case against Violet Frostwicke, when Mrs. Kennett promptly upset all his calculations.

Miss Violet could have had nothing to do with the murder of her aunt, seeing that Mrs. Dunstan was alive and actually spoke to the cook when the latter knocked at her bedroom door after she had seen the young girl walk out of the house.

Then came the question of Mr. Athol. But, if you remember, it was quite impossible even to begin to build a case against the young man. His own statement that he left the house at about midnight, having totally forgotten to rouse the cook, when he did so, was amply corroborated from every side.

The cabman who took him up to the corner of Eaton Terrace at 11.50 p.m. was one witness in his favour; his landlady at his rooms in Jermyn Street, who let him in, since he had mislaid his latchkey, and who took him up some tea at seven o'clock the next morning, was another, whilst, when Mary saw Miss Violet going into her aunt's room, the clock at St. Peter's, Eaton Square, was just striking twelve.

I dare say you think I ought by now to have mentioned the charwoman, Mrs. Thomas, who represented the final, most complete, most hopeless contradiction in this remarkable case.

Mrs. Thomas was seen by Mary, the housemaid, at half-past six o'clock in the morning, coming down from the upper floor, where she had no business to be, and carrying the bag of sand used for strewing over the slippery front-door steps.

The bag of sand, of course, was always kept in the area.

The moment that bag of sand was mentioned Dr. Folwell gave a curious gasp. Here, at least, was the solution to one mystery. The victim had been stunned whilst still in bed by a blow on the head dealt with that bag of sand; and whilst she was unconscious the callous miscreant had robbed her and finally asphyxiated her with the gas fumes.

Where was the woman who, at half-past six in the morning, was seen in possession of the silent instrument of death?

Mrs. Thomas had disappeared. The last that was then or ever has been seen of her was when she passed underneath the dim light of a by-pass on the landing, as if tired out with the weight which she was carrying.

Since then, as you know, the police have been unswerving in their efforts to find Mrs. Thomas. The address which she had given in St. Peter's Mews was found to be false. No one of that name or appearance had ever been seen there.

The woman who was supposed to have sent her with a letter of recommendation to Mrs. Dunstan knew nothing of her. She swore that she had never sent anyone with a letter to Mrs. Dunstan. She gave up her work there one day because she found it too hard at such an early hour in the morning; but she never heard anything more from her late employer after that.

Strange, wasn't it, that two people should have disappeared out of that house on that same memorable night?

Of course, you will remember the tremendous sensation that was caused some twenty-four hours later, when it transpired that the young person who had thrown herself into the river from Waterloo Bridge on that same eventful morning, and whose body was subsequently recovered and conveyed to the Thames Police Station, was identified as Miss Violet Frostwicke, the niece of the lady who had been murdered in her own house in Eaton Terrace.

Neither money nor diamonds were found on poor Miss Violet. She had herself given the most complete proof that she, at least, had no hand in robbing or killing Mrs. Dunstan.

The public wondered why she took her aunt's wrath and her probable disinheritance so fearfully to heart, and sympathized with Mr. David Athol for the terribly sad loss which he had sustained.

But Mrs. Thomas, the charwoman, had not yet been found.

5

I think I looked an extremely respectable, good plain cook when I presented myself at the house in Eaton Terrace in response to the advertisement in the *Daily Telegraph*.

As, in addition to my prepossessing appearance, I also asked very low wages and declared myself ready to do anything except scour the front steps and the stone area, I was immediately engaged by Mrs. Jones, and was duly installed in the house the following day under the name of Mrs. Curwen.

But few events had occurred here since the discovery of the dual tragedy, now more than a year ago, and none that had thrown any light upon the mystery which surrounded it.

The verdict at the inquest had been one of wilful murder against a person known as Mrs. Thomas, the weight of evidence, coupled with her disappearance, having been very heavy against her; and there was a warrant out for her arrest.

Mrs. Dunstan had died intestate. To the astonishment of all those in the know, she had never signed the will which Messrs. Blenkinsop and Blenkinsop had drafted for her, and wherein she bequeathed £20,000 and the lease of her house in Eaton Terrace to her beloved niece, Violet Frostwicke, £1,000 to Miss Cruikshank, and other, smaller, legacies to friends or servants.

In default of a will, Mr. Nicholas Jones, only brother of the deceased, became possessed of all her wealth.

He was a very rich man himself, and many people thought that he ought to give Miss Cruikshank the £1,000 which the poor girl had thus lost through no fault of her own.

What his ultimate intentions were with regard to this no one could know. For the present he contented himself with moving to Eaton Terrace with his family; and, as his wife was a great invalid, he asked Miss Cruikshank to continue to make her home in the house and to help in its management.

Neither the diamonds nor the money stolen from Mrs. Dunstan's safe were ever traced. It seems that Mrs. Dunstan, a day or two before her death, had sold a freehold cottage which she owned near Teddington. The money, as is customary, had been handed over to her in gold, in Mr. Blenkinsop's office, and she had been foolish enough not to bank it immediately. This money and the diamonds had been the chief spoils of her assailant. And all the while no trace of Mrs. Thomas, in spite of the most strenuous efforts on the part of the police to find her.

Strangely enough, when I had been in Eaton Terrace about three days, and was already getting very tired of early rising and hard work, the charwoman there fell ill one day and did not come to her work as usual.

I, of course, grumbled like six, for I had to be on my hands and knees the next morning scrubbing stone steps, and my thoughts of Lady Molly, for the moment, were not quite as loyal as they usually were.

Suddenly I heard a shuffling footstep close behind me. I turned and saw a rough-looking, ill-dressed woman standing at the bottom of the steps.

"What do you want?" I asked sourly, for I was in a very bad humour.

"I saw you scrubbing them steps, miss," she replied in a raucous voice; "my 'usband is out of work, and the children hain't 'ad no breakfast this morning. I'd do them steps, miss, if you'd give me a trifle."

The woman certainly did not look very prepossessing, with her shabby, broad-brimmed hat hiding the upper part of her face, and her skirt, torn and muddy, pinned up untidily round her stooping figure.

However, I did not think that I could be doing anything very wrong by letting her do this one bit of rough work, which I hated, so I agreed to give her six-pence, and left her there with kneeling-mat and scrubbing-brush and went in, leaving, however, the front door open.

In the hall I met Miss Cruikshank, who, as usual, was down before everybody else.

"What is it, Curwen?" she asked, for through the open door she had caught sight of the woman kneeling on the step.

"A woman, miss," I replied, somewhat curtly. "She offered to do the steps. I thought Mrs. Jones wouldn't mind, as Mrs. Callaghan hasn't turned up."

Miss Cruikshank hesitated an instant, and then walked up to the front door.

At the same moment the woman looked up, rose from her knees, and boldly went up to accost Miss Cruikshank.

"You'll remember me, miss," she said, in her raucous voice. "I used to work for Mrs. Dunstan once. My name is Mrs. Thomas."

No wonder Miss Cruikshank uttered a quickly smothered cry of horror. Thinking that she would faint, I ran to her assistance; but she waved me aside and then said quite quietly:

"This poor woman's mind is deranged. She is no more Mrs. Thomas than I am. Perhaps we had better send for the police."

"Yes, miss; p'r'aps you'd better," said the woman with a sigh. "My secret has been weighin' heavy on me of late."

"But, my good woman," said Miss Cruikshank, very kindly, for I suppose she thought, as I did, that this was one of those singular cases of madness which sometimes cause innocent people to accuse themselves of undiscovered crimes. "You are not Mrs. Thomas at all. I knew Mrs. Thomas well—and——"

"Of course you knew me, miss," replied the woman. "The last conversation you and I had together was in the kitchen that morning, when Mrs. Dunstan was killed. I remember your saying to me——"

"Fetch the police, Curwen," said Miss Cruikshank peremptorily.

Whereupon the woman broke into a harsh and loud laugh of defiance.

To tell you the truth, I was not a little puzzled. That this scene had been foreseen by my dear lady, and that she had sent me to this house on purpose that I should witness it, I was absolutely convinced. But—here was my dilemma; ought I to warn the police at once or not?

On the whole, I decided that my best plan would undoubtedly be to communicate with Lady Molly first of all, and to await her instructions. So I ran upstairs, scribbled a hasty note to my dear lady, and, in response to Miss Cruikshank's orders, flew out of the house through the area gate, noticing as I did so, that Miss Cruikshank was still parleying with the woman on the doorstep.

I sent the note off to Maid Vale by taxicab; then I went back to Eaton Terrace. Miss Cruikshank met me at the front door, and told me that she had tried to detain the woman, pending my return; but that she felt very sorry for the unfortunate creature, who obviously was labouring under a delusion, and she had allowed her to go away.

About an hour later I received a curt note from Lady Molly ordering me to do nothing whatever without her special authorization.

In the course of the day, Miss Cruikshank told me that she had been to the police-station, and had consulted with the inspector, who said there would be no harm in engaging the pseudo Mrs. Thomas to work at Eaton Terrace, especially as thus she would remain under observation.

Then followed a curious era in Mr. Nicholas Jones's otherwise well-ordered household. We three servants, instead of being called at six as heretofore, were allowed to sleep on until seven. When we came down we were not scolded. On the contrary, we found our work already done.

The charwoman—whoever she was—must have been a very hard-working woman. It was marvellous what she accomplished single-handed before seven a.m., by which time she had invariably gone.

The two maids, of course, were content to let this pleasant state of things go on, but I was devoured with curiosity.

One morning I crept quietly downstairs and went into the kitchen soon after six. I found the pseudo Mrs. Thomas sitting at a very copious breakfast. I noticed that she had on altogether different—though equally shabby and dirty—clothes from those she had worn when she first appeared on the doorstep of 180, Eaton Terrace. Near her plate were three or four golden sovereigns over which she had thrown her grimy hand.

Miss Cruikshank the while was on her hands and knees scrubbing the floor. At sight of me she jumped up, and with obvious confusion muttered something about "hating to be idle," etc.

That day Miss Cruikshank told me that I did not suit Mrs. Jones, who wished me to leave at the end of my month. In the afternoon I received a little note from my dear lady, telling me to be downstairs by six o'clock the following morning.

I did as I was ordered, of course, and when I came into the kitchen punctually at six a.m. I found the charwoman sitting at the table with a pile of gold in front of her, which she was counting over with a very grubby finger. She had her back to me, and was saying as I entered:

"I think if you was to give me another fifty quid I'd leave you the rest now. You'd still have the diamonds and the rest of the money."

She spoke to Miss Cruikshank, who was facing me, and who, on seeing me appear, turned as white as a ghost. But she quickly recovered herself, and, standing between me and the woman, she said vehemently:

"What do you mean by prying on me like this? Go and pack your boxes and leave the house this instant."

But before I could reply the woman had interposed.

"Don't you fret yourself, miss," she said, placing her grimy hand on Miss Cruikshank's shoulder. "There's the bag of sand in that there corner; we'll knock her down as we did Mrs. Dunstan—eh?"

"Hold your tongue, you lying fool!" said the girl, who now looked like a maddened fury.

"Give me that other fifty quid and I'll hold my tongue," retorted the woman, boldly.

"This creature is mad," said Miss Cruikshank, who had made a vigorous and successful effort to recover herself. "She is under the delusion that not only is she Mrs. Thomas, but that she murdered Mrs. Dunstan—"

"No—no!" interrupted the woman. "I only came back that morning because I recollected that you had left the bag of sand upstairs after you so cleverly did away with Mrs. Dunstan, robbed her of all her money and jewels, and even were sharp enough to imitate her voice when Mrs. Kennett terrified you by speaking to Mrs. Dunstan through the door."

"It is false! You are not Mrs. Thomas. The two maids who are here now, and who were in this house at the time, can swear that you are a liar."

"Let us change clothes now, Miss Cruikshank," said a voice, which sounded almost weirdly in my ear in spite of its familiarity, for I could not locate whence it came, "and see if in a charwoman's dress those two maids would not recognize *you*."

"Mary," continued the same familiar voice, "help me out of these filthy clothes. Perhaps Miss Cruikshank would like to resume her own part of Mrs. Thomas, the charwoman."

"Liars and impostors—both!" shouted the girl, who was rapidly losing all presence of mind. "I'll send for the police."

"Quite unnecessary," rejoined Lady Molly coolly; "Detective-Inspector Danvers is outside the door."

The girl made a dash for the other door, but I was too quick for her, and held her back, even whilst Lady Molly gave a short, sharp call which brought Danvers on the scene.

I must say that Miss Cruikshank made a bold fight, but Danvers had two of our fellows with him, and arrested her on the warrant for the apprehension of the person known as Mrs. Thomas.

The clothes of the charwoman who had so mysteriously disappeared had been found by Lady Molly at the back of the coal-cellar, and she was still dressed in them at the present moment.

No wonder I had not recognized my own dainty lady in the grimy woman who had so successfully played the part of a blackmailer on the murderess of Mrs. Dunstan. She explained to me subsequently that the first inkling that she had had of the horrible truth—namely, that it was Miss Cruikshank who had deliberately planned to murder Mrs. Dunstan by impersonating a charwoman for a while, and thus throwing dust in the eyes of the police—was when she heard of the callous words which the old lady was supposed to have uttered when she was told of Miss Violet's flight from the house in the middle of the night.

"She may have been very angry at the girl's escapade," explained Lady Molly to me, "but she would not have allowed her to starve. Such cruelty was out of all proportion to the offence. Then I looked about me for a stronger motive for the old lady's wrath; and, remembering what she said on New Year's Eve, when Violet fled crying from the room, I came to the conclusion that her anger was not directed against her niece, but against the other girl, and against the man who had transferred his affections from Violet Frostwicke to Miss Cruikshank, and had not only irritated Mrs. Dunstan by this clandestine, double-faced love-making, but had broken the heart of his trusting *fiancée*.

"No doubt Miss Cruikshank did not know that the will, whereby she was to inherit £1,000, was not signed, and no doubt she and young Athol planned out that cruel murder between them. The charwoman was also a bag of sand which was literally thrown in the eyes of the police."

"But," I objected, "I can't understand how a cold-blooded creature like that Miss Cruikshank could have allowed herself to be terrorized and blackmailed. She knew that you could not be Mrs. Thomas, since Mrs. Thomas never existed."

"Yes; but one must reckon a little sometimes with that negligible quantity known as conscience. My appearance as Mrs. Thomas vaguely frightened Miss Cruikshank. She wondered who I was and what I knew. When, three days later, I found the shabby clothes in the coal-cellar and appeared dressed in them, she lost her head. She gave me money! From that moment she was done for. Confession was only a matter of time."

And Miss Cruikshank did make full confession. She was recommended to mercy on account of her sex, but she was plucky enough not to implicate David Athol in the recital of her crime.

He has since emigrated to Western Canada.

Gelett Burgess

(1866–1951)

FRANK GELETT BURGESS, though widely known early in this century as a humorist (*Goops and How to Be Them*, and other works), is remembered by mystery fans for two books. *The Picaroons* (1904), written with Will Irwin, begins with three down-at-the-heel adventurers telling their stories to "Coffin John," who gives each of them a "lucky dime" and challenges them to make their fortune. All three set out to experience "the Romances of Roguery" in what the authors call a "San Francisco Nights Entertainment." Among these Picaroons is Professor Vanga, a former medium who is clearly the progenitor of Astrogen Kerby, the fake medium and crystal gazer whose detective exploits are recounted in *The Master of Mysteries* (1912).

Victor Berch, the scholar of popular fiction, has discovered that the Astro, "The Seer of Secrets," stories were first published in 1905–1906 issues of *The Sunday Magazine* under the pseudonym "Alan Braghampton." The book collection, however, has no author's name, but the preface implies that the book contains three ciphers. Two are easy: the first letters of the first words of each story read "The author is Gelett Burgess"; and the last letters of the last words read "False to life and false to art." I don't believe that anyone has yet discovered the third cipher.

The Denton Boudoir Mystery

UNDERNEATH a shaded, swinging, bronze lamp in his favorite corner of the studio, the Master of Mysteries sat with half-closed eyes, seeming to drowse over a huge vellum-bound folio whose leaves bore lines of Arabic characters. But, though his dreamy eyes appeared heavy and dull, his index finger sped with such rapidity from line to line as to reveal that the palmist was eagerly absorbed in the message of those antique parchment pages. Behind him loomed the damasks and embroidered hangings with which the room was adorned; in a corner hung a gilded censer breathing its delicate aromatic perfume; an astrolabe occupied a small table at one hand, and near it lay a strange assortment of queer instruments picked up by the Seer in his vagabond travels,— the dread "spider" of the Inquisition, the *Angoise* "pear," a set of fearsome thumbscrews, strips of human hide, and other such horrors.

"So," he murmured contemplatively, "Ptolemy was a Torquemada himself, in a good many ways. That's interesting; and it confirms an old theory of mine. To think that many persons don't believe in metempsychosis—and do believe in the signs of the zodiac!" His thin lips parted in a smile.

He had turned to his book again, and had read for a few minutes, when his whole attitude changed. He sat upright; his eyes gleamed with interest. Voices were heard outside in the office, where his assistant was still working. He listened intently; then with a quick movement of his right hand touched a button, and the room was flooded with light. It was the first sight of a new client that often told Astro more than an hour's interview.

"Wait a moment till I announce you!" Valeska was exclaiming. "The

Master can not be interrupted in his work. It is impossible. I could not do it for the President himself!"

"I must see him immediately! I tell you I must see him!" a man's voice replied. "By heaven! I'll break in by main force!"

Another moment, and the black velvet portières leading to the waiting-room were violently flung aside, and a flushed and excited young man of about thirty years strode into the apartment. Behind him the face of Valeska Wynne appeared in the doorway, with an alarmed expression.

Astro sat, in turban and silken robe, reading, apparently unmoved by this interruption. When the young man stopped in the center of the room, the Seer slowly raised his olive-hued face to the visitor, and a smoldering glance shot from his dark eyes, in a mute question. The young man took a few steps nearer, and broke out again:

"See here! You've got to take this case!" he exclaimed appealingly. "I am at my wits' ends. I'll go mad if you don't help me; no one else can solve it. You're the only man in New York that can explain this mystery. For God's sake, sir, tell me you'll do it!" He dropped in exhaustion into an armchair, looking anxiously at the crystal-gazer. The fingers of one hand twitched nervously, while his other fist was clenched. His forehead was lined with vertical wrinkles.

Astro, still unperturbed, looked at him gravely, his quick eye darting from point to point of the young man's clothing. Finally he said languidly, with an almost imperceptible foreign accent, "My dear sir, the Turks have a proverb, 'He who is in a hurry is already half mad.' If you were in such haste to see me, you should have taken a cab to come here, instead of a street-car."

The young man pulled himself together, sat up, and stared hard at the Seer. Then his face relaxed, as he said, with a tone of great relief, nodding his head, "That's wonderful! It's exactly what I did. Oh, I know you can do it, if you only will! The police are all stupid,—there isn't a man with a brain on the whole force, I believe. You're the man to help me!"

Astro made a graceful gesture with his long slender hand. "It is not a question of brains, my dear sir. It is a question of the right comprehension of the forces of the occult, of undeveloped senses and powers. Men need sign-boards to show them the way from town to town. The birds wing their straight paths by instinct. It is my fortune to be sensitive to vibrations that most minds do not register. Where you see a body, I see a spirit, a life, an invisible color. All these esoteric laws have been known by the priestcraft of the occult for ages. Nothing is hidden from the Inner Eye."

"I don't know how you get it," the young man interrupted. "I believe that there are many things we don't understand yet, and that some men are developed beyond their fellows. I've studied mysticism myself, and that's why I came directly to you. I want the mystery of my sweetheart's death cleared up, and the hellish scoundrel that killed her executed. Until that is accomplished, my life will stop, or I'll go insane. The police can prove nothing, even on their own suspect. What motive there could have been for such a crime I can't imagine; it seems so unnecessary, so monstrous!" He had worked himself again into a fever of excitement.

Astro rose and walked over to his visitor. Placing his thumbs on two muscles in the young man's neck, near the spinal column, he manipulated the flesh for a few moments. His client's hysteria gradually subsided, and he became calmer.

"Now," said Astro, sinking back into his chair and taking up the amber mouthpiece of his water-pipe, "give me the details of your story from the beginning. You need not mind my assistant; she is quite in my confidence and may be trusted implicitly."

Valeska had entered, and sat at a table prepared to take notes of the conversation. Astro's eyes turned indulgently on the pretty blond head as it bent seriously over the writing pad.

The young man spoke now as if he had the history already clearly mapped out in his mind. He used occasional impulsive gestures, displaying an ardent and intense temperament.

"My name is Edward Masson. For three months I have been engaged to marry Miss Elizabeth Denton, of Hamphurst, Long Island. That is, I was, until three days ago, when we had a quarrel,—nothing to speak of, really, you know, but the match was temporarily broken off. It would have come out all right, I'm sure. I intended to make it up with her. I was prepared to make any compromise whatever; for I was crazy about her. She was my whole life." He paused and put his hands across his eyes.

Valeska looked across to the Master, her own eyes already swimming with tears of sympathy. Astro, however, showed no sign, and puffed tranquilly at his hookah, waiting for Masson to become more calm. In the anteroom a great clock broke the silence with a ringing melodious chime and struck the hour of six in booming notes.

Masson looked up with a tense face. "That next day she was murdered!" he said brokenly. "She was found dead in her boudoir on the second floor of her house, just before dinner-time, at about dusk. Both doors were locked; but the double windows were open. The police say she was strangled. Think of it! God! she was beautiful! How could any one have done it? It seems impossible, even now, that she is dead. There were slight marks on her throat that looked like fingerprints. I didn't see them,—there was lace around her neck when I saw her, in her casket. Oh, God!" He rose and paced up and down the room restlessly, his eyes cast down.

"What have the police done?" Astro inquired gently.

"They've arrested Miss Denton's maid. She had a key to Elizabeth's room, it seems, and some of the servants thought they heard her talking in the room. I think that's the strongest point against her. But I doubt if she did it. It was too brutal. I must run down the real murderer and have it proved beyond the possibility of a doubt. I can't rest till that's done."

He turned almost savagely to the quiet figure of the palmist. "Can't you do it? You can see things in crystals; you know the secret laws of nature; you lead a life of study and research with the old adepts. Can't you do this for me?"

Astro smiled subtly. "My dear Mr. Masson," he said, "I do not ordinarily concern myself with such affairs. Those who wish come to me, and I, of my knowledge of the Laws of Being, can reveal what is hidden. Such agonizing experiences as yours are distracting to the student of the Higher Way."

"I'm rich!" Masson broke in. "I'll pay you anything you wish! Make your price—one thousand, two, anything! Only help me! My God, man! you were a part of the world once. Can't you remember what it means to love a beautiful woman and want to marry her?"

"I remember—only too well. It was partly on that account that I hesitated. But I'll forget myself and consent to assist you."

The young man sank into a chair again, with gratitude in his poise. "You'll want to go down to Hamphurst?" he asked.

"Certainly. I must get the vibrations of the scene itself before I seek the murderer. He has left behind him emanations that will rapidly evaporate. I shall go down to-morrow if you will accompany me. To-night I shall go to the Tombs and see Miss Denton's maid. She, too, must be studied by one who is sensitive to aura. My friend McGraw will be able to get permission for that, no doubt."

He shot a glance at Valeska as he mentioned the inspector's name. She replied with a fluttering smile and was serious again.

Young Masson buttoned up his overcoat, and with an embarrassed, hesitating manner, did his best to express his thanks. Astro cut short his stammering sentences, laid his own hand with a friendly gesture on Masson's shoulder, and guided him out of the room. At parting it was agreed that they should meet on the nine-twelve train for Hamphurst.

The palmist walked back to the studio, shut off all lights but the one in his favorite corner, and sat down in silence. Valeska waited for him to speak.

"Not bad for two days' work," he said finally, smiling.

"Are you sure you can do it?" she asked, raising her golden brows.

"My dear," he replied, taking up his water-pipe again, "am I not a

Mahatma of the Fourth Sphere, and were not the divine laws of cosmic life revealed to me while I was a chela on the heights of the Himalayas?"

Valeska broke into a silvery laugh. "Do you know," she said, "that patter of yours is almost as becoming as that turban and robe. But, to be serious, have you any clue as yet?"

Astro did not answer for a moment; then he said meaningly, "The principle by which muscle reading can be accomplished is this: The person that is held moves in a minute circle until he finds the point of least resistance to his motion. He moves, then, in this line as long as his holders unconsciously guide him in that direction. The same principle is true of any problem of this sort. Let us wait, until we are guided by something that seems characteristic of this special crime. The street-car business was simple enough to you, I suppose?"

Valeska pouted. "Oh, I'm not altogether a fool. Why, he had a Broadway transfer in his hand when he came in here. He was in too much of a hurry to take a cross-town car for the four blocks."

The Seer chuckled. "But now we'd better go to work. I'll see the maid first. There's no need of your going. You'd better get back to your work on the zodiac. Look up Napoleon's notes on the subject. His was the biggest intellect the stars ever fooled. It will teach you how to fool lesser ones. But get a good night's rest. There'll be something more to search for at Hamphurst to-morrow. I'll look over the papers and see what is known about this murder. Masson was too excited to tell half."

After reading for a half-hour, Astro yawned, shook himself, and changed from the cynical psychologist to a man of keen brisk manner and alert glance. His green limousine, which was always kept waiting at the door of the studio, took him rapidly down-town. A half-hour later he was looking through the cell door at Marie Dubois, the French maid of the late Miss Denton.

She was eager to talk and volubly protested her innocence. Astro let her run on without questions, until she had finally told all she knew of the affair, which was little enough, apparently. She had started up to Miss Denton's room at about half past six to get a cashmere shawl which was to be sent to the cleaner's. Half-way up the side stairs she had stopped, hearing voices inside the boudoir. She did not, however, recognize Miss Denton's voice; instead, there was a higher-pitched voice, exclaiming "Great God!" several times. This was followed by laughter; then came a shrill whistle. She heard something like the fall of a body, then footsteps. All this so alarmed her that she ran up and tried the boudoir door. Finding that locked, she called down to the butler, went and got her own key, and asked him to investigate. The voice she had heard seemed like an old woman's. The butler had heard it, and also the chauffeur, who was in the stable across the yard.

"And how about the letters from Mr. Masson to Miss Denton, which were found in your room?" Astro inquired.

"Oh, Mees Denton, she give me zem zat I send to her fiancé!" the girl protested. "Zat same afternoon she make ze *paquet. Mon Dieu!* ze police say I steal ze letters! It ees not so! Nevaire have I seen a man so good like Monsieur Masson to me. He ees gentleman. Why I steal his letters?" She began to weep.

"Let me see your hand, Marie."

The girl gave him a slender trembling palm. Astro looked at it for a few moments; then he said, "Marie, did Mr. Masson ever make love to you?"

A sudden wave of color flooded the girl's face; but she cried out excitedly, "Nevaire! *Mon Dieu! non, par exemple!* Why should he do zat? Had he not ze beautiful Mees Denton? *Oh, non, Monsieur!*"

Astro smiled cryptically and walked out. The rest of the evening he spent translating certain obscure Hebrew texts from the *Midrash* and comparing them with the published English versions.

On the train down to Hamphurst, next day, Masson was morose and talked but little. He was nervous and impatient to get to the house, watching sullenly out of the window all the way. Valeska did her best to be agreeable; but Astro came out of his reverie only once, to ask;

"Why was the date of your marriage postponed, Mr. Masson?"

Masson scowled, then sighed and shook his head.

"Miss Denton, a month or so ago, was not at all well. The doctors found her heart to be weak. They thought that the excitement of a wedding and its preparation would be too much for her, and feared a collapse."

Astro resumed his abstracted pose. Valeska bent her brows. Masson gazed mournfully out of the window.

Alighting at Hamphurst, they took a carriage and were driven to the Denton house, an old-fashioned, two-and-a-half-story, frame building, painted yellow with white trimmings. It was surrounded with beautiful wine-glass elms which were scattered over the grounds. A wide lawn stretched in front and on one side, with a gravel driveway to the residence and a stable in the rear. The place had an air of quiet peaceful respectability. It seemed to the last degree improbable as the scene of such a tragedy as had been so recently enacted.

The officers had finished their investigations, and the funeral had taken place the day before. An aged aunt of Miss Denton's and the four servants now occupied the house. Astro and his assistant were introduced to the old lady, then went immediately up to the boudoir where the body had been found. Here, at Astro's request, the exact situation discovered at that time was explained by James, the man-of-all-work, whom Marie had referred to as the butler.

He pointed out the position in which he had found the corpse. It lay face downward; the hair was somewhat disarranged. The square, cheerful, blue-and-white boudoir was now filled with sunlight streaming in from the high French windows which led to a small balcony outside. Many of Miss Denton's belongings still lay about,—a fold of ribbon, a lace collar, a handkerchief on the bureau; and on a small table, a book face down where she had left it, made it seem as if the owner had only just left the room on some trifling errand.

The old lady silently handed Astro a photograph of her niece,—a beautiful woman of twenty-three, with the frank and winning expression of a young girl. Astro handed it to Valeska, who looked at it in admiration and regret. The aunt explained further that her niece Elizabeth was in a low-necked, white mull dress. She had come down for dinner; but, finding that she had forgotten her handkerchief, had gone back up-stairs to get it. She had not hurried, as dinner had not yet been served. Her aunt did not think it strange that Elizabeth did not return for ten or fifteen minutes. Then she had heard Marie scream to James, and she herself had followed him up, and had been there when he opened the door.

The old lady was too overcome to go further; but James corroborated Masson's previous story. Both doors had been locked and the keys withdrawn. The windows were open. No footprints or traces of any kind had been found outside by the police. James himself had been in the lower front hall at the time, rolling up some rugs, and had heard the sound of voices up-stairs, and had wondered at them. One voice, he thought, sounded much like Marie's. It was about three minutes, he thought, between the time when he heard the voice and the laughter—for he had heard that also—to the moment when Marie called for him to come up. She had appeared much excited.

He was a simple-faced fellow, with an awkward air and a generally shiftless appearance,—the ordinary country youth who has had too little energy to better himself in any way. Astro scarcely gave him a glance, but stood gazing at the door in front of him.

He made a sign finally, and all but Valeska left the room. She shut the door behind them. Then she followed his eyes about the walls and floor.

"I think," said Astro, thoughtfully regarding the window-frame, "that Masson regrets exceedingly having tried to kiss Marie about four days ago. Poor chap!"

Valeska's eyes narrowed. "Oh!" she said. "That was what broke off the engagement?"

"I'm afraid so."

"But was Marie in love with him, too?" she asked eagerly.

Astro's expression was more animated as he replied, "I love, thou lovest, he loves; we love, you love, they love. I think, my dear, that in matters of the heart you know the symptoms better than I, although you were *not* taught the philosophy of the Yogis by a Hindu fakir. What do you say, pretty priestess?"

"Masson was sincerely in love with Miss Denton. He never cared a snap for Marie."

"I believe you. And yet he kissed her—or tried to. There was no mistaking that blush. It is a common error to suppose that French girls are a whit less modest than their English or American sisters. In point of fact, they are often more so,—more ignorant, more innocent. Marie was carefully brought up; she is still a child. But the Latin races have temperament; they soon learn. Marie is a passionate little thing, quick at loving as at hating, full of revenges and regrets."

"But what has that kiss to do with this murder?"

"That's precisely what I'm here to find out. Permit me to resume my meditation, that my astral vision may be released."

Valeska smiled, and kept silent. It was Astro's way of requesting that he was not to be questioned further until he himself had run down his clue.

It was a quarter of an hour before he spoke; then to say in triumph. "Ho! I have found it! I have at least solved half the mystery." He pointed to three parallel scratches on the frieze, above the picture-molding.

Valeska shook her head, puzzled.

He shrugged his shoulders and went to the window, pointing to a tiny spot on the white frame.

"It's blood!" exclaimed Valeska.

"It's blood; and yet Miss Denton was strangled, and no blood was shed,—none, at least, of hers."

"Whose blood, then, was it?"

"Kindly get out of the window on the balcony, my dear."

She stepped over the low sill, unconsciously placing her left hand on the frame to steady herself. Her fingers touched the paint about two inches below the bloody smutch.

"Well, my dear, it certainly isn't your blood, at least," said Astro.

"Marie's, then? She is taller than I."

"She had no wound on her hand. I examined them both carefully."

"And there was none on James'."

"Nor the aunt's. If you have looked all you wish to, you might go down to the kitchen and talk to the cook. It was said in the paper that she had a bad temper, and had lately quarreled with Miss Denton. To be sure, all good cooks have bad tempers; but, as the police didn't see fit to arrest her, she may possibly be the murderer. See what you can do. I shall remain here for a while. There's much to be done, and I'm in a hurry to earn my thousand dollars."

When Valeska had left, Astro resumed his study of the room, going over it inch by inch, looking again at the window, finally turning to the balcony. The care with which he worked showed that the Master of Mysteries was unusually perplexed. After examining the floor and rail of the balcony, he drew a bird glass from his pocket and spent a half-hour gazing at the elm whose branches stretched toward the window. Off the balcony was another window, from the room next to the boudoir. This, too, he examined carefully. Then he smiled slightly, put up the glass, and reentered the room. It was evident that he had found what he had sought.

Descending to the lower hall, he gave a quick look at doors and windows, then went out into the yard in the rear to the base of the tree he had spent so much time in investigating. He looked now up, and then down. He gazed up at the two windows of the balcony. His eyes were on the great door of the stable when Valeska appeared, her eyes shining.

"The cook has a cut on her left forefinger!" she announced breathlessly. "The second girl says that, just before they discovered the crime, the cook was away from the kitchen for about fifteen minutes. The cook herself says that she had gone out back of the stable to get a few strawberries for her own supper."

"Did she come back with the berries?"

"Yes; but she might have picked them before."

"What shape was the cut on her finger?"

"Why, it was a straight cut, of course. She said she did it slicing ham. But you know she might have gone up-stairs and into the guest-room, which has a window on the same balcony, and—"

"What about the second girl?" Astro interrupted.

Valeska laughed. "She's a country girl, awfully, awfully in love with James. She's frightened to death for fear that he'll be suspected of the murder."

"Did she hear the voices and the laughter?"

"No. Anyway, she was with the aunt most of the time, in the dining-room. It was the cook who did it, I'm sure."

"And how about the whistle? And why should the cook laugh at such a time?"

Valeska's face fell. "Well," she said finally, "for that matter why should any murderer laugh? The whistle might have been a signal to some one outside."

"Except that, in this case, it wasn't. My dear, the laughter and the whistle are the easiest parts of the mystery. What I want to know is, where is the key to the door? It was in the lock when Miss Denton went up-stairs the second time."

"Where, indeed, is it? That would show a good deal."

"If you'll come with me, I'll show it to you. But first I think we had better get Mr. Masson. I may need a little help in a few moments. Will you kindly call him? I'll be in the stable."

As Valeska left, the palmist strolled slowly over to the stable and looked in the great door. In the center of the floor stood a large brown touring-car. A young man in overalls was polishing the brass work.

Astro nodded. "A very fine-looking machine," he offered. "A Lachmore, isn't it?"

The chauffeur grunted and kept on with his work.

"I am a friend of Mr. Masson's," Astro went on, "and I should like to look over this car. I am thinking of letting one myself some day."

Still the young man did not answer except by inarticulate grunts.

Astro drew nearer. "What's the matter with your finger?" he asked abruptly.

The young man looked up, now angrily, as if about to make a discourteous retort. Seeing Masson approaching, however, he replied, "Oh, it got jammed in the machine a day or two ago. What's that to you?"

"I'd like to see it. I can cure it. I am a healer."

Astro extended his hand suavely.

The young man scowled darkly. "Oh, it's not much. No need of bothering you."

By this time Masson had entered with Valeska.

"Mr. Masson," said the Seer, "this young man interests me very much. I have been conscious ever since I arrived at Hamphurst of certain very harsh and painful vibrations. In the boudoir, these grew more intense. I felt something in that room that was neither an odor nor a color, but partook of the nature of both. Now, singularly enough, I find the same influence here, only more active and vibrant. This young man has a peculiar aura. I wonder that you can not perceive it even with one of your five material senses."

The young man stared, more and more uncomfortable at the talk. Finally he dropped his rag, walked round to the back of the car, and took up a heavy wrench.

Astro raised his voice slightly. "Mr. Masson," he said, "I can see this fellow's astral body as well as his material frame. Now, I notice on the forefinger of his left hand, in its astral condition, a small V-shaped cut. I am very anxious to know whether such a corresponding wound is to be found on his fleshly hand. Do you think you could induce him to remove that bandage?"

Masson, mystified, but evidently comprehending that something important was at stake, raised his voice. "Walters," he said, "kindly oblige me by removing that rag from your left hand."

Walters looked up surlily. "I can't, Mr. Masson. It would make it bleed again. It bled like anything when I jammed it in the machine."

"My friend," said Astro genially, "jammed wounds do not bleed to any extent. It is a V-shaped scar then?"

"What of it?" The chauffeur stood poised in a sinister attitude.

"That's what I want to know, too," cried Masson. "By heaven! do you mean that this fellow here had anything—"

Astro raised his hand. "One moment," he interrupted. "First, I want to ask you, Walters, to show me where the gasoline tank is in this car?"

A look of terror swept over the young man's face. He raised the wrench in his hand and rushed at the palmist. Astro avoided him lithely and grappled with him. The man struck out, tore himself free, and dashed for the door. He would have made his escape had not Masson jumped for him. There was another scuffle. Masson, now convinced that he had his sweetheart's murderer before him, fought like a maniac. Astro, who had been thrown to the ground by the force of the blow he had received, now rose, and the next moment drew out a revolver and covered his prisoner.

"Let go, or I shoot you like a dog!" he barked out between his teeth. "Let him go, Masson! This is not for you. The law will attend to him. The man's evil enough; but not so bad as you think. He's no murderer, really."

At these words Walters turned to Astro with a gleam of hope in his eye. "Oh, I'm not, sir! Before God, I had no intention of murdering her! I didn't know I had till afterward. I only tried to keep her from screaming, and she dropped like a log. It was that accursed parrot! Miss Denton was frightened to death, sir, and so was I, pretty near."

Astro spoke sharply. "Valeska, get that halter, and I'll fasten him so he'll be safe till the police can get here."

"A parrot," ejaculated Valeska, as she brought the halter. "Ah, I see! That accounts for the strange, high-pitched voice, the laughter, and the whistling!"

"Get up now, and tell your story!" commanded Astro. "And remember that you speak in the presence of one to whom everything is revealed. At the slightest departure from the truth I shall feel instantly the shifting of your spectrum, and a change in the amplitude of your vibrations. In my crystals I saw the scene; but it was dusk, and the glass was cloudy. Tell me exactly what happened, and if it coincides with my vision you shall have my help in your trial."

"I'll tell the truth, so help me God!' cried Walters. "Listen! It was this way. It was only her money I was after. I had planned it for a week back, knowing just when she left the room empty. I got up the side stairs, and out on the balcony, and into the tree where I could watch her. As soon as she finished dressing and put out the light and went down-stairs, I slid on to the balcony and slipped into the room. Well, I had got her purse and emptied it, when all of a sudden the door opened, and in she came; for I hadn't thought to lock it. She gave a little scream at seeing me there in the dusk, and I grabbed her to keep her from making more noise. Just then Hades seemed to break loose all around me. There was a voice yelling, 'Great God! Great God!' and then something feathery came scratching and flapping into my face. I put out one hand to ward it off, and got a bite that made me drop my hold of the lady. Then as she fell to the floor, there was a laugh that made my blood run cold. It laughed and laughed fit to kill. I couldn't stand it! I didn't care whether I was caught or not then; I locked the door, climbed out on the tree and got down to the ground. I didn't dare to run away, for fear I'd be suspected! but after I heard how it came out it was all I could stand to stay here. I didn't know what to do about Marie; but I hoped she'd get off some way, for I knew they never could prove it on her. And that's the truth, so help me God! Where the parrot came from I have no idea."

"It belongs in the next neighbor's house, and has been missing for a week," said Masson. "Now I'll go and telephone to the police."

He stopped a moment and looked wistfully at the Seer. "Ah, I knew you could do it," he said. "I wish you could tell me now how ever to be happy again."

"There is no such thing as happiness, my friend," said Astro seriously. "There is no joy but calm, the Eastern books say."

Masson bowed his head. Then, as he left, he remarked, 'I shall send you a check in the morning. You will see if I am not grateful."

"What I don't see is, how you knew the key was in the gasoline tank of the auto?" Valeska asked him, on the way to town.

"I am not yet sure that it was, but can you think of any safer place for a chauffeur to hide it?" Astro replied with a smile.

Melville Davisson Post

(1871–1930)

OF EARLY DETECTIVE STORY WRITERS, West Virginian Melville Davisson Post created the greatest number of series characters. Randolph Mason, who first appeared in *The Strange Cases of Randolph Mason* (1896), is a lawyer who uses the law to defeat justice, but who reforms in *The Corrector of Destinies* (1908) and works for the innocent. Post's other creations include Sir Henry Marquis of Scotland Yard, Marquis' ancestor Pendleton, whose detection is found in old diaries, Monsieur Jonquelle of the Paris Police, Walker "of the Secret Service" who begins as a crook but becomes a detective, the Virginia lawyer Colonel Braxton, and greatest of them all, Uncle Abner, who lives in western Virginia before the Civil War. Unlike Randolph Mason, who sees law as a tool to be manipulated, Uncle Abner seeks justice—God's justice. "Naboth's Vineyard" first appeared in *Illustrated Sunday Magazine*, June 4, 1916, and it was collected two years later in *Uncle Abner, Master of Mysteries.*

Naboth's Vineyard

ONE HEARS A GOOD DEAL about the sovereignty of the people in this republic; and many persons imagine it as a sort of fiction, and wonder where it lies, who are the guardians of it, and how they would exercise it if the forms and agents of the law were removed. I am not one of those who speculate upon this mystery, for I have seen this primal ultimate authority naked at its work. And, having seen it, I know how mighty and how dread a thing it is. And I know where it lies, and who are the guardians of it, and how they exercise it when the need arises.

There was a great crowd, for the whole country was in the court-room. It was a notorious trial.

Elihu Marsh had been shot down in his house. He had been found lying in a room, with a hole through his body that one could put his thumb in. He was an irascible old man, the last of his family, and so, lived alone. He had rich lands, but only a life estate in them, the remainder was to some foreign heirs. A girl from a neighboring farm came now and then to bake and put his house in order, and he kept a farm hand about the premises.

Nothing had been disturbed in the house when the neighbors found Marsh; no robbery had been attempted, for the man's money, a considerable sum, remained on him.

There was not much mystery about the thing, because the farm hand had disappeared. This man was a stranger in the hills. He had come from over the mountains some months before, and gone to work for Marsh. He was a big blond man, young and good looking; of better blood, one would say, than the average laborer. He gave his name as Taylor, but he was not communicative, and little else about him was known.

The country was raised, and this man was overtaken in the foothills of the mountains. He had his clothes tied into a bundle, and a long-barreled fowling-piece on his shoulder. The story he told was that he and Marsh had settled that morning, and he had left the house at noon, but that he had forgotten his gun and had gone back for it; he had reached the house about four o'clock, gone into the kitchen, got his gun down from the dogwood forks over the chimney, and at once left the house. He had not seen Marsh, and did not know where he was.

He admitted that his gun had been loaded with a single huge lead bullet. He had so loaded it to kill a dog that sometimes approached the house, but not close enough to be reached with a load of shot. He affected surprise when it was pointed out that the gun had been discharged. He said that he had not fired it, and had not, until then, noticed that it was empty. When asked why he had so suddenly determined to leave the country, he was silent.

He was carried back and confined in the county jail, and now, he was on trial at the September term of the circuit court.

The court sat early. Although the judge, Simon Kilrail, was a landowner and lived on his estate in the country some half dozen miles away, he rode to the courthouse in the morning, and home at night, with his legal papers in his saddle-pockets. It was only when the court sat that he was a lawyer. At other times he harvested his hay and grazed his cattle, and tried to add to his lands like any other man in the hills, and he was as hard in a trade and as hungry for an acre as any.

It was the sign and insignia of distinction in Virginia to own land. Mr. Jefferson had annulled the titles that George the Third had granted, and the land alone remained as a patent of nobility. The Judge wished to be one of these landed gentry, and he had gone a good way to accomplish it. But when the court convened he became a lawyer and sat upon the bench with no heart in him, and a cruel tongue like the English judges.

I think everybody was at this trial. My Uncle Abner and the strange old doctor, Storm, sat on a bench near the center aisle of the courtroom, and I sat behind them, for I was a half-grown lad, and permitted to witness the terrors and severities of the law.

The prisoner was the center of interest. He sat with a stolid countenance like a man careless of the issues of life. But not everybody was concerned with him, for my Uncle Abner and Storm watched the girl who had been accustomed to bake for Marsh and red up his house.

She was a beauty of her type; dark haired and dark eyed like a gypsy, and with an April nature of storm and sun. She sat among the witnesses with a little handkerchief clutched in her hands. She was nervous to the point of hysteria, and I thought that was the reason the old doctor watched her. She would be taken with a gust of tears, and then throw up her head with a fine defiance; and she kneaded and knotted and worked the handkerchief in her fingers. It was a time of stress and many witnesses were unnerved, and I think I should not have noticed this girl but for the whispering of Storm and my Uncle Abner.

The trial went forward, and it became certain that the prisoner would hang. His stubborn refusal to give any reason for his hurried departure had but one meaning, and the circumstantial evidence was conclusive. The motive, only, remained in doubt, and the Judge had charged on this with so many cases in point, and with so heavy a hand, that any virtue in it was removed. The Judge was hard against this man, and indeed there was little sympathy anywhere, for it was a foul killing—the victim an old man and no hot blood to excuse it.

In all trials of great public interest, where the evidences of guilt over-whelmingly assemble against a prisoner, there comes a moment when all the people in the courtroom, as one man, and without a sign of the common purpose, agree upon a verdict; there is no outward or vis-ible evidence of this decision, but one feels it, and it is a moment of the tensest stress.

The trial of Taylor had reached this point, and there lay a moment of deep silence, when this girl sitting among the witnesses suddenly burst into a very hysteria of tears. She stood up shaking with sobs, her voice choking in her throat, and the tears gushing through her fingers.

What she said was not heard at the time by the audience in the court-room, but it brought the Judge to his feet and the jury crowding about her, and it broke down the silence of the prisoner, and threw him into a perfect fury of denials. We could hear his voice rise above the confu-sion, and we could see him struggling to get to the girl and stop her. But what she said was presently known to everybody, for it was taken down and signed; and it put the case against Taylor, to use a lawyer's term, out of court.

The girl had killed Marsh herself. And this was the manner and the reason of it: She and Taylor were sweethearts and were to be married. But they had quarreled the night before Marsh's death and the follow-ing morning Taylor had left the country. The point of the quarrel was some remark that Marsh had made to Taylor touching the girl's repu-tation. She had come to the house in the afternoon, and finding her lover gone, and maddened at the sight of the one who had robbed her of him, had taken the gun down from the chimney and killed Marsh. She had then put the gun back into its place and left the house. This was about two o'clock in the afternoon, and about an hour before Taylor returned for his gun.

There was a great veer of public feeling with a profound sense of having come at last upon the truth, for the story not only fitted to the circumstantial evidence against Taylor, but it fitted also to his story and it disclosed the motive for the killing. It explained, too, why he had refused to give the reason for his disappearance. That Taylor denied what the girl said and tried to stop her in her declaration, meant nothing except that the prisoner was a man, and would not have the woman he loved make such a sacrifice for him.

I cannot give all the forms of legal procedure with which the closing hours of the court were taken up, but nothing happened to shake the girl's confession. Whatever the law required was speedily got ready, and she was remanded to the care of the sheriff in order that she might come before the court in the morning.

Taylor was not released, but was also held in custody, although the case against him seemed utterly broken down. The Judge refused to permit the prisoner's counsel to take a verdict. He said that he would withdraw a juror and continue the case. But he seemed unwilling to release any clutch of the law until some one was punished for this crime.

It was on our way, and we rode out with the Judge that night. He talked with Abner and Storm about the pastures and the price of cattle, but not about the trial, as I hoped he would do, except only once, and then it was to inquire why the prosecuting attorney had not called either of them as witnesses, since they were the first to find Marsh, and Storm had been among the doctors who examined him. And Storm had explained how he had mortally offended the prosecutor in his canvass, by his remark that only a gentleman should hold office. He did but quote Mr. Hamilton, Storm said, but the man had received it as a deadly insult, and thereby proved the truth of Mr. Hamilton's expression, Storm added. And Abner said that as no circumstance about Marsh's death was questioned, and others arriving about the same time had been called, the prosecutor doubtless considered further testimony unnecessary.

The Judge nodded, and the conversation turned to other questions. At the gate, after the common formal courtesy of the country, the Judge asked us to ride in, and, to my astonishment, Abner and Storm accepted his invitation. I could see that the man was surprised, and I thought annoyed, but he took us into his library.

I could not understand why Abner and Storm had stopped here, until I remembered how from the first they had been considering the girl, and it occurred to me that they thus sought the Judge in the hope of getting some word to him in her favor. A great sentiment had leaped up for this girl. She had made a staggering sacrifice, and with a headlong courage, and it was like these men to help her if they could.

And it was to speak of the woman that they came, but not in her favor. And while Simon Kilrail listened, they told this extraordinary story: They had been of the opinion that Taylor was not guilty when the trial began, but they had suffered it to proceed in order to see what might develop. The reason was that there were certain circumstantial evidences, overlooked by the prosecutor, indicating the guilt of the woman and the innocence of Taylor. When Storm examined the body of Marsh he discovered that the man had been killed by poison, and was dead when the bullet was fired into his body. This meant that the shooting was a fabricated evidence to direct suspicion against Taylor. The woman had baked for Marsh on this morning, and the poison was in the bread which he had eaten at noon.

Abner was going on to explain something further, when a servant entered and asked the Judge what time it was. The man had been greatly impressed, and he now sat in a profound reflection. He took his watch out of his pocket and held it in his hand, then he seemed to realize the question and replied that his watch had run down. Abner gave the hour, and said that perhaps his key would wind the watch. The Judge gave it to him, and he wound it and laid it on the table. Storm observed my uncle with, what I thought, a curious interest, but the Judge paid no attention. He was deep in his reflection and oblivious to everything. Finally he roused himself and made his comment.

"This clears the matter up," he said. "The woman killed Marsh from the motive which she gave in her confession, and she created this false evidence against Taylor because he had abandoned her. She thereby avenged herself desperately in two directions. . . . It would be like a woman to do this, and then regret it and confess."

He then asked my uncle if he had anything further to tell him, and although I was sure that Abner was going on to say something further when the servant entered, he replied now that he had not, and asked for the horses. The Judge went out to have the horses brought, and we remained in silence. My uncle was calm, as with some consuming idea, but Storm was as nervous as a cat. He was out of his chair when the door was closed, and hopping about the room looking at the law books standing on the shelves in their leather covers. Suddenly he stopped and plucked out a little volume. He whipped through it with his forefinger, smothered a great oath, and shot it into his pocket, then he crooked his finger to my uncle, and they talked together in a recess of the window until the Judge returned.

We rode away. I was sure that they intended to say something to the Judge in the woman's favor, for, guilty or not, it was a fine thing she had done to stand up and confess. But something in the interview had changed their purpose. Perhaps when they had heard the Judge's comment they saw it would be of no use. They talked closely together as they rode, but they kept before me and I could not hear. It was of the woman they spoke, however, for I caught a fragment.

"But where is the motive?" said Storm.

And my uncle answered, "In the twenty-first chapter of the Book of Kings."

We were early at the county seat, and it was a good thing for us, because the courtroom was crowded to the doors. My uncle had got a big record book out of the county clerk's office as he came in, and I was glad of it, for he gave it to me to sit on, and it raised me up so I could see. Storm was there, too, and, in fact, every man of any standing in the county.

The sheriff opened the court, the prisoners were brought in, and the Judge took his seat on the bench. He looked haggard like a man who had not slept, as, in fact, one could hardly have done who had so cruel a duty before him. Here was every human feeling pressing to save a woman, and the law to hang her. But for all his hag-ridden face, when he came to act, the man was adamant.

He ordered the confession read, and directed the girl to stand up. Taylor tried again to protest, but he was forced down into his chair. The girl stood up bravely, but she was white as plaster, and her eyes dilated. She was asked if she still adhered to the confession and understood the consequences of it, and, although she trembled from head to toe, she spoke out distinctly. There was a moment of silence and the Judge was about to speak, when another voice filled the courtroom. I turned about on my book to find my head against my Uncle Abner's legs.

"I challenge the confession!" he said.

The whole courtroom moved. Every eye was on the two tragic figures standing up: the slim, pale girl and the big, somber figure of my uncle. The Judge was astounded.

"On what ground?" he said.

"On the ground," replied my uncle, "that the confession is a lie!"

One could have heard a pin fall anywhere in the whole room. The girl caught her breath in a little gasp, and the prisoner, Taylor, half rose and then sat down as though his knees were too weak to bear him. The Judge's mouth opened, but for a moment or two he did not speak, and I could understand his amazement. Here was Abner assailing a confession which he himself had supported before the Judge, and speaking for the innocence of a woman whom he himself had shown to be guilty and taking one position privately, and another publicly. What did the man mean? And I was not surprised that the Judge's voice was stern when he spoke.

"This is irregular," he said. "It may be that this woman killed Marsh, or it may be that Taylor killed him, and there is some collusion between these persons, as you appear to suggest. And you may know

something to throw light on the matter, or you may not. However that
may be, this is not the time for me to hear you. You will have ample
opportunity to speak when I come to try the case."

"But you will never try this case!" said Abner.

I cannot undertake to describe the desperate interest that lay on the
people in the courtroom. They were breathlessly silent; one could hear
the voices from the village outside, and the sounds of men and horses
that came up through the open windows. No one knew what hidden
thing Abner drove at. But he was a man who meant what he said, and
the people knew it.

The Judge turned on him with a terrible face.

"What do you mean?" he said.

"I mean," replied Abner, and it was in his deep, hard voice, "that you
must come down from the bench."

The Judge was in a heat of fury.

"You are in contempt," he roared. "I order your arrest. Sheriff!"
he called.

But Abner did not move. He looked the man calmly in the face.

"You threaten me," he said, "but God Almighty threatens you." And
he turned about to the audience. "The authority of the law," he said, "is
in the hands of the electors of this county. Will they stand up?"

I shall never forget what happened then, for I have never in my life
seen anything so deliberate and impressive. Slowly, in silence, and
without passion, as though they were in a church of God, men began
to get up in the courtroom.

Randolph was the first. He was a justice of the peace, vain and
pompous, proud of the abilities of an ancestry that he did not inherit.
And his superficialities were the annoyance of my Uncle Abner's life.
But whatever I may have to say of him hereafter I want to say this thing
of him here, that his bigotry and his vanities were builded on the foun-
dations of a man. He stood up as though he stood alone, with no glance
about him to see what other men would do, and he faced the Judge
calmly above his great black stock. And I learned then that a man may
be a blusterer and a lion.

Hiram Arnold got up, and Rockford, and Armstrong, and Alkire, and
Coopman, and Monroe, and Elnathan Stone, and my father, Lewis,
and Dayton and Ward, and Madison from beyond the mountains. And
it seemed to me that the very hills and valleys were standing up.

It was a strange and instructive thing to see. The loud-mouthed and
the reckless were in that courtroom, men who would have shouted in
a political convention, or run howling with a mob, but they were not
the persons who stood up when Abner called upon the authority of the
people to appear. Men rose whom one would not have looked to see—

the blacksmith, the saddler, and old Asa Divers. And I saw that law and order and all the structure that civilization had builded up, rested on the sense of justice that certain men carried in their breasts, and that those who possessed it not, in the crisis of necessity, did not count.

Father Donovan stood up; he had a little flock beyond the valley river, and he was as poor, and almost as humble as his Master, but he was not afraid; and Bronson, who preached Calvin, and Adam Rider, who traveled a Methodist circuit. No one of them believed in what the other taught; but they all believed in justice, and when the line was drawn, there was but one side for them all.

The last man up was Nathaniel Davisson, but the reason was that he was very old, and he had to wait for his sons to help him. He had been time and again in the Assembly of Virginia, at a time when only a gentle-man and landowner could sit there. He was a just man, and honorable and unafraid.

The Judge, his face purple, made a desperate effort to enforce his authority. He pounded on his desk and ordered the sheriff to clear the courtroom. But the sheriff remained standing apart. He did not lack for courage, and I think he would have faced the people if his duty had been that way. His attitude was firm, and one could mark no uncertainty upon him, but he took no step to obey what the Judge commanded.

The Judge cried out at him in a terrible voice.

"I am the representative of the law here. Go on!"

The sheriff was a plain man, and unacquainted with the nice expres-sions of Mr. Jefferson, but his answer could not have been better if that gentleman had written it out for him.

"I would obey the representative of the law," he said, "if I were not in the presence of the law itself!"

The Judge rose. "This is revolution," he said; "I will send to the Governor for the militia."

It was Nathaniel Davisson who spoke then. He was very old and the tremors of dissolution were on him, but his voice was steady.

"Sit down, your Honor," he said, "there is no revolution here, and you do not require troops to support your authority. We are here to sup-port it if it ought to be lawfully enforced. But the people have elevated you to the Bench because they believed in your integrity, and if they have been mistaken they would know it." He paused, as though to col-lect his strength, and then went on. "The presumptions of right are all with your Honor. You administer the law upon our authority and we stand behind you. Be assured that we will not suffer our authority to be insulted in your person." His voice grew deep and resolute. "It is a grave thing to call us up against you, and not lightly, nor for a trivial reason shall any man dare to do it." Then he turned about. "Now, Abner," he said, "what is this thing?"

Young as I was, I felt that the old man spoke for the people standing in the courtroom, with their voice and their authority, and I began to fear that the measure which my uncle had taken was high handed. But he stood there like the shadow of a great rock.

"I charge him," he said, "with the murder of Elihu Marsh! And I call upon him to vacate the Bench."

When I think about this extraordinary event now, I wonder at the calmness with which Simon Kilrail met this blow, until I reflect that he had seen it on its way, and had got ready to meet it. But even with that preparation, it took a man of iron nerve to face an assault like that and keep every muscle in its place. He had tried violence and had failed with it, and he had a recourse now to the attitudes and mannerisms of a judicial dignity. He sat with his elbows on the table, and his clenched fingers propping up his jaw. He looked coldly at Abner, but he did not speak, and there was silence until Nathaniel Davisson spoke for him. His face and his voice were like iron.

"No, Abner," he said, "he shall not vacate the Bench for that, nor upon the accusation of any man. We will have your proofs, if you please."

The Judge turned his cold face from Abner to Nathaniel Davisson, and then he looked over the men standing in the courtroom.

"I am not going to remain here," he said, "to be tried by a mob, upon the *viva voce* indictment of a bystander. You may nullify your court, if you like, and suspend the forms of law for yourselves, but you cannot nullify the constitution of Virginia, nor suspend my right as a citizen of that commonwealth.

"And now," he said, rising, "if you will kindly make way, I will vacate this courtroom, which your violence has converted into a chamber of sedition."

The man spoke in a cold, even voice, and I thought he had presented a difficulty that could not be met. How could these men before him understand to keep the peace of this frontier, and force its lawless elements to submit to the forms of law for trial, and deny any letter of those formalities to this man? Was the grand jury, and the formal indictment, and all the right and privilege of an orderly procedure for one, and not for another?

It was Nathaniel Davisson who met this dangerous problem.

"We are not concerned," he said, "at this moment with your rights as a citizen; the rights of private citizenship are inviolate, and they remain to you, when you return to it. But you are not a private citizen. You are our agent. We have selected you to administer the law for us, and your right to act has been challenged. Well, as the authority behind you, we appear and would know the reason."

The Judge retained his imperturbable calm.

"Do you hold me a prisoner here?" he said.

"We hold you an official in your office," replied Davisson, "not only do we refuse to permit you to leave the courtroom, but we refuse to permit you to leave the Bench. This court shall remain as we have set it up until it is our will to readjust it. And it shall not be changed at the pleasure or demand of any man but by us only, and for a sufficient cause shown to us."

And again I was anxious for my uncle, for I saw how grave a thing it was to interfere with the authority of the people as manifested in the forms and agencies of the law. Abner must be very sure of the ground under him.

And he was sure. He spoke now, with no introductory expressions, but directly and in the simplest words.

"These two persons," he said, indicating Taylor and the girl, "have each been willing to die in order to save the other. Neither is guilty of this crime. Taylor has kept silent, and the girl has lied, to the same end. This is the truth: There was a lovers' quarrel, and Taylor left the country precisely as he told us, except the motive, which he would not tell lest the girl be involved. And the woman, to save him, confesses to a crime that she did not commit.

"Who did commit it?" He paused and included Storm with a gesture. "We suspected this woman because Marsh had been killed by poison in his bread, and afterwards mutilated with a shot. Yesterday we rode out with the Judge to put those facts before him." Again he paused. "An incident occurring in that interview indicated that we were wrong; a second incident assured us, and still later, a third convinced us. These incidents were, first, that the Judge's watch had run down; second, that we found in his library a book with all the leaves in it uncut, except at one certain page; and, third, that we found in the county clerk's office an unindexed record in an old deed book." There was deep quiet and he went on:

"In addition to the theory of Taylor's guilt or this woman's, there was still a third; but it had only a single incident to support it, and we feared to suggest it until the others had been explained. This theory was that some one, to benefit by Marsh's death, had planned to kill him in such a manner as to throw suspicion on this woman who baked his bread, and finding Taylor gone, and the gun above the mantel, yielded to an afterthought to create a further false evidence. It was overdone!

"The trigger guard of the gun in the recoil caught in the chain of the assassin's watch and jerked it out of his pocket; he replaced the watch, but not the key which fell to the floor, and which I picked up beside the body of the dead man."

Abner turned toward the judge.

"And so," he said, "I charge Simon Kilrail with this murder; because the key winds his watch; because the record in the old deed book is a conveyance by the heirs of Marsh's lands to him at the life tenant's death; and because the book we found in his library is a book on poisons with the leaves uncut, except at the very page describing that identical poison with which Elihu Marsh was murdered."

The strained silence that followed Abner's words was broken by a voice that thundered in the courtroom. It was Randolph's.

"Come down!" he said.

And this time Nathaniel Davisson was silent.

The Judge got slowly on his feet, a resolution was forming in his face, and it advanced swiftly.

"I will give you my answer in a moment," he said.

Then he turned about and went into his room behind the Bench. There was but one door, and that opening into the court, and the people waited.

The windows were open and we could see the green fields, and the sun, and the far-off mountains, and the peace and quiet and serenity of autumn entered. The Judge did not appear. Presently there was the sound of a shot from behind the closed door. The sheriff threw it open, and upon the floor, sprawling in a smear of blood, lay Simon Kilrail, with a dueling pistol in his hand.

Susan Glaspell

(1882–1948)

SUSAN GLASPELL was a journalist, novelist, and playwright, who (with her husband George Cram Cook) began the little theatre movement in America, founding in 1915 the Provincetown Playhouse in Cape Cod. Glaspell and Cook sponsored the early works of Eugene O'Neill, and she herself won the Pulitzer Prize for Drama with *Allison's House* in 1930.

"A Jury of Her Peers" is based on the people Glaspell knew during her childhood in Davenport, Iowa, and on a genuine murder case in the year 1900. In 1916, she dramatized the case as a one-act play called *Trifles*. The next year, she rewrote it as a short story for *Everyweek*. With its group detection, it is one of the finest combinations of whodunit and whydunit ever written. And it is a ringing assertion that women think differently from men not because, as men complacently believe, they are more emotional, but because they observe trifles.

A Jury of Her Peers

WHEN MARTHA HALE opened the storm-door and got a cut of the north wind, she ran back for her big woolen scarf. As she hurriedly wound that round her head her eye made a scandalized sweep of her kitchen. It was no ordinary thing that called her away—it was probably farther from ordinary than anything that had ever happened in Dickson County. But what her eye took in was that her kitchen was in no shape for leaving: her bread all ready for mixing, half the flour sifted and half unsifted.

She hated to see things half done; but she had been at that when the team from town stopped to get Mr. Hale, and then the sheriff came running in to say his wife wished Mrs. Hale would come too—adding, with a grin, that he guessed she was getting scarey and wanted another woman along. So she had dropped everything right where it was.

"Martha!" now came her husband's impatient voice. "Don't keep folks waiting out here in the cold."

She again opened the storm-door, and this time joined the three men and the one woman waiting for her in the big two-seated buggy.

After she had the robes tucked around her she took another look at the woman who sat beside her on the back seat. She had met Mrs. Peters the year before at the county fair, and the thing she remembered about her was that she didn't seem like a sheriff's wife. She was small and thin and didn't have a strong voice. Mrs. Gorman, sheriff's wife before Gorman went out and Peters came in, had a voice that somehow seemed to be backing up the law with every word. But if Mrs. Peters didn't look like a sheriff's wife, Peters made it up in looking like a sheriff. He was to a dot the kind of man who could get himself elected sheriff—a heavy man with a big voice, who was particularly genial with the law-abiding, as if to make it plain that he knew the difference between criminals and non-criminals. And right there it came into Mrs. Hale's mind, with a stab, that this man who was so pleasant and lively with all of them was going to the Wrights' now as a sheriff.

"The country's not very pleasant this time of year," Mrs. Peters at last ventured, as if she felt they ought to be talking as well as the men.

Mrs. Hale scarcely finished her reply, for they had gone up a little hill and could see the Wright place now, and seeing it did not make her feel like talking. It looked very lonesome this cold March morning. It had always been a lonesome-looking place. It was down in a hollow, and the poplar trees around it were lonesome-looking trees. The men were looking at it and talking about what had happened. The county attorney was bending to one side of the buggy, and kept looking steadily at the place as they drew up to it.

"I'm glad you came with me," Mrs. Peters said nervously, as the two women were about to follow the men in through the kitchen door.

Even after she had her foot on the door-step, her hand on the knob, Martha Hale had a moment of feeling she could not cross that threshold. And the reason it seemed she couldn't cross it now was simply because she hadn't crossed it before. Time and time again it had been in her mind, "I ought to go over and see Minnie Foster"—she still thought of her as Minnie Foster, though for twenty years she had been Mrs. Wright. And then there was always something to do and Minnie Foster would go from her mind. But *now* she could come.

The men went over to the stove. The women stood close together by the door. Young Henderson, the county attorney, turned around and said, "Come up to the fire, ladies."

Mrs. Peters took a step forward, then stopped. "I'm not—cold," she said.

And so the two women stood by the door, at first not even so much as looking around the kitchen.

The men talked for a minute about what a good thing it was the sheriff had sent his deputy out that morning to make a fire for them, and then Sheriff Peters stepped back from the stove, unbuttoned his outer coat, and leaned his hands on the kitchen table in a way that seemed to mark the beginning of official business. "Now, Mr. Hale," he said in a sort of semi-official voice, "before we move things about, you tell Mr. Henderson just what it was you saw when you came here yesterday morning."

The county attorney was looking around the kitchen.

"By the way," he said, "has anything been moved?" He turned to the sheriff. "Are things just as you left them yesterday?"

Peters looked from cupboard to sink; from that to a small worn rocker a little to one side of the kitchen table.

"It's just the same."

"Somebody should have been left here yesterday," said the county attorney.

"Oh—yesterday," returned the sheriff, with a little gesture as of yesterday having been more than he could bear to think of. "When I had to send Frank to Morris Center for that man who went crazy—let me tell you, I had my hands full *yesterday*. I knew you could get back from Omaha by to-day, George, and as long as I went over everything here myself—"

"Well, Mr. Hale," said the county attorney, in a way of letting what was past and gone go, "tell just what happened when you came here yesterday morning."

Mrs. Hale, still leaning against the door, had that sinking feeling of the mother whose child is about to speak a piece. Lewis often wandered along and got things mixed up in a story. She hoped he would tell this straight and plain, and not say unnecessary things that would just make things harder for Minnie Foster. He didn't begin at once, and she noticed that he looked queer—as if standing in that kitchen and having to tell what he had seen there yesterday morning made him almost sick.

"Yes, Mr. Hale?" the county attorney reminded.

"Harry and I had started to town with a load of potatoes," Mrs. Hale's husband began.

Harry was Mrs. Hale's oldest boy. He wasn't with them now, for the very good reason that those potatoes never got to town yesterday and he was taking them this morning, so he hadn't been home when the sheriff stopped to say he wanted Mr. Hale to come over to the Wright place and tell the county attorney his story there, where he could point it all out. With all Mrs. Hale's other emotions came the fear that maybe Harry wasn't dressed warm enough—they hadn't any of them realized how that north wind did bite.

"We come along this road," Hale was going on, with a motion of his hand to the road over which they had just come, "and as we got in sight of the house I says to Harry, 'I'm goin' to see if I can't get John Wright to take a telephone.' You see," he explained to Henderson, "unless I can get somebody to go in with me they won't come out this branch road except for a price *I* can't pay. I'd spoke to Wright about it once before; but he put me off, saying folks talked too much anyway, and all he asked was peace and quiet—guess you know about how much he talked himself. But I thought maybe if I went to the house and talked about it before his wife, and said all the women-folks liked the telephones, and that in this lonesome stretch of road it would be a good thing—well, I said to Harry that that was what I was going to say— though I said at the same time that I didn't know as what his wife wanted made much difference to John—"

Now, there he was!—saying things he didn't need to say. Mrs. Hale tried to catch her husband's eye, but fortunately the county attorney interrupted with:

"Let's talk about that a little later, Mr. Hale. I do want to talk about that, but I'm anxious now to get along to just what happened when you got here."

When he began this time, it was very deliberately and carefully:

"I didn't see or hear anything. I knocked at the door. And still it was all quiet inside. I knew they must be up—it was past eight o'clock. So I knocked again, louder, and I thought I heard somebody say 'Come in.' I wasn't sure—I'm not sure yet. But I opened the door—this door," jerking a hand toward the door by which the two women stood, "and there, in that rocker"—pointing to it—"sat Mrs. Wright."

Every one in the kitchen looked at the rocker. It came into Mrs. Hale's mind that that rocker didn't look in the least like Minnie Foster—the Minnie Foster of twenty years before. It was a dingy red, with wooden rungs up the back, and the middle rung was gone, and the chair sagged to one side.

"How did she—look?" the county attorney was inquiring.

"Well," said Hale, "she looked—queer."

"How do you mean—queer?"

As he asked it he took out a note-book and pencil. Mrs. Hale did not like the sight of that pencil. She kept her eye fixed on her husband, as if to keep him from saying unnecessary things that would go into that note-book and make trouble.

Hale did speak guardedly, as if the pencil had affected him too.

"Well, as if she didn't know what she was going to do next. And kind of—done up."

"How did she seem to feel about your coming?"

"Why, I don't think she minded—one way or other. She didn't pay much attention. I said, 'Ho' do, Mrs. Wright? It's cold, ain't it?' and she said, 'Is it?'—and went on pleatin' at her apron.

"Well, I was surprised. She didn't ask me to come up to the stove, or to sit down, but just set there, not even lookin' at me. And so I said: 'I want to see John.'

"And then she—laughed. I guess you would call it a laugh.

"I thought of Harry and the team outside, so I said, a little sharp, 'Can I see John?' 'No,' says she—kind of dull like. 'Ain't he home?' says I. Then she looked at me. 'Yes,' says she, 'he's home.' 'Then why can't I see him?' I asked her, out of patience with her now. ''Cause he's dead,' says she, just as quiet and dull—and fell to pleatin' her apron. 'Dead?' says I, like you do when you can't take in what you've heard.

"She just nodded her head, not getting a bit excited, but rockin' back and forth.

"'Why—where is he?' says I, not knowing *what* to say.

"She just pointed upstairs—like this"—pointing to the room above.

"I got up, with the idea of going up there myself. By this time I—didn't know what to do. I walked from there to here; then I says: 'Why, what did he die of?'

"'He died of a rope around his neck,' says she; and just went on pleatin' at her apron."

Hale stopped speaking, and stood staring at the rocker, as if he were still seeing the woman who had sat there the morning before. Nobody spoke; it was as if every one were seeing the woman who had sat there the morning before.

"And what did you do then?" the county attorney at last broke the silence.

"I went out and called Harry. I thought I might—need help. I got Harry in, and we went upstairs." His voice fell almost to a whisper. "There he was—lying over the—"

"I think I'd rather have you go into that upstairs," the county attorney interrupted, "where you can point it all out. Just go on now with the rest of your story."

"Well, my first thought was to get that rope off. It looked—"

He stopped, his face twitching.

"But Harry, he went up to him, and he said, 'No, he's dead all right, and we'd better not touch anything.' So we went downstairs.

"She was still sitting that same way. 'Has anybody been notified?' I asked. 'No,' says she unconcerned.

"'Who did this, Mrs. Wright?' said Harry. He said it business-like, and she stopped pleatin' at her apron. 'I don't know,' she says. 'You don't *know?*' says Harry. 'Weren't you sleepin' in the bed with him?' 'Yes,' says she, 'but I was on the inside.' 'Somebody slipped a rope round his neck and strangled him, and you didn't wake up?' says Harry. 'I didn't wake up,' she said after him.

"We may have looked as if we didn't see how that could be, for after a minute she said, 'I sleep sound.'

"Harry was going to ask her more questions, but I said maybe that weren't our business; maybe we ought to let her tell her story first to the coroner or the sheriff. So Harry went fast as he could over to High Road—the Rivers' place, where there's a telephone."

"And what did she do when she knew you had gone for the coroner?" The attorney got his pencil in his hand all ready for writing.

"She moved from that chair to this one over here—Hale pointed to a small chair in the corner—"and just sat there with her hands held together and looking down. I got a feeling that I ought to make some conversation, so I said I had come in to see if John wanted to put in a telephone; and at that she started to laugh, and then she stopped and looked at me—scared."

At the sound of a moving pencil the man who was telling the story looked up.

"I dunno—maybe it wasn't scared," he hastened; "I wouldn't like to say it was. Soon Harry got back, and then Dr. Lloyd came, and you, Mr. Peters, and so I guess that's all I know that you don't."

He said that last with relief, and moved a little, as if relaxing. Every one moved a little. The county attorney walked toward the stair door.

"I guess we'll go upstairs first—then out to the barn and around there."

He paused and looked around the kitchen.

"You're convinced there was nothing important here?" he asked the sheriff. "Nothing that would—point to any motive?"

The sheriff too looked all around, as if to re-convince himself.

"Nothing here but kitchen things," he said, with a little laugh for the insignificance of kitchen things.

The county attorney was looking at the cupboard—a peculiar, ungainly structure, half closet and half cupboard, the upper part of it being built in the wall, and the lower part just the old-fashioned kitchen cupboard. As if its queerness attracted him, he got a chair and opened the upper part and looked in. After a moment he drew his hand away sticky.

"Here's a nice mess," he said resentfully.

The two women had drawn nearer, and now the sheriff's wife spoke.

"Oh—her fruit," she said, looking to Mrs. Hale for sympathetic understanding. She turned back to the county attorney and explained: "She worried about that when it turned so cold last night. She said the fire would go out and her jars might burst."

Mrs. Peters' husband broke into a laugh.

"Well, can you beat the women! Held for murder, and worrying about her preserves!"

The young attorney set his lips.

"I guess before we're through with her she may have something more serious than preserves to worry about."

"Oh, well," said Mrs. Hale's husband, with good-natured superiority, "women are used to worrying over trifles."

The two women moved a little closer together. Neither of them spoke. The county attorney seemed suddenly to remember his manners—and think of his future.

"And yet," said he, with the gallantry of a young politician, "for all their worries, what would we do without the ladies?"

The women did not speak, did not unbend. He went to the sink and began washing his hands. He turned to wipe them on the roller towel—whirled it for a cleaner place.

"Dirty towels! Not much of a housekeeper, would you say, ladies?"

He kicked his foot against some dirty pans under the sink.

"There's a great deal of work to be done on a farm," said Mrs. Hale stiffly.

"To be sure. And yet"—with a little bow to her—"I know there are some Dickson County farm-houses that do not have such roller towels." He gave it a pull to expose its full length again.

"Those towels get dirty awful quick. Men's hands aren't always as clean as they might be."

"Ah, loyal to your sex, I see," he laughed. He stopped and gave her a keen look. "But you and Mrs. Wright were neighbors. I suppose you were friends, too."

Martha Hale shook her head.

"I've seen little enough of her of late years. I've not been in this house—it's more than a year."

"And why was that? You didn't like her?"

"I liked her well enough," she replied with spirit. "Farmers' wives have their hands full, Mr. Henderson. And then"—She looked around the kitchen.

"Yes?" he encouraged.

"It never seemed a very cheerful place," said she, more to herself than to him.

"No," he agreed; "I don't think any one would call it cheerful. I shouldn't say she had the home-making instinct."

"Well, I don't know as Wright had, either," she muttered.

"You mean they didn't get on very well?" he was quick to ask.

"No; I don't mean anything," she answered, with decision. As she turned a little away from him, she added: "But I don't think a place would be any the cheerfuler for John Wright's bein' in it."

"I'd like to talk to you about that a little later, Mrs. Hale," he said. "I'm anxious to get the lay of things upstairs now."

He moved toward the stair door, followed by the two men.

"I suppose anything Mrs. Peters does'll be all right?" the sheriff inquired. "She was to take in some clothes for her, you know—and a few little things. We left in such a hurry yesterday."

The county attorney looked at the two women whom they were leaving alone there among the kitchen things.

"Yes—Mrs. Peters," he said, his glance resting on the woman who was not Mrs. Peters, the big farmer woman who stood behind the sheriff's wife. "Of course Mrs. Peters is one of us," he said, in a manner of entrusting responsibility. "And keep your eye out, Mrs. Peters, for anything that might be of use. No telling; you women might come upon a clue to the motive—and that's the thing we need."

Mr. Hale rubbed his face after the fashion of a show man getting ready for a pleasantry.

"But would the women know a clue if they did come upon it?" he said; and, having delivered himself of this, he followed the others through the stair door.

The women stood motionless and silent, listening to the footsteps, first upon the stairs, then in the room above them.

Then, as if releasing herself from something strange, Mrs. Hale began to arrange the dirty pans under the sink, which the county attorney's disdainful push of the foot had deranged.

"I'd hate to have men comin' into my kitchen," she said testily— "snoopin' round and criticizin'."

"Of course it's no more than their duty," said the sheriff's wife, in her manner of timid acquiescence.

"Duty's all right," replied Mrs. Hale bluffly; "but I guess that deputy sheriff that come out to make the fire might have got a little of this on." She gave the roller towel a pull. "Wish I'd thought of that sooner! Seems mean to talk about her for not having things slicked up, when she had to come away in such a hurry."

She looked around the kitchen. Certainly it was not "slicked up." Her eye was held by a bucket of sugar on a low shelf. The cover was off the wooden bucket, and beside it was a paper bag—half full.

Mrs. Hale moved toward it.

"She was putting this in there," he said to herself—slowly.

She thought of the flour in her kitchen at home—half sifted, half not sifted. She had been interrupted and had left things half done. What had interrupted Minnie Foster? Why had that work been left half done? She made a move as if to finish it,—unfinished things always bothered her,—and then she glanced around and saw that Mrs. Peters was watching her—and she didn't want Mrs. Peters to get that feeling she had got of work begun and then—for some reason—not finished.

"It's a shame about her fruit," she said, and walked toward the cupboard that the county attorney had opened, and got on the chair, murmuring: "I wonder if it's all gone."

It was a sorry enough looking sight, but "Here's one that's all right," she said at last. She held it toward the light. "This is cherries, too." She looked again. "I declare I believe that's the only one."

With a sigh, she got down from the chair, went to the sink and wiped off the bottle.

"She'll feel awful bad, after all her hard work in the hot weather. I remember the afternoon I put up my cherries last summer."

She set the bottle on the table, and, with another sigh, started to sit down in the rocker. But she did not sit down. Something kept her from sitting down in that chair. She straightened—stepped back, and, half turned away, stood looking at it, seeing the woman who sat there "pleatin' at her apron."

The thin voice of the sheriff's wife broke in upon her: "I must be getting those things from the front room closet." She opened the door into the other room, started in, stepped back. "You coming with me, Mrs. Hale?" she asked nervously. "You—you could help me get them."

They were soon back—the stark coldness of that shut-up room was not a thing to linger in.

"My!" said Mrs. Peters, dropping the things on the table and hurrying to the stove.

Mrs. Hale stood examining the clothes the woman who was being detained in town had said she wanted.

"Wright was close!" she exclaimed, holding up a shabby black skirt that bore the marks of much making over. "I think maybe that's why she kept so much to herself. I s'pose she felt she couldn't do her part; and then, you don't enjoy things when you feel shabby. She used to wear pretty clothes and be lively—when she was Minnie Foster, one of the town girls, singing in the choir. But that—oh, that was twenty years ago."

With a carefulness in which there was something tender, she folded the shabby clothes and piled them at one corner of the table. She looked at Mrs. Peters, and there was something in the other woman's look that irritated her.

"She don't care," she said to herself. "Much difference it makes to her whether Minnie Foster had pretty clothes when she was a girl."

Then she looked again, and she wasn't so sure; in fact, she hadn't at any time been perfectly sure about Mrs. Peters. She had that shrinking manner, and yet her eyes looked as if they could see a long way into things.

"This all you was to take in?" asked Mrs. Hale.

"No," said the sheriff's wife; "she said she wanted an apron. Funny thing to want," she ventured in her nervous little way, "for there's not much to get you dirty in jail, goodness knows. But I suppose just to make her feel more natural. If you're used to wearing an apron—. She said they were in the bottom drawer of this cupboard. Yes—here they are. And then her little shawl that always hung on the stair door."

She took the small gray shawl from behind the door leading upstairs, and stood a minute looking at it.

Suddenly Mrs. Hale took a quick step toward the other woman. "Mrs. Peters!"

"Yes, Mrs. Hale?"

"Do you think she—did it?"

A frightened look blurred the other things in Mrs. Peters' eyes.

"Oh, I don't know," she said, in a voice that seemed to shrink away from the subject.

"Well, I don't think she did," affirmed Mrs. Hale stoutly. "Asking for an apron, and her little shawl. Worryin' about her fruit."

"Mr. Peters says—" Footsteps were heard in the room above; she stopped, looked up, then went on in a lowered voice: " Mr. Peters says—it looks bad for her. Mr. Henderson is awful sarcastic in a speech, and he's going to make fun of her saying she didn't—wake up."

For a moment Mrs. Hale had no answer. Then, "Well, I guess John Wright didn't wake up—when they was slippin' that rope under his neck," she muttered.

"No, it's *strange*," breathed Mrs. Peters. "They think it was such a— funny way to kill a man."

She began to laugh; at sound of the laugh, abruptly stopped.

"That's just what Mr. Hale said," said Mrs. Hale, in a resolutely natural voice. "There was a gun in the house. He says that's what he can't understand."

"Mr. Henderson said, coming out, that what was needed for the case was a motive. Something to show anger—or sudden feeling."

"Well, I don't see any signs of anger around here," said Mrs. Hale. "I don't—"

She stopped. It was as if her mind tripped on something. Her eye was caught by a dish-towel in the middle of the kitchen table. Slowly she moved toward the table. One half of it was wiped clean, the other half messy. Her eyes made a slow, almost unwilling turn to the bucket of sugar and the half empty bag beside it. Things begun— and not finished.

After a moment she stepped back, and said, in that manner of releasing herself:

"Wonder how they're finding things upstairs? I hope she had it a little more red up there. You know,"—she paused, and feeling gathered,— "it seems kind of *sneaking*; locking her up in town and coming out here to get her own house to turn against her!"

"But, Mrs. Hale," said the sheriff's wife, "the law is the law."

"I s'pose 'tis," answered Mrs. Hale shortly.

She turned to the stove, saying something about that fire not being much to brag of. She worked with it a minute, and when she straightened up she said aggressively:

"The law is the law—and a bad stove is a bad stove. How'd you like to cook on this?"—pointing with the poker to the broken lining. She opened the oven door and started to express her opinion of the oven; but she was swept into her own thoughts, thinking of what it would mean, year after year, to have that stove to wrestle with. The thought of Minnie Foster trying to bake in that oven—and the thought of her never going over to see Minnie Foster—.

She was startled by hearing Mrs. Peters say: "A person gets discouraged—and loses heart."

The sheriff's wife had looked from the stove to the sink—to the pail of water which had been carried in from outside. The two women stood there silent, above them the footsteps of the men who were looking for evidence against the woman who had worked in that kitchen. That look of seeing into things, of seeing through a thing to something else, was in the eyes of the sheriff's wife now. When Mrs. Hale next spoke to her, it was gently:

"Better loosen up your things, Mrs. Peters. We'll not feel them when we go out."

Mrs. Peters went to the back of the room to hang up the fur tippet she was wearing. A moment later she exclaimed, "Why, she was piecing a quilt," and held up a large sewing basket piled high with quilt pieces.

Mrs. Hale spread some of the blocks on the table.

"It's log-cabin pattern," she said, putting several of them together. "Pretty, isn't it?"

They were so engaged with the quilt that they did not hear the footsteps on the stairs. Just as the stair door opened Mrs. Hale was saying:

"Do you suppose she was going to quilt it or just knot it?"

The sheriff threw up his hands.

"They wonder whether she was going to quilt it or just knot it!"

There was a laugh for the ways of women, a warming of hands over the stove, and then the county attorney said briskly:

"Well, let's go right out to the barn and get that cleared up."

"I don't see as there's anything so strange," Mrs. Hale said resentfully, after the outside door had closed on the three men—"our taking up our time with little things while we're waiting for them to get the evidence. I don't see as it's anything to laugh about."

"Of course they've got awful important things on their minds," said the sheriff's wife apologetically.

They returned to an inspection of the blocks for the quilt. Mrs. Hale was looking at the fine, even sewing, and preoccupied with thoughts of the woman who had done that sewing, when she heard the sheriff's wife say, in a queer tone:

"Why, look at this one."

She turned to take the block held out to her.

"The sewing," said Mrs. Peters, in a troubled way. "All the rest of them have been so nice and even—but—this one. Why, it looks as if she didn't know what she was about!"

Their eyes met—something flashed to life, passed between them; then, as if with an effort, they seemed to pull away from each other. A moment Mrs. Hale sat there, her hands folded over that sewing which was so unlike all the rest of the sewing. Then she had pulled a knot and drawn the threads.

"Oh, what are you doing, Mrs. Hale?" asked the sheriff's wife, startled.

"Just pulling out a stitch or two that's not sewed very good," said Mrs. Hale mildly.

"I don't think we ought to touch things," Mrs. Peters said, a little helplessly.

"I'd just finish up this end," answered Mrs. Hale, still in that mild, matter-of-fact fashion.

She threaded a needle and started to replace bad sewing with good. For a little while she sewed in silence. Then, in that thin, timid voice, she heard:

"Mrs. Hale!"

"Yes, Mrs. Peters?"

"What do you suppose she was so—nervous about?"

"Oh, I don't know," said Mrs. Hale, as if dismissing a thing not important enough to spend much time on. "I don't know as she was—nervous. I sew awful queer sometimes when I'm just tired."

She cut a thread, and out of the corner of her eye looked up at Mrs. Peters. The small, lean face of the sheriff's wife seemed to have tightened up. Her eyes had that look of peering into something. But the next moment she moved, and said in her thin, indecisive way:

"Well, I must get those clothes wrapped. They may be through sooner than we think. I wonder where I could find a piece of paper—and string."

"In that cupboard, maybe," suggested Mrs. Hale, after a glance around.

One piece of the crazy sewing remained unripped. Mrs. Peters' back turned, Martha Hale now scrutinized that piece, compared it with the dainty, accurate sewing of the other blocks. The difference was startling. Holding this block made her feel queer, as if the distracted thoughts of the woman who had perhaps turned to it to try and quiet herself were communicating themselves to her.

Mrs. Peters' voice roused her.

"Here's a bird-cage," she said. "Did she have a bird, Mrs. Hale?"

"Why, I don't know whether she did nor not." She turned to look at the cage Mrs. Peters was holding up. "I've not been here in so long." She sighed. "There was a man round last year selling canaries cheap—but I don't know as she took one. Maybe she did. She used to sing real pretty herself."

Mrs. Peters looked around the kitchen.

"Seems kind of funny to think of a bird here." She half laughed—an attempt to put up a barrier. "But she must have had one—or why would she have a cage? I wonder what happened to it."

"I suppose maybe the cat got it," suggested Mrs. Hale, resuming her sewing.

"No; she didn't have a cat. She's got that feeling some people have about cats—being afraid of them. When they brought her to our house yesterday, my cat got in the room, and she was real upset and asked me to take it out."

"My sister Bessie was like that," laughed Mrs. Hale.

The sheriff's wife did not reply. The silence made Mrs. Hale turn round. Mrs. Peters was examining the bird-cage.

"Look at this door," she said slowly. "It's broke. One hinge has been pulled apart."

Mrs. Hale came nearer.

"Looks as if some one must have been—rough with it."

Again their eyes met—startled, questioning, apprehensive. For a moment neither spoke nor stirred. Then Mrs. Hale, turning away, said brusquely:

"If they're going to find any evidence, I wish they'd be about it. I don't like this place."

"But I'm awful glad you came with me, Mrs. Hale." Mrs. Peters put the bird-cage on the table and sat down. "It would be lonesome for me—sitting here alone."

"Yes, it would, wouldn't it?" agreed Mrs. Hale, a certain determined naturalness in her voice. She picked up the sewing, but now it dropped in her lap, and she murmured in a different voice: "But I tell you what I *do* wish, Mrs. Peters. I wish I had come over sometimes when she was here. I wish—I had."

"But of course you were awful busy, Mrs. Hale. Your house—and your children."

"I could've come," retorted Mrs. Hale shortly. "I stayed away because it weren't cheerful—and that's why I ought to have come. I"—she looked around—"I've never liked this place. Maybe because it's down in a hollow and you don't see the road. I don't know what it is, but it's a lonesome place, and always was. I wish I had come over to see Minnie Foster sometimes. I can see now—" She did not put it into words.

"Well, you mustn't reproach yourself," counseled Mrs. Peters. "Somehow, we just don't see how it is with other folks till—something comes up."

"Not having children makes less work," mused Mrs. Hale, after a silence, "but it makes a quiet house—and Wright out to work all day— and no company when he did come in. Did you know John Wright, Mrs. Peters?"

"Not to know him. I've seen him in town. They say he was a good man."

"Yes—good," conceded John Wright's neighbor grimly. "He didn't drink, and kept his word as well as most, I guess, and paid his debts. But he was a hard man, Mrs. Peters. Just to pass the time of day with him—." She stopped, shivered a little. "Like a raw wind that gets to the bone." Her eye fell upon the cage on the table before her, and she added, almost bitterly: "I should think she would've wanted a bird!"

Suddenly she leaned forward, looking intently at the cage. "But what do you s'pose went wrong with it?"

"I don't know," returned Mrs. Peters; "unless it got sick and died."

But after she said it she reached over and swung the broken door. Both women watched it as if somehow held by it.

"You didn't know—her?" Mrs. Hale asked, a gentler note in her voice.

"Not till they brought her yesterday," said the sheriff's wife.

"She—come to think of it, she was kind of like a bird herself. Real sweet and pretty, but kind of timid and—fluttery. How—she— did—change."

That held her for a long time. Finally, as if struck with a happy thought and relieved to get back to everyday things, she exclaimed:

"Tell you what, Mrs. Peters, why don't you take the quilt in with you? It might take up her mind."

"Why, I think that's a real nice idea, Mrs. Hale," agreed the sheriff's wife, as if she too were glad to come into the atmosphere of a simple kindness. "There couldn't possibly be any objection to that, could there? Now, just what will I take? I wonder if her patches are in here— and her things."

They turned to the sewing basket.

"Here's some red," said Mrs. Hale, bringing out a roll of cloth. Underneath that was a box. "Here, maybe her scissors are in here—and her things." She held it up. "What a pretty box! I'll warrant that was something she had a long time ago—when she was a girl."

She held it in her hand a moment; then, with a little sigh, opened it. Instantly her hand went to her nose.

"Why—!"

Mrs. Peters drew nearer—then turned away.

"There's something wrapped up in this piece of silk," faltered Mrs. Hale.

"This isn't her scissors," said Mrs. Peters in a shrinking voice.

Her hand not steady, Mrs. Hale raised the piece of silk. "Oh, Mrs. Peters!" she cried. "It's—"

Mrs. Peters bent closer.

"It's the bird," she whispered.

"But, Mrs. Peters!" cried Mrs. Hale. "*Look* at it! Its neck—look at its neck! It's all—other side *to*."

She held the box away from her.

The sheriff's wife again bent closer.

"Somebody wrung its neck," said she, in a voice that was slow and deep.

And then again the eyes of the two women met—this time clung together in a look of dawning comprehension, of growing horror. Mrs. Peters looked from the dead bird to the broken door of the cage. Again their eyes met. And just then there was a sound at the outside door.

Mrs. Hale slipped the box under the quilt pieces in the basket, and sank into the chair before it. Mrs. Peters stood holding to the table. The county attorney and the sheriff came in from outside.

"Well, ladies," said the county attorney, as one turning from serious things to little pleasantries, "have you decided whether she was going to quilt it or knot it?"

"We think," began the sheriff's wife in a flurried voice, "that she was going to—knot it."

He was too preoccupied to notice the change that came in her voice on that last.

"Well, that's very interesting, I'm sure," he said tolerantly. He caught sight of the bird-cage. "Has the bird flown!"

"We think the cat got it," said Mrs. Hale in a voice curiously even.

He was walking up and down, as if thinking something out.

"Is there a cat?" he asked absently.

Mrs. Hale shot a look up at the sheriff's wife.

"Well, not *now*," said Mrs. Peters. "They're superstitious, you know; they leave."

She sank into her chair.

The county attorney did not heed her. "No sign at all of any one having come in from the outside," he said to Peters, in the manner of continuing an interrupted conversation. "Their own rope. Now let's go upstairs again and go over it, piece by piece. It would have to have been some one who knew just the—"

The stair door closed behind them and their voices were lost.

The two women sat motionless, not looking at each other, but as if peering into something and at the same time holding back. When they spoke now it was as if they were afraid of what they were saying, but as if they could not help saying it.

"She liked the bird," said Martha Hale, low and slowly. "She was going to bury it in that pretty box."

"When I was a girl," said Mrs. Peters, under her breath, "my kitten— there was a boy took a hatchet, and before my eyes—before I could get there—" She covered her face an instant. "If they hadn't held me back I would have"—she caught herself, looked upstairs where footsteps were heard, and finished weakly—"hurt him."

Then they sat without speaking or moving.

"I wonder how it would seem," Mrs. Hale at last began, as if feeling her way over strange ground—"never to have had any children around?" Her eyes made a slow sweep of the kitchen, as if seeing what that kitchen had meant through all the years. "No, Wright wouldn't like the bird," she said after that—"a thing that sang. She used to sing. He killed that too." Her voice tightened.

Mrs. Peters moved uneasily.

"Of course we don't know who killed the bird."

"I knew John Wright," was Mrs. Hale's answer.

"It was an awful thing was done in this house that night, Mrs. Hale," said the sheriff's wife. "Killing a man while he slept—slipping a thing round his neck that choked the life out of him."

Mrs. Hale's hand went out to the bird-cage.

"His neck. Choked the life out of him."

"We don't *know* who killed him," whispered Mrs. Peters wildly. "We don't *know*."

Mrs. Hale had not moved. "If there had been years and years of— nothing, then a bird to sing to you, it would be awful—still—after the bird was still."

It was as if something within her not herself had spoken, and it found in Mrs. Peters something she did not know as herself.

"I know what stillness is," she said, in a queer, monotonous voice. "When we homesteaded in Dakota, and my first baby died—after he was two years old—and me with no other then—"

Mrs. Hale stirred.

"How soon do you suppose they'll be through looking for evidence?"

"I know what stillness is," repeated Mrs. Peters, in just the same way. Then she too pulled back. "The law has got to punish crime, Mrs. Hale," she said in her tight little way.

"I wish you'd seen Minnie Foster," was the answer, "when she wore a white dress with blue ribbons, and stood up there in the choir and sang."

The picture of that girl, the fact that she had lived neighbor to that girl for twenty years, and had let her die for lack of life, was suddenly more than she could bear.

"Oh, I *wish* I'd come over here once in a while!" she cried. "That was a crime! That was a crime! Who's going to punish that?"

"We mustn't take on," said Mrs. Peters, with a frightened look toward the stairs.

"I might 'a' *known* she needed help! I tell you, it's *queer*, Mrs. Peters. We live close together, and we live far apart. We all go through the same things—it's all just a different kind of the same thing! If it weren't—why do you and I *understand?* Why do we *know*—what we know this minute?"

She dashed her hand across her eyes. Then, seeing the jar of fruit on the table, she reached for it and choked out:

"If I was you I wouldn't *tell* her her fruit was gone! Tell her it *ain't.* Tell her it's all right—all of it. Here—take this in to prove it to her! She—she may never know whether it was broke or not."

She turned away.

Mrs. Peters reached out for the bottle of fruit as if she were glad to take it—as if touching a familiar thing, having something to do, could keep her from something else. She got up, looked about for something to wrap the fruit in, took a petticoat from the pile of clothes she had brought from the front room, and nervously started winding that round the bottle.

"My!" she began, in a high, false voice, "it's a good thing the men couldn't hear us! Getting all stirred up over a little thing like a—dead canary." She hurried over that. "As if that could have anything to do with—with—My, wouldn't they *laugh?*"

Footsteps were heard on the stairs.

"Maybe they would," muttered Mrs. Hale—"maybe they wouldn't."

"No, Peters," said the county attorney incisively; "it's all perfectly clear, except the reason for doing it. But you know juries when it comes to women. If there was some definite thing—something to show. Something to make a story about. A thing that would connect up with this clumsy way of doing it."

In a covert way Mrs. Hale looked at Mrs. Peters. Mrs. Peters was looking at her. Quickly they looked away from each other. The outer door opened and Mr. Hale came in.

"I've got the team round now," he said. "Pretty cold out there."

"I'm going to stay here awhile by myself," the county attorney suddenly announced. "You can send Frank out for me, can't you?" he asked the sheriff. "I want to go over everything. I'm not satisfied we can't do better."

Again, for one brief moment, the two women's eyes found one another. The sheriff came up to the table.

"Did you want to see what Mrs. Peters was going to take in?"

The county attorney picked up the apron. He laughed.

"Oh, I guess they're not very dangerous things the ladies have picked out."

Mrs. Hale's hand was on the sewing basket in which the box was concealed. She felt that she ought to take her hand off the basket. She did not seem able to. He picked up one of the quilt blocks which she had piled on to cover the box. Her eyes felt like fire. She had a feeling that if he took up the basket she would snatch it from him.

But he did not take it up. With another little laugh, he turned away, saying:

"No; Mrs. Peters doesn't need supervising. For that matter, a sheriff's wife is married to the law. Ever think of it that way, Mrs. Peters?"

Mrs. Peters was standing beside the table. Mrs. Hale shot a look up at her; but she could not see her face. Mrs. Peters had turned away. When she spoke, her voice was muffled.

"Not—just that way," she said.

"Married to the law!" chuckled Mrs. Peters' husband. He moved toward the door into the front room, and said to the county attorney:

"I just want you to come in here a minute, George. We ought to take a look at these windows.

"Oh—windows," said the county attorney scoffingly.

"We'll be right out, Mr. Hale," said the sheriff to the farmer, who was still waiting by the door.

Hale went to look after the horses. The sheriff followed the county attorney into the other room. Again—for one moment—the two women were alone in that kitchen.

Martha Hale sprang up, her hands tight together, looking at that other woman, with whom it rested. At first she could not see her eyes, for the sheriff's wife had not turned back, since she turned away at that suggestion of being married to the law. But now Mrs. Hale made her turn back. Her eyes made her turn back. Slowly, unwillingly, Mrs. Peters turned her head until her eyes met the eyes of the other woman. There was a moment when they held each other in a steady, burning look in which there was no evasion nor flinching. Then Martha Hale's eyes pointed the way to the basket in which was hidden the thing that would make certain the conviction of the other woman—that woman who was not there and yet who had been there with them all through the hour.

For a moment Mrs. Peters did not move. And then she did it. With a rush forward, she threw back the quilt pieces, got the box, tried to put it in her handbag. It was too big. Desperately she opened it, started to take the bird out. But there she broke—she could not touch the bird. She stood helpless, foolish.

There was the sound of a knob turning in the inner door. Martha Hale snatched the box from the sheriff's wife, and got it in the pocket of her big coat just as the sheriff and the county attorney came back into the kitchen.

E. C. Bentley

(1875–1956)

EDMUND CLERIHEW BENTLEY'S classic work, *Trent's Last Case* (1913), is often considered the beginning of the Golden Age of the Detective Story. I agree about the importance of Bentley's novel, but I insist that it inaugurated the *second* Golden age. The *first* great period of fictional sleuthing, several examples of which are included in this collection, opened with Sherlock Holmes in 1887. In either case, Bentley both humanized the detective story and made it more complex. He humanized it by presenting Philip Trent as a fallible sleuth. Trent not only presents the wrong solution but he becomes emotionally involved with one of the suspects, the victim's widow. Bentley made the form more complex by introducing the gimmick of having several solutions, each beautifully clued, before the truth is finally revealed.

Following the success of *Trent's Last Case*, Bentley wrote three short stories about Trent for *The Strand*, including "The Ordinary Hairpins," October 1916. Two decades later, he wrote additional Trent tales, and eventually all but one were collected in *Trent Intervenes*.

The Ordinary Hairpins

A SMALL COMMITTEE of friends had persuaded Lord Aviemore to sit for a presentation portrait, and the painter to whom they gave the commission was Philip Trent. It was a task that fascinated him, for he had often seen and admired, in public places, the high half-bald skull, vulture nose, and grim mouth of the peer who was said to be deeper in theology than any other layman, and all but a few of the clergy; whose devotion to charitable work had made him nationally honoured. It was not until the third sitting that Lord Aviemore's sombre taciturnity was laid aside.

"I believe, Mr. Trent," he said abruptly, "you used to have a portrait of my late sister-in-law here. I was told that it hung in the studio."

Trent continued his work quietly. "It was just a rough drawing I made after seeing her in *Carmen*—before her marriage. It has been hung in here ever since. Before your first visit I removed it."

The sitter nodded slowly. "Very thoughtful of you. Nevertheless, I should like very much to see it, if I may."

"Of course." Trent drew the framed sketch from behind a curtain. Lord Aviemore gazed long in silence at Trent's very spirited likeness of the famous singer, while the artist worked busily to capture the first expression of feeling that he had so far seen on that impassive face. Lighted and softened by melancholy, it looked for the first time noble.

At last the sitter turned to him. "I would give a good deal," he said simply, "to possess this drawing."

Trent shook his head. "I don't want to part with it." He laid a few strokes carefully on the canvas. "If you care to know why, I'll tell you. It is my personal memory of a woman whom I found more admirable than any other I ever saw. Lillemor Wergeland's beauty and physical perfection were unforgettable. Her voice was a marvel; her spirit matched them; her fearlessness, her kindness, her vigour of mind and character, her feeling for beauty, were what I heard talked about even by people not given to enthusiasm. She had weaknesses, I dare say—I never spoke to her. I heard her sing very many times, but I knew no more about her than many other strangers. A number of my friends knew her, though, and all I ever gathered about her made me inclined to place her on a pedestal. I was ten years younger then; it did me good."

Lord Aviemore said nothing for a few minutes, then he spoke slowly. "I am not of your temperament or your circle, Mr. Trent. I do not worship anything of this world. But I do not think you were far wrong about Lady Aviemore. Once I thought differently. When I heard that my eldest brother was about to marry a prima donna, a woman whose portrait was sold all over the world, who was famous for extravagance in dress and what seemed to me self-advertising conduct, I was appalled when I heard from him of this engagement. I will not deny that I was shocked, too, at the idea of a marriage with the daughter of Norwegian peasants."

"She was country-bred, then," Trent observed. "One never heard much about her childhood."

"Yes. She was an orphan of ten years old when Colonel Stamer and his wife went to lodge at her brother's farm for the fishing. They fell in love with the child, and having none of their own, they adopted her. All this my brother told me. He knew, he said, just what I would think; he only asked me to meet her, and then to judge if he had done well or ill. Of course I asked him to introduce me at the first opportunity."

Lord Aviemore paused and stared thoughtfully at the portrait. "She charmed every one who came near her," he went on presently. "I resisted the spell; but before they had been long married she had conquered all my prejudice. It was like a child, I saw, that she delighted in the popularity and the great income her gifts had brought her. But she was not really childish. It was not that she was what is called intellectual; but she had a singular spaciousness of mind in which nothing little or mean could live—it had, I used to fancy, some kinship with her Norwegian landscapes of mountain and sea. She was, as you say, extremely beautiful, with the vigorous purity of the fair-haired northern race. Her marriage with my brother was the happiest I have ever known."

He paused again while Trent worked on in silence, and soon the low meditative voice resumed. "It was about this time six years ago—the middle of March—that I had the terrible news from Taormina, the day after my return from Canada. I went out to her at once. When I saw her I was aghast. She showed no emotion; but there was in her calmness the most unearthly sense of desolation that I have ever received. From time to time she would say, as if she spoke to herself, 'It was all my fault.'"

At Trent's exclamation of surprise Lord Aviemore looked up. "Few people," he said, "know the whole of the tragedy. You have heard that a slight shock of earthquake caused the collapse of the villa, and that my brother and his child were found dead in the ruins; you have heard, I suppose, that Lady Aviemore was not in the house at the time. You have heard that she drowned herself afterwards. But you have evidently not heard that my brother had a presentiment that this visit to Sicily would end in death, and wished to abandon it at the last moment; that his wife laughed away his forebodings with her strong common sense. But we belong to the Highlands, Mr. Trent; we are of that blood and tradition, and such interior warnings as my brother had are no trifles to us. However, she charmed his fears away; he had, she told me, entirely lost all sense of uneasiness. On the tenth day of their stay her husband and only child were killed. She did not think, as you may think, that there was coincidence here. The shock had changed her whole mental being; she believed then, as I believed, that my brother inwardly foreknew that death awaited him if went to that place." He relapsed into silence.

"I know slightly," Trent remarked, "a man called Selby, a solicitor, who was with Lady Aviemore just after her husband's death."

Lord Aviemore said that he remembered Mr. Selby. He said it with such a total absence of expression of any kind that the subject of Selby was killed instantly; and he did not resume that of the tragedy of the woman whom the world remembered still as Lillemor Wergeland.

It was a few months later, when the portrait of Lord Aviemore was to be seen at the show of the N.S.P.P., that Trent received a friendly letter from Arthur Selby. After praising the picture, Selby went on to ask if Trent would do him the favour of calling at his office by appointment for a private talk. "I should like," he wrote, "to put a certain story before you, a story with a problem in it. I gave it up as a bad job long ago myself, but seeing your portrait of A. reminded me of your reputation as an unraveller."

Thus it happened that, a few days later, Trent found himself alone with Selby in the offices of the firm in which that very capable, somewhat dandified lawyer was a partner. They spoke of the portrait, and Trent told of the strange exaltation with which his sitter had spoken of the dead lady. Selby listened rather grimly.

"The story I referred to," he said, "is the Aviemore story. I acted for the countess when she was alive. I was with her at the time of her suicide. I am an executor of her will. In the strictest confidence, I should like to tell you that story as I know it, and hear what you think about it."

Trent was all attention; he was deeply interested, and said so. Selby, with gloomy eyes, folded his arms on the broad writing-table between them, and began.

"You know all about the accident," he said. "I will start with the 15th of March, when Lord Aviemore and his son were buried in the cemetery at Taormina. That was before I came on the scene. Lady Aviemore had already discharged all the servants except her own maid, with whom she was living at the Hotel Cavour. There, as I gathered, she seldom left her rooms. She was undoubtedly overwhelmed by what had happened, though she seems never to have lost her grip on herself. Her brother-in-law, the present Lord Aviemore, had come out to join her. He had only just returned from Canada"—Selby raised a finger and repeated slowly—"from Canada, you will remember. He had gone out to get ideas about the emigration prospect, I understood. He remained at the hotel, meaning to accompany Lady Aviemore home when she should feel equal to the journey.

"It was not until the 18th that we received a long telegram from her, asking us to send some one representing the firm to her at Taormina. She stated that she wished to discuss business matters without delay, but did not yet feel able to travel. At the cost of some inconvenience, I went out myself, as I happen to speak Italian pretty well. You understand that Lady Aviemore, who already possessed considerable means of her own, came into a large income under her husband's will."

"She was a client who could afford to indulge her whims," Trent observed. "If you were already her adviser, she probably expected you to come."

"Just so. Well, I went out to Taormina, as I say. On my arrival Lady Aviemore saw me, and told me quite calmly that she was acquainted with the provisions of her late husband's will, and that she now wished to make her own. I took her instructions, and prepared the will at once. The next day the British Consul and I witnessed her signature. You may remember, Trent, that when the contents of her will became public after her death they attracted a good deal of attention."

"I don't think I heard of it," Trent said. "If I was giving myself a holiday at the time, I wouldn't know much about what was going on."

"Well, there were some bequests of jewellery and things to intimate friends. She left £2,000 to her brother Knut Wergeland, of Myklebostad in Norway, and £100 to her maid, Maria Krogh, also a Norwegian, who had been with her a long time. The whole of the rest of her property she left to her brother-in-law, the new Lord Aviemore, unconditionally. That surprised me, because I had been told that he had disapproved bitterly of the marriage, and hadn't concealed his opinion from her or any one else. But she never bore malice, I knew; and what she said to me at Taormina was that she could think of nobody who would do so much good with the money as her brother-in-law. From that point of view she was justified. He is said to spend three-fourths of his income on charities of all sorts, and I shouldn't wonder if it was true. Anyhow, she made him her heir."

"And what did he say to it?"

Selby coughed. "There is no evidence that he knew anything about it before her death. No evidence," he repeated slowly. "And when told of it afterwards he showed precious little feeling of any kind. Of course, that's his way. But now let me get on with the story. Lady Aviemore asked me to remain to transact business for her until she should leave Taormina. She did so on the 27th of March, accompanied by Lord Aviemore, myself, and her maid. To shorten the railway journey, as she told us, she had planned to go by boat first to Brindisi, then to Venice, and so home by rail. The boats from Brindisi to Venice all go in the daytime, except once a week, when a boat from Corfu arrives in the evening and goes on about eleven. She decided to get to Brindisi in time to catch that boat. So that was what we did; had a few hours in Brindisi, dined there, and went on board about ten o'clock. Lady Aviemore complained of a bad headache. She went at once to her cabin, which was a deck-cabin, asking me to send some one to collect her ticket at once, as she wanted to sleep as soon as possible and not be awakened again. That was soon done. Shortly before the boat left, the maid came to me on her way to her own quarters and told me her mistress had retired. Soon after we were out of the harbour I turned in myself. At that time Lord Aviemore was leaning over the rail on the deck on to which Lady Aviemore's cabin opened, and some distance from the cabin. There was nobody else about that I could see. It was just beginning to blow, but it didn't trouble me, and I slept very well.

"It was a quarter to eight next morning when Lord Aviemore came into my cabin. He was fearfully pale and agitated. He told me that the Countess could not be found; that the maid had gone to her cabin to call her at 7.30 and found it empty.

"I got up in a hurry, and went with him to the cabin. The dressing-case she had taken with her was there, and her fur coat and her hat and her jewellry-case and her handbag lay on the berth, which had not been slept in. The only other thing was a note, unaddressed, lying open on the table. Lord Aviemore and I read it together. After the inquiry at Venice I kept the note. Here it is."

Selby unfolded and handed over a sheet of thin ruled paper, torn from a block. Trent read the following words, written in a large, firm, rounded hand:

"Such an ending to such a marriage is far worse than death. It was all my fault. This is not sorrow; it is complete destruction. I have been kept up till now only by the resolution I took on the day when I lost them, by the thought of what I am going to do now. I take my leave of a world I cannot bear any more."

There followed the initials "L.A." Trent read and re-read the pitiful message, so full of the awful egotism of grief, then he looked up in silence at Selby.

"The Italian authorities found that she had met her death by drowning. They could not suppose anything else—nor could I. But now listen, Trent. Soon after her death I got an idea into my head, and I have puzzled over the affair a lot without much result. I did find out a fact or two, though; and it struck me the other day that if I could discover something, you could probably do much better."

Trent, still studying the paper, ignored this tribute. "Well," he said, "what is your idea, Selby?"

Selby, evading the direct question, said, "I'll tell you the facts I referred to. That sheet, you see, is torn from an ordinary ruled writing-pad. Now I have shown it to a friend of mine who is in the paper business. He has told me that it is a make of paper never sold in Europe, but sold very largely in Canada. Next, Lady Aviemore never was in Canada. And there was no writing-pad in her dressing-case or anywhere in the cabin. Neither was there any pen or ink, or any fountain pen. The ink, you see, is a pale sort of grey ink."

Trent nodded. "Continental hotel ink, in fact. This was written in a hotel, then—probably the one where you had dinner in Brindisi. You could identify her writing, of course."

"Except that it seems to have been written with a bad pen—a hotel pen, no doubt—it is her usual handwriting."

"Any other exhibits?" Trent asked after a brief silence.

"Only this." Selby took from a drawer a woman's handbag of elaborate bead-work. "Later on, when I saw Lord Aviemore about the disposal of her valuables and personal effects, I mentioned that there was this bag, with a few trifles in it. 'Give it away,' he said. 'Do what you like with it.' Well," Selby went on, smoothing the back of his head with a air of slight embarrassment, "I kept it. As a sort of memento—what? The things in it don't mean anything to me, but you have a look at them." He turned the bag out upon the writing-table. "Here you are—handkerchief, notes and change, nail-file, keys, powder-thing, lipstick, comb, hairpins——"

"Four hairpins." Trent look them in his hand. "Quite new ones, I should say. Have they anything to tell us, Selby?"

"I don't see how. They're just ordinary black hairpins—as you say, they look too fresh and bright to have been used."

Trent looked at the small heap of objects on the table. "And what's that last thing—the little box?"

"That's a box of Ixtil," the anti-sea-sick stuff. Two doses are gone. It's quite good, I believe."

Trent opened the box and stared at the pink capsules. "So you can buy it abroad?"

"I was with her when she bought it in Brindisi, just before we went on board."

Again Trent was silent a few minutes. "Then all you discovered that was odd was this about the Canadian paper, and the note having obviously been prepared in advance. Queer enough, certainly. But going back before that last day or two—all through the time you were with Lady Aviemore, did nothing come under your notice that seemed strange?"

Selby fingered his chin. "If you put it like that, I do remember a thing that I thought curious at the time, though I never dreamed of its having anything to do——"

"Yes, I know, but you asked me here to go over the thing properly, didn't you? That question of mine is one of the routine inquiries."

"Well, it was simply this. A day or two before we left Sicily I was standing in the hotel lobby when the mail arrived. As I was waiting to see if there was anything for me, the porter put down on the counter a rather smart-looking package that had just come—done up the way they do it at a really first-class shop, if you know what I mean. It looked like a biggish book, or box of chocolates, or something; and it had French stamps on it, but the postmark I didn't notice. And this was addressed to Mlle. Maria Krogh—you remember, the Countess's maid. Well, she was there waiting, and presently the man handed it to her. Maria went off with it, and just then her mistress came down the big stairs. She saw the parcel, and just held out her hand for it, and Maria passed it over as if it was a matter of course, and Lady Aviemore went upstairs with it. I thought it was quaint if she was ordering goods in her maid's name; but I thought no more of it, because Lady Aviemore decided that evening about leaving the place, and I had plenty to attend to. And if you want to know," Selby went on as Trent opened his lips to speak, "where Maria Krogh is, all I can tell you is that I took her ticket in London for Christiansand, where she lives, and where I sent her legacy to her, which she acknowledged. Now then!"

Trent laughed at the solicitor's tone, and Selby laughed too. His friend walked to the fireplace and pensively adjusted his tie. "Well, I must be off," he announced. "How about dining with me on Friday at the Cactus? If by that time I've anything to suggest about all this, I'll tell you. You will? All right, make it eight o'clock." And he hastened away.

But on the Friday he seemed to have nothing to suggest. He was so reluctant to approach the subject that Selby supposed him to be chagrined at his failure to achieve anything, and did not press the matter.

It was six months later, on a sunny afternoon in September, that Trent walked up the valley road at Myklebostad, looking farewell at the mountain far ahead, the white-capped mother of the torrent that roared down a twenty-foot fall beside him. He had been a week in this remote backwater of Europe, seven hours by motorboat from the nearest place that ranked as a town. The savage beauty of that watery landscape, where sun and rain worked together daily to achieve an unearthly purity in the scene, had justified far better than he had hoped his story that he had come there in search of matter for his brush. He had worked and he had explored, and had learned as much as he could of his neighbours. It was little enough, for the postmaster, in whose house he had a room, spoke only a trifle of German, and no one else, as far as he could discover, had anything but Norwegian, of which Trent knew no more than what could be got from a traveler's phrase-book. But he had seen every dweller in the valley, and he had paid close attention to the household of Knut Wergeland, the rich man of the valley, who had the largest farm. He and his wife, elderly and grim-faced peasants, lived with one servant in an old turf-roofed steading not far from the post office. Not another person, Trent was sure, inhabited the house.

He had decided at last that his voyage of curiosity to Myklebostad had been ill-inspired. Knut and his wife were no more than a thrifty peasant pair. They had given him a meal one day when he was sketching near the place, and they had refused with gentle firmness to take any payment. Both had made on him an impression of complete trustworthiness and competency in the life they led so utterly out of the world.

That day, as Trent gazed up to the mountain, his eye was caught by a flash of sunlight against the dense growth of birches running from top to bottom of the steep cliff that walled the valley to his left. It was a bright blink, about half a mile from where he stood; it remained steady, and at several points above and below he saw the same bright appearance. He perceived that there must be a wire, and a well-used wire, led up the precipitous hill face among the trees. Trent went on towards the spot on the road whence the wire seemed to be taken upwards. He had never been so far in this direction until now. In a few minutes he came to the opening among the trees of a rough track leading upwards among rocks and roots, at such an angle that only a vigorous climber could attempt it. Close by, in the edge of the thicket, stood a tall post, from the top of which a wire stretched upward through the branches in the same direction as the path.

Trent slapped the post with a resounding blow. "Heavens and earth!" he exclaimed. "I had forgotten the *saeter!*"

And at once he began to climb.

A thick carpet of rich pasture began where the deep birch-belt ended at the top of the height. It stretched away for miles over a gently sloping upland. As Trent came into the open, panting after a strenuous forty-minute climb, the heads of a score of browsing cattle were sleepily turned towards him. Beyond them wandered many more, and two hundred yards away stood a tiny hut, turf-roofed.

This plateau was the *saeter;* the high grassland attached to some valley farm. Trent had heard long ago, and never thought since, of this feature of Norway's rural life. At the appointed time, the cattle would be driven up by an easier detour to the mountain pastures for their summer holiday, to be attended there by some peasant—usually a young girl—who lived solitary with the herd. Such wires as that he had seen were kept bright by the daily descent of milk churns, let down by a line from above, received by a farm-hand at the road below.

And there, at the side of the hut, a woman stood. Trent, as he approached, noted her short rough skirt and coarse sack-like upper garment, her thick grey stockings and clumsy clogs. About her bare head her pale-gold hair was fastened in tight plaits. As she looked up on hearing Trent's footfall, two heavy silver earrings dangled about the tanned and careworn face of this very type of the middle-aged peasant women of the region.

She ceased her task of scraping a large cake of chocolate into a bowl and straightened her tall body. Smiling, with lean hands on her hips, she spoke in Norwegian, greeting him.

Trent made the proper reply. "And that," he added in his own tongue, "is a large part of all the Norwegian I know. Perhaps, madam, you speak English." Her light blue eyes looked puzzlement, and she spoke again, pointing down to the valley. He nodded; and she began to talk pleasantly in her unknown speech. From within the hut she brought two thick mugs; she pointed rapidly to the chocolate in the bowl, to himself and herself.

"I should like it of all things," he said. "You are most kind and hospitable, like all your people. What a pity it is we have no language in common!" She brought him a stool and gave him the chocolate-cake and a knife, making signs that he should continue the scraping, then within the hut she kindled a fire of twigs and began to boil water in a black pot. Plainly this was her dwelling, the roughest Trent had ever seen. He could discern that on two small shelves were ranged a few pieces of chipped earthenware. A wooden bedplace, with straw and two neatly folded blankets, filled a third of the space in the hut. All the carpentry was of the rudest. From a small chest in a corner she drew a biscuit tin, half full of flat cakes of stale rye bread. There seemed to be nothing else in the tiny place but a heap of twigs for fuel.

She made chocolate in the two mugs, and then, at Trent's insistence in dumb show, she sat on the only stool at a rude table outside the hut, while her guest made a seat of an upturned milking pail. She continued to talk amiably and unintelligibly, while he finished with difficulty the half of a bread-cake.

"I believe, madam," he said at last, setting down his empty mug, "you are talking simply to hear the sound of your own voice. In your case, that is excusable. You don't understand English, so I will tell you to your face that it is a most wonderful voice. I should say," he went on thoughtfully, "that you ought to have been one of the greatest sopranos that ever lived."

She heard him calmly, and shook her head as not understanding.

"Well, don't say I didn't break it gently," Trent protested. He rose to his feet. "Madam, I know that you are Lady Aviemore. I have broken in on your solitude, and I ask pardon for that; but I could not be sure unless I saw you. I give you my word that no one else knows or ever shall know from me, what I have discovered." He made as if to return by the way he had come.

But the woman held up a hand. A singular change had come over her brown face. A lively spirit now looked out of her desolate blue eyes; she smiled another and much more intelligent smile. After a few moments she spoke in English, fluent but with a slight accent of her country.

"Sir," she said, "you have behaved very nicely up till now. It has been an amusement for me; there is not much comedy on the *saeter*. Now, will you have the goodness to explain?"

He told her in a few words that he had suspected she was still alive, that he had thought over such facts as had come to his knowledge, and had been led to think she was probably in that place. "I thought you might guess I had recognized you," he added, "so it seemed best to assure you that your secret was safe. Was it wrong to speak?"

She shook her head, gazing at him with her chin on a hand. Presently she said, "I think you are not against me. I can feel that, though I do not understand why you wanted to search out my secret, and why you kept it when you had dragged it into the light."

"I dragged it because I am curious," he answered. "I have kept it and will keep it because—oh well, because it is your own, and because to me Lillemor Wergeland is a sort of divinity."

She laughed suddenly. "Incense! And I in these rags, in this hovel, with what unpleasantness I can see in this little spotty piece of cheap mirror! . . . Ah well! You have come a long way, curious man, and it would be cruel not to gratify your curiosity a little more. Shall I tell you? After all, it was simple.

"It was very soon after the disaster that the resolve came to me. I never hesitated. It was my fault that we had gone to Sicily—you have heard that? Yes, I see it in your face. I felt I must leave the world I knew, and that knew me. I never really thought of suicide. As for a convent, unhappily there is none for people with minds like mine. I meant simply to disappear, and the only way to succeed was to get the reputation of being dead. I thought it out for some days and nights. Then I wrote, in the name of my maid, to an establishment in Paris where I used to buy things for the stage."

"Ha!" Trent exclaimed. "I heard of that, and I guessed."

"I sent money," she went on, "and I ordered a dark-brown transformation—that is a lady's word for wig—some stuff for darkening the skin, various pigments, pencils, *et tout le bazar*. My maid did not know what I had sent for; she only handed the parcel to me when it came. She would have thrown herself in the fire for me, I think, my maid Maria. When the things arrived, I announced that I would return to England by the route you have heard of, perhaps."

He nodded. "The route that gave you a night passage to Venice. And you disguised yourself in your cabin at Brindisi, and slipped off in the dark before the boat started."

"Indeed, I was not such a fool!" she returned. "What if my absence had been discovered somehow before the boat left Brindisi? That could easily happen, and then good-bye to the fiction of my suicide. No; when we reached Brindisi, we had, as I knew, some hours there. We left our things at an hotel, where we were to dine, and then I put on a thick veil and went out alone. At the office near the harbour I took a second-class passage to Venice for myself, in the name of Miss Julia Simmons, in the same boat I had planned to take. It would be at the quay, they told me, in an hour. Then I went into the poorer streets of the town and bought some clothes, very ugly ones, some shoes, toilet things——"

"Some black hairpins," Trent murmured.

"Naturally, black," she assented. "My own gilt pins would have looked queer in a dark-brown wig, and I had to have pins to fasten it properly. I bought also a little cheap portmanteau-thing, and put my purchases in it. Then I took a cab to the quay, found the boat had arrived, and gave one of the stewards a tip to show me the berth named on my ticket, and to carry my baggage there. After that I went shopping again on shore. I bought a long mackintosh coat and a funny little cap—the very things for Miss Simmons—took them to the hotel, and pushed them under the things my maid had already packed in my big case.

"On the steamer, when Maria had left me and I had locked the cabin door, I arranged a dark, rather catty sort of face for myself, and fitted on Miss Simmons's hair. I put on her mackintosh coat and cap. When the boat began to move away from the quay, I opened my door an inch and peeped out. As I expected, every one was looking over the rail, and so—the sooner the better—I just slipped out, shut the cabin door, and walked straight to Miss Simmons's berth at the other end of the ship. . . . There is not much more to say. At Venice I did not look for the others, and never saw them. I went on to Paris, and wrote to my brother Knut that I was alive, telling him what I meant to do if he would help me. Such things do not seem so mad to a true child of Norway."

"What things?" Trent asked.

"Things of deep sorrow, malady of the soul, escape from the world. . . . He and his wife have been true and good to me. I am supposed to be her cousin, Hilda Bjoernstad. In my will I left them money, more than enough to pay for me, but they did not know that when they welcomed me here."

She ceased and smiled vaguely at Trent, who was considering her story with eyes that gazed fixedly at the skyline.

"Yes, of course," he remarked presently in an abstracted manner. "That was it. As you say, so simple. And now let me tell you," he went on with a change of tone, "one or two little details you have forgotten.

"At Brindisi you bought, just before going on board with the others, a box of the stuff called Ixtil, because it looked as if there might be bad weather. You took a dose at once, and another a little later, as the directions told you. You might have needed more of it before reaching Venice, but as Mr. Selby was with you when you bought it, you thought it wiser to leave it behind when you vanished. Also, you left behind you four new black hairpins, which had somehow, I suppose, got loose inside your handbag, and were found there by Selby. You see, Lady Aviemore, it was Selby who brought me into this. He told me all the facts he knew, and he showed me your bag and its contents. But he didn't attach any importance to the two things I have just mentioned."

She raised her eyebrows just perceptibly. "I cannot see why he should. And I cannot see why he should bring in you or anybody."

"Because he had some vague notion of your brother-in-law having either caused your death, or at least having known of your intention to commit suicide. He never told me so outright, but it was plain that that was in his mind. Selby wanted me to clear that up if I could. You see, your brother-in-law stood to benefit enormously by your death, and then there was the matter of the note announcing your suicide."

"It announced," she remarked, "the truth; that I was leaving a world I could not bear any longer. The words might mean one thing or another. But what about the note?"

"The perfectly truthful note was written with pen and ink, of which there was none in your cabin. It was written on paper which had been torn from a writing-pad, and no pad was found. Also that make of paper is sold in Canada, never in Europe. You had never been in Canada. Your brother-in-law had just come back from Canada. You see?"

"But did not Selby perceive that Charles is a saint?" inquired the lady with a touch of impatience. "Surely that was plain! More Dominic than Francis, no doubt; but an evident saint."

"In my slight knowledge of him," Trent admitted, "he did strike me in that way. But Selby is a lawyer, you see, and lawyers don't understand saints. Besides, your brother-in-law had taken a dislike to him, I think, and so perhaps he felt critical about your brother-in-law."

"It is true," she said, "he did not care about Mr. Selby, because he disliked all men who were foppish and worldly. But now I will tell you. That evening in the hotel at Brindisi I wanted to write that note, and I asked Charles for a sheet from the block he had in his hand and was just going to write on. That is all. I wrote it in the hotel writing-room, and took it afterwards in my bag to my cabin."

"We supposed you had written it beforehand," Trent said, "and that was one of the things that led me to feel morally certain you were still alive. I'll explain. If, as we thought, you had written the note in the hotel, your suicide was a premeditated act. Yet it was afterwards that Selby saw you buying that Ixtil stuff, and it was plain that you had taken two doses. And it struck me, though it didn't seem to have struck Selby, that it was unlikely any one already resolved to drown herself at sea would begin treating herself against sea-sickness.

"Then there were those new black hairpins. The sight of them was a revelation to me. For I knew, of course, that with that hair of yours you had probably never used a black hairpin in your life."

The Countess felt at her pale-gold plaits and gravely held out to him a black hairpin. "In the valley we use nothing else."

"It is very different in the valley, I know," he said gently. "I was speaking of my world—the world that you have left. I was led by those hairpins to think of your having changed your appearance, and I even guessed at what was in the parcel that came for your maid, which Selby had told me about."

She regarded her guest with something of respect. "It still remains," she said, "to explain how you knew it was in Norway, and here, as a poor farm servant, that I should hide myself. It seemed to me the last thing in the world—your world—that a woman who had lived my life would be expected to do."

"All the same, I thought it was a strong possibility," he answered. "Your problem, you see, was just what you say—to hide yourself. And you had another—you had to make a living somehow. Everything you possessed—except some small amount in cash, I suppose—you left behind when you disappeared. And a woman can't go on acting and disguising herself for ever. A man can grow hair on his face, or shave it off; for a woman, disguise must be a perpetual anxiety. If she has to get employment, and especially if she has no references, it's something very like an impossibility."

She nodded gravely. "That was how I saw it."

"So," he pursued, "it came to this: that the world-famous Lillemor Wergeland had to come to the surface again somewhere, and in no long time—Lillemor Wergeland, whose type of beauty and general appearance were so marked and unmistakable, whose photographs were known everywhere. The fact is that for some time I couldn't see for the life of me how it could possibly have been done. There were only a few countries, I supposed, of which you knew enough of the language to attempt to live in any of them; and if you did, you would always be conspicuous by your physical type and your accent. If you attracted attention, discovery might follow at any moment. The more I thought of it, the more marvellous it seemed that you had not been recognized—assuming you were still alive—during the six years or so that had passed before I heard the full story and guessed at the truth.

"And then an idea came. There was one country in which your looks and speech would not betray you as a foreigner—your own country. And if there were any corners of the world where you could go with a fair certainty of being unrecognized, the remoter villages of Norway would be among them. And at Myklebostad, on the Langfjord, which the map told me was one of the remotest, you had a brother who was two thousand pounds richer by your supposed death. You see how it was, then, that I came to this place on a sketching holiday."

Trent stood up and gazed across the valley to the sunlit white peaks beyond. "I have visited Norway before, but never had such an interesting time. And now, before I return to the haunts of men, let me say again that I shall forget at once all that has happened to-day. Don't think it was merely a vulgar curiosity that brought me here. There was once a supreme artist whose gifts made me her debtor and servant. Anything that happened to her touched me; I had a sort of right to go seeking what it really was that had happened."

She stood before him in her coarse and stained clothes, her hands clasped behind her, with a face and attitude of perfect dignity. "Very well; you stand on your right and I on mine—to arrange my own life, since I am alone in it. I will spend it here, where it began. My soul was born here before it went out to have adventures, and it has crept home again for comfort. Believe me, it is not only that as you say, I am safe from discovery here. That counts for very much; but also I felt I must go and live out my life in my own place, this faraway lonely valley, where everything is humble and unspoilt, and the hills and the fjords are as God made them before there were any men. It is all my own, own land!

"And now," she ended suddenly, "we understand one another, and we can part friends." She extended her hand, saying, "I do not know your name."

"Why should you?" he asked. He bent over the hand, then went quickly from her. At the beginning of the descent he glanced back once; she waved to him.

Half-way down the rugged track he stopped. Far above a wonderful voice was singing to the glory of the Norse land.

> "Ja, herligt er mit Fodeland
>   Der ewig trodser Tidens Tand,"

sang the voice.

Trent looked out upon the wild landscape. "Her fatherland!" he soliloquized. "Well, well! They say the strictest parents have the most devoted children."

H. C. Bailey

(1878–1961)

HENRY CHRISTOPHER BAILEY was a successful historical novelist before his first book of Reginald Fortune detective stories, *Call Mr. Fortune*, was published in 1920. Reggie Fortune quickly became one of the great sleuthing figures of the period between the two world wars. It is easy (and, on the whole, fair) to criticize the Fortune stories for their class consciousness. Reggie does say "Oh, my dear chap" too often, and his repeated claim to be a common man cannot be taken seriously. But the Fortune stories have a humanity, especially about abused children, that separates them from the works of many other authors of the period. Reggie, despite his moaning and groaning and love of muffins, is a formidable detective, and such stories as "The Archduke's Tea" (the opening tale in *Call Mr. Fortune*) have a potent nostalgic appeal.

The Archduke's Tea

MR. REGINALD FORTUNE, M.A., M.B., B.CH., F.R.C.S., was having a lecture from his father.

"You only do just enough," Dr. Fortune complained. "Never brilliant. No zeal. Now, Reginald, it won't do. Just enough is always too little. Take my word for it. And do be attentive to the Archduke. God bless you!"

"Have a good time, sir," said Mr. Reginald Fortune, and watched his father settle down in the car (a long process) beside his mother and drive off. They were gone at last, which Reginald had begun to think impossible, and the opulent practice of Dr. Fortune lay for a month in the virgin hands of Reginald.

"Beautifully patient the mater is," Reginald communed with himself as he ate his third muffin. "Fretful game to spend your life waitin' for a man to get ready. Quaint old bird, the pater. Death-bed manner for a tummy-ache. Wonder the patients lap it up."

But old Dr. Fortune was good at diagnosis, and he had his reasons for saying that Reggie lacked zeal. At Oxford, at his hospital, Reggie did what was necessary to take respectable degrees, but no more than he could help. It was remarked by his dean that he did things too easily. He always had plenty of time, and spent it here, there, and everywhere, on musical comedy and prehistoric man, golf and the newer chemistry, bargees and psychical research. There was nothing which he knew profoundly, but hardly anything of which he did not know enough to find his way about in it. Nobody, except his mother, had ever liked him too much, for he was a self-sufficient creature, but everybody liked him enough; he got on comfortably with everybody from barmaids to dons.

He was of a round and cheerful countenance and a perpetual appetite. This gave him a solidity of aspect emphasized by his extreme neatness. Neither his hair nor anything else of his was ever ruffled. He was more at his ease with the world than a man has a right to be at thirty-five.

It is presumed that he had never wanted anything which he had not got. Old Dr. Fortune possessed a small fortune and a rich practice, and Reggie enjoyed the proceeds and proposed to inherit both. The practice lay in that pleasant outer suburb of London called Westhampton, a region of commons and a large park, sacred to the well-to-do, and still boasting one or two houses inhabited by what auctioneers call the nobility.

In Boldrewood, the best of these places, there lived at this moment in Reggie Fortune's existence, the Archduke Maurice, the heir-apparent to the Emperor of Bohemia. You may remember that the Archduke came to live in England shortly after his marriage. It is, however, not true, as scandal reported, that his uncle the Emperor sent him into exile. There is reason to believe that the Archduchess, a woman equally vehement and beautiful, was not liked in several European courts. On her return from the honeymoon she made a booby trap for that drill serjeant of a king, Maximilian of Swabia, and for some weeks the Central Powers were threatening to mobilize. But she was a Serene Highness of the house of Erbach-Wittelsbach, which traces its descent to Odin, and had an independent realm of nearly two square miles, with parliament and army complete, and even the Emperor of Bohemia could not pretend that Maurice had married beneath him. History will affirm the simple truth that the Archduke and the Archduchess sought seclusion in England because they were bored to death by the Bohemian court, which was perpetually occupied in demonstrating that you can be very dull without being in the least respectable. The Archduke Maurice was a man of geniality and extraordinarily natural tastes. His garden—a long walk—a pint of beer in one of the old Westhampton inns made him a happy day. The Archduchess was not so simple, for she loved to drive her own car, a ferocious vehicle. But Archduchesses may not do that in Bohemia.

Reggie, having eaten all the muffins, lit his pipe and meditated on the cases left him by his father. Old Mrs. Smythe had her autumn influenza, and old Talbot Browne had his autumn gout, and the little Robinsons were putting in their whooping-cough. A kindly world! . . . He was dozing in the dark when the telephone bell rang.

Was that Dr. Fortune? Would he come to Boldrewood at once—at once. The Archduke had been knocked down by a motor-car and picked up unconscious.

"Poor old pater!" Reggie grinned, as he put his tools together. The pater would never forgive himself for being out of this. He loved a lord, did the pater, and since he had been called in to remove a fish bone from the archducal throat he could not keep the Archduke out of his conversation. The royal geniality of the Archduke, the royal disdain of the Archduchess—Dr. Fortune had been much gratified thereby, and Reggie was prepared to loathe their Royal Highnesses. Thank Heaven, the pater was safe on his holiday! If his head swelled so over an archducal fish bone, he would have burst over an archduke knocked down.

Reggie was practical, if without sympathy; he made haste in his neat way, and the sedate chauffeur of Dr. Fortune was horrified by instructions to let the car rip. The streets of Westhampton are not adapted to this. The district has tried hard to keep itself rural still, and its original narrow winding lanes remain ill-lighted and overhung by trees. Boldrewood stands high, and its grounds border upon Westhampton Heath, across which there is one lamp per furlong. Just as Reggie's car swung round to the heath it was stopped with a jerk.

"What's the trouble, Gorton?" Reggie said to the chauffeur.

Gorton was leaning sideways and peering into the gloom of the gutter. A gleam from the sidelight winked at a body which lay still. "Give me a turn," Gorton muttered. His face showed white. Reggie jumped out, but Gorton was quicker. "Lumme, it's the Archduke!" he said, and his voice went up high.

"Don't be futile, Gorton." Reggie bent over the body. "Get the lamps on him."

Gorton backed the car and the body came into the light. Its face was crushed. Gorton gasped and swallowed. "But it's not him neither," he muttered.

After a minute Reggie stood up. "He was a fine chap about an hour ago," he said gently.

"All over, sir?" Reggie nodded. "Some hog done him in?"

"As you say, Gorton. Running-down case. Big car. Took him in the back. Went over his head. But I don't see how he got into the gutter." He walked round the body, moved it a little, and picked up two matches—unusual matches in England—very thin vestas with dark blue heads. "Why did you think he was the Archduke, Gorton?"

"Such a big chap, sir. Not many his measure. And there's something about the make of the poor chap that's very like. But thank God it's not the Archduke, anyway."

"Why?" said Reggie, who was without reverence for Archdukes. "Well, let's take him along."

They brought the dead man to the lodge at the main gates of Boldrewood, and there left him with a message to be telephoned to the police.

The hall at Boldrewood is in the Victorian baronial style, absurd but comfortable. Reggie was still blinking at the light when a woman ran at him. His first notion of the Archduchess Ianthe was vehemence. She came upon him, a great fur cloak falling away from her speed, panting, black eyes glowing, and then stopped short, and her pale face was distorted with passion. "Dr. Fortune! You are not Dr. Fortune!" she cried.

"Dr. Fortune, Junior, madame. My father is away, and I am in charge of his practice." She muttered something in a language he did not know, and looked as if she was going to kill him. His second notion of her was that she was wickedly beautiful. A Greek perfection in the pale face, but, Lord, what a temper! The daintiest grace of body, but it moved and quivered like a whip lash.

"My dear Ianthe!" A man came smiling from behind the screen by the fire. He was tall and slight and dandyish: a lot of colour in his clothes, an odd absence of colour in him. A bright blue tie with an emerald in it, a bright blue handkerchief hanging half out of the pocket of the silver-grey coat. But his face had a waxy pallor, his hair, his moustache, and little pointed beard were so fair that they looked like patches of paint on a mask. "We are much obliged by Dr. Fortune's coming so quickly."

The Archduchess whirled round. "He is too young," she said in German. "Look at him. He is a boy."

"I beg your pardon, madame," said Reggie in the same language. "May I see the patient?"

The man laughed. "I am sure we have every confidence in your skill, Dr. Fortune." All the laughter was smoothed out of his face. "And your discretion," he said in a lower voice. "I am the Archduke Leopold. You may be frank with me. And rely upon my help."

Reggie bowed. "How did the accident happen, sir?"

The Archduke turned to his sister-in-law. "You know that I do not know," she cried. "I was out in the car."

"As my sister says, Dr. Fortune, she was out in the car." The Archduke paused. "She drives herself. It is with her a little passion. My brother was out walking alone."

"Those long walks! How I hate them!" the Archduchess broke out.

"Again, it is with him a little passion. Well, he did not come back. I grew anxious. I am staying here, you understand. My sister was late too. I sent out servants. My brother was found lying in the road not far from the gate of the lodge. He remains unconscious. I fear——" He spread out his hands.

"You—you always fear!" the Archduchess cried. They exchanged glances like blows.

"May I go up, madame?" Reggie said solemnly. She whirled round and rushed away.

"The Archduchess is much agitated," said the Archduke.

"It is most natural," Reggie murmured.

"Most natural. Pray follow me, Dr. Fortune. I will take you to my brother."

The Archduke Maurice lay in a room of austere simplicity. A writing-table, a tiny dressing-table, three chairs, and a narrow iron bed were all its furniture. Only three small rugs lay on the floor. At the head of the bed a man stood watching. The Archduchess was on her knees, her face pressed to her husband's body, and she sobbed violently.

The Archduke Leopold looked at Reggie, made a gesture towards her, and said, "My dear Ianthe!"

She looked up flushed and tear stained.

"I beg your pardon, madame. This is dangerous to the patient," Reggie said.

She gave a stifled cry and rushed out of the room.

The Archduke Leopold seemed to intend to stay, but in a moment the voice of the Archduchess was heard calling for him. "Better go to her, sir. Keep her out of here," Reggie said, and turned to his patient. It is obvious that the Archduke did not relish so brusque an order. But the passionate voice was not to be denied.

The man by the bed and Reggie took each other's measure. "English?" said Reggie.

"Yes, sir. Holt, I am. The Archduke's valet."

"You undressed him?"

"Yes, sir. Was that wrong?"

"Depends how you did it." Reggie began his examination.

The Archduke Maurice was a big man. That is a habit in his family. He had their fairness, but even in coma his cheeks showed more colour than his brother Leopold's, and his yellow hair and beard had a reddish glow. A bold, honest face with plenty of brow. Reggie went over his body with an anatomical enthusiasm for so splendid a specimen.

"Get me some warm water, will you?" Holt went out of the room. Reggie bent over the broad chest. From it, from just above the heart, he drew out a thin sliver of steel. He made a face at it and put it away. Holt came back, and there was sponging and bandaging.

"You washed him before, I see. Anyone else touched him but you?"

"Only carrying him, sir. I've been with him the whole time. I found him."

"Oh. Lying on his face, I suppose?"

"No, sir. On his back. Just like he is now."

"Oh. Notice anything?"

"No, sir, I wish I had. I'd like to have the handling of the bounder that did it."

"Well, well, we mustn't get excited. Preserve absolute calm, Holt. He's well liked, is he?"

"Why, sir, we'd do anything for him. He—oh, he's a gentleman."

"Quite so. You mustn't leave him a moment. No one—see, no one—is to come into the room. I'll be back soon."

"Very good, sir. Beg pardon, sir." The good Holt flushed. "What's the verdict?"

"It's not all over yet!" Reggie went downstairs.

And it appeared to him that he interrupted the Archduke and the Archduchess in a quarrel. But the Archduke was very pleased to see him, effusive in offering a chair, and so forth. Reggie was not gratified. "I must have nurses, sir," he announced. "I should like another opinion."

"You see!" the Archduchess cried. "It is as I told you. This boy!"

"The Archduchess is naturally anxious," the Archduke apologized. "By all means nurses. But another opinion—you must have confidence in yourself, my good friend."

"I have. But I want Sir Lawson Hunter to see the case."

The Archduke shrugged. "It is serious then, Dr. Fortune? We do not wish a great noise. Is it not so, Ianthe?"

"I would give my soul to be quiet," she cried.

"Quite," says Reggie.

"Very well. Discretion, then, you understand, my good friend."

"I'll telephone to Sir Lawson at once."

"Indeed? It is serious, then?"

"It's a bad concussion." Reggie bowed and made for the door.

"You—Dr. Fortune——" the Archduchess cried. "Will he—what will happen?"

"There's no reason we shouldn't hope, madame," Reggie said, and paused a moment watching them. Emotion plays queer tricks with faces. They were both in the grip of emotions.

Sir Lawson Hunter is rather fat and his legs are rather short. His complexion is greyish and his eyes look boiled. People call him dyspeptic, though his capacious stomach has never known an ache: or imagine that he drinks, though alcohol and physicians are his chief abominations. His European reputation as a surgeon has been won by knowing his own mind.

Reggie met him at the door and took him upstairs before that puzzling pair, the Archduke and the Archduchess, had a sight of him. "Glad you could come, sir. It's an odd case."

"Every case is odd," said Sir Lawson Hunter.

"He was knocked down by a car. The——"

"If he was, I can find it out for myself. Damme, Fortune, don't bias me. Most unprofessional. That's the worst of general practice. You fellows must always be saying something."

Reggie held his peace. He knew Sir Lawson's little ways, having been his house surgeon. The faithful Holt was turned out of the room. Sir Lawson Hunter went over the senseless body with his usual speed and washed his hands.

"Splendid animal," he remarked. "They run to that, these Pragas. I remember his uncle's abdominal muscles. Heroic. Well. He was walking. A big car driven fast hit him from behind on the right side, fractured two ribs, and knocked him down. Impact of his head on the road has caused a serious concussion. That car should have stopped."

Reggie smiled. "Oh, one of the odd things is that it didn't."

"There's a damned lot of road hogs about, my boy," said Sir Lawson heartily. He was himself fond of high speed. "Well. They sent out, I suppose. Found him lying on his face unconscious."

"No, sir."

"What?" Sir Lawson jumped.

"He was lying on his back."

"Oh, that's absurd."

"Yes, sir. But I've seen his valet who found him."

"These fellows have no observation," Sir Lawson grunted, but there was some animation in his boiled eye. "Damme, Fortune, he ought to have been on his face."

"Yes, sir."

"Miracles don't happen."

"No, sir."

"Now these abrasions on the legs. As if the car had been driven at him again while he lay. A queer thing. Or have there been two cars at him?"

"And there is this too, sir." Reggie held out the sliver of steel.

"I saw the puncture. I was coming to that. Humph! Whoever put this in meant business."

"And didn't know his job. It slipped along the bone and missed everything."

Sir Lawson turned the thing over. "A woman's hatpin. About half a woman's hatpin."

"Fresh fracture. Broke as it was pushed in."

"They're a wild lot," said Sir Lawson, and smiled. "You have no nerves, Fortune?"

"I believe not, sir."

"This ought to be the making of you. You want shaking up. You must stay in the house. By the way, who's in the house?"

"The Archduchess, of course——"

"Ianthe. Yes. Aunt's in a mad-house. Ianthe. Yes. Crazy on motoring. Drives her own car. And have you seen Ianthe—since?" Sir Lawson nodded at the body on the bed.

"She is very excited."

"Is she really?" Sir Lawson laughed. "Is she, though? How surprising!"

"She is surprising, sir."

"What? What? Be careful, my boy. Handsome creature, isn't she?"

"Yes, sir." Reggie declined to be amused. "The Archduke Leopold is staying with them."

"Leopold. He's the dandy entomologist. He's tame enough. Well, he's the head of the house after this fellow. Better tell him." He blinked at Reggie. "You have nurses you can trust? Well, we'll stay in the room till one comes, my boy. Our friend of the hatpin won't miss a chance. These Royal families they're a criss-cross of criminal tendencies. Hohenzollerns, Hapsburgs, Pragas, Wittelsbachs—look at the heredity."

"There was another running-down case here to-night. The man was killed—fractured skull. He was left on the road too. And another queer thing—he was much the same build as the Archduke Maurice."

"Good Gad!" Sir Lawson was startled out of his omniscient manner, an event unknown in Reggie's experience. "There's something devilish in it, Fortune. One murder—the wrong man dead—and then try again at once the same way. Imagine the creature looking at that poor dead wretch and jumping on the car again to drive it on at the other man. Diabolical! Diabolical!"

"I don't think I have much imagination, sir," said Reggie, who was not impressed by ineffective emotion.

There was a gentle tap at the door, a nurse came and was given her instructions, and the two men went down to the Archduke Leopold.

He had changed his clothes. He was now in a claret-coloured velvet which did violence to his complexion and his pale beard. He sat in the smoking-room with a book on the entomology of Java and a glass of eau sucrée. He smiled at them and waved them to chairs.

"I have to tell you, sir, that your brother lies in grave danger," said Sir Lawson.

Reggie looked at him sideways.

"Ah, the concussion! It is serious, then? I am deeply distressed."

"The concussion is most serious. There's another matter. In your brother's chest above the heart, at which it must have been aimed, we have found—this."

"Mon Dieu! It is a hatpin—a woman's hatpin. But it is incredible! It is murder."

"Attempted murder."

"But what do you suggest, sir? Do you accuse some one?"

"Not my function. That pin was driven at your brother's heart by some one. Can you tell me any more, sir?"

The Archduke buried his face in his hands. "I will not believe it," he muttered—"I will not believe it." After a little he controlled himself.

"Gentlemen, you have a right to my confidence. I will tell you every-thing. I trust you to do all that is possible for my poor brother and for the honour of our family, which to him, as to me, is dearer than life. You know that he is the heir to the throne of Bohemia. My uncle, the Emperor, has long been vexed with his living in England. I came here to persuade my brother to go back to his country. My poor brother had made his home here at the wish of the Archduchess, who dislikes the duties of royalty. He was passionately, madly, in love with her. But, alas! in these love marriages there is often difficulty. They were not of the same mind upon many things, and the Archduchess is of a vehement temper. I fear—but you will forgive me if I say no more. I take one small thing. My brother loved to go walking. The Archduchess is pas-sionately fond of her motor-car, drives it herself, loves wild speed. My brother detested motor-cars. I fear that my coming gave them cause for fresh quarrels. My brother was ready to go back to Bohemia. The Archduchess was violently opposed to it. I confess to you, gentlemen, I have feared some scandal, some madness. I thought she would leave him. But this—it is appalling."

"The Archduchess was out in her motor-car to-night?" Sir Lawson said.

"Yes. Yes. It is true. But this—must we think it?"

"We have to think of nothing but our duty to our patient," said Sir Lawson.

The Archduke grasped his hand. "You are right. I thank you. I shall not forget your fidelity."

The Archduchess whirled into the room. She, as Reggie remarked, had not cared to change her clothes. She had not even touched her hair, which was escaping in a wild disorder from under her hat. "They will not let me see him," she cried. "Leopold——"

"It is by my instructions, madame," Sir Lawson said. "I am respon-sible for the Archduke's safety."

She bit her lip. "Is he so hurt?" she said unsteadily.

"He lies in very grave danger, madame. I permit no one in his room."

She stared at him, her throat quivering, her great eyes bold and bright. Then with a little shrug she turned away and, plucking at the gold things which jingled from her waist, took out a cigarette and lit it. Reggie saw one of those foreign matches with the violet heads.

Sir Lawson made his bow, and Reggie went with him to his car. "Why did you tell them that the Archduke was in grave danger?" he said.

"He'll be safer if they believe he is going to die," said Sir Lawson.

"Oh, do you think so?" said Reggie, as the car shot away.

Then he made an excellent supper and slept sound.

He found his patient peaceful in the morning. No sign of con-sciousness yet, but more colour in the cheeks, a deeper breathing and a stronger pulse, more warmth. "The Archduchess has come twice in the night to ask about him, doctor," the nurse said. "I told her he was no better."

"Did she make a noise?" Reggie frowned.

"No, she was very good."

Reggie went out to take the air, and the air is not bad on the Westhampton heights. He made a good pace under the great beeches of Boldrewood, and came out on the open road across the heath. Just there he had found the dead man. A dull red stain could still be seen. It was farther on that the Archduke was struck. Just beyond the turn to Brendon. He found the place. There was a loosening of the road, as if a heavy car had been brought up sharply or made a violent swerve. He walked to and fro scanning the ground. Another of those foreign matches.

He was just picking it up when a motor-car stopped a few yards away. Two men jumped out and came towards him. One was middle aged and singularly without distinction. The other had a youthful and very jaunty air, and it was only when he came near that Reggie saw the fellow was old enough to be his father. An actor's face, with that look of calculated expression, and an actor's way of dressing, a trifle too emphatic. His present part was the gay young fellow.

"Dr. Fortune, I think?" He smiled all over his face.

"I am Dr. Fortune."

"Reconstructing the crime, eh? Oh, you needn't be discreet. I'm Lomas—Stanley Lomas—Criminal Investigation Department, don't you know? Sir Lawson Hunter came round to me last night. Patient's doing well, I see. That's providential. Just a moment—just a moment." He skipped away from Reggie to his companion, and they went over the ground. But Reggie thought them very superficial. Lomas skipped back again. "He didn't bleed, then. The other man did, though—the man you found."

"In the middle of the road. And I found him dead in the gutter."

"It's quaint what the criminal don't think of. I'm surprised every time. Did you find anything here?"

Reggie held out his match. "There were two more like that by the other man."

Lomas turned it over. "Belgian make. You buy them all over the Continent, don't you know."

"The Archduchess carries them."

"Now, that's very interesting. If you don't mind I'll walk up to the house with you." Upon the way he praised the beauties of nature and the quality of the morning air.

As they came to the door of Boldrewood a big car passed them with the Archduchess driving alone. Lomas put up his eyeglass. "She's not overcome with grief, what?"

"Not quite."

"Might be bravado, don't you know."

"I don't know."

"It takes some of them that way," Lomas said pensively. He turned on the steps of the house and looked after the car as it wound in and out among the beeches. "Striking woman. Yes. I'll come up to your room, if you don't mind."

"I thought you wanted to say something," Reggie said.

Lomas did not answer till they were upstairs. "Well, no. Not to say anything," he resumed, and lit a cigarette. "I want another opinion, as you fellows say. Sir Lawson Hunter has made up his mind."

"Oh, he always does that."

Lomas lifted an eyebrow. "Well, look at it. Somebody in a car laid for our Archduke. The other poor devil was cut down by mistake. And the somebody had nerve enough to go on. That's striking. The Archduchess comes of pretty wild stock. In love or out of love she wouldn't stick at a trifle. You find her matches by each body. You find a hatpin in the Archduke. That's a blunder, what? Yes, but it's a woman's blunder. She finds he isn't quite dead after all her trouble, she is desperate, and—*voilâ.*" He made a gesture of stabbing.

"So you've made up your mind, too, Mr. Lomas?"

Lomas blew smoke rings. "I'm wasting your time, doctor. I want to know—has it occurred to you—the Archduchess and the Archduke Leopold—working it together? If she's fallen in love with Leopold. That straightens it out, don't you know."

"Guess again," Reggie said.

Lomas lit another cigarette. "Well, that's what I want to know. You saw them together just after the crime." He lifted an eyebrow.

"Nothing doing," said Reggie.

"I'm afraid so. I'm afraid so. It's a disturbing case, doctor. Nothing doing, as you say. If I had all the evidence in my hands, I expect there's no one I could touch. You can't indict royalty. The Archduke's smash—well, let's say it's all in the family. But this poor devil they killed! Who's to pay for him? These royal dagoes come over and run amuck on an English road, and I can't touch them. Disheartening, what? That's the trouble, doctor."

Reggie nodded and, as his breakfast made its appearance, Lomas rose to go. He would not have even coffee. "Better get busy, don't you know. We must see if we can put the fear of God into them. If they'll go scurrying back to Bohemia it's the best way out." He skipped off, his jauntiness put on again like a coat.

Reggie was standing at the window with his after-breakfast pipe when the Archduchess brought her car back. She was very pale in spite of the morning air, and her face had grown haggard. "Something'll snap," Reggie was saying to himself, when a voice behind him said aloud, "Nice car, sir." He jumped round and saw standing at his elbow the insignificant little companion of Mr. Lomas. "After all, there's nothing like an English car," said the little man.

"Oh. You've noticed that?" Reggie said. "You do notice something, then?"

"Of course we aren't gifted, sir. But we're professional. Something in that, don't you think? Yes, sir, as you say: we have noticed something. It was a foreign car, and foreign tyres did the trick last night. And the Archduchess drives English. And yet—did you know we had the other half of the hatpin? I picked it up last night." He held out a scrap of steel with a big head of wrought silver. "German work, they tell me."

"Viennese," Reggie said.

"You know everything, sir. Such a convenience. But Vienna being quite near Bohemia, as I've heard—looks awkward, don't it?"

"Is that what you came to say?"

"Not wholly, sir. No. I am Superintendent Bell. Mr. Lomas sent me to you. He considered you might find it convenient to have some one in the house who could keep an eye open."

"Very kind of Mr. Lomas."

There was a tap at the door. The Archduke Leopold's valet appeared. The Archduke Leopold was much surprised that Dr. Fortune had not brought him news of the patient. The Archduke Leopold desired that Dr. Fortune would come to him immediately.

"Really?" Reggie said. "Dr. Fortune's compliments to the Archduke, and he is much occupied. He can give the Archduke a few moments."

The valet, having the appearance of a man who has never been so surprised in his life, retired.

"It's a gift," Superintendent Bell murmured. "It's a gift, you know. I never could handle the nobs."

Reggie began to get together some odds and ends: a bottle full of tiny white tablets, a graduated glass, a jug of water, a hypodermic syringe. "You'd better clear out, you know," he said to Superintendent Bell.

"Will he come?"

"He'll come all right," Reggie said, and took off his coat. When he turned, Superintendent Bell had vanished.

"Just setting the stage, sir?" said a voice from behind the curtain.

"Confound your impertinence," Reggie growled. "Here——"

But the Archduke came in. He was now a decoration in russet brown. "You are very mysterious, Dr. Fortune," he complained. "I expect more frankness, sir."

"My patient is my first consideration, sir."

"I desire that you will consider my anxieties. Well, sir, how is my brother?"

"You may give yourself every hope of his recovery, sir."

The Archduke looked round for a chair and was some time in finding one. "This is very good news," he said slowly, and slowly smiled. "*Mon Dieu*, doctor, it seems too good to be true! Last night you told me to fear the worst."

"Last night—was last night, sir," Reggie said. "This morning we begin to see our way. All the symptoms are good. I believe that in a few hours the patient will be able to speak."

"To speak? But the concussion? It was so dangerous. But this is bewildering, doctor."

"Most fortunate, sir. You might talk of the hand of Providence. Well, we shall see what we shall see. He may be able to tell you something of how it all happened. You'll pardon me, I'm anxious to prepare the injection." He dropped a tablet in the glass and poured in water. "Fact is, this ought to make all the difference. Wonderful things drugs, sir. A taste of strychnine—one of these little fellows—and a man has another try at living. Two or three of 'em—just specks, aren't they?—sudden death. Excuse me a moment. I must take a look at the patient."

He was gone some time.

When he came back the Archduke was still there. "All goes well, doctor?"

"I begin to think so."

"I must not delay you. My dear doctor! If only your hopes are realized. What happiness!" He slid out of the room.

Reggie went to the table and picked up the glass of strychnine solution. From behind the curtain Superintendent Bell rushed out and caught his arm. "Don't use it, sir," he said hoarsely. Superintendent Bell was flushed.

"Don't be an ass," said Reggie. He put the glass down, took up the bottle of tablets, turned them out on a sheet of paper, and began to count them.

"Good Lord!" said Superintendent Bell. "You laid for him, did you? What a plant!"

"You know, you're an impertinence," Reggie said, and went on counting.

"I'll get on to Mr. Lomas, sir," said the Superintendent humbly.

"Don't you telephone or I'll scrag you."

"Telephone? Not me. I say, sir, you're some doctor." He fled.

Reggie finished his counting and whistled. "He did himself proud," said he. "The blighter!" He shot the tablets back into their bottle, found another bottle and poured into it the solution, and locked both away. "Number one," he said, with satisfaction. "Now for number two." He went off to his patient and spent a placid half-hour chatting with the day nurse on dancing in musical comedy. But it was hardly half an hour before the Archduchess tapped at the door.

Reggie opened it. "This way, if you please, madame." He led the way to his room. "I have something to say." She stood before him, fierce, defiant, and utterly wretched. "I can promise you that the Archduke will recover consciousness."

She caught at her breast. "He—he will live?" It was the most piteous cry he had ever heard.

"He will live, madame!"

She trembled, swayed, and fell. Reggie grasped at her, took her in his arms, and put her in a chair and waited frowning. . . . She panted a little and began to smile. Then faintly, softly, "No, no. No more now. Ah, dearest." It was in her own language. She opened heavy eyes. "What is it?"

"The Archduke has spoken, madame. He said—your name."

Then she began to cry and, holding out both hands to Reggie, "Let me go to him—please—please."

"Not now. Not yet. He must have no emotions. You will go to your room and sleep."

"You—you are a boy." She laughed through her tears, and thrust her hands into Reggie's.

"I beg your pardon, madame," Reggie said stiffly. The creature was absurdly adorable.

"You? Oh—Englishman." It was made plain to him that he was expected to kiss her hand. He did it like an Englishman. Then the other was put to his lips.

He cleared his embarrassed throat. "I must insist, madame, you will say nothing of this to anyone. It's necessary the household should suppose the Archduke still in danger."

"Why?" A spasm crossed her face. "You are afraid of Leopold!"

"And you, madame?" Reggie said.

"Afraid? No, but"—she shuddered—"but he is not a man."

"Have no anxieties, madame. I have none," Reggie said, and opened the door. Then, "She's a bit of a dear," he said to himself, and rang for his lunch.

Four times that afternoon the Archduke Leopold sent to ask for news of his brother, and each time Reggie answered that the patient was much the same. "Leopold will be doin' some thinking," Reggie chuckled. "Happy days for Leopold."

Towards tea-time the Hon. Stanley Lomas arrived jauntier than ever.

"Well, doctor, been enjoying yourself, what?" He shook hands heartily. "Best congratulations and all that. Sound scheme. Ve—ry sound scheme. Well, I expect you'll be glad to be rid of Leopold, what? I conceive I can put the fear of God into him now. Free hand, don't you know. Let's take him on."

It was announced to the Archduke Leopold that the Hon. Stanley

Lomas of the Criminal Investigation Department desired to confer with him. The Archduke, who was drinking tea, was pleased to receive Mr. Lomas. He also received Reggie. "Dr. Fortune? You have something to tell me?"

"There is no change, sir."

"No change yet! And you gave me such hopes this morning. These are anxious hours, Mr. Lomas."

"I can imagine it, sir. But I hope to relieve some of your anxieties. I believe we shall discover who was responsible for last night's outrage."

"So! And so soon! But you are wonderful, you English police. You will sit down, Mr. Lomas." He looked at Reggie, whose lingering naturally surprised him. "Is there anything more, Dr. Fortune?"

"Dr. Fortune is part of my evidence, sir," said Lomas.

"Is it possible? But you interest me—you interest me exceedingly. Permit me one moment." He slid out of the room.

Lomas turned in his chair and lifted an eyebrow at Reggie, who was settling his tie before an old Italian mirror. "Probably gone to change his clothes," Reggie said. "He's only worn one suit to-day."

A footman brought in more tea-things, and a moment after the Archduke came back.

"I am all impatience, Mr. Lomas. But pray take a more comfortable chair. Dr. Fortune—I recommend the chair by the screen. Let me give you some tea." He was all smiles.

"Have you made arrangements to leave England, sir?" Lomas said sharply.

"Mr. Lomas!"

"You have time to catch the mail to-night."

"I hope that I do not understand you, sir. You appear insolent."

"Oh, sir, there will be no delicacy in handling the affair. You went to Dr. Fortune's room this morning." The Archduke gave a glance at Reggie, who sat intent on stirring his tea. "He was preparing an injection of strychnine for his patient."

"Hallo, what's that?" Reggie cried, and nodded at the window. "Oh, I suppose it's the car, Lomas. Your fellows will have found her and brought her round."

"The car, sir?" the Archduke said, and Lomas put up his eyeglass.

"The car that did the deed."

The Archduke slid across to the window. Lomas, too, stood up and looked out. They turned and stared at Reggie, who was sipping his tea. Lomas frowned. "There's nothing there, Fortune."

The Archduke smiled. "Dr. Fortune has hallucinations," and he pulled out his handkerchief and dabbed his face, sat down, and drank his tea in gulps.

"We'll keep to the point, if you please." Lomas was annoyed. "Dr.

Fortune told you that two of his strychnine tablets would kill a man. He went out of the room. While he was gone you dropped half a dozen tablets into the injection prepared for your brother. I have to demand, sir, that you leave England by the next boat."

The Archduke burst out laughing. "The good Dr. Fortune! As you have seen, he has hallucinations. He hears what is not, dreams what never was. But if I were a policeman, Mr. Lomas, I should not make Dr. Fortune a witness. You become ridiculous."

"He is not the only witness, sir. One of my men was behind the curtain."

The Archduke poured himself out another cup of tea. "May I give you some more, Dr. Fortune? No? I fear you are malicious, my friend." He laughed a little. "And you, sir. We sometimes find a policeman corrupt in our country. We do not permit him to trouble us."

"You brought a German car into England, sir," Lomas said. "Where is that car?"

"Your spies do not seem very good, Mr. Lomas. Come, sir, enough of this. I——" The Archduke started from his seat with a cry. His body was bent in a bow. A horrible grin distorted his face. He fell down and was convulsed. . . . He gasped; his pale cheeks became of a dusky blue. He writhed and lay still. . . .

"So that's that," Reggie said. "I wondered what he wanted with half a dozen."

"What is it?" Lomas muttered.

"Oh, strychnine poisoning. He's swallowed a grain or so."

"My God! Can you do anything?"

Reggie shrugged. "He's as dead as the table." . . .

After a while, "Well! It's a way out," Lomas said. "But I can't understand the fellow."

"Oh, I don't understand it all," Reggie admitted. "He was out to kill his brother. That meant being Emperor. But why kill him now more than before? And the Archduchess. She is straight enough, I know. But just how she was to this fellow I don't see."

"There's not much in that," Lomas said. "Maurice couldn't stand the Court, and it was common talk he meant to resign the succession. While he was quiet over here in England Leopold felt safe. But lately they tell me Maurice has been making up his mind to go back. Duty to his country, don't you know? The Archduchess was strong against it. She hates all the business of royalty. But Maurice is a resolute sort of fellow even with a woman. Leopold came over to see what he could do. I suppose he set the Archduchess on to make Maurice give up the idea and stay quiet. They worked together—or that's the notion at the Bohemian Embassy. She's a gipsy, what, but she's straight. She is not in this. It wasn't her car. Well, when Leopold found there was nothing doing he set about the murder. He was a bad egg, don't you know? There was a woman in Rome—they kicked him out there. But it was a sound scheme. He had it all straight—except the wrong tyres on his car. Good touch, the hatpin. Seemed like a woman in a rage. He knew a lot about women—one kind of woman."

There was a tap at the door. The two walked forward.

"Sir Lawson Hunter, sir." The footman tried in vain to see the Archduke.

"Yes, bring him up," Reggie said.

Sir Lawson bustled in. "New case for you, sir." The two men moved apart and Sir Lawson saw the body.

"Poisoned himself. Taken strychnine," Lomas said.

"Oh, don't bias him," said Reggie. "He doesn't like that."

"Good Gad!" Sir Lawson's eyes bulged.

"Yes, that beats me, Fortune." Lomas waved his hand at the body. "I would have sworn he hadn't the pluck."

"Oh, he hadn't. He meant it for me. I changed the cups."

"You——" Lomas stared at him. "That was when you heard the car!"

"That was why I heard the car."

"And you let him take the dose!'

"Yes. Seemed fair. You see, I picked up that poor fellow he smashed last night."

"Good Gad!" said Sir Lawson.

The footman was again at the door. Dr. Fortune was wanted at the telephone. "There's one here, isn't there? Put me through." The footman, hardly able to speak at the sight of the dead Archduke, retired gulping.

The bell rang. Reggie took up the receiver. "Yes. Yes. At once," and he put it down. "I must be going. Serious case. Mrs. Jones's little girl may have German measles."

DOVER · THRIFT · EDITIONS

POETRY

"MINIVER CHEEVY" AND OTHER POEMS, Edwin Arlington Robinson. 64pp. 28756-4 $1.00

EARLY POEMS, Ezra Pound. 80pp. (Available in U.S. only) 28745-9 $1.00

EARLY POEMS, William Carlos Williams. 64pp. (Available in U.S. only) 29294-0 $1.00

"THE WASTE LAND" AND OTHER POEMS, T. S. Eliot. 64pp. (Available in U.S. only) 40061-1 $1.00

RENASCENCE AND OTHER POEMS, Edna St. Vincent Millay. 64pp. (Available in U.S. only) 26873-X $1.00

SELECTED POEMS, John Milton. 128pp. 27554-X $1.50

SELECTED CANTERBURY TALES, Geoffrey Chaucer. 144pp. 28241-4 $1.00

GREAT SONNETS, Paul Negri (ed.). 96pp. 28052-7 $1.00

CIVIL WAR POETRY: An Anthology, Paul Negri. 128pp. 29883-3 $1.50

WAR IS KIND AND OTHER POEMS, Stephen Crane. 64pp. 40424-2 $1.00

THE RAVEN AND OTHER FAVORITE POEMS, Edgar Allan Poe. 64pp. 26685-0 $1.00

ESSAY ON MAN AND OTHER POEMS, Alexander Pope. 128pp. 28053-5 $1.50

GOBLIN MARKET AND OTHER POEMS, Christina Rossetti. 64pp. 28055-1 $1.00

CHICAGO POEMS, Carl Sandburg. 80pp. 28057-8 $1.00

THE SHOOTING OF DAN MCGREW AND OTHER POEMS, Robert Service. 96pp. (Available in U.S. only) 27556-6 $1.00

COMPLETE SONNETS, William Shakespeare. 80pp. 26686-9 $1.00

SELECTED POEMS, Percy Bysshe Shelley. 128pp. 27558-2 $1.50

100 BEST-LOVED POEMS, Philip Smith (ed.). 96pp. 28553-7 $1.00

101 GREAT AMERICAN POEMS, The American Poetry & Literacy Project (ed.). (Available in U.S. only) 40158-8 $1.00

NATIVE AMERICAN SONGS AND POEMS: An Anthology, Brian Swann (ed.). 64pp. 29450-1 $1.00

SELECTED POEMS, Alfred Lord Tennyson. 112pp. 27282-6 $1.00

LITTLE ORPHANT ANNIE AND OTHER POEMS, James Whitcomb Riley. 80pp. 28260-0 $1.00

CHRISTMAS CAROLS: COMPLETE VERSES, Shane Weller (ed.). 64pp. 27397-0 $1.00

GREAT LOVE POEMS, Shane Weller (ed.). 128pp. 27284-2 $1.00

LOVE: A Book of Quotations, Herb Galewitz (ed.). 64pp. 40004-2 $1.00

EVANGELINE AND OTHER POEMS, Henry Wadsworth Longfellow. 64pp. 28255-4 $1.00

CIVIL WAR POETRY AND PROSE, Walt Whitman. 96pp. 28507-3 $1.00

SELECTED POEMS, Walt Whitman. 128pp. 26878-0 $1.00

THE BALLAD OF READING GAOL AND OTHER POEMS, Oscar Wilde. 64pp. 27072-6 $1.00

FAVORITE POEMS, William Wordsworth. 80pp. 27073-4 $1.00

WORLD WAR ONE BRITISH POETS: Brooke, Owen, Sassoon, Rosenberg and Others, Candace Ward (ed.). (Available in U.S. only) 29568-0 $1.00

THE CAVALIER POETS: An Anthology, Thomas Crofts (ed.). 80pp. 28766-1 $1.00

ENGLISH ROMANTIC POETRY: An Anthology, Stanley Appelbaum (ed.). 256pp. 29282-7 $2.00

EARLY POEMS, William Butler Yeats. 128pp. 27808-5 $1.50

"EASTER, 1916" AND OTHER POEMS, William Butler Yeats. 80pp. (Available in U.S. only) 29771-3 $1.00

DOVER·THRIFT·EDITIONS

FICTION

FLATLAND: A ROMANCE OF MANY DIMENSIONS, Edwin A. Abbott. 96pp. 27263-X $1.00

PERSUASION, Jane Austen. 224pp. 29555-9 $2.00

PRIDE AND PREJUDICE, Jane Austen. 272pp. 28473-5 $2.00

SENSE AND SENSIBILITY, Jane Austen. 272pp. 29049-2 $2.00

WUTHERING HEIGHTS, Emily Brontë. 256pp. 29256-8 $2.00

BEOWULF, Beowulf (trans. by R. K. Gordon). 64pp. 27264-8 $1.00

CIVIL WAR STORIES, Ambrose Bierce. 128pp. 28038-1 $1.00

THE AUTOBIOGRAPHY OF AN EX-COLORED MAN, James Weldon Johnson. 112pp. 28512-X $1.00

TARZAN OF THE APES, Edgar Rice Burroughs. 224pp. (Available in U.S. only) 29570-2 $2.00

ALICE'S ADVENTURES IN WONDERLAND, Lewis Carroll. 96pp. 27543-4 $1.00

O PIONEERS!, Willa Cather. 128pp. 27785-2 $1.00

MY ÁNTONIA, Willa Cather. 176pp. 28240-6 $2.00

PAUL'S CASE AND OTHER STORIES, Willa Cather. 64pp. 29057-3 $1.00

IN A GERMAN PENSION: 13 Stories, Katherine Mansfield. 112pp. 28719-X $1.50

THE STORY OF AN AFRICAN FARM, Olive Schreiner. 256pp. 40165-0 $2.00

"THE YELLOW WALLPAPER" AND OTHER STORIES, Charlotte Perkins Gilman. 80pp. 29857-4 $1.00

HERLAND, Charlotte Perkins Gilman. 128pp. 40429-3 $1.50

FIVE GREAT SHORT STORIES, Anton Chekhov. 96pp. 26463-7 $1.00

"THE FIDDLER OF THE REELS" AND OTHER SHORT STORIES, Thomas Hardy. 80pp. 29960-0 $1.50

FAVORITE FATHER BROWN STORIES, G. K. Chesterton. 96pp. 27545-0 $1.00

THE WARDEN, Anthony Trollope. 176pp. 40076-X $2.00

THE COUNTRY OF THE POINTED FIRS, Sarah Orne Jewett. 96pp. 28196-5 $1.00

GREAT SHORT STORIES BY AMERICAN WOMEN, Candace Ward (ed.). 192pp. 28776-9 $2.00

SHORT STORIES, Louisa May Alcott. 64pp. 29063-8 $1.00

THE AWAKENING, Kate Chopin. 128pp. 27786-0 $1.00

A PAIR OF SILK STOCKINGS AND OTHER STORIES, Kate Chopin. 64pp. 29264-9 $1.00

THE REVOLT OF "MOTHER" AND OTHER STORIES, Mary E. Wilkins Freeman. 128pp. 40428-5 $1.50

HEART OF DARKNESS, Joseph Conrad. 80pp. 26464-5 $1.00

THE SECRET SHARER AND OTHER STORIES, Joseph Conrad. 128pp. 27546-9 $1.00

THE "LITTLE REGIMENT" AND OTHER CIVIL WAR STORIES, Stephen Crane. 80pp. 29557-5 $1.00

THE OPEN BOAT AND OTHER STORIES, Stephen Crane. 128pp. 27547-7 $1.50

THE RED BADGE OF COURAGE, Stephen Crane. 112pp. 26465-3 $1.00

A CHRISTMAS CAROL, Charles Dickens. 80pp. 26865-9 $1.00

THE CRICKET ON THE HEARTH AND OTHER CHRISTMAS STORIES, Charles Dickens. 128pp. 28039-X $1.00

THE DOUBLE, Fyodor Dostoyevsky. 128pp. 29572-9 $1.50

NOTES FROM THE UNDERGROUND, Fyodor Dostoyevsky. 96pp. 27053-X $1.00

THE GAMBLER, Fyodor Dostoyevsky. 112pp. 29081-6 $1.50

THE ADVENTURE OF THE DANCING MEN AND OTHER STORIES, Sir Arthur Conan Doyle. 80pp. 29558-3 $1.00

THE HOUND OF THE BASKERVILLES, Arthur Conan Doyle. 128pp. 28214-7 $1.00

SIX GREAT SHERLOCK HOLMES STORIES, Sir Arthur Conan Doyle. 112pp. 27055-6 $1.00

SILAS MARNER, George Eliot. 160pp. 29246-0 $1.50

DOVER · THRIFT · EDITIONS

FICTION

MADAME BOVARY, Gustave Flaubert. 256pp. 29257-6 $2.00

WHERE ANGELS FEAR TO TREAD, E. M. Forster. 128pp. (Available in U.S. only) 27791-7 $1.50

A ROOM WITH A VIEW, E. M. Forster. 176pp. (Available in U.S. only) 28467-0 $2.00

THE OVERCOAT AND OTHER STORIES, Nikolai Gogol. 112pp. 27057-2 $1.50

GREAT GHOST STORIES, John Grafton (ed.). 112pp. 27270-2 $1.00

"THE MOONLIT ROAD" AND OTHER GHOST AND HORROR STORIES, Ambrose Bierce (John Grafton, ed.) 96pp. 40056-5 $1.00

THE MABINOGION, Lady Charlotte E. Guest. 192pp. 29541-9 $2.00

WINESBURG, OHIO, Sherwood Anderson. 160pp. 28269-4 $2.00

THE LUCK OF ROARING CAMP AND OTHER STORIES, Bret Harte. 96pp. 27271-0 $1.00

THIS SIDE OF PARADISE, F. Scott Fitzgerald. 208pp. 28999-0 $2.00

"THE DIAMOND AS BIG AS THE RITZ" AND OTHER STORIES, F. Scott Fitzgerald. 29991-0 $2.00

THE SCARLET LETTER, Nathaniel Hawthorne. 192pp. 28048-9 $2.00

YOUNG GOODMAN BROWN AND OTHER STORIES, Nathaniel Hawthorne. 128pp. 27060-2 $1.00

THE GIFT OF THE MAGI AND OTHER SHORT STORIES, O. Henry. 96pp. 27061-0 $1.00

THE NUTCRACKER AND THE GOLDEN POT, E. T. A. Hoffmann. 128pp. 27806-9 $1.00

THE BEAST IN THE JUNGLE AND OTHER STORIES, Henry James. 128pp. 27552-3 $1.00

DAISY MILLER, Henry James. 64pp. 28773-4 $1.00

WASHINGTON SQUARE, Henry James. 176pp. 40431-5 $2.00

THE TURN OF THE SCREW, Henry James. 96pp. 26684-2 $1.00

DUBLINERS, James Joyce. 160pp. 26870-5 $1.00

A PORTRAIT OF THE ARTIST AS A YOUNG MAN, James Joyce. 192pp. 28050-0 $2.00

DEATH IN VENICE, Thomas Mann. 96pp. (Available in U.S. only) 28714-9 $1.00

THE METAMORPHOSIS AND OTHER STORIES, Franz Kafka. 96pp. 29030-1 $1.50

THE MAN WHO WOULD BE KING AND OTHER STORIES, Rudyard Kipling. 128pp. 28051-9 $1.50

SREDNI VASHTAR AND OTHER STORIES, Saki (H. H. Munro). 96pp. 28521-9 $1.00

THE OIL JAR AND OTHER STORIES, Luigi Pirandello. 96pp. 28459-X $1.00

SELECTED SHORT STORIES, D. H. Lawrence. 128pp. 27794-1 $1.00

GREEN TEA AND OTHER GHOST STORIES, J. Sheridan LeFanu. 96pp. 27795-X $1.00

SHORT STORIES, Theodore Dreiser. 112pp. 28215-5 $1.50

THE CALL OF THE WILD, Jack London. 64pp. 26472-6 $1.00

FIVE GREAT SHORT STORIES, Jack London. 96pp. 27063-7 $1.00

WHITE FANG, Jack London. 160pp. 26968-X $1.00

THE NECKLACE AND OTHER SHORT STORIES, Guy de Maupassant. 128pp. 27064-5 $1.00

BARTLEBY AND BENITO CERENO, Herman Melville. 112pp. 26473-4 $1.00

THE GOLD-BUG AND OTHER TALES, Edgar Allan Poe. 128pp. 26875-6 $1.00

TALES OF TERROR AND DETECTION, Edgar Allan Poe. 96pp. 28744-0 $1.00

DETECTION BY GASLIGHT, Douglas G. Greene (ed.). 272pp. 29928-7 $2.00

THE THIRTY-NINE STEPS, John Buchan. 96pp. 28201-5 $1.50

THE QUEEN OF SPADES AND OTHER STORIES, Alexander Pushkin. 128pp. 28054-3 $1.50

FIRST LOVE AND DIARY OF A SUPERFLUOUS MAN, Ivan Turgenev. 96pp. 28775-0 $1.50

FATHERS AND SONS, Ivan Turgenev. 176pp. 40073-5 $2.00

FRANKENSTEIN, Mary Shelley. 176pp. 28211-2 $1.00

THREE LIVES, Gertrude Stein. 176pp. (Available in U.S. only) 28059-4 $2.00

DOVER · THRIFT · EDITIONS

FICTION

THE STRANGE CASE OF DR. JEKYLL AND MR. HYDE, Robert Louis Stevenson. 64pp. 26688-5 $1.00

TREASURE ISLAND, Robert Louis Stevenson. 160pp. 27559-0 $1.50

THE LOST WORLD, Arthur Conan Doyle. 176pp. 40060-3 $1.50

GULLIVER'S TRAVELS, Jonathan Swift. 240pp. 29273-8 $2.00

ROBINSON CRUSOE, Daniel Defoe. 288pp. 40427-7 $2.00

THE KREUTZER SONATA AND OTHER SHORT STORIES, Leo Tolstoy. 144pp. 27805-0 $1.50

THE IMMORALIST, André Gide. 112pp. (Available in U.S. only) 29237-1 $1.50

ADVENTURES OF HUCKLEBERRY FINN, Mark Twain. 224pp. 28061-6 $2.00

THE ADVENTURES OF TOM SAWYER, Mark Twain. 192pp. 40077-8 $2.00

THE MYSTERIOUS STRANGER AND OTHER STORIES, Mark Twain. 128pp. 27069-6 $1.00

HUMOROUS STORIES AND SKETCHES, Mark Twain. 80pp. 29279-7 $1.00

YOU KNOW ME AL, Ring Lardner. 128pp. 28513-8 $1.00

MOLL FLANDERS, Daniel Defoe. 256pp. 29093-X $2.00

CANDIDE, Voltaire (François-Marie Arouet). 112pp. 26689-3 $1.00

"THE COUNTRY OF THE BLIND" AND OTHER SCIENCE-FICTION STORIES, H. G. Wells. 160pp. (Available in U.S. only) 29569-9 $1.00

THE ISLAND OF DR. MOREAU, H. G. Wells. (Available in U.S. only) 29027-1 $1.00

THE INVISIBLE MAN, H. G. Wells. 112pp. (Available in U.S. only) 27071-8 $1.00

THE TIME MACHINE, H. G. Wells. 80pp. (Available in U.S. only) 28472-7 $1.00

LOOKING BACKWARD, Edward Bellamy. 160pp. 29038-7 $2.00

THE WAR OF THE WORLDS, H. G. Wells. 160pp. (Available in U.S. only) 29506-0 $1.00

ETHAN FROME, Edith Wharton. 96pp. 26690-7 $1.00

SHORT STORIES, Edith Wharton. 128pp. 28235-X $1.00

THE AGE OF INNOCENCE, Edith Wharton. 288pp. 29803-5 $2.00

THE MOON AND SIXPENCE, W. Somerset Maugham. 176pp. (Available in U.S. only) 28731-9 $2.00

THE PICTURE OF DORIAN GRAY, Oscar Wilde. 192pp. 27807-7 $1.50

MONDAY OR TUESDAY: Eight Stories, Virginia Woolf. 64pp. (Available in U.S. only) 29453-6 $1.00

JACOB'S ROOM, Virginia Woolf. 144pp. (Available in U.S. only) 40109-X $1.50

NONFICTION

THE DEVIL'S DICTIONARY, Ambrose Bierce. 144pp. 27542-6 $1.00

DE PROFUNDIS, Oscar Wilde. 64pp. 29308-4 $1.00

OSCAR WILDE'S WIT AND WISDOM: A Book of Quotations, Oscar Wilde. 64pp. 40146-4 $1.00

THE SOULS OF BLACK FOLK, W. E. B. Du Bois. 176pp. 28041-1 $2.00

NARRATIVE OF THE LIFE OF FREDERICK DOUGLASS, Frederick Douglass. 96pp. 28499-9 $1.00

NARRATIVE OF SOJOURNER TRUTH, Sojourner Truth. 80pp. 29899-X $1.00

UP FROM SLAVERY, Booker T. Washington. 160pp. 28738-6 $2.00

A VINDICATION OF THE RIGHTS OF WOMAN, Mary Wollstonecraft. 224pp. 29036-0 $2.00

THE SUBJECTION OF WOMEN, John Stuart Mill. 112pp. 29601-6 $1.50

TAO TE CHING, Lao Tze. 112pp. 29792-6 $1.00

THE ANALECTS, Confucius. 128pp. 28484-0 $2.00

SELF-RELIANCE AND OTHER ESSAYS, Ralph Waldo Emerson. 128pp. 27790-9 $1.00

SELECTED ESSAYS, Michel de Montaigne. 96pp. 29109-X $1.50

DOVER · THRIFT · EDITIONS

NONFICTION

A MODEST PROPOSAL AND OTHER SATIRICAL WORKS, Jonathan Swift. 64pp. 28759-9 $1.00
UTOPIA, Sir Thomas More. 96pp. 29583-4 $1.50
THE AUTOBIOGRAPHY OF BENJAMIN FRANKLIN, Benjamin Franklin. 144pp. 29073-5 $1.50
COMMON SENSE, Thomas Paine. 64pp. 29602-4 $1.00
THE STORY OF MY LIFE, Helen Keller. 80pp. 29249-5 $1.00
GREAT SPEECHES, Abraham Lincoln. 112pp. 26872-1 $1.00
THE PRINCE, Niccolò Machiavelli. 80pp. 27274-5 $1.00
PRAGMATISM, William James. 128pp. 28270-8 $1.50
TOTEM AND TABOO, Sigmund Freud. 176pp. (Available in U.S. only) 40434-X $2.00
POETICS, Aristotle. 64pp. 29577-X $1.00
NICOMACHEAN ETHICS, Aristotle. 256pp. 40096-4 $2.00
MEDITATIONS, Marcus Aurelius. 128pp. 29823-X $1.50
SYMPOSIUM AND PHAEDRUS, Plato. 96pp. 27798-4 $1.50
THE TRIAL AND DEATH OF SOCRATES: Four Dialogues, Plato. 128pp. 27066-1 $1.00
THE BIRTH OF TRAGEDY, Friedrich Nietzsche. 96pp. 28515-4 $1.50
BEYOND GOOD AND EVIL: Prelude to a Philosophy of the Future, Friedrich Nietzsche. 176pp. 29868-X $1.50
CONFESSIONS OF AN ENGLISH OPIUM EATER, Thomas De Quincey. 80pp. 28742-4 $1.00
CIVIL DISOBEDIENCE AND OTHER ESSAYS, Henry David Thoreau. 96pp. 27563-9 $1.00
SELECTIONS FROM THE JOURNALS (Edited by Walter Harding), Herny David Thoreau. 96pp. 28760-2 $1.00
WALDEN; OR, LIFE IN THE WOODS, Henry David Thoreau. 224pp. 28495-6 $2.00
THE LAND OF LITTLE RAIN, Mary Austin. 96pp. 29037-9 $1.50
THE THEORY OF THE LEISURE CLASS, Thorstein Veblen. 256pp. 28062-4 $2.00

PLAYS

PROMETHEUS BOUND, Aeschylus. 64pp. 28762-9 $1.00
THE ORESTEIA TRILOGY: Agamemnon, The Libation-Bearers and The Furies, Aeschylus. 160pp. 29242-8 $1.50
LYSISTRATA, Aristophanes. 64pp. 28225-2 $1.00
WHAT EVERY WOMAN KNOWS, James Barrie. 80pp. (Available in U.S. only) 29578-8 $1.50
THE CHERRY ORCHARD, Anton Chekhov. 64pp. 26682-6 $1.00
THE THREE SISTERS, Anton Chekhov. 64pp. 27544-2 $1.00
UNCLE VANYA, Anton Chekhov. 64pp. 40159-6 $1.50
THE INSPECTOR GENERAL, Nikolai Gogol. 80pp. 28500-6 $1.50
THE WAY OF THE WORLD, William Congreve. 80pp. 27787-9 $1.50
BACCHAE, Euripides. 64pp. 29580-X $1.00
MEDEA, Euripides. 64pp. 27548-5 $1.00
THE MIKADO, William Schwenck Gilbert. 64pp. 27268-0 $1.50
FAUST, PART ONE, Johann Wolfgang von Goethe. 192pp. 28046-2 $2.00
SHE STOOPS TO CONQUER, Oliver Goldsmith. 80pp. 26867-5 $1.50
A DOLL'S HOUSE, Henrik Ibsen. 80pp. 27062-9 $1.00
HEDDA GABLER, Henrik Ibsen. 80pp. 26469-6 $1.50
GHOSTS, Henrik Ibsen. 64pp. 29852-3 $1.50
VOLPONE, Ben Jonson. 112pp. 28049-7 $1.50
DR. FAUSTUS, Christopher Marlowe. 64pp. 28208-2 $1.00
THE MISANTHROPE, Molière. 64pp. 27065-3 $1.00